SINNERS' CRUSADE

For salvation, the good of man and forty thousand bucks, an expatriate alcoholic, a happy-go-lucky hooker, a pleasure-hungry pimp and an uptight abortionist follow an eccentric priest from France to Jerusalem to a terrifying realm of international intrigue on a wild crusade that explodes into the most devilish, devastating orgy of atonement of all time!

"Absolutely bizarre . . . amazingly funny . . . headlong adventure . . . Religious scandal, blackmail, Bedouins vs. Arabs vs. Israelis, industrial espionage and revenge and reparation—they're all here . . . McHale keeps the plot twisting and turning until the very last page."
—*San Francisco Examiner & Chronicle*

"What distinguishes McHale is not only the fertility of his invention but the humanity."
—*Time*

"Endlessly inventive . . . startling and relentlessly funny."
—*Philadelphia Inquirer*

Also by Tom McHale:

PRINCIPATO

FARRAGAN'S RETREAT

ALINSKY'S DIAMOND

A Novel by

Tom McHale

BALLANTINE BOOKS • NEW YORK

Library of Congress Catalog Card Number: 74-11007

SBN 345-24608-X-195

This edition published by arrangement with
J. B. Lippincott Company

First Printing: November, 1975

Printed in the United States of America

BALLANTINE BOOKS
A Division of Random House, Inc.
201 East 50th Street, New York, N.Y. 10022
Simultaneously published by
Ballantine Books, Ltd., Toronto, Canada

To Suzanne, my wife,
who survived the writing
of this novel

"*Vengeance on a dumb brute!*" *cried Starbuck,* "*that simply smote thee from blindest instinct! Madness! To be enraged with a dumb thing, Captain Ahab, seems blasphemous.*"

—MOBY DICK

PART I
MURPHY

1

Genesis: France

THE GREAT ANGOULÊME DIAMOND HEIST set the soul of France afire. It also set Murphy's soul afire, something that had not happened for a longer time than he cared to remember.

The theft of the famous Suleiman's Pebble from the Angoulême Cathedral had come to light the evening before when Radio-Télévision Française suspended its regular programming to show the hastily developed film of two Scandinavian tourists—husband and wife—who had immortalized with their portable movie cameras the whole of the elaborate distraction the thieves had engineered to get everyone out of the treasure room, but merely failed to immortalize whoever it was that slipped into that same room after the two guards had come rushing out with guns blazing, detonated the detonation-proof glass that contained the gem, and made off with it.

In the series of personal interviews that followed the films, it was obvious that the robbers were not culpable—not absolutely, anyhow—for there was no compromise with the twin racial qualities of ingeniousness and élan. Functionaries like the local prefect of police and his inspectors made grudging admissions that there was something of criminal genius at hand, and men in the street wished the thieves outright success. A Sorbonne professor spoke of universal justice and retribution, reminding the nation that the diamond had been taken from a Muslim mosque in Jerusalem by earlier Frenchmen as part of the spoils of the Crusades—holy wars whose holiness was indeed questionable—and he speculated it had been stolen by Arabs and taken to Mecca.

But the professor had been the only Arabophile in the series of interviews. The general assumption was that the jewel had been taken by Basques to finance their nationalist movement. Murphy concurred. Whoever it was had backed a hijacked truck, loaded with six bulls on their way to a Basque festival in Bayonne, up to a rear entrance of the cathedral nave during noon Mass on Sunday and stampeded them into the worshipers and tourists. All hell had broken loose. Little old French ladies in black summer coats had raced from pillar to pillar to hide from the ranging horns, while First Communion candidates in their white robes and what appeared to be busloads of German tourists fought and clawed each other at the doors for the privilege of first escape. The Scandinavian and his wife, apparently impervious to harm, had filmed this passionate religiosity of southern Europe with a Bergmanesque detachment, the culmination of the script being the eternally long minute that one of their camera eyes was trained on the ancient priest at the main altar—blind, deaf, or else in remarkable communication with his God—who went right on reading Mass after his altar boys had long since fled. In the end, with the Scandinavians still in attendance, a platoon of gendarmes had spilled into the cathedral and gunned down the bulls in a number of blind corners and other entrapments. The last frames showed the sudden dawn of universal recognition that the treasure room had been left unguarded all this time; there was a general scurrying of booted police feet in that direction and the discovery of the shattered and empty display case; in place of the diamond, with unquestionable mockery, was a Basque beret.

The morning papers were full of the progress of the investigation around Bayonne and Biarritz and also included the news that the owner of the six hijacked bulls and his driver had been found, bound and gagged but otherwise unharmed and full of compliments for the thoughtfulness and gentlemanliness of the hijackers, who had paid in full for what they had stolen. Also, for the first time it was acknowledged that what appeared in the televised films to be a kind of ceremonial bunting on the horns of the toros was, in reality, a covering of foam rubber taped to the animals' heads to protect the worshipers, which explained the hitherto incredible fact that no one was injured beyond scratches and bruises. The editorial in that morning's *Lyon-Presse* called the thieves chivalrous and humane and differentiated painstakingly between high crime and low crime.

The feat, spectacular of invention, had reminded Murphy—now a naturalized French citizen—of his old self: a young satyr fresh off an Iowa farm who had hustled the lovely Monique de Rastignac into marriage; the Murphy of the great car restoration scheme who had refurbished the decaying Château de Rastignac in Haute-Savoie, splayed its beauty in triumph across the pages of *Maison Belle,* reclaimed its vineyards, and assured after a fashion (through his son, Jean-Philippe) the continuance of that family's ancestral line.

This morning after, accompanied by his father-in-law, *monsieur le baron,* Murphy stared fondly at his own image in the zinc of the bar in the *tabac* of their village. The hour was 7 A.M., he was already three cognacs to the good, and today the remembrance of things past pleased him immensely. Privately, he wished France or the rest of the world would provide a daily inspirational deed the ilk of the Angoulême heist: anything to keep him from thinking of his new life, wherein, despite the remnant of a more intelligent self, he was fulfilling the exacting condition of a proposed long-term suicide. For Francis Xavier Murphy, busted two summers before by the Société d'Appelation Controlée for artificially elevating the alcohol content of his own awful product, was now lord and master of 12,000 bottles of an unmarketable and decidedly mediocre white Seyssel wine, the ruin of his wife's family fortune and most of the economy of little Vardelle-sur-Lac, Haute-Savoie, France. In accordance, by way of penance and after the rule of a solemn vow made one hungover Sunday morning during the consecration of the Mass, Murphy was drinking his way toward blessed Death through his own 12,000-bottle mistake.

But he did not drink alone. His father-in-law, who had helped spike the wine, helped drink it up also—only not by way of penance. He clearly loved the evil grape, and minutes after they had quit the *tabac,* strained up the hill out of the village in the old Citroën, and come to a halt in the courtyard of the château, Murphy felt the familiar jab of sharp elbow in his ribs. "Hey, Frank, a little glass of wine, huh?"

"Oui monsieur," Murphy answered—ruefully—because there was no reason to refuse.

They crossed the entry hall of the château and went down the circular stone stairway to the cellars. This morning Murphy chose only to sigh unhappily at the sight of the immense dust-covered legacy he meant to leave his son if Jean-Philippe could figure out what to do with it in the next five years—since that was when Murphy expected it all to begin turning. Other mornings he actually wept and could only console himself after a few glasses by his reasonings that there must be other Murphys about: men who had built immense housing developments atop belatedly discovered quicksand beds or erected Disneylands in Siberias of tourism—in short, men like himself who had been simply unwilling to lose sleep over the caprices of wine fermentation and so spiked the product with pure alcohol to hedge against the unhappy years that other French vintners had conditioned themselves to accept.

He took a bottle from the racks, blew it off, and uncorked it expertly. His father-in-law sat down on one of the lower steps and proffered his greedy glass. Murphy filled it, then his own. They were well on their way into a typical day, and Murphy, who now had neither an occupation, nor future prospects of one, nor a hobby, nor athletic inclination, nor sexual appetite—and very little else to recommend him—knew more or less at what hour he would take to his hammock to sleep it off, while wondering vaguely at the same time how many more typical days he might endure. A salvation would have to come from somewhere outside; he had few resources left inside himself.

2

A passage to Israel

MIRACULOUSLY, SALVATION—a winged angel, Murphy supposed—hove into view the very next day when he received from Emile Monard, resident priest in the village of Vardelle-sur-Lac, first a dinner invitation, then a proposition to carry a crucifix at the head of a religious pilgrimage from the Normandy coast to Jerusalem, in Israel.

The proposal unnerved him hardly at all, even though the year was A.D. 1969 and no one, if he remembered correctly, had gone properly crusading since the second and last fiasco of Louis IX of France in the thirteenth century. But that gap in time and lapse in priority mattered little to Murphy. Had he been asked he would have gone along with the Americans on the Apollo flight to the moon: anything to get the hell out of Vardelle-sur-Lac.

He awoke in the early evening from sleeping off the day, scowled at the ashen-faced image in his bathroom mirror, and doused himself innumerable times with cold water to chase away the twitchings of his hangover. Then he dressed and climbed into his Peugeot to begin the drive down the hill to dine with Emile, looking forward, regardless of the way he felt, to the prospect. Emile Monard was his only real friend, in spite of the jealousy of his father-in-law, who wanted to be Murphy's only real friend and who kept a rote list of insults handy for vilifying the priest.

Communiste! the old man had raged already perhaps ten thousand times, and ten thousand times in response Murphy had merely shrugged his shoulders. For his own part he was in sympathy with whatever Monard happened to be. Emile had done a lot of good in Haute-Savoie. Building the compound near Vardelle for the migrant Spanish and North African workers who tended the vines and harvested the grapes had been a colossal achievement. *Le baron* had right to thank the priest instead of castigating him, for he no longer had to put up those same workers on his own lands. Murphy himself had given Emile money on the sly; where he got the rest of it was local legend.

"Il est putain!" the old man accused, in keeping with his own private interpretation of that legend. Monard, raising funds for his projects among the Tout Paris, had been immortalized in the tabloid pages of *Paris-Match,* dancing with a beauty in the capital. The effect in Vardelle-sur-Lac had been electrifying. *Le baron* had been mortified and had dashed off a ranting letter to the archbishop at Lyon demanding Monard's removal. Monard's regular congregation had trebled overnight. But the old man's letter and subsequent phone calls had been all for naught; Emile had too many friends in the big time to be outflanked by an isolated royalist baron who was déclassé, manqué, and very nearly broke. He had endured and prospered, so to speak, in Vardelle-sur-Lac, where he preferred to remain, and for Murphy the priest served as a convenient and only escape valve when the accumulating madness that came from living on the inside of the Château de Rastignac with Monique, his wife, their son, Jean-Philippe—and of course

le baron—threatened to blow apart the walls and top-ple the towers. . . .

Halfway to the village he was flagged down by two men whose car, a new black Citroën with tourist plates, had run into a ditch. Murphy's initial reaction was one of annoyance. The road ran only to the château gates, and a sign on the outskirts of the village warned that it was a dead end. He thought of delivering a harangue—the one usually reserved for those who had the audacity to make their turnaround in the château courtyard—but the taller of the two-some, smiling sheepishly and slung over with five or six varieties of camera, was at his door before Murphy could get his windows rolled down.

"I am not able to speak the French language," the man said in heavily accented English.

"I have a bad hangover," Murphy told him for no particular reason at all.

"Ah . . . you drink. . . . That is too bad." The man gazed at him sadly for a long moment, till Murphy grew irked at his ready pity. Recognition that he was on the skids was getting to be a universal thing; nobody had made a joke about his drinking in ages. Beside him, the tourist grew speculative about his condition. "Do you have a family problem, sir?"

"Among other things," Murphy answered. "Are you a psychiatrist?"

"No, I am just a tourist in your country." The man spoke in a self-effacing manner that pleased Murphy. "We are Israelis. I am Ben Bokva and he is Teplitsky. Here we parked the car to take pictures of the village and the lake, but the brakes slipped and it rolled into the ditch."

"That's too bad," Murphy judged, because he could not think of another thing to say.

"Yes, it is most unfortunate," the one called Teplit-sky agreed. He had crossed the road at the same time that Murphy had opened his door and stood out of the car. A collective sigh escaped the three of them that just failed in its power to wish the Citroën back on the road.

"I've got a heavy rope in my trunk," Murphy told them, remembering that he was already overdue to eat with Emile in the *presbytère*. "Maybe we can pull it out with my car."

"Yes, perhaps," the Israelis said in unison. In another minute they had attached the bumpers. Murphy strained the Peugeot in reverse while Ben Bokva and Teplitsky pushed at the nose of their car. It came easily out of the ditch, and Teplitsky climbed inside and set the hand brake again. Ben Bokva untied the tow rope. Murphy noticed for the first time that both men were tall and well muscled as if they were accustomed to heavy manual labor. Ben Bokva rolled the rope and returned it to the Peugeot's trunk, while Teplitsky sprinted the distance between the two cars waving a piece of paper in his hand.

"Sir, I have written down our names and addresses. If ever you come to Tel Aviv, please notify I or Ben Bokva and we will be honored to show you our country."

"Thank you," Murphy told him, somehow touched by this adult naïveté. He accepted the paper, knowing he would crumple it up later. "The chances of my ever getting to Israel are very slim."

"Well, if you do, you have two friends who are called Ben Bokva and Teplitsky." Ben Bokva spoke. "Shalom."

"Shalom," Murphy echoed, then started off down the hill again. He looked back once in the rearview mirror to see the Israelis photographing the château in the beginning sunset. Then they disappeared around a bend. He filed their names and addresses in the dashboard ashtray just as he pulled into the parking lot before the *presbytère*.

The housekeeper, Mme. Robert, who did not like Murphy since the wine scandal that had cost her brother his job in the vineyards, admitted him to the house without a word. The priest was seated in the library waiting for him.

"How's my favorite nihilist, François?"

"A bit shaky, *mon père*. I've spent the whole day passed out in my hammock. The great white wines of the Château de Rastignac, *tu sais?*"

"You're crazy, Frankie boy. That rotgut is going to take out your stomach." The priest spoke in a nearly perfect vernacular of the time of Murphy's youth that he had learned during a two-year stint on the assembly line of a Ford Motors plant in New Jersey.

Emile Monard was more American than an American. He kept closets full of Levi's—the tapered kind and the flare-bottomed kind—boxes of appropriately scuffed tennis shoes, and drawers full of button-down broadcloth shirts and crew-neck sweaters. His hero had been Jack Kennedy. Murphy had always assumed that Emile's notion of perfectible self had come from some young man he had once seen walking along a New Jersey beach. Today he lounged barefooted on a sofa clad in a striped polo shirt and tapered Bermudas that Murphy was almost certain American kids no longer wore. Easily into his forties, the priest had the look of grudgingly parting with his twenties; he took good care of himself but was an incredible narcissist. Murphy wished Emile might die young. The recognition of his real aging would be a misery for the priest.

"You know you've become a goddam alky, don't you?" Monard was on his feet now, rasping his toes in the thickness of an Oriental rug.

"Lots of French people are alcoholics, Emile. My father-in-law keeps a nice buzz on all day long. Besides, I've told you I'm drinking a penance."

"That's no penance, that's self-destruction. And your father-in-law still functions, at whatever rate. But you're becoming an American alcoholic like those guys on the Bowery in New York. That's the fallin'-down passin'-out kind of alky. One of the guys I worked with on the assembly line at Matawan ended up there. Christ, Frank, you should've seen him. It was so sad. He couldn't take food any more. All he could do to fight off the nausea was drink. I used to try to go over there about once a week to pump some soup into him, and he'd practically always vomit it right up again. He always had a load of shit in his pants, too. Finally he fell into the street one night and somebody ran over him. . . ."

The priest walked a quick angry circle about the library, his hands shoved deep into the pockets of his Bermudas as if to guard against the alternative of using them on Murphy. Then he headed for a sideboard and yanked out a bottle of Scotch.

"Here, have a wee little nip. I know damn well you need one."

He poured Murphy a straight Scotch with no ice and thrust it out to him. Murphy did not refuse. He took the glass and winced inwardly as Emile's anger changed to a pitying glance at the sight of Murphy's shaking hand.

"Man, you are going at it with a vengeance, Francis Xavier Murphy. What you need is another project to ward off your imminent collapse."

"I'm still smarting after the failure of the great wine enterprise. I'm being very cautious about any new projects."

"Exceedingly so, I'd say. The wine bit was two years ago, and the whole thing, though crooked, was worthy of a man of your talents. If that idiot of a father-in-law of yours hadn't shot off his mouth in the wrong bar, you'd still be in business. However, I think I have something that might interest you. But it means leaving Vardelle-sur-Lac."

"Wonderful. With one exception: Don't tell me to go back to America. I've got no more relatives there, and from what I read in *Time* magazine that place would swallow me right up in a day. And another thing—no more dormitories for Algerian grape pickers either. We can't afford to hire them any more."

Monard poured him another Scotch, and Murphy gulped it gratefully. The priest looked at him for a long time, his face becoming distant and speculative.

"Do you need money, Frank?"

"Absolutely."

"How about forty thousand American dollars?"

"What do I have to do for it?"

"Walk to Jerusalem."

"In Israel? That Jerusalem?"

"Yep."

"Emile, by any chance were you put up to this by two Israelis in a new black Citroën?"

"No, this is totally a Catholic enterprise. Why do you ask?"

"Because I just pulled two Israelis out of a ditch on the way down the hill. One guy's name was Bensomething or other and the other one had a Russian or Polish name I can't remember right offhand. Anyhow, I've got their names written down on a piece of paper in the car. They're from Tel Aviv. They've invited me to visit them if ever I get to Israel."

"A kind of remarkable coincidence," Emile judged, shrugging his shoulders to indicate his ignorance. "But you might get your chance to take them up on their offer."

"Aren't you a little daft? It's a couple thousand miles from France to Israel."

"I know it. But this is nineteen sixty-nine. There are lots of good roads along the way, and as far as I know no hostile armies to worry about. Remember the crusaders, Frank. Most of them did the trip over dog paths seven or eight hundred years ago."

"Hmm." The scornfulness of a lapsed Catholic was still pregnant within Murphy. "All the dregs of Europe pouring out through the Pope's sphincter into the Middle East. Who would I be going with, an army of drunks?"

"No, just a few other lost souls like yourself."

"Emile, I think you really are crazy. It would take a year, maybe even more, to walk that far."

"Look at it another way, Frankie. If it took a year to walk that far, and you had to walk every day, you wouldn't have too much time for the booze. You might dry yourself out nicely in that amount of time. And you'd be earning money, too. How else could you come by forty thousand dollars just for walking?"

"Who's behind this, *mon père?* You've turned over a lot of good money in your time, but I know you don't have anything like forty thousand bucks. Are you sure it's not those two Israelis? They might be setting up a bunch of innocent Christians, who they know wouldn't be denied access to the Arab countries en route, to provide them with information about missile deployment and stuff like that."

Murphy was aware of a sudden rising excitement in his voice. The thought of leaving Vardelle-sur-Lac to become an Israeli spy sent rockets of adrenalin coursing through him. All told, he was pro-Israeli in the Middle Eastern affair; in the last election he had refrained from voting for de Gaulle and his referendum because "Charlie" had stopped the Mirage shipments to Tel Aviv. Now, as a spy, he would enjoy perfect concealment because, of all things, of his Christianity. Also, he was not circumcised.

He extended his glass to Emile, who filled it happily this time, then prepared one of his own. The priest looked at him sagely over the rim of his drink. "I think we're about to do a little business, Frank."

"Maybe. I'm really excited by the prospect of working for the Israelis."

"Sorry to disappoint you, but this act of fraud you're about to join up with is a peripheral part of the international Roman Catholic conspiracy. Your boss would be none other than *monsieur le père* Marfeau."

"Ugh. He's crazy. Or at least half of France thinks he is."

"And the rest think he's a saint. I know he's crazy,

but I also think he's a saint. He and I have done a lot of business together."

"What's his gimmick, Emile? A sleuth like Marfeau always has a gimmick."

"A national spiritual exercise. It's a master stroke, actually—the Fourteenth Crusade, Christian Activist reform again at the end of the turbulent sixties, transmitted to the French nation absolutely free, care of Radio-Télévision Française. Marfeau has been twisting arms on this idea for years."

"And here I thought I was going to be one of the Christian innocents." Murphy smiled lamely. "Are you sure I'm not the only one involved? It would be awfully lonely to walk that far by myself."

"There are no Christian innocents, Frank. That's something you should always bear in mind. But no, you wouldn't be the only one. The others will be equally as sordid as yourself. But I won't tell you anything about them unless you promise to go. Otherwise you might get drunk before some members of the press and wreck everything, since you'd know too much."

"I'll go. I'll sign on right now. Not because I think it will help dry me out, but because I want to get the hell out of Vardelle-sur-Lac before it's too late and I end up under one of those stone slabs up there with the illustrious de Rastignac ancestry."

"Can't say I blame you. I hear the only reason that magnificent line has continued into the twentieth century without interruption has to do with the fact that when the revolutionary armies marched into Haute-Savoie looking for nobles to guillotine, the château was so rundown and the inhabitants so mean-looking the revolutionaries thought they were squatters, and the de Rastignacs at that moment weren't proud enough to tell them any different. Some even say that *monsieur le baron's* ancestors joined up to hunt other nobles with the revolutionaries because they had had a lot to drink with them. Just think what would have happened if you hadn't come along with your rich red Iowa blood. The line would probably be extinct by now."

"Yeah? Well, that's enough of de Rastignac jokes for tonight. Getting away from them isn't the only reason for going." He was becoming testy on this point, but for good reason. When there had been only Murphy—survivor of a family wiped out by an Iowa tornado—the de Rastignacs, admittedly too French and too Catholic, had taken him in with few questions asked. For this he would always be grateful. He thought to turn the thumbscrews on his friend the rogue priest. "I'd like to know the details of a scheme that two scoundrels like you and Marfeau are cooking up."

"Now, Frank, try to think of the higher purpose rather than the scheme itself. The workings of God are truly strange. Sometimes they need a little push."

"Marfeau reminds me of one of those crooked American faith healers."

"Perhaps. But the American lowbrows who go to see those healers have a special set of needs that they often feel get fulfilled. And if you think Marfeau's a French Elmer Gantry, you should try to remember there are Catholic French who get their kicks from lowbrow, too."

"Who would be the others going along with me?" Murphy asked. He had slowed down on sipping his Scotch. Now it was Emile who poured himself another.

"Well, first there's Blessed Marilyn Aldrich, who comes from Birmingham, England, and her companion, Jonathan Whitmore also of Birmingham, who can't be gotten rid of, so I guess you might say it's the first time in history that someone was rewarded with forty thousand dollars merely for being a goddam leech."

"Why is Marilyn Aldrich going?"

"She's going to ride a mule all the way because she's the one the miracle happened to. The pilgrimage is one of thanksgiving, you see. It's the fulfillment of a promise she made to Marfeau that if her sickness were cured she would ride an ass to Jerusalem. Later, when Marfeau prayed over her and the subsequent miracle occurred the very next morning, she had to come through on the promise. Understand?"

"Marfeau cured her?"

"Of course not. There's no such thing as a miraculous cure. I thought you were some kind of drunken realist. Marfeau couldn't cure prickly heat. There was never anything wrong with her to begin with. It's just that she had to pretend to be cured so the crusade could get under way. Now that she's cured, it can begin."

"When did the cure happen?" Murphy was smiling almost gleefully. This was better than working for the Israelis. The notion of being on the inside of a great hoax protected by religion, of all things, pleased him immensely. The world had not left him behind in Vardelle-sur-Lac, Haute-Savoie, France, after all.

"The cure happened the day before yesterday, Murph."

"How convenient. Emile, you've got to be the crookedest priest in the whole Catholic Church."

"Not me. Marfeau is. No pope in his most fiendish hour of history has equaled some of the things Marfeau has done in the name of God. Come on, let's have some dinner."

They stood and walked out of the library and into the dining room, where Mme. Robert, the housekeeper, emerged from the kitchen the instant they pulled their chairs to the table. She carried two plates of vichyssoise and almost thrust Murphy's into his lap by way of demonstrating her disapproval of that night's dinner guest. Monard merely winked at Murphy as she huffed wordlessly back into the kitchen.

"What do you think Mme. Robert would say, Emile, if she knew what kind of scheme you were up to in the name of religion?"

"I'm not sure. All I know about that woman is that if the Lord Jesus Christ himself came to dinner one evening, she'd find a way to remind him that his hair was too long and needed a trimming. I think about her a lot. As far as I'm concerned, she's my cross in life for being less than a perfectly pietistic priest."

"You need a cross in life, Emile. Doesn't any of this phony pilgrimage business bother your conscience?"

"Frank, try to keep thinking of the higher purpose here. Marfeau's no bum. He's fed and housed and clothed DPs from the war. When the *pieds noirs* came back from Africa he found them jobs that didn't exist. In fact, he created the industries that created the jobs. That, to me, is a lot more Christian than some village priest pisswhistling about lewd films and masturbation every Sunday morning from the pulpit."

Murphy said nothing but instead tried another spoonful of vichyssoise, reassured by now that Mme. Robert had not laced his plate with rat poison or some such thing. Only he was easily on the verge of nausea; his forehead had broken out in a sweat, and his hand trembled as he spooned the soup to his lips.

"You really need to go on this crusade," Monard told him quietly, shaking his head. "Pretty soon you won't be able to get much of anything down except the booze. Like the guy who died on the Bowery."

"I'm going. I promise you. Now stop talking about it. Who else is going with me?"

"Besides the two *anglais,* there's Bisson, a parish priest from Saint-Aubin in Normandy, where the cure happened. He's supposed to be Marilyn Aldrich's confessor and the one to swear that she's been there for four months and never been seen out of a wheelchair. Along with certain pious old ladies, of course, who saw her all those times at early morning Mass. But then they won't be of much use on the tube and Bisson will, since he's going to give occasional five-minute interpretations of the Christian experience along the route. Only one word of caution. The priest is old and supposed to be somewhere out on cloud nine most of the time. In fact, he actually believes a cure did take place."

"My God, you're a cad! What does the good Père Bisson get out of all this except happiness?"

"An orphanage, I believe. Yes, that's it. Not a big one, of course, but one that's adequate for his purposes. He's been trying to get the government or the Church to build him one for years, but who the hell ever listens to small parish priests? He was the perfect choice, since a priest in a seacoast resort town would be rather likely to have contact with English Catholics over on holiday."

"This is getting good, Emile. I'm loving my fellow travelers already. Who else?"

"An English doctor named Kyle-Boyer. Austin Kyle-Boyer, I believe. Getting him was a stroke of genius on Marfeau's part. He's to be the pilgrimage's resident cynic: rational medical man in the face of spirited Christian hopefulness—or Catholic witchcraft, as he intends to call it. Anyhow, he'll be sparring with Bisson on the telly, and that ought to alert the French to the business of the crusade, since, if I know my countrymen, they'll all side up with Bisson even though they despise him for being a naïve peasant priest. Only watch out for this guy, Frank, because he really is crooked. Back home in Angleterre he was a first-rate abortionist, long before it was legal, and he cost eighty thousand dollars to buy away from his profession for a year. Marfeau is pretending he was Marilyn Aldrich's unconvinced physician from Birmingham. Also, he speaks French like a member of the Académie."

"It's becoming easy to see why we're top-heavy with English."

"Yes. Taking advantage of the French national prejudices is most unfortunate. But they're there and waiting to be used, it has to be admitted."

As if speaking of prejudices had reminded him,

Monard rang the tiny bell beside his plate and, re-flexively, Mme. Robert charged from the kitchen with a *rôti de veau, pommes frites, et légumes,* all atop the same tray, which she deposited on the table with-out a word and then scooped up the two soup plates and retreated again. Murphy sought to quell his nausea at the smell of the mounds of food. He took a glass of wine instead.

"You know, Emile, that you're going to have trouble with the Catholic Church over this. Even though it calls a place like Lourdes miraculous, it's pretty skep-tical about nine tenths of what's supposed to be happening down there."

"Don't worry about the Catholic Church. I'm an affiliate in good standing and she's a sly old fox. If this extravaganza turns out the way Marfeau thinks it will, the Church'll climb right on the band-wagon and hustle it for all it's worth. And if it flops, they'll get their chance to nail Marfeau to the cross, which is something a number of French bishops have been dying to do for years. But it won't flop. Mar-feau is too smart for that."

"Would it be ridiculous to ask if there's anyone else going along on the trip?"

"Just one more person of importance. That's Ger-vais, the Radio-Télévision Française producer. He's got two cameramen with him, plus a station wagon and a utility van that's carrying all the food, bed-ding, and extra clothes you pilgrims are going to need. He rides; he doesn't walk. That was all part of the agreement, plus his forty thousand dollars. RTF pays the cameramen. Considering his position with the network, he might have cost Marfeau a lot more. But he figures to score a coup with this series, and the government is always looking for bread and circuses to keep folks' minds off the economy and the government, so he wasn't too hard to procure."

"This is all a bit of fantasy, Emile."

"What of it? *Le père* Marfeau deals exclusively in

fantasy. This is absolutely his kind of caper, and he'll make an absolute success of it."

"Can I ask who's paying for it? I hear Marfeau drives a Deux Chevaux and avoids the tables of the rich."

"Yes, the tables in the great halls, perhaps. But he's shared more than one meal with them down in the kitchen on the servants' day off. He raised all he needed with a few phone calls."

"Whew! Nothing is pure, is it?"

"Nothing much, Murph, that's for sure. But all this will be good therapy for you. You've lost touch with pragmatism by playing châtelain up there on that gloomy hillside. You've become ineffectual. Come on, the food's getting cold. Let's eat."

"Can't. I'm feeling nauseated. I'll have to make do with the vichyssoise and some wine."

"All right, but I'm not going to lecture you any more. Remember, when you sign up, there's no drinking on the job. Otherwise you'll probably die along the way."

"Death might be a welcome prospect. But tell me one thing. If we don't make it to Jerusalem—that is, if the whole crusade disbands for some reason or other—do I still get my forty thousand dollars?"

"Absolutely. But this crusade, as you've obligingly begun to call it, won't disband. You'll see. Marfeau has willed that it go to Jerusalem. France needs it; Christianity needs it also." The priest intoned the words solemnly through a mouthful of roast veal, winking facetiously at the same time. Then he added in real seriousness, "The one true thing that has to be said for Mme. Robert is that she's a hell of a good cook."

"Marvelous, if becoming nauseated by way of the odors is any quotient," Murphy judged, feeling more nauseated still. "I'm glad you're able to enjoy it. How do I hook up with this crusade anyhow?"

"Can you leave tomorrow?"

"Absolutely. At first dawn."

"Then drive to Caen, in Normandy. A lawyer named Gillet will meet you in the bar of a restaurant called Les Fruits de Mer at, say, seven in the evening for your last cocktail."

"Why do I have to meet with a lawyer?"

"To read the clauses of the contract Marfeau has had drawn up. If you're in full agreement with Marfeau's conditions, you sign, and the next morning Gillet will take you to the others. A driver will bring your own car back to the château. You ought to meet up with the group somewhere outside Caen. Hopefully you'll have your walking legs by the time the entourage reaches Le Mans. By the way, you'll identify yourself to Gillet by wearing that old blue blazer of yours, the one with the University of Iowa seal on the breast pocket."

"I don't think I've worn that since the first time I walked into the Ritz in Paris for a drink. And that was seventeen years ago."

"All lives come full circle, apparently," Monard judged, with a curious faraway look in his eyes. Then he snapped back. "Also, before I forget, the first films of the pilgrims should appear on tonight's late news coverage. You can get a good—if distant—look at your compatriots. The one carrying your cross is Jonathan Whitmore. If he appears to be scowling, it's because he's a professed atheist and doesn't believe in crosses."

"Neither do I."

"It's only a symbol, Frank, my boy. Just keep thinking of your forty thousand dollars."

"Well, my father-in-law at least should be pleased by the notion that I'm carrying the cross to Jerusalem. It's a family tradition. The château is littered with etchings of former de Rastignacs who allegedly went off to liberate and stayed to rape and pillage in the Holy Land in the name of France and God."

"You won't be doing any raping, unless Marfeau condescends to let you fellows stop off in a bawdy house every now and then. What do you think Monique will say?"

"Good riddance, probably."

"That's what you wish she'd say," Monard said testily, folding his napkin and flipping it on the table. "That way you'd be released from your connubial responsibilities that you haven't fulfilled in a long time anyhow. Boy, it makes me sick to see the look on that woman's face. How can she still love you like she does? Can't you make that thing between your legs go up any more, or have you drunk it into obedience?"

"Don't you know? You're her confessor."

"Bad joke, François. And as for your next probable accusation, I don't mix it up with married women." He stood abruptly from the table to pace back and forth again across the room. At that moment, Mme. Robert chose to make a pointed entry from the kitchen. She stared a long moment in exaggerated disbelief at Murphy's unused plate, then rounded his chair to plant her hands firmly on the tablecloth. *"Croyez-vous que je ne suis pas bonne cuisiniére, Monsieur Murphy?"* she rasped into his face.

"Tais-toi, Janine," the priest told her.

"Non, monsieur le curé! I spend all day in the kitchen cooking for the likes of this *salaud,* who shows up too drunk and sick to eat any of it." She gestured furiously at Murphy, who thought he was about to be struck. For his own part he resisted staggering to his feet and smashing her face. The bare bones of some ancient pride were calling out for vengeance. He had accomplished something in life, been a good husband and father at one time. . . .

"Janine, go to the kitchen!" Monard ordered sharply. "You know it's not the fault of your cooking. Everyone who has ever eaten here has had nothing but praise for your skill. He's sick, don't you understand?"

"I understand, *monsieur le curé!* You should not

be his friend. A sick drunk who has almost ruined our village with his foolish schemes!" She yanked Murphy's plate from before him and raced off toward the kitchen, thought better of it, turned around and smashed the plate on the floor, then retreated through the door. Monard merely shook his head sadly. Murphy stared at the shattered plate in mute disbelief.

"They never forget, do they?" Murphy said at length.

"No. I suppose they never will, either. You raised up their hopes and pride, then dashed them in one punch. Not your dishonesty alone, of course, since your father-in-law was in complicity, but they blame you almost exclusively, since they've never given him credit for any intelligence. It's another good reason for you to leave Vardelle-sur-Lac. Two years of living in an island of hostility like this should be enough for anyone. For *le baron* it's different, since he was born contemptuous of them anyhow. But you were not. You liked and respected them, and they in their turn, when they were able, liked and respected you. It makes it all that much more difficult."

"Yes, you're right." Murphy spoke softly, getting up from the table. He was half drunk again, but a real sadness, close to tears, came over him at the notion that the seventeen years he had invested in France had all come to nothing. He was once again the American who lived in the château and, worse, he had not a single living relative or friend left in America, so there was no reason to return there. Going to Jerusalem struck him as the only thing left in the whole world to do besides kill himself.

"Good-bye, Emile. Thanks for the new direction in life."

"It's only good for a year, Murph, but perhaps you can parlay it into something more permanent. This life is at an end. It has to be. And who knows, perhaps Monique and Jean-Philippe might even be willing to join you afterward."

They shook hands somberly, and Murphy felt his

way carefully down the steps of the *presbytère* toward the Peugeot. He thought of mentioning that he was sorry about Mme. Robert, but behind him Emile Monard closed the door with a soft click, and there was nothing else to say. Vaguely, he wondered when he would see the priest again.

He started the Peugeot and drove out of the courtyard and into the street, moving toward the château. In the headlights he saw the two Israelis dining on the small terrace of the village's only restaurant and thought of stopping for a drink, since they would certainly welcome him. Then he remembered that in the recent past without *le baron* along the proprietors had let him stand unnoticed as long as ten minutes before they would serve him, and decided against it. He sounded his horn as he drove past.

On the village outskirts where the road began to climb and came nearest to the lake at the same time, he halted the car, thinking he might descend the bank and jump into the July night waters to sober himself up in preparation for the leave-taking he intended for the early morning. But he saw the lit ends of cigarettes moving in the darkness and knew some of the village teen-agers would be there, naked and drinking wine and making love on blankets. They would laugh at his alcoholic's puffy white nakedness and chant the derisive *monsieur la châtelaine américaine* that their parents had taught them, so again he decided against doing anything. He contented himself instead with looking at the stars and the white glow of moon on the far-off peaks and remembered how, when they were first married, he and Monique had stolen off excitedly at night to swim in the coves and make love on the grassy banks. It all seemed such a long, long time ago. . . .

3

Flight from the Château de Rastignac

IN THE MORNING, ABOUT FIVE THIRTY, Murphy departed for Normandy and his meeting with the lawyer Gillet, following *le baron's* Citroën through the château gates and into the range of curves that wound down to the village below.

It was a gray dawn, colder than normal for the month. An intermittent drizzle had been falling since after midnight, when thick clouds had rolled in from the east: an ominous, nearly perfect day for so profound a departure. Murphy sighed, now the prisoner (despite the promise of $40,000) of an irresistible romantic notion that the Frankish knight was leaving his virtuous lady and good strong son in charge of the castle until he should return from the Holy City, having helped to avenge the outrages of the infidels in the land of Our Savior. . . .

But it was all a bit of fantasy, of course, Murphy chided himself, probably normal enough in an age when there was little, if anything, left to be idealistic about. He watched through the blur of windshield wipers as the trail of vapor from the Citroën's tail pipe suddenly died and *le baron's* black monstrosity took off like a shot down the hillside. There went the last idealist and believer he knew personally in all the world, Murphy decided: a man who would

27

replace the twentieth century with the nineteenth if
he were able, a man who rushed down the sides
of mountains at fearsome speeds, absolutely assured
that the hands of his God were plying the same steer-
ing wheel as his own. . . .

The night before, hearing that his son-in-law would
leave the very next morning on a pilgrimage to Jerusalem, the old man's eyes had moistened, and he
had praised Murphy's youthful strength and Christian
zeal and assured him that in this instance, more than
any other, he would bring honor to the name de
Rastignac as was done in the past. Then, by way of
emphasis, he led him along the rogues' gallery of
de Rastignac ancestors, pointing out Murphy's ante-
cedents (even though Murphy was a Murphy and
not a de Rastignac at all) who had gone on crusades
or pilgrimages or fought in holy wars or helped massacre Huguenots or done whatever was called for
in the name of Christ's Blood, until they came to
the portrait of Guillaume, Baron de Rastignac, who
had died in 1812.

Guillaume was Murphy's favorite ancestral in-law,
probably because he was the only one about whom
Murphy was certain he had found out the truth,
also because he was the only one in the long line
of inbred, wizened generations of de Rastignacs to
have been painted with a smile on his face. He
too had taken the cross in hand, setting out on a
private crusade to Moscow, one of the other holy
cities, riding on a jackass in response to the supposed
miraculous recovery of a son dying of pneumonia,
all shortly after Napoleon's invasion of Russia. But
being a de Rastignac, he set out in defiance of reason
and everyone else's exhortation, and in keeping with
the family's well-developed ironic tradition he was
robbed and murdered on the plains of Poland, not by
avenging Russians or Polish bandits but by French
deserters returning from the demise of that particularly
snowy winter. Still, the family thought well of him, and
le baron had conceived an ingenious lie about the

czar's Tartar legions coming upon a single Frenchman astride a jackass and venting upon him all their frustrated pagan rage. He also made a special point of noting that Guillaume was moving toward Moscow, not away from it.

"His death was a horrible, barbarous affair that lasted more than five hours." *Le baron* spoke sadly, gesturing toward the still-smiling Guillaume. "He died with the word *Jesu* on his lips."

"I have been told, monsieur, that your ancestor was robbed and murdered by French deserters," Murphy told him flatly, suddenly enormously weary, on the eve of his departure for Jerusalem, of playing the de Rastignac ancestor game, the monarchy fantasy game, the Christian politics game, and all the other games *le baron* had so energetically played all his life to avoid the truth of exactly who and what he was.

"That's an absolute lie, François, invented no doubt by some of our family's enemies," the old man retorted. But that was all. He had squared his shoulders, tried to avert eyes glazed by hurt, and marched out of the room to another glass of wine. Murphy, for his part, had patted a good-bye kiss on Guillaume's forehead; then he had squared his own shoulders and gone to break the news to Monique.

She was painting in her studio in the east tower, and Murphy, panting heavily by the time he was but a third of the way up the well-worn circular stone stairway, had tried to think how best to tell the news of his departure to her. As ever, when he thought of leaving, he remembered his favorite short story, read years before in an American anthology, about the man who awakened one morning at 4 A.M., nudged his sleeping wife to tell her he was leaving immediately on a trip, received her mumbled well-wishes, and left, never to return. But the story, always recalled for the clean deftness of that departure and escape, had been borrowed upon already. (Five years before, when he was thirty-two and existing in another not-so-drunken though equally purposeless limbo, between the vintage car scheme and the great wine scandal, he had tried it on Monique in the middle of the night and left fifteen minutes later—passport, travelers' checks, and suitcases—to join up in Paris with two English youths on their way overland to India in a camper van who had advertised in the *Herald-Tribune* for a third companion. By the time he had returned, flying in from Burma six months later, her anger had cooled and they had resurrected their marriage, both agreeing the separation had done much good.) As he reached her studio door, Murphy decided to try for the blunt leave-taking one more time. She might remember the happy period that had followed his last departure. Also, there was the matter of the forty thousand dollars. Monique was the least frivolous woman Murphy knew, but perhaps she could be won by the promise of a few good paintings and a new wardrobe. It was worth a try.

He pushed through the door and found her sketching with charcoal on a large pad propped upon an easel. She wore a long Moroccan caftan, medieval-looking, Murphy supposed, the perfect raiment for your lady to be wearing when you got to the top of the east tower to tell her you were leaving the very next day on a crusade to the Holy Land. She smiled wanly at him as he moved across the room.

"You're panting heavily, Frank. You shouldn't take the steps so quickly."

"I'm not as thin and lithe as some of your ancestors, Monique."

"Apparently not. There's a lot to be said for them, after all. It seems they were mostly wine growers, but not particularly tasters until the generation of my father."

"I did some things in my time, Monique. I rebuilt this house and replanted the vineyards. We have a fine son."

It was his standard retort, much practiced, that he chanted or whined. But this time he decided it really was time to go. He was tired of the sound of his own voice.

"Yes, you did all those things, then made the name de Rastignac something of a joke on national television. For the house and Jean-Phillippe I thank you. For keeping my father company in his old age, I suppose I owe you some thanks also. But for what's become of our marriage, for drinking yourself right into sexual impotence, I'm afraid I can't thank you at all. . . . Frank, we haven't made love in more than a year. Do you realize that?"

Murphy said nothing, looking out the high narrow window instead to where the last inch of light on the horizon grew smaller still. The tone of Monique's voice bore no accusation, rather a kind of anguish that Emile Monard had described exactly. She was a starved woman. Also, more painful to Murphy, he was almost certain the priest had already proposed she take a lover, for Emile saw no point in any continence that brought unhappiness.

"I'm leaving tomorrow on a pilgrimage to Jerusalem, Monique."

"I know. Emile called to tell me in case you got drunk and forgot to mention it. I'm to get you up in the morning so you can drive to Normandy. You're to stop at the *presbytère* on the way out of Vardelle. Mme. Robert will give you a letter to take to the lawyer."

"Are you angry?"

"No, there's no point in being angry any more. I have as little chance of preventing you from going as I had the time you went to India. Besides, Emile thinks it will be good therapy, since you obviously can't drink and walk at the same time. Only promise me one thing—that you'll never mention the name de Rastignac in front of a television camera."

"I promise."

"Bring back the Holy Grail for me, Frank."

"Wasn't that something to drink from?"

"In this case it means that cannibal sexual appetite you had when I married you. We're only in our thirties—too young for something like that to be gone entirely."

"What are you sketching, Monique?" Murphy asked, wanting to change the subject. He walked to the other side of the easel to stand beside her. On the pad, nearly finished, was a crusader knight that was clearly Murphy himself. Two large ears, like those of a jackass, grew out of his head; a wine bottle was the emblem on his shield.

"I guess we take our revenges in any way that we can," Murphy said distantly.

"Yes, I suppose so. I've had so few chances." She tore the sheet from the pad and crumpled it on the floor. "You'd better say good-bye to Jean-Philippe. I'll see you off in the morning."

"Are you angry?"

"Oh, Frank, you've already asked me that. It doesn't matter, is what I'm trying to tell you. Just go and get your self-respect back. . . ." She was crying, tears sliding down the smooth planes of her cheeks. It was a long time since he had heard her cry; Murphy had thought her inured to the possibility of being hurt again. In recent years her beauty had hardened into a real aristocratic aloofness; Murphy imagined these days that, when strangers saw them together, they mistook him for her bodyguard or chauffeur or whatever. Certainly not her husband. He recalled the first time he had seen her, more than sixteen years before, in Paris: a timid young beauty, purposely released from her walled-up convent school along with others more or less like her, who marched chanting up the Rue de la Sorbonne, bearing signs that proclaimed them pro-French Algeria. At the end of the street they had clashed with an Algerian Independence contingent, and as Murphy watched, fascinated, she had gotten into a personal confrontation with a swarthy Arab who began flailing her with her own protest sign. In a blind, unthinking moment, Murphy, nominally a coward, had rushed into the

street and kicked the Algerian squarely in the
crotch. That act had brought him a wife.

He tried to take her in his arms, but she put him
off.

"Go tell Jean-Philippe you're leaving, Frank."

Cowed, Murphy descended the steps again—carefully, the vertigo clutching at him as it always did
when he started down—and went to look for Jean-
Philippe in his room. Finally he ferreted him out in a
dark corner of the great hall. Murphy's son was playing with his turtles. He had nearly fifty of them, and
as the father drew close he heard the scraping and
clacking of many horned turtle underpans sliding over
the flagstone of the floor. Murphy switched on the
light. His son was enveloped in a tortoise sea. They
crawled up his legs and chest and covered yards of
the distance he might have to cross to touch Jean-
Philippe. Murphy began instantly to itch.

"I wanted to tell you that I'm leaving on a long
trip tomorrow, Jean-Philippe."

"*Où, papa? L'Amérique?* Where are you going,
Father? To America?" he asked. Jean-Philippe spoke
English nearly as well as his mother. But as a compromise between his lingual ability and the French
xenophobia learned from his grandfather, he had developed the annoying habit of repeating almost every
French word in English.

"*Non, à Jerusalem, Jean-Philippe.*"

"By airplane?"

"No, I'm going to walk there with some pilgrims,
carrying the cross of Christ."

Something in Jean-Philippe's face, full of bourgeois
reasonableness learned from Baudrey, the estate
keeper, and his wife, suggested immediately that Murphy was very stupid, and he hastened to assure his
son that he was being paid $40,000 for his trouble.

"Then it begins to make good sense, after all,
Papa. When do you return from Jerusalem?"

"About this time next summer, with any kind of

luck. Père Monard thinks it will take nine months to a year."

"Is there any chance of obtaining some of the money before that time?"

"No, not until we reach Jerusalem. Why?"

"Because the house needs a new roof, in case you haven't looked up lately. Also, Roger wants to begin the new transplants, and we'll need to hire experienced workers, not those *gosses américains* who spend most of their time having grape fights among the vineyards. That takes money."

"Don't you think you should ask me before you and Baudrey begin something like transplanting? What's the point of it anyhow? We're out of the wine-making business."

"Yes, until now, thanks to you," Jean-Philippe gnashed out, standing so abruptly that three or four turtles crashed to the floor around him. Reflexively Murphy took a step backward: At fourteen Jean-Philippe was already taller than his father, hardened by hours of physical exercise each day, and Murphy, weakened by drinking, had no doubts that Jean-Philippe could pound him to pulp. Frightened, he took a more conciliatory tone.

"But Jean-Philippe, you've got to realize there's no point in enlarging the vineyards. We can't make or sell wine."

"No, not by labeling it Château de Rastignac. But Roger has found a German in Strasbourg who knows how to get it into Allemagne, and he'll label it himself and sell it as Moselle d'Alsace. He'll take all that shit down in the caves and any more we can make. We'll hire back as many of the villagers as will trust us. The château will become a proud place to live again."

"No one who knew anything about wine could mistake that shit, as you call it, for a Moselle," Murphy told his son irritably, because he did not know what else to say. He felt like an archery target stuck full of indicting arrows.

"Let the German worry about that. It's his problem if he's caught."

"It's partially yours, too, along with your friend Baudrey, of course. And the authorities won't be very lenient this time."

"Yes they will, monsieur, they will be exceptionally lenient if we're caught. Because this time there won't be a drunk old baron and his drunk American son-in-law giving away their special secret for elevating the alcohol in their wine on the national television and making us all ashamed because you both thought you were so funny. This time there will be *un jeune français* trying to restore his family's fortune, *un type très sportif, qui va chaque dimanche à la messe. . . .*"

"I'm sure you'll make a success of your project, Jean-Philippe," Murphy told him, anxious to head off his complete reversion to French, because that meant a tirade was on its way. "I'll see you in the morning before I leave," he added, turning to move off. But Jean-Philippe bounded over the outer rim of his turtle world and was on Murphy in seconds; he grabbed his father's arm and spun him around. Murphy's fright dissolved into misery; as had his mother, Jean-Philippe had tears in his eyes.

"Father, do you remember when I was a little boy and we would rent the house in Juan-les-Pins for the summer and drive over to Cannes in *grand-père's* Citroën to sit in the cafés and watch the people go by? Remember how everybody was happy? You and *maman* and I also? You never drank very much then. Maybe if you go on this crazy promenade to Jerusalem, you'll be able to stop drinking like Père Monard said and we might all go back to Cannes for a holiday."

"I believe I'm still persona non grata with the police in Cannes," Murphy told him ruefully.

"I'll fix it for you with them. Like I did the last time."

"Please don't remind me of that, Jean-Philippe."

Murphy meant it; it was his ultimate self-loathing. Two years before, when the wine scandal had rained down local brimstone on their heads, the family had fled to the Riviera to get out of reproachful Vardelle-sur-Lac for a time. Only Murphy, on their second day in Cannes, more drunk than ever before in his life, inexplicably walked out of a café to the Croisette, took off his clothes, and jumped or fell totally naked over the railing into the sand below. Horrifically, it was twelve-year-old Jean-Philippe, desperate that his mother should not know what had happened, who persuaded the police not to book his father and instead got them to telephone Emile Monard, who had driven down to Cannes and had Murphy put in a hospital for two days on the pretext that he had tripped and fallen down a flight of stairs. Monique still had not learned the sad secret the father and son shared.

"In one year, when you return"—Jean-Philippe spoke again—"we'll go to Cannes for a holiday. The police won't remember you, because you'll be a different person."

"I hope so," Murphy told him, kissing his son good-bye and considering at the same moment that the thing he owed Jean-Philippe most in all his neglected responsibility of parenthood was a sober week in Cannes. . . .

And he meant to deliver, Murphy resolved doubly in the morning, as he pulled up before the *presbytère* in Vardelle to pick up Emile's letter from Mme. Robert. Minutes before, when he had left the château, following after *le baron,* there had been only Monique in the courtyard to bid him a wistful good-bye. Jean-Philippe, almost by way of emphasizing that something was owed him by his father before relations between them could ever be normalized, had exiled himself to the squash court. Murphy had watched him racing sweatily about in the distance, hammering the ball into the backboard with a thumping fury that made him think his son saw an

illusion of the father's head, into which he was trying
to bang some sense and sobriety. The instant before
he drove through the gates, Murphy stepped out of
the Peugeot and called to his son, "Next year in
Cannes, Jean-Philippe, I promise you!" But there
had been no response, only a ringing *thwack!* on
the ball that Murphy thought would surely send it
through the boards.

He left the car idling in the street and rang the
doorbell of the priest's house, steeling himself against
the last abuse that Mme. Robert would be able to
vent against him for at least a year, and which he
expected to be vituperative in the extreme. But instead the housekeeper appeared in the door with tears
in her eyes, handed him the letter for Gillet with
one hand and a special rosary blessed by the Pope
with the other, and kissed him an almost passionate
good-bye on both cheeks. Incredibly, Murphy
learned, the wily Emile had told her that *monsieur
le baron's* son-in-law was walking to Jerusalem to
expiate his guilt for his part in the wine scandal.
The news had apparently mollified her on the instant, and when Murphy turned away from the door
he saw that it had mollified a good part of Vardelle-
sur-Lac as well.

Baudrey stood waiting for him beside the car and
promised Murphy to keep a good firm eye on the
château and particularly Jean-Philippe, while Murphy
resolved to himself to dump Baudrey as soon as he
returned from Israel since it was obvious the estate
keeper was beginning to think of himself as indis-
pensable. He shook hands with the district gendarme,
who doffed his hat and wished him *bonne chance,*
and waved a restrained good-bye to a number of
women who fluttered handkerchiefs from their door-
stoops beside the road.

In another minute he caught up with *le baron,* who
was parked and waiting for him at the turnoff to the
National 6 that led to Lyon and Paris. The old man
stood beside his car and swigged at the awful wine from

his own vineyard at five forty-five in the morning. Murphy left the Peugeot and, remembering Jean-Philippe's anger of moments before, steeled himself against taking a drink from that bottle.

"François, they think you're walking to Jerusalem to pay the price *pour notre petite scandale*." *Le baron* winked at him, proffering the wine. His contempt was a monster.

"Perhaps I am," Murphy reckoned grimly. He shook his head to indicate he wanted nothing to drink.

"I would say you are walking to Jerusalem to continue the great heritage of the family de Rastignac, who were crusaders and pilgrims and warriors all throughout their history."

"I am only a humble person," Murphy countered. "No exploit of mine could ever equal that of your ancestor Guillaume."

"That's true," *le baron* answered, obviously appeased and taking another bite on the bottle. "His death was a horrible affair. The czar's Tartars came upon him—a single Frenchman riding his mule toward Moscow—and tortured and killed him."

"It's said they tortured him for seven hours."

"No, it was five hours. Or at least that's what the chronicles of our family say. Poor Guillaume! I hope it was only five hours. . . . Of course, it might have been seven hours. He was a very brave man, you know."

"*Oui, monsieur.* Well, I must say good-bye."

"Good-bye, François," the old man said, locking the wine bottle under his arm and bussing Murphy on both cheeks. "*A bientôt.*"

"*A bientôt, monsieur,*" Murphy told him softly, watching for a long moment as *le baron* climbed into his Citroën, engaged his gears, and lurched majestically off toward his morning appointment in the *tabac.* Then he jumped into the Peugeot and fled swiftly out of Vardelle-sur-Lac.

Murphy drove hurriedly west toward Lyon; the only real traffic on the National 6 at that time of morning—long lines of trucks straining under heavy loads of steel and junk cars—was moving in the opposite direction toward the Italian frontier and the industrial towns around Turin. With his sun roof open and fresh air rushing in, it occurred to him after perhaps half an hour that this was the first morning in a long memory that he was not beating back the first rushes of hangover nausea with another drink. But Jean-Philippe's reaction the night before to the news of his departure had shocked Murphy into a recognition of his real condition, and he had downed nothing more after his return from the *presbytère*. Instead he filled his time with packing a small bag for the trip (walking shorts and polo shirts for a trek to a hot country, he supposed), gathering up his passport and identification papers, making out a will that he posted to his lawyer in Grenoble (everything to Monique and Jean-Philippe), and cumbersomely sewing his University of Iowa blazer patch that was to identify him to Gillet at the restaurant in Normandy to a more accommodating jacket, since he would certainly never be twenty years of age or weigh as little as 145 pounds again.

At Lyon the first hunger came upon him, and he stopped at a café beside the Rhône for a small breakfast of croissants and coffee, using the time to decide whether to take the Autoroute north toward Paris or continue on the old National 6. In the end he chose the old 6, nostalgia—for a last glimpse at some of its towns strung out beside the Saône and a chance to stop in a few of his favorite bars en route—outweighing the prospect of a dull though speedy journey north.

He paced himself. Upriver at Mâcon he stopped as he always did at the regional wine growers' *salle d'initiative* for the complimentary snack of tripe and two glasses of chilled white wine. At Chalon-sur-Saône it was a quick coffee and cognac. At Auxerre, he decided on a brief excursion off the main route to Tonnerre for lunch at L'Abbaye, one of his favorite restaurants, only to find it inexplicably closed for the entire summer, so he returned to Auxerre to a clean *routier* he knew and shared a country-style *potage de légumes* and *côtelette de veau,* and several carafes of *vin rouge* at a groaning table with three beefy truck drivers from Marseille, who were fascinated by the anomaly of his University of Iowa blazer patch roughly threaded to the lightweight Cardin jacket that Monique had given him for one of his more recent birthdays.

After lunch, in an hour more, he was at Sens, where he pulled to the side of the road and napped briefly in the car; then on to Fontainebleau, where he turned west toward Normandy, skirting the edges of Paris. Murphy's blood began to stir with an unnamed pleasure as it did each time he approached the environs of the capital. He was still not too old for that. Paris, in the days of his youthful twenties, when he had bumbled timidly into the town straight from an Iowa farm, had provided the fulfillment in one way or another of every cliché-cum-dream that living in fields of monotonous corn had forced upon him: He had met and married a Monique, known and drunk with a *monsieur le baron,* mastered somewhat (despite his long Iowa vowels) the French language, sinned cautiously, though pleasurably, according to his Iowan's notion of how to wear a Gallic second skin, when that same Monique was not about, lived in Saint-Germain-des-Prés, attended lectures on existentialism at the Sorbonne, learned, *hélas,* to like wine, and once, on a Saturday morning, recognized Jean-Paul Sartre walking in the Rue Bonaparte. . . . And now at least, if he seemed to have little else but a fallow life in a dank château in Haute-Savoie, he still had the memory of that alert and wonderful time to draw upon for solace. Like first love and other youthful experiences, it never quite went away.

4

A troubled knightly vigil

IT WAS LATER THAN THE APPOINTMENT HOUR of 7 P.M. when he reached Caen, his progress west toward the coast slowed abruptly by long lines of cars streaming out of Paris on holiday.

A motorcycle policeman directed him to Les Fruits de Mer. He found a parking place not a block away, then hurried to the restaurant's bar and stood for a long moment in the entrance, trying to decide who among the patrons might be a lawyer named Gillet. But nearly all the men were middle-aged and dark-suited and had the look of being lawyers, doctors, or bankers, and Murphy ended up self-consciously pointing at his Iowa blazer patch and turning slowly about the room scanning every table for a reaction. There were no takers, however, although there was some curiosity, and as Murphy moved to the bar, deciding Gillet had not yet arrived, he heard some wag—obviously an American—refer to him as Hester Prynne with her scarlet letter.

He ordered a Scotch and soda and sat down to wait at the bar, turning about occasionally to check out any new arrivals. But eight Scotches and an hour and a half later no one had come forth to identify himself as Gillet, and Murphy thought—while he was still able—to try telephoning Emile Monard back in Vardelle-sur-Lac to ask if perhaps the priest had been mistaken about the meeting plans. He stood up from the bar after asking the barman about a telephone and noticed for the first time that the woman of a handsome young thirtyish couple sitting at a table to his left had apparently departed. They had been there since his arrival, chatting quietly to each other, and had paid him no particular attention. But now he saw the man stared at him pensively and forced a tight smile as Murphy cautiously threaded past his table to the phone.

"Monsieur Murphy?"

"Oui?"

"I am Armand Gillet. I represent *le père* Marfeau in the business of these negotiations for the pilgrimage to Israel."

"I see that I've been under surveillance for the last hour or so," Murphy said, trying to sound rueful. He was vaguely conscious of slurring his words.

"You'll have to forgive me that little indulgence, Monsieur Murphy, but we really did not know much about you, except for what Père Monard told us over the telephone."

"And now do you know any more?"

"Yes, it seems true that you drink too much. Eight Johnny Walkers is quite a bit for anybody's capacity in little more than an hour. Why don't you join me here and we'll talk over the details of the contract you've come to sign. Perhaps you won't be interested after you hear certain conditions."

Gillet had stood up to welcome him with a handshake. Marfeau's lawyer was tall and athletic-looking, well groomed and dressed in a lightweight, also Cardin suit that was pin-striped and properly dignified, in keeping with what Murphy had always judged to be the essential boredom of his profession. His grip was firm and intimidating, and Murphy, aware of the blazer patch crudely sewn to his wrinkled jacket, guessed he looked like a slovenly rumdum by comparison.

"I think I'd like another drink." Murphy gestured toward a waiter who stood talking to the barman.

"I think you've had enough, Monsieur Murphy," Gillet told him, hauling down his arm and shaking his head no for the benefit of the waiter. Murphy might have fainted at that rebuff. Incredibly the waiter kept to his place.

"I don't have to go on this bogus crusade of yours, Gillet."

"It's quite true. You needn't. But from what we understand about you, what else will you do? Emile Monard—who is your friend, by the way—thinks you will be a terminal case within a year. That is, you might have drunk yourself to death for whatever reason: cirrhosis, pancreatitis, falling asleep at the wheel of your car. Even a heart attack is possible. He's trying to help you dry out, as the Americans say. I've prepared your contract carefully. I think there is only one clause therein that might seem harsh to you."

"What's that clause?" Murphy asked, already knowing what it had to be.

"It has to do with alcohol, of course. You will be permitted no more than a half liter of wine per day, and that only with the evening meal, after which you may fall asleep at whim."

"I'm thirty-seven years old. A married man and a father. Why don't we let me decide how much booze I can have during a given day?"

"Because you've lost control. That's the essential point. And for the price of forty thousand American dollars, *le père* Marfeau is not going to permit you to stagger across the face of Europe carrying a crucifix to be shown daily on Radio-Télévision Française. Besides, you have to develop your strength. Some days you may be required to walk more than thirty kilometers."

"I'm not sure I'm that interested in going, Gillet. This was supposed to be a contract signing, not an indictment. I might be drinking a bit heavily now, but it wasn't always that way. There was a time when I drank nothing at all. I've accomplished things in life, too. Ask Emile Monard about some of the things I've done."

"I have, Monsieur Murphy," Gillet told him, with a curious faraway look that dissolved in another moment into annoyance. "I've asked Père Monard about you quite extensively. I know about the car restoration scheme, that went exceedingly well until you became bored with it, and the château restoration that was featured in *Maison Belle,* after which you immediately became bored with that. And then, of course, the wine scheme that unfortunately turned to scandal before you had a chance to become bored with it. . . . In short, Murphy, no consistency anywhere; only temporary projects to which you've applied a frenetic energy that inevitably spent itself. And now, unhappily, lacking another direction for your talents, you've become an alcoholic. . . . Why don't we adjourn, Murphy? Suddenly I'm not all that sure you're so desirable. Père Marfeau's pilgrimage—bogus as it may be—still has a loftier purpose and doesn't need some drunk to go blurting out the truth on national television. We'll find ourselves another crossbearer. I don't know if forty thousand dollars might have been useful to you or not, but there's always someone to whom it will be useful. Why don't you have that drink now and permit me to pick up the bill?"

"No, I won't have another drink," Murphy told him belligerently, so that heads turned to observe them, "and I can pay my own bar tab."

"As you wish, Monsieur Murphy. I won't press the issue." Gillet stood up and called for his own bill, paid it, and traded pleasantries with the waiter, whom he obviously knew well. Murphy, for his part, was still angry. He held Gillet from going by a grip on his forearm. "What's to keep me from blurting out the truth that *le père* Marfeau is running a phony pilgrimage since I won't be going along with it?"

Gillet descended to the table again and deftly maneuvered the hand of his clasped forearm to take a viselike grip on Murphy's own, so that they held each other like two Roman centurions engaged in a ritual greeting—only Murphy, who knew he was making no particular impression on the lawyer, began squirming in his chair with the pain. Gillet's face smiled graciously at him; unaccountably, the eyes in its midst were suddenly the most menacing Murphy had ever seen. A woman, newly arrived two tables away, smiled at the sight of two friends taking emotional leave of each other.

"You would be assassinated for your trouble," Gillet answered, his face still frozen into a charming mask.

"Even if I filed a letter with the police beforehand telling them about you and Marfeau?"

"Even if you did that silly thing, Monsieur Murphy. For who would believe the village drunk, the man who devastated the economy of Vardelle-sur-Lac, against the word of Armand Gillet, a lawyer who never left Paris for Caen, or *le père* Marfeau, who was seen preaching day after day to the Christian Activist Workers of France, those same workers so beloved by the police for their lawful and orderly nature? Filing a letter would simply do you no good. And please don't be so naïve as to think your death would occur by knife or gunshot. It could be made conclusively to look like an accident, or even suicide. And worse than that, you yourself might not even be the victim. There is your son, Jean-Philippe, for example. Or Monique, your very beautiful wife. . . ."

"Who is behind this?" Murphy demanded in a whisper. A sudden horror filled him in this most innocent-seeming place. He released his grip on Gillet and felt close to vomiting from his sudden fear. "Are you trying to tell me that Marfeau would stoop to killing? He's a priest!"

"So, after a fashion, was Cardinal Richelieu, but look at some of the work of his hand. Please believe that Marfeau is quite capable of giving the order to have you removed, were you to interfere with his master plan for stimulating Western Christianity. He's been working on the idea for years and has finally been able to bring all the parts together. So again, be assured that if you are the single piece of the puzzle that fails to fit, you are quite expendable."

Gillet had released his painful grip on Murphy's arm. His face was pleasant and handsome as before, but the eyes were now become wise, like those of a bemused old man; a faint quizzicalness was also there, as if he expected Murphy to say the next word.

"Last night"—Murphy spoke after a long moment—"when I talked with Emile Monard, this was all something of a lark, even though I agreed I had to get out of Vardelle-sur-Lac."

"From talking with Père Monard, Monsieur Murphy, I would guess that treating most propositions as a lark is rather normal for you. There's a curious contempt in you that probably derives from that time in your youth when you tried committing suicide in the funnel of the tornado that killed your parents and sister instead. I suppose the aftermath of that irony would make for some kind of massive indifference in a man. But unwittingly over the years you've dealt yourself a new hand of cards. You now have a wife and son, people for whom you're responsible, despite your obvious reluctance to be responsible for anything. That makes you vulnerable and gives us the means to assure your silence. Now, how do you choose? To join up with us or remain silent?"

"I'll remain silent. I want nothing at all to do with this. I'll return to Vardelle in the morning," Murphy told him, his voice husky now with fear.

"*Bien. C'est ça.* I have to leave, Monsieur Murphy. Only, before I go, let me make an additional proposal, since you may be overreacting to your new knowledge that *le père* Marfeau is a very deliberate man. Let's extend the time limit for making your final decision until dawn tomorrow. Perhaps by then you will have had enough time to become more reflective and decide that, after all, you really do want to join up with the pilgrimage."

"Why am I being given this second chance?"

"Because I think on all accounts you're the perfect man to carry the cross to Jerusalem. Père Marfeau would think that also, I'm sure. He would be very disappointed to lose you. Now, are you sure I can't pay for all those drinks you had at the bar?"

"No, I'm going back for another. I'll take care of it."

"Good-bye, then. It's a shame things have become so confused, but I've got a dinner engagement and can't stay any longer. Until dawn tomorrow."

"How will I find you to tell you my answer?"

"I'll find you, Monsieur Murphy. Trust me to be there on time. Good-bye."

Gillet stood and walked from the bar, nodding to someone near the door whom he evidently knew. Murphy stared after him a long moment, vaguely aware that the muscles of his forearm where the lawyer had taken his grip had gone into spasm. In another moment he stood up carefully and walked to the bar, where the barman gestured with approval after the already departed figure. "*Il est très bon gars, ce M. Gillet.* A lawyer. A fine boxer, too. But not professional."

"And you saw us together at that table, am I right?" Murphy begged, thinking suddenly he might still file a letter with the police, using the barman's testimony to bolster his statement.

Before him the man's face became a blank mask. "You are wrong, Monsieur Murphy, I saw nothing."

"How did you know my name?" he asked in a hoarse whisper.

"Your bar bill has already been paid, Monsieur Murphy. Good night, sir. . . ."

Ah. Inwardly he heard the clanking of the doors to his old safe life closing swiftly behind him. He determined to force them open again; he was not going to march on Marfeau's bogus pilgrimage, would spit in the face of Gillet, who had minutes before chiseled his epitaph in words of such undisguised scorn. Then Murphy beheld himself miserably in the bar mirror. The pale and puffy-faced image disgusted him; by way of compensation he ripped off the dumb-looking University of Iowa blazer patch and stuffed it into his pocket. Then he flung down a tip, shook a chilled hand with the partisan barman, and shuffled outside.

He had no idea where he was going. In front of Les Fruits de Mer, in the lamplit darkness that was cooling down after the heat of the day, his head cleared somewhat and he scanned the street warily in both directions, fearful of Gillet and perhaps minions of his boxing companions lurking somewhere in the darkness. But there was no one he could discern who looked particularly menacing, so he thought next to hole up in a small hotel somewhere on a back street until morning, when he would flee back to Vardelle-sur-Lac, furiously reproach Emile Monard for delivering him into the clutches of fiends, and, in the next breath, beg him to call off those same fiends since he meant to impart nothing to anyone about Marfeau's Fourteenth Crusade, phony or other-wise.

He retrieved his bag from the Peugeot, deciding to leave the car in its parking spot, turned the nearest corner, and in minutes more lost himself in the comforting maze of narrow and twisting streets of the city's old quarter. He found a hotel after perhaps fifteen minutes that seemed to him a place of perfect safety, its entrance a small door at the end of a long cobbled walkway between two buildings.

Inside, a room clerk with a breath smelling of cheap wine shrugged his indifference at Murphy's insistence that he wanted no dinner and promised to deliver a bottle of *vin rouge* to his room immediately. Murphy drank that in twenty minutes, growing angrier by the glassful at the recall that Armand Gillet's ruthless estimation of Murphy's life was that he had no recourse but to head off on Marfeau's trek to Jerusalem, else he would be a total wreck, drunk to death.

But he would show them! Murphy shouted to the walls of the room. He would return to Haute-Savoie, put himself off the drink and on the wagon, take command of Jean-Philippe's scheme to sell the swill in the château cellars to the Strasbourg German, supervise the vineyard transplants. He told as much to the room clerk when the second bottle was delivered, urging the man to wake him early for his return to the château, only vaguely curious that the clerk this time brought along an unrequested plate of bread and cheese.

Murphy shucked off his clothes all over the room when the man left and climbed into bed with the second bottle. Two sips later he passed out, overturning the bottle, whose dark red wine poured out to the dregs all over the sheets.

At dawn, or thereabouts, a key was inserted in the lock, the door swung open, and Armand Gillet, Monique, and Emile Monard stood framed in the doorway.

Murphy had kicked off the top sheet during the night. He lay naked in a still-damp circle of wine stain, his phallus erect from the promptings of some dream. His first awful consciousness was the smart of pain from the fierce whack of Emile's backhand at the tip of his prick. Awake, when he understood who they were, he yanked the sheet over him again and

begged in sudden terror to know if Jean-Philippe were
with them.

"No, he's home in the château, Frank," Emile
said. Despite his action, his voice was toneless. The
priest seemed tired, as if he had spent the entire
night driving from Haute-Savoie. He receded a little
toward the door, and Monique and Gillet moved
inches farther into the room.

"Thank God's he's not here," Murphy said after a
moment, shaking the webs from his head. "You won't
say anything to him, will you, Monique?"

"No, of course not. How is a mother supposed to
describe this to her son?"

"How did you get hooked up with him?" Murphy
demanded, pointing at Gillet. Suddenly he was crying.
"He's a prick, this guy! Have you known him a long
time?"

"No, he works for *le père* Marfeau but has become
a new member in the ranks of the Preservation of
Francis Xavier Murphy Society. New and willing to
help," Monique judged, eyeing Gillet with a kind of
curiosity, as if she were considering embarking on an
affair with him. And despite his tears, Murphy understood the same possibility had occurred to the others
also; side by side, both aristocratic-looking, they were
an incredibly handsome couple, and Murphy, carrying
a cross to the Holy Land, was not likely to be an
impediment to anyone's conscience.

"Please get up and get dressed, Monsieur Murphy,"
Armand Gillet urged. "We'll get you some coffee,
repack your bag, and leave for the pilgrimage as
soon as possible."

"I'm not going on that crusade," Murphy blubbered.
"It's too damn far to walk to Jerusalem. I want to
go back to Vardelle and the château."

"You are not welcome there." Monique spoke with
a low-voiced coldness, more forceful than Murphy had
ever heard in all the time of their marriage. With
an absolute clarity he remembered her mother: a
timid Italian lady, married off to old de Rastignac

by her wealthy industrialist father from Turin as a safe hedge against the caprices of Mussolini and the Fascisti, a woman who, in the course of a single generation, had reversed the tide of inbred de Rastignac ugliness and produced the beautiful Monique. Once, more astounding because of her frailty, she had gotten in a row with her husband while tending her roses one day and reached up and smashed him across the face with a crack that—for Murphy's purposes—had resounded throughout the land of France. In response, the old man had taken to his bed with a bottle for two full days. The memory enforced a profound misery in Murphy.

He felt himself being yanked to his feet by Emile and Gillet the lawyer.

"My father-in-law would welcome me back," Murphy told his wife, swaying between his own benefactors.

"No, he would not, Frank. I had a long talk with him yesterday after he returned from the *tabac*," Monique said evenly. "We are now in agreement. You came to the Château de Rastignac, where there was land and tradition and a marriageable young woman, and gained entry and settled down because we appraised your goodness and honesty and found you satisfactory. Now it's certain you've abused us. And remember you came with nothing in hand. No roots, though it was most unfortunate how you lost them, and very little money either, except for what you had left over from the sale of that not-so-valuable land in Iowa—"

"I'm not worthless," Murphy whined. "I did things, Monique. Didn't I, Emile? You French aren't the easiest people in the whole world to get along with, you know."

"Perhaps not," Monique spat out, "but you Americans are often impossible! One can give consideration to the possibility that Francis Xavier Murphy of Dubuque, Iowa, was not meant to be heir to the Château de Rastignac. But for what he has done to his son, turning him into a rigid fascist of a young man in response to the example of indolence and irresponsibility, this is inexcusable!"

Monique was crying too; the truth was out. Emile Monard left Murphy and crossed the room, took her into his arms, and patted her back, comforting her the way one would a young child. Armand Gillet let go his grip to urge the priest to take Monique down to the car. Then he turned and said softly to Murphy, "Get dressed, Monsieur Murphy. We leave immediately for the crusade." This time he spoke in French. The message was faultlessly clear.

Armand Gillet drove an expensive black Mercedes, the odor of whose leather upholstery made Murphy doubly nauseated so that three times he was sick out the window onto the car's high, burnished flank. Then he slept most of the way after they left Caen, waking only once, after his awareness of a long silence in the car, to hear his friend Emile Monard ask quietly of the driver in French, "Well, how do you find him, Monsieur Gillet?"

"Parfait, mon père. Meilleur que Jésus-Christ lui-même."

Perfect, Father. Better than Jesus Christ himself. . . .

PART II
THE OTHERS

5

Once a journey to Connecticut

THEY WERE DYING TO GET RID OF HIM; the very speed at which they hurtled overland after Marfeau's crusade indicated that—only it took at least an hour and a half longer than anyone had anticipated, for outside Caen Gillet took the wrong route toward Le Mans and had to backtrack the entire distance when he realized his mistake.

But by ten in the morning, after three hours in the car, with the exception of two stops for pots of mind-clearing black coffee (during the second of which he signed Marfeau's contract, with everyone witnessing), it was not the pangs of rejection Murphy was feeling. Rather, his only emotion was one of incredulous daze at his own submissiveness in the face of their combined will.

There was precedent here, Murphy thought ironically. The plight of another man come to the end of any apparent purpose, lacking the means to further propulsion, and necessarily taken in hand by others lingered in his memory. An uncle, who for his temperament's survival had fled from Iowa dullness to the mystic, history-book cities of Boston and Philadelphia on the East Coast, had finally reached his nadir in Stamford, Connecticut. As a child Murphy had known of him mainly by allusion: the eastward jerk of his father's head when he referred to his wife's brother, his parents' muted voices when they discussed Emmett, hushed tones that implied vicarious sinning and, worst of all for dawn-to-dusk Iowa farmers, an apparent lazy streak and inability to stick to any sort of job for longer than a year at a time. But for Murphy, who even as a child was chafing at the landlocked, season-regulated ritual of their existence, the uncle who sent back postcards of Boston Common, the harbor at Marblehead, Massachusetts, Independence Hall in Philadelphia, and the Statue of Liberty grew larger than life, a person of endless enterprise. Doubtless he changed jobs so frequently because it was his option to do so. He had wisely chosen not to become the prisoner of the three hundred Iowa acres to which Murphy's father sentenced himself.

When Murphy first met his uncle at thirteen, Emmett was nearly dead from drink. During that summer he rode toward the East on a Greyhound bus with his frightened mother, stopping only once (for a longer time than twenty minutes) in the maelstrom of New York to find another bus to take them on to Stamford, Connecticut. There they had met with the representative of a county agency, and Murphy's mother, weeping at the ill fortune of being Emmett's only living relative, had signed the papers authorizing his commitment to the state mental institution at Hartford. The representative had not minced words, and Murphy's mother, perhaps determined that her son should understand that the Emmett departed from the safety of Iowa was no romantic figure to be imitated, had not ordered him to leave the room. Emmett, gone mad, had taken to exposing himself to children in parks and women in elevators, walked naked with a stiffened phallus in the environs of his skid-row room, masturbated in public.

They went the same day to find him in the der-

elict's hotel. The first sight of Emmett, a god fled the
prairies to the fabled cities of the American East,
seared itself forever in Murphy's mind. The stench
of the room, the disarray, the armies of roaches and
silverfish after the neatness and order of their Iowa
home sickened him. Emmett, who sat witlessly disheveled in the midst of it, his body wasted and his
face battle-scarred from countless drunken falls down
flights of stairs, began crying hopelessly when he
finally realized who was the woman that stood before
him. Curiously, Murphy remembered, his mother, who
had broken down in the county office on signing the
commitment papers, by then had gathered her
strength and, packing a bag of her brother's pitifully
few belongings, urged him out of the room and into
the car where the impassive county agent sat waiting
for them. They were going on a picnic outside Hartford, she told Emmett, and Emmett, it seemed to
Murphy, may actually have believed her.

But at the gates of the state hospital he knew
better.

"A picnic . . . a picnic . . ." he had repeated
over and over again, the tone of his voice ironic
but not bitter, simply bottomless, beyond hope, as if
he realized that he had arrived at a place from which,
all the world knew, one began the descent into
Hell.

"I tried, Marie," he said to his sister. "I tried
so hard to make it here. I couldn't stand it out
there, the farm and the chores. . . . Monotonous.
That's the word for it. It was so monotonous. How
do you stand it?"

"It keeps me from thinking," Murphy's mother had
answered automatically. "That's why I like it, I guess."

But that was all. Emmett had made a speculative
joke about whether or not the institution contained a
liquor store, and the county agent, breaking silence,
assured him it did not but told him the hospitaliza-
tion would have him back on his feet in a couple of

months. He died, still institutionalized, within a year. The state of Connecticut buried him. . . .

And like the picnic of sad Emmett, his kinsman, Marfeau's crusade was yet another version of that Hartford hospital, Murphy surmised. Only Marfeau was handing him a Swiss bank receipt for forty thousand dollars to inspire the cure. That counted for something, helped assuage his feeling of total humiliation as they came upon the pilgrim caravan from the rear, warned of its imminence by a large sign attached to the back of a blue-and-white Radio-Télévision Française utility van that read: CAUTION: RELIGIOUS PILGRIMAGE ON FOOT.

Ahead of the van, driven by one of Gervais's cameramen, who was surprisingly large, muscular, and determined-looking, was a Peugeot station wagon, also the colors of the national network. To Murphy, its big driver looked to be the brother of the one at the wheel of the van. Beside him, Gervais, instantly recognizable from his TV appearances, slept from fatigue or boredom.

Armand Gillet slowed the Mercedes beside the station wagon and sounded his horn to awaken Gervais, who annoyedly rubbed his eyes into focus, then motioned them to park at the head of the line. The paid pilgrims turned around to observe them curiously; beside Murphy, in the rear seat, Emile Monard began to shake with laughter.

"*Mon dieu,* Murphy, you really bought it this time."

Despite his nausea, Murphy found it in himself to laugh also. Yesterday's rain had been replaced this far inland by an excessive July heat that was even now drawing mirages from the distant surface of the asphalt road that led through the Normandy pasturelands, and as they slid past the pilgrims in the Mercedes, the sounds of many feet sucking at the moistening tar came to them audibly: the feet of Kyle-Boyer's pack mule, which followed dumbly after her swaggering leader with a limp lead rope between them; then Kyle-Boyer himself, who doffed his pith helmet, smiled graciously at the car's occupants, and said in the politest English intonation, "Go fuck yourselves, you frog bastards. This isn't any kind of traveling circus, you know."

That set off gales of mirth inside the Mercedes; even Monique joined in. But from the outside they were responded to only by the black mule Father Bisson was riding, which stomped through the tar ahead of Kyle-Boyer. It stopped, laid back its ears, turned its head, and watched them for a moment as they crept past, and Murphy, remembering mules from the Iowa days of his youth, thought to silence them lest the animal panic and throw the old priest off. But he did not, and Bisson, oblivious of them and clad in a black cassock and biretta that looked to be absorbing most of the wrath of that day's sun, went right on reading his breviary, alternating smiling and gravely nodding his head as if the text contained a Latin treasure of amusement and enlightenment at the same moment. The mule, incurious now, continued walking on.

Marilyn Aldrich's animal was snowy white. As if to confirm the irascible, high-strung tendency of its rare breeding, it wore blinders against peripheral vision that the other mules did not. Astride it, letting the reins go slack and holding to the pommel of a cuplike Turkish saddle, was the cured suppliant herself, all clad in a shining white robe that Murphy thought might even be luminous in the night. Like Bisson she was oblivious of them, staring straight ahead with saucerlike eyes through the wedge of space between the mule's ears.

"Boy, oh, boy, is she high on something or other!" Emile decided, looking back, his head hung far out the window. Then he spoke to Gillet. "Is Gervais giving her drugs?"

"I don't know," the lawyer answered. "The other night when I spoke with him on the phone, I made a joke about her eyes, and Gervais admitted she uses belladonna to produce the effect for the television cameras. It was Marfeau's idea."

"Très bien! Fantastique! Marfeau is absolutely a sorcerer."

"Elle est très belle," Monique said simply.

They moved past Jonathan Witmore, the first in line, angrily carrying Murphy's cross over his shoulder like a baseball bat. The torn hem of his oversized pilgrim's robe dragged in the asphalt, and his feet, when seen, had nearly the girth of snowshoes from all the accumulation of debris adhering to his tar-coated sandals.

Armand Gillet pulled off the road ahead of the line; Jonathan Witmore was upon them almost instantly. "Who's Murphy?" he demanded fiercely. Unmistakably his accent was cockney.

"I am," Murphy said.

"Well, 'ere's your goddam cross. You was supposed to be here yesterday."

He thrust the business end of the crucifix—a truly sad-eyed cast-in-bronze Jesus mounted atop a six-foot pole of some lightweight alloy—through the open car window. It flashed past Murphy's nose and had the misfortune of connecting with Emile Monard's outstretched arm. He yelped with the pain, then grabbed the branches of the Savior's tree and shoved it furiously back out through the window. The blunt end of the pole caught Jonathan Witmore squarely in the stomach and bowled him into a ditch. Clambering over Murphy, Emile was out of the car in an instant. On his back in the ditch, the frightened cockney sought to fend him off with the crucifix, but the priest removed it from Whitmore in one ripping motion, threw it aside, and jumped in on top of him.

"If I can find your nuts under that dress you're wearing, I'm going to kick them right off," Emile swore. But there was no chance despite his anger; the driver-cameramen had abandoned their vehicles and raced up the line of pilgrims and mules and were on him in another moment, and Gervais came right behind them. His RTF employees restrained Emile—each by an arm—and even lifted him slightly from the ground so that he kicked futilely in the air.

"Who is this person?" The voice belonged to Gervais. On camera he conspired with the TV viewers *sotto voce* to enforce the notion that nothing so anomalous or peculiar as this line of pilgrims had marched along a French highway in centuries; off camera, his face wan, devoid of makeup, the voice was weary and harassed, a full-toned, exasperated sigh that implied he had enough problems already without the intrusion of Emile Monard and his hot temper.

"This is *M. le curé* Monard, a friend of M. Murphy," Armand Gillet told the producer. "He's come along to say good-bye to him." For no apparent reason he added, "Père Monard once appeared in the pages of *Paris-Match*."

Then he introduced Monique. Lastly he pointed to Murphy, who had begun to shake in response to a renewed onslaught of nausea. In a chromed portion of the interior finish of the open door, Murphy, still seated, saw a ghostly image: It was himself— or Uncle Emmett at the institution doors—sickly white, with graying hair and deep pockets of bilious color beneath his eyes. When he looked up, everyone—the pilgrims, Gervais and his lackeys, Monique, Gillet, and Emile Monard—was staring at him, their individual reactions covering the spectrum from dull curiosity to outright pity. Behind them, on the highway, heavy trucks rumbled past, the only noise in the vacuum of group silence.

"That man is quite ill from alcoholism," Kyle-Boyer, the doctor, pronounced. "He's in no condition at all to carry that cross today, Gervais, let alone walk."

"Obviously," Gervais said. "Jonathan, when he extricates himself from that ditch, will have to continue with his saintly task, at least until late afternoon, when M. Murphy might be well enough to try walking for an hour or so."

"Well, I'm not doin' it!" Jonathan Whitmore yelled, standing upright and climbing back onto the road. He had landed in a green, slimy muck that had already stained most of the back of his robe. "My contract says I was supposed to lead Marilyn's mule and that's all I had to do. I'm standin' on my rights, I am!"

"*Tais-toi!*" one of the burly cameramen warned. Shut up. By way of emphasis he thrust the discarded crucifix back into Whitmore's hands. Then he made an intimidating fist, as did the other cameraman and Emile Monard. Immediately Jonathan Whitmore looked properly chastened.

"Violence! Violence!" Gervais suddenly shrieked, with an elaborate Mediterranean gesture that told, despite his careful professional accent, that he was probably Marseillaise or at least came from somewhere in Provence. "This is supposed to be a holy pilgrimage, the means to a national spiritual regeneration, but so far there's been nothing but threats and infighting. If the French people knew what went on off camera we might turn this crusade into a serialized epic comedy. Oh, God, why was I talked into doing this? That damn Marfeau. I'm chaperoning a circus. Thank God there are no more of them coming!"

The English word God, twice mentioned and apparently understood, triggered a platitude in French from Father Bisson. Gervais's face fell and became exaggeratedly weary again. He turned about to pat the old priest gently on the leg through his cassock by way of demonstrating approval. Appeased, Bisson went back to reading his breviary. Marilyn Aldrich began giggling witlessly, and despite the evil of his hangover Murphy deduced she really was on some kind of drugs. Everyone looked at her curiously for a long moment; then Emile Monard spoke the words. "She's stoned, isn't she, Gervais? I mean she's on drugs."

"Obviously, Père Monard. You ought to hear some of the language that comes out of that holy woman's mouth when she's not on drugs and her saddle blisters begin hurting her. Four days astride a mule, and he's got them climbing right up her back."

"Maybe they aren't saddle sores, if you know what I mean," Emile suggested.

"I assure you, Father Monard, that Marilyn is suffering from saddle boils," Kyle-Boyer said. "My medical faculty degree avows among other things that I am a gynecologist."

Monique suddenly broke silence. She had been staring all the while at Jonathan Whitmore's robe, a red crusader's cross stitched to its front.

"Will you have to wear one of those robes, Frank?"

"I suppose so," Murphy answered, getting out of the Mercedes and steadying himself by holding onto the baking edge of the roof line.

"They look hot. But for forty thousand dollars one is obliged to endure a few discomforts, I guess."

"How does she know about the forty thousand dollars?" Gervais demanded. His previous exasperation became a sudden irritation that was easy to see. He narrowed his eyes at Armand Gillet in questioning.

"She's his wife, obviously," Gillet responded.

"Who else knows?"

"Père Monard here, who made the original arrangements, if you remember."

"Yes, yes. Who else?"

"Our son, Jean-Philippe," Monique told the producer quietly. "His father needed to convince him that he was not totally foolish in agreeing to walk to Jerusalem. He mentioned the money. It made sense then."

"Anyone else?" Gervais prompted.

"No one else," Emile Monard answered.

"I would say, Père Monard, that you haven't been very cautious about choosing our final participant in this pilgrimage. Marfeau, I believe, gave you certain instructions about the very private nature of this entire undertaking and who was most desirable. That person was to be—shall we say?—socially isolated. But instead your candidate turns out to have a wife and son who are privy to his affairs."

"Marfeau told me to find a certain type of man," Emile Monard answered coldly. "I found him. Look at him. He's nearly dead. Could you have done any better?"

It was an incredible rebuff; Murphy felt ashamed and betrayed. He wanted to ask Emile Monard how much his fee had been for finding the perfect dissolute drunk, notwithstanding the fact that they were supposed to be friends. But in the end he did not.

Gervais merely shrugged his shoulders before responding. "No, I could probably not have done any better. But I would like to make the point before you leave that he's too widely connected. You should have been more thoughtful. You too, Monsieur Gillet."

"Why me? What do you mean?" Gillet demanded.

"Because of Murphy, two additional persons know about the contracts and the money. Word might leak out. All of this is supposed to be spontaneous. Marfeau demands that it be that way. Everyone is supposed to be connected to Marilyn Aldrich in a very plausible way. In a not-too-distant taping session, Monsieur Murphy will be introduced as a long-time friend of Marilyn so overcome with joy that he left everything—his life in Haute-Savoie, his wife, and his son—to join up with her pilgrimage."

"Ballocks!" Jonathan Whitmore said. "A person'd have to be hit with lightnin' to want to walk to fuckin' Jerusalem for joy. It's damn lucky there's some yank dollars changin' hands here, is all I can say."

"Oh, shut up, Jonathan," Kyle-Boyer invited. "I say, Gervais, let's get moving again. Let Murphy say good-bye to these people; then put him in the Peugeot to sleep it off for a time. The only thing worse than walking through this blasted heat is standing still in it. And all this talk of money is so depressing, because it will be such a long time before I get to spend any of it."

Kyle-Boyer's voice was as imperious as the man himself looked, and in response Gervais seemed to gather up his widely flung emotional parts and started dispensing orders. They were reinforced in another moment by two police on motorcycles, who stopped and told them to move on, since traffic had only one lone recourse around them on the narrow road. Armand Gillet was anxious to leave also. He had more business farther south in Tours before nightfall and thought it best to deposit Monique and Emile Monard at the railway station in Argentan, the next town, where they might take the train back to Paris.

It was time for saying good-bye. Resolutely, remembering that his Uncle Emmett had wept unceasingly, Murphy determined to control himself. He shook hands with Emile Monard, then rallied enough to pay back the priest with a rueful thanks for having chosen the best terminal drunk in all of France for Marfeau's pilgrimage. But it mattered little to Emile; in his own mind he had arrived at the perfect solution for saving another Bowery bum from falling beneath the wheels of a truck. A splendid Christian, then, was the rogue priest by virtue of this day's work.

"You'll be in good shape in about a week, Murph," Emile consoled. "It will take about that long to build up your legs. And just keep thinking about that forty thousand bucks. Only don't think about the distance. I figured it out this morning in the car. It would be about the same as walking from Baltimore to Denver if you were still in America."

"Oh, cripes," Murphy said, the realization hitting him like dead weight. It had to be at least that far. It seemed at the same moment to hit everyone else just as bluntly, with the exception of Father Bisson, who spoke no English. Even Marilyn Aldrich, staring vacuously into the distance, mimicked the estimate.

"Baltimore to Denver. . . . Baltimore to Denver. . . ."

"Please say good-bye to your wife, Monsieur Murphy," Gervais urged. "This kind of talk is very demoralizing. I can just imagine the variety of sores I'll have from riding all that distance in the station wagon."

"Yes, you probably will," Murphy agreed. Then he drew Monique, always reticent about public displays of emotion, to the front of the Mercedes, where they simply held each other for a long moment in mutual diplomatic deference to the awful order of his breath. But still she cried when he wished she would not.

"This . . . enterprise"—she spoke softly, searching for the right English word—"this enterprise will do you a lot of good, Frank. I don't think you're an alcoholic. Not really. Drinking has become a kind of crutch because you've had nothing else to do for the last two years. And my father has been no help because he condones it since it supplies him with agreeable companionship. When you return from Israel you'll have the energy for a new project, and drinking moderately again will also have become a habit."

"Give my love to Jean-Philippe, Monique," Murphy answered, releasing her with a futile gesture. There was a wasteland between them by now. A love gone dry and not even replaced by compensating affection; the shame he had rained down on an old French name that Monique, at least, revered, for which she would never forgive him; their son, the perfect fulfillment of any couple's aspiration, who hunted desperately for a surrogate father in the likes of Baudrey, their estate manager. Truly it was time to go. Murphy nodded a curt good-bye to Armand Gillet, who smiled icily in return. At best that bastard's pity was an impersonal thing. Murphy thought he ought to have the last word, so he admonished the lawyer. "Drive carefully. At least until you get them to the train station."

But Gillet only continued to smile icily before

encouraging his passengers into the car. Monique, who now sat up front with the driver, did not look back as the Mercedes started off, nor did Emile Monard. There was an absolute soundless vacuum in their wake.

It was all too absurd, Murphy thought. They were not really going away for a whole year; he himself was not really going to walk to Jerusalem; that sort of thing just wasn't done any more. He wanted to scream after them, beg them to come back for him, but the cry for help simply strangled in his throat because he knew, alas, that he had been purposefully left behind.

Baltimore to Denver: The distance was impossible.

The consummate despair began welling up in Murphy, worse even than that which had filled the shocked aftermath of the deaths of his parents and sister in the Iowa tornado. Worse even, perhaps, than Emmett could have felt in being left to his eternity at the gates of the Connecticut institution. And he decided for certain from the knot of level, curious gazes about him that no one affiliated with the Fourteenth Crusade was likely to offer him anything so helpful as a bottle of alcohol to beat back the enticing demons that frequently rushed about in his dreams these days, suggesting multitudinous painless ways of committing suicide, just to get the whole goddam mess of his life over with.

6

Who is Armand Gillet and why is he dead?

FOR MOST OF THE FIRST DAY Murphy thought little of Monique, Gillet, Marfeau, the pilgrims, or anyone else for that matter as he rid himself of his awesome hangover, sleeping the deepest of deep sleeps on a mattress in the back of Gervais's Peugeot. The station wagon was unexpectedly air-conditioned, and the mattress cool and soft in case any of the pilgrims keeled over from heat prostration or fatigue, and Murphy was out until about five thirty in the late afternoon when Gervais—composed and more kindly —woke him. Gervais proffered a cup of red wine, the last consideration Murphy expected, and two cups of warm bouillon from a thermos bottle before suggesting that Murphy try carrying his cross for an hour or so before they made camp for the night.

Complying, Murphy donned his pilgrim's robe, beneath which he wore only his jockey shorts, and was given a pair of sandals from a collection in the utility van that trailed after the station wagon. Then he took his cross from a still-wrathful Jonathan Whitmore and set gamely off at the head of the procession toward Le Mans, his own shoes sucking now at the tar and his head still too fogged in to feel anything like embarrassment at the inevitable incredulous stares that came from every vehicle that passed them by. An hour later, with his legs aching, but marveling that he remained upright and that the cross seemed to have hardly any weight at all, he was first to come upon the scene of Armand Gillet's charred body being removed from the burned-out shell of the Mercedes.

It was eight miles or so south of Argentan, the town in which the lawyer was to have dropped off Monique and Emile Monard, but Murphy had no way of knowing for certain that the two were on a train to Paris as per plan, and he rushed desperately down the hillside, cross in hand and robe flapping madly behind him, to the culvert where the car lay smoldering upside down on its caved-in roof to beg the number of victims from the knots of police standing about.

"Un seulement, monsieur. Un jeune homme. Brûlé vif." One only, burned alive.

Thank God! was Murphy's grateful response, until he noticed that all the police held handkerchiefs to their faces against the terrible smell. Gillet's unrecognizable form was being nudged into a canvas sack by two white-clad medical personnel who wore face masks and what appeared to be absurdly oversized asbestos gloves. The tide of his fear receding, he was overcome in another moment by the burned flesh odor and turned away from the scene to begin retching violently onto the grassy hillside. When he was done, he started up to the road again, using the crucifix for support and not daring to look back. Gervais stood at the top, a curious lack of expression on his face.

"Who, Murphy?" Gervais asked.

"Just Gillet."

"Just Gillet. . . . Hmm. . . ." But that was all. The producer's face collapsed into a frown, and he kneaded the back of his head with his fingers as if he were trying to urge the answer for the young lawyer's terrible dying out of some unaccountable portion of his brain. Despite his immense relief, which had put him close to tears, Murphy thought Gervais an insensitive prick for not being agreeably surprised that Murphy's wife and friend were not also being toted away from the car in canvas sacks.

But the others made up for the apparent lack of any feeling on Gervais's part: Marilyn Aldrich, Kyle-Boyer, Father Bisson, Jonathan Whitmore, and the two cameramen, Ricard and Lebel, all crowded around Murphy for news of the victims and then issued a communal sigh of relief on hearing that only Armand Gillet had been in the car.

"Thank God!" Kyle-Boyer, the professional atheist, ejaculated, then added more soberly, "He was such a fine-looking young fellow. It's a pity to see them snatched away at that age."

" 'Ere I was thinkin' this mornin' that I'd like to be just like him," Jonathan Whitmore said. "With my forty thousand yank dollars I could buy me a Mercedes-Benz automobile and a new French suit. But now I wouldn't want any of that. It'd be bad luck after what happened to the likes of him."

Unnoticed, Lebel had slipped off to the cab of his van and returned with a bottle of wine and a handful of plastic drink glasses. He distributed them wordlessly to everyone, then filled each one to the brim, beginning with Murphy. Ricard, not the least macabre in his intent, proposed a toast that there had been but one victim instead of three and extolled Murphy's good fortune that his wife and friend still lived. Murphy, sipping greedily, decided that for the first time in a long while he actually had something good and fortunate to celebrate with a drink.

"Gervais is the coldest man," Marilyn Aldrich judged from somewhere in the reaches of her tranquilized mind. Her words startled the group of one-death revelers, coming as they did in the midst of an effective total silence. The wind, blowing in from the coast, had risen, blotting out the normal peripheral noises; the cars and trucks that usually rumbled past now crept at miniscule speeds, the better to savor the tragedy. She pointed past the grazing white mule to where Gervais squatted down on the edge of the highway with two gendarmes. One of them was obviously making a chalk drawing of the accident for Gervais's benefit.

"He'll probably have Lebel and Ricard bring out the cameras to film the bloody mess," Kyle-Boyer said. "He's supposed to concentrate on the lot of us, but Gervais is the type to make the best of any newsworthy tragedy he encounters along the way. No doubt he'll send Father Bisson down the hill to bless the roast for dramatic effect before the police take it away."

Murphy the newcomer was now certain that none of his fellow mercenaries particularly cared for Gervais, with the possible exception of Father Bisson, who probably lacked a capacity for hate altogether. He was also certain that the good priest had no intention of descending the hill to bless anything. The wind, shifting, was wafting the terrible odor directly toward them, and Bisson seemed most repulsed by it. They watched dumbly as the three mules, blowing and wheezing, moved ahead at a trot past Gervais and two gesticulating gendarmes to get somewhere upwind of the stench.

In another moment, Gervais bade the two police good-bye and returned, still frowning and shaking his head.

"It was an accident," the producer said. "He must have been drunk. He started to pass two lorries on this curve when one of the lorries tried to pass the other. His car was knocked right through the guard railing and down the hill. The lorry drivers tried to save him, but the heat and flames were too intense."

"That's ghastly awful," Jonathan Whitmore judged. "But let's get the hell out of here. The poor bloke stinks terrible, he does."

"Yes, start moving now," Gervais ordered. "We'll

delay the introductory filming of M. Murphy until sometime later. Go to the park in the next village and set up camp for the night. I've got to telegraph Marfeau the news of Gillet's death. I'll join you as soon as I'm able."

Gervais nodded Ricard toward the station wagon, and the two abruptly departed, climbed into the vehicle, and sped off down the road toward the village. Lebel collected the glasses and headed back toward his van. There was nothing left to do but catch up with the mules and continue on. As Marilyn Aldrich and Father Bisson were helped into their saddles, the police, released from their morbid preoccupation with the remains of Armand Gillet, observed them with open curiosity. The white ambulance bearing the canvas sack had already set off slowly down the highway, not bothering to sound its klaxon.

There was but one more shock to absorb that first day. It came at bedtime when an exhausted and enfeebled Murphy, having shakily consumed his allotted half liter of wine and suffered the curt refusal of his request for another, should have passed out instantly on crawling into his sleeping bag. But he did not. Instead he lay awake for hours thinking.

As did Kyle-Boyer, apparently; the English doctor was the only other person besides Murphy who understood French to get a look at the telegram that Marfeau sent in reply to Gervais's wire of earlier that evening, informing the preacher that Armand Gillet was dead. . . .

When they settled down in the deserted municipal campground of the next village as per Gervais's instructions, the producer and his driver had not yet returned from searching for an open office of the Postes, Téléphone, and Télégraphe, and Murphy got his first exposure to the evening meal and the sleeping arrangements that would hold for many months to come. Frankly he marveled, deciding that Louis IX or Richard the Lion-Hearted or Raymond of

Toulouse or any of the other medieval crusade leaders could not have come remotely close to the comfort and convenience enjoyed by their twentieth-century imitators, the numbers of servants they toted along not withstanding.

For a start there were three separate cuisines, to suit the geographical and cultural disparity of the crusaders, each of them supplied from an enormous food locker in the rear of the big RTF utility van that Murphy learned was replenished weekly. Gervais, Lebel, and Ricard, all Provençals, ate the hot and garlic-laden cooking of the south. Marilyn Aldrich and Jonathan Whitmore lived, English fashion, from a frying pan and, the repulsed Kyle-Boyer intimated to Murphy, ate their greasy fish and chips as often as four nights a week. Kyle-Boyer, as his girth implied, was a gourmet, though his art was sadly thwarted by time, fatigue, and especially Father Bisson, for whom he also cooked, since the old priest was unable to digest rich and heavy sauces. Exiled to the realm of high-protein, easily chewable foods—as his dismal sighing clearly implied—Kyle-Boyer invited Murphy to join with himself and old Bisson in setting up their separate table and propane gas cooking stove and then take dinner with them. Murphy, thinking for once realistically of his nearly exploded liver, decided that one of the paths to personal rehabilitation lay in eating with the priest and the doctor, the supposedly ideological enemies who were not enemies at all.

While he helped them set up for the meal, Murphy saw the rest of the lode that the utility van contained. In addition to tables and stoves, there were extra pilgrim costumes and walking sandals, medical supplies for humans and animals, two complete bathroom facilities like those in the cabins of jet airliners, tents and bedding, TV cameras and a television set for viewing, spare jerry cans full of gasoline, a large reserve water tank, all variety of kitchen utensils, and a portable electric generator for night lighting. Kyle-Boyer's mule, its canvas-covered pack all slung over with pots and lanterns, was a sham, then, like the rest of the crusade. It existed merely for effect. The inside of the pack, the doctor told Murphy, was stuffed full of foam rubber.

The three—Kyle-Boyer, Father Bisson, and Murphy—sat down to dinner, a simple affair of steak, salad, cheese, and bread, after Ricard, apparently suddenly remembering a duty, showed Murphy the dead space behind a sliding panel in the utility van's wall where the crucifix was to be deposited each night for safekeeping. Shrugging at that necessity, the point of which escaped him, Murphy waited at the table with Kyle-Boyer while old Bisson said grace over the food and then launched into a long prayerful eulogy over the demise of Armand Gillet. His first repast on the road then, Murphy thought ruefully, was a funeral supper.

But Murphy could eat only a little of the food, grown cold anyhow with the length of the eulogy. He sipped at his wine and remained at the table with the others while Ricard set up the portable television on a convenient stump so they might watch that evening's telecast of the RTF film shot on the march the day before. But except for Murphy, the others were clearly bored with three nights of viewing themselves—medieval and anomalous and creeping like snails—sharing a French highway with swiftly moving cars and trucks that frequently only enforced the notion of their trudging gait by slowing to observe the pilgrims with unrestrained curiosity and then hastening away in a burst of renewed speed. Only Father Bisson seemed remotely interested. He regarded his wizened image astride the mule, immersed as ever in reading his breviary, for a long moment. *"C'est moi?"* he asked finally of Kyle-Boyer.

"Yes, Father, it's you," Kyle-Boyer told him in French.

Appeased apparently that his soul had not been stolen and planted in another Father Bisson, the priest responded eagerly to Kyle-Boyer's suggestion that they continue their game of chess. Murphy watched as Gervais commandeered the screen, his face made up to its perfect media image, his voice conspiring, full of wonderment as ever, dispensing further tidbits of information about Marilyn Aldrich and Jonathan Whitmore.

When it came to Father Bisson and Kyle-Boyer, there were at home interviews. Obviously selected members of old Bisson's congregation back on the coast at Saint-Aubin testified to his goodness and saintliness and avoided making any mention of his age and senility. All believed that Marilyn Aldrich, *la jeune anglaise,* had been visited by a miraculous cure. All the interviewed were women. All had that special look of spending more time in church than at home on any given day. All of them, it seemed to Murphy, had been waiting for a miracle all the days of their lives. Father Bisson had not the vaguest idea he was being spoken about.

For the backgrounding of Austin Kyle-Boyer, there was a single on-the-spot interview from Birmingham, England, annoyingly rendered because of the necessity for almost line-by-line translation into French. The interviewee was an Irishwoman, working in Birmingham as a domestic and intending to make her way home to Dublin as soon as she "filled her sock," a phrase for which, Murphy thought, the French in translation was infinitely more precise. She labeled Kyle-Boyer an atheist, a quack, and an abortionist and insinuated darkly that there was something wrong with a man who was still a bachelor at his age and, worse, who did all his own cooking, which was foreign, her thoughtful euphemism when she meant to say French.

Kyle-Boyer, distracted from his chess game, merely snorted. "That witch! Domestic, indeed! She's a sot who lives in the neighborhood pub and has owed me five pounds four and six for the last two years. Thank God this isn't being televised in England, or my professional reputation would suffer irreparable harm."

"Are you really an abortionist?" Murphy asked.

"Of course I am. Someone has got to do that sort of thing. You're not some kind of rabid Catholic overpopulator, are you?"

"No, it doesn't matter to me one way or the other. How did you get into it anyhow?"

"I was forced into it, after a manner of speaking. I originally chose gynecology as my field to spark my interest in women, because all through adolescence my sex drive had been a rather muted affair. But alas, that did no good." Kyle-Boyer sighed heavily, staring off into the distance as if he could see a tableau of wasted years of study hanging there. "It turned out that my real passion was for fine food and wine. And as I began balding and growing pudgy with prodigious eating and lusting after the like of *coq au vin* when I should have been lusting after women, you can readily imagine what a downturn my profession took. Finally, becoming a baby scraper seemed the only alternative. It was lucrative, and good wines cost money. Otherwise I should have had to return to English cooking."

Kyle-Boyer made a face that was apparently his judgment of English cooking and then seemed alternately sad, perhaps over the unfair shortchanging of hormones he had received in life. Murphy, rarely in a position to offer anyone sympathy, sought to cheer him up. "Well, don't worry, you being an abortionist really doesn't matter, like I said."

"It doesn't really matter to Gervais either." Kyle-Boyer spoke annoyedly, nodding his head toward the TV screen. "But just look at the judgment-by-implication on that scoundrel's face."

On camera, knitting his brow, squinting, frowning, and shrugging, Gerbais was trying hard for a silent condemnation. Murphy wondered how many of the French, his countrymen of a contraceptive-loving, underpopulated nation, gave a damn about abortion anyhow. Not very many, he suspected, though Kyle-

Boyer was still likely to be the target of a few egg throwers along the way.

The camera eye riveted for a long moment on Kyle-Boyer and his mule, whose overslung pots and lanterns clanged rhythmically, then focused on the whole line of pilgrims disappearing over a hill like Bedouins heading into infinity over the crest of a dune. By the time Pompidou departed the Elysée Palace yet another time somewhere in a troupe of black Citroëns, and a police inspector in the Basque country shrugged his shoulders by way of indicating his ignorance over the whereabouts of Suleiman's Pebble, Gervais and Ricard had returned, with Gervais cursing effusively after their long search for a telegraph office.

"We had to go all the way to Le Mans," Gervais said to no one in particular. "Marfeau was preaching and could not be reached by telephone, so I had to send a telegram."

But the news prompted no reaction. Gervais and Ricard sat down to eat the Provençal stew that Lebel had prepared, and Murphy helped Kyle-Boyer clean up after their meal and then set up sleeping accommodations for the night. Operating on Kyle-Boyer's certainty that it would not rain and no tent was necessary, they simply laid a large square of canvas—to guard against the early morning dew—on a flat portion of ground on the opposite side of the camping area from which the grazing mules were tethered. Then they spaced three sleeping bags at appropriate distances across the canvas: one for Kyle-Boyer, one for Murphy, and the last for Gervais. Murphy condescended to sleep in the middle sack, for which the English doctor was profusely grateful. Besides genuinely disliking Gervais, he had apparently been forced, during the three nights prior to Murphy's arrival, to stay awake and listen to the producer's petulant ramblings over the arduousness of his task as crusade marshal, riding all day long in an air-conditioned station wagon, until the self-pitying Frenchman talked himself to sleep.

Within half an hour everyone was abed, and Murphy found himself marveling once again, as he had from the first incredulous moment of Emile Monard's proposition that he carry a cross to Jerusalem, at the apparently bottomless nature of the sham into which he had entered by contract. Kyle-Boyer, his new friend, provided the details when they heard a loud slap—that put an end to Marilyn Aldrich's whimperings—coming from within the tent in which she and Jonathan Whitmore had zipped themselves up for the night.

"Poor Marilyn." Kyle-Boyer clucked softly. "Her saddle boils must be killing her by now, but nonetheless Jonathan is bent on taking his pleasure before sleeping."

"With the sound of that crack he gave her, he might have knocked her out cold," Murphy said.

"I doubt it. Back in Birmingham, as you probably know, she was a prostitute and he was her pimp. She's rather used to getting cracked like that. Rather invites it, I wager."

"Yes, I think so, too," Gervais contributed; then he raised himself up on one elbow to yell in the direction of the tent: "Jonathan, whatever you do, don't strike her in the face. She'll have to wear layers of makeup to disguise any discoloration."

"Fuck yourself, Gervais!" Jonathan Whitmore hurled back. Then the zipper came ripping down and the small cockney issued forth stark naked into the moonlight. The three abed on the canvas gasped in unison at the sight: his erect phallus was an impossible anomaly, longer than his forearm, wider around, it seemed, than the thickness of his calves.

"You might be boss when we're on the road, Gervais, but I'm boss on the night shift in this 'ere tent," Whitmore harangued. In rhythm, his prick bobbed up and down by way of emphasis. Together Gervais and Kyle-Boyer motioned him frantically back inside the tent, pointing at the same time to the Peugeot, where Father Bisson supposedly lay sleeping in the rear. Apparently understanding their meaning at last, Whitmore's anger dissolved instantly and he tried vainly to cover up the immense front of himself, then ducked under the canvas and zipped it quickly up again. Gervais and Kyle-Boyer continued looking toward the station wagon; then, satisfied that Father Bisson had seen nothing, Gervais let out a long sigh. *"Mon Dieu!* If I could get one shot of that thing on the television screens of the French nation, interest in Marfeau's pilgrimage to Jerusalem would jump somewhat into the ninetieth-percentile range."

"For the moment, I think it far more important that Lebel and Ricard don't find out about the existence of such a thing in our midst," Kyle-Boyer said, "or poor Jonathan is liable to be the victim of homosexual rape."

"God, yes," Gervais agreed, slapping his forehead in the night. His renewed sighing told that a new volley of plaints was probably on its way. But Murphy lying between the two men who now checked out the utility van where it was hoped that Ricard and Lebel slept, was deep in instant fantasy, staring up at the stars. The phallus had excited him too, triggered the flutterings of an erection in his normally pacific sexual self. He remembered early in his marriage when he and Monique had taken a camping trip through Germany and Austria, sleeping just so in a tent and screwing themselves into exhaustion every night. It had never been so good after that. Especially back in the château, where the walls were eternally damp and ridden with de Rastignac ancestry, where the nexus of nobleness, churchliness, ancientness, and gloom had conspired to produce a nameless frigidity in Monique that among other things had helped wear down Murphy's appetite. One mile away from that house, in the meanest *auberge,* Monique could be like a tigress in the sack. Yet she chose to live in the château, even though Murphy had protested that it had compromised their marriage in so many ways. Sincerely now, the pain of loss and wasted years keen within him, he wished that Monique de Rastignac had taken him home to a tent instead. Also he wished that Marilyn Aldrich and Jonathan Whitmore had showed up in the de Rastignac vineyards to pick grapes during that summer that he and Monique had talked so seriously about mating in tandem with another couple before they finally gave up the idea for good and all. . . .

Kyle-Boyer, sighing as deeply on Murphy's right-hand side as Gervais on his left, was first to break the lengthy silence.

"Do you know, I find it extremely curious that though we're all bound to Marfeau through contracts and commitments and verified receipts of payment, it's really Father Bisson who governs us all. His moral rectitude, I mean. After all, look at us shivering here at the possibility that he should catch sight of Jonathan's penis, much less find out that Jonathan and Marilyn aren't man and wife as he's been told. Or worse, that he should know Ricard and Lebel aren't sleeping in the van to guard the equipment but because they're homosexual lovers who have to be kept out of sight. Or that I'm an abortionist when he thinks I'm merely a misguided atheist in need of his charity. I think it well that the good priest gets to sleep alone in the station wagon, considering his age and arthritis, Gervais, but all this can't be kept secret from him for as long as this caprice continues. It's impossible."

"Perhaps Father Bisson has a fault we haven't learned about," Gervais speculated. There was real hopefulness in his voice.

"I doubt it," Murphy said, anxious to quiet them. "I was told by Emile Monard, the priest you met today, that if Père Bisson has a fault, it's simply that he would sell his ass for God."

"Let's hope God is proven to be an out-and-out

fraud sometime this week. That would give us some sort of working advantage," Gervais concluded. Then: "Murphy, let me ask you one last thing about this lawyer, Gillet."

"What is it?"

"When you first met him, in Caen at some bar, I believe, was there anyone else with him?"

"A woman. But she left the bar at least ten minutes before Gillet acknowledged himself to me."

"And you noticed no men about who seemed to be abnormally interested in you or your conversation with Gillet?"

"No. Gillet seemed to know people in the bar. The barman and waiters all knew him, but he gave the impression of being quite a young man about town. Why are you so curious?"

"Simply because the whole affair of Gillet is curious. Alive and splendid one minute, then *poof!*"— he snapped his fingers to emphasize—"dead and burned to cinders ten kilometers farther down the road."

"Oh, sleep easy on it, will you, Gervais?" Kyle-Boyer insisted. "It was an accident. The gendarmes drew it all out on the road for you. These things will happen. Now be quiet, please."

Then there was silence, and Murphy began drifting off to sleep, savoring the night noises of crickets and the tearings and munchings of the three mules as they grazed in the meadow, and turning only once to see Gervais, wide awake and eyes narrowed in consternation. Murphy slept deeply for more than an hour, only to be rudely awakened along with the others by the arrival of a courier from the Postes, Téléphone, and Télégraphe on a sputtering motorcycle with a wire for Gervais.

The producer read Marfeau's response by flashlight as the cycle roared off back down the road to Le Mans, pronounced a single invective—*"Merde!"* —then climbed again into his sleeping bag, crumpling the telegram in his hand. But the news, once received, seemed to release him at least from the suspense of waiting, and within minutes he fell asleep, his finger releasing the wadded paper onto the canvas.

Kyle-Boyer nudged Murphy to pick it up, and when they had spread it open between them, the Englishman lit a match so they might read it. There were but three words, that any secondary school student of French anywhere might have translated: *Qui est Gillet?*

Who is Gillet?

"Well, if Marfeau doesn't know," Kyle-Boyer whispered softly, "who the bloody hell does?"

"I can't imagine," Murphy answered, "but we'd better not say anything to the others."

"Yes, quite right. But I intend to ask Gervais about this in the morning."

Murphy then began his sleepless hours of wonderment. Kyle-Boyer did also: he placed his pith helmet beneath his head and gazed perplexedly out over the bulging crest of his stomach.

7

Murphy's debut

IN THE MORNING, over the coffee and *pain beurré* that was to be their habitual breakfast fare for many months to come, Gervais lied in response to Kyle-Boyer's casual question about Marfeau's wire of the night before.

"Père Marfeau said that he was deeply grieved. Especially considering M. Gillet's age."

Then, a fine actor in his own right, the producer walked casually away, barking out some orders to Ricard and Lebel. In response, Murphy and Kyle-Boyer merely exchanged shrugs. There had to be a reason for Marfeau's ignorance of Gillet. There also had to be a reason for Gervais's choosing not to confide in them. But for the moment they let it go. The world about them seemed that morning much the same as it had the night before: a plausible place, a place where the answer to Gillet would yet turn up. Also, they readily admitted to each other that neither could suffer the embarrassment of having Gervais know they had read his telegram.

But it was the beginning, Murphy would frequently recall to himself, though no one, for a long time, knew of what; the lay of the land ahead looked innocent enough. In fact, of all the march to Jerusalem—from France through Italy, Yugoslavia, Greece, Turkey, Syria, what was left of Hashemite Jordan, and then into Israel—Murphy decided he would best remember the time it took to reach Clermont-Ferrand from the time he joined up with his fellow pilgrims.

He would best remember that time because they still traveled in a reality that was appreciable, uncoiling measurably: when the mind still trusted enough to make judgments about the wayfarers they encountered; when Murphy and Kyle-Boyer together dared ponder mysteries the like of Who Is Armand Gillet? and dared also believe there must be a simple answer somewhere just out of reach; when no one had any reason to doubt that Marfeau—however vast the gap between the nobility of his purpose and the unscrupulousness of his methods—was their prime machinator and the magnet at hand that drew them on to Clermont-Ferrand, if only for the chance to meet such a noble scoundrel; and when no one among them—excluding Gervais, who alone knew better—actually thought they would make it even as far as Istanbul, once Marfeau had milked them for all the publicity possible. . . .

But such thoughts grew remote as Murphy prepared for his debut as the crusade's crossbearer on French national television, and he was well pleased that it was delayed until six days after his arrival, to give him time to recover from the ravages of the recent past. Both Gervais the producer and Kyle-Boyer the doctor agreed he looked ghastly from his long term of abuse, and the benefit of exercise from several days of progressively longer periods of walking, plus the beginnings of a decent diet and the curative powers of the sun, would do much more for his image and that of the crusade in the long run than filling in the dark hollows of his eyes with pancake makeup and then propping him up in front of a television camera for his impassioned initial interview with Gervais, using for support to carry Murphy the staff of the cross he himself was meant to carry instead.

Crusading for an evangelist was show business, after all, Gervais conceded nonchalantly. Especially this crusade. Witness their master, Marfeau, who used sunlamps and makeup and whole spectrums of eye shadow to create alternately robust or ascetic images for use in the service of God and Marfeau. His following was vast. Or Billy Graham, who dazzled them still in the American Midlands. Or Fulton Sheen, from the TV time of Murphy's Iowa youth. Gervais knew them all and understood their art: handsome men, spun from beautiful threads, who projected a benevolent charisma, compelling confidence as they sold their respective visions. Murphy easily saw the point of Gervais's decision to wait. A sick drunk, albeit drying out, inspired revulsion or pity. And the miraculous cure that set this pilgrimage in motion had supposedly already taken place. So while he walked along with the others, reviving flaccid muscle —three hours this first full day, a little more on each succeeding day, until he might finally be able to keep up the twenty-mile-per-day pace Gervais was priming them for—Murphy was not to be included in the filming.

Together, Murphy and Kyle-Boyer despaired of ever being able to withstand Gervais's twenty-mile day. That rate, if attained on schedule, should bring them to Marfeau in Clermont-Ferrand, approximately 460 kilometers distant, in about fifteen days. In Kyle-Boyer's judgment only Jonathan Whitmore, because he was young and strong, the three mules (and their two human burdens if they held on tightly enough), the station wagon, and the utility van were up to a twenty-mile daily hike. They would never make it in fifteen days.

On the morning of his TV debut, the two cameramen, Ricard and Lebel, got into a lovers' quarrel and broke each other's noses. On the evening of that same day, before dinner, Murphy, properly made up and looking, as everyone assured him, fantastically more healthy than when he had arrived six days before, was interviewed before a stone cross in a little village called Ecommoy. He responded to Gervais's questions from a script Gervais had prepared that afternoon: He was Francis Xavier Murphy, age thirty-seven, a naturalized French citizen, formerly of America, who had married a Frenchwoman (name withheld), fathered a son by her (name also withheld), and was now a prosperous vintner in the Seyssel wine-growing area of Haute-Savoie. He was also a long-time acquaintance of *la jeune anglaise,* Marilyn Aldrich, whom M. Murphy and his wife had befriended years before when Mlle. Aldrich was but a little girl vacationing at the resort town of La Baule in Normandy. Hearing belatedly of her miraculous cure, he had left his estates and workers and hastened off to intercept her on her march, pledging to carry a crucifix as a symbol of his gratitude all the way to Jerusalem. His estates and workers could take care of themselves. . . .

The lie, once spoken, began to Murphy to seem more palatable every moment, and he chuckled over the advantage of the French nation in having but two government-controlled TV networks so that no rivals might chance to dig up the truth about Francis Xavier Murphy, who had been drinking himself to death in the Château de Rastignac in Haute-Savoie rather than successfully managing its estates.

But the next evening during the news telecast, Murphy, narcissistically anticipating, was keenly disappointed. Television made one look heftier than one actually was, and in his sack of a pilgrim's robe Murphy looked like a heavyweight. Also the sound of his own voice irritated him. It was nearly a monotone, lacked animation, and seventeen years after crossing the ocean the lilt of his French was still pregnant with long Iowa vowels. But the others were sympathetic. None had come off exactly as he had hoped, and among them, in this instance at least, only Gervais was impressive. But then he was a professional.

When the final news coverage—of Northern Ireland and Indochina—had passed into instant ancient history, Marilyn Aldrich, still behind the gossamer of Darvon she took against her continuing saddle boils, made a curious observation. "Murphy's the only one of us with family. Isn't that strange?"

"Is it true?" Murphy asked.

"I think so," Jonathan Whitmore said. "I'm an orphan, 'n' Marilyn's old dad went 'n' died about two years back. Ricard's got no one, 'n' Gervais told me Lebel's dad disowned him because of his pederasty. Told him never to come home again, he did."

"I'm alone, too, since Mum died," Kyle-Boyer added. "But she went eight years ago. How about you, Gervais?"

"What do you want, Kyle-Boyer?"

"Do you have any family?"

"Yes, I have a wife."

"Is she in Paris?" Murphy asked, surprised that Gervais, highstrung and irritable, might have a family situation that approached anything like normalcy.

"No, she is not. My wife is an Israeli girl. She's waiting for me in Jerusalem with her family."

"Then cheer up, Gervais," Jonathan Whitmore encouraged. "You've got something to look forward to, after all."

"Yes, I suppose," Gervais answered. But in the gathering darkness he frowned, and the special look, not unlike fear, passed over his face again.

8

Some wayfarers: The pious youth and the unfortunate gypsies

ONE THING MIGHT BE SAID FOR MARFEAU, Murphy decided: he worked hard. And on the road to Clermont-Ferrand he absolutely outdid himself in making certain La Belle France was wide awake to the existence of the Fourteenth Crusade. Only, being Marfeau, his methods were ever questionable, since controversy obviously breeds interest, and the closer they crept to the preacher, the worse the smell became.

First the smell was of rotten eggs, because after Tours he began sending out his Christian Activist agents to do a job on Kyle-Boyer, the institutional atheist. Mainly they were little surreptitious men, Gallic look-alikes of the English pimp, Jonathan Whitmore, henchmen who suddenly appeared in twos or threes and occasionally even in bands in villages and some of the larger towns along the way where they were certain to draw a crowd for the benefit of Gervais's ever-ready cameras.

Pregnant and bristling with outraged indignation and Christian zéal, they also came equipped with a rote list of impressions that they hurled at Kyle-Boyer—*Vive le Christianisme! A bas l'athéisme! Sale anglais!*—before letting fly the eggs. But in the main, except for the unpleasantness of the odor, which seemed to upset the mules more than the pilgrims, Kyle-Boyer took his peltings with good humor. He began wearing a light raincoat over his walking shorts and knee socks that shielded him from most of the spatter, and since the egg throwers were long-time professionals with deadly aim and under strict orders not to hit his face or pith helmet, little harm was done. Only once did the abortionist react with anything like anger against his assailants; this was in a tiny village not even listed in Michelin about halfway between Tours and Châteauroux when a grocer stepped outside his shop and began unaccountably hurling fresh eggs from a display case in Kyle-Boyer's general direction. But the grocer was clearly insane or near to it, and Murphy, recalling the incident, sometimes thought that Kyle-Boyer's response of walking up to the pitcher, cracking him squarely over the head with his walking stick, and leaving him to collapse unconscious into his own egg crates was more like compassionate shock therapy than simple vengeance.

Gervais, however, made the best of it on film, capturing Kyle-Boyer in the haughty imperial act of striking down a French wog, but neglecting to capture the blank stare of an automated man whose left hand traded eggs from a crate to his pitching arm with a mechanical precision that told he was firing not at an atheist leading a mule but at everything: life, God, France, his wife, her family, his children, produce wholesalers, car dealers, tax collectors, and anyone else who had added himself to the obviously unsupportable burden he labored under. But the brief film clip of Kyle-Boyer's act had been enough; in other towns and villages, other grocers and assorted citizenry waited with glee for the fat Englishman. Some of the assailants had switched from eggs to rocks, and before the preacher finally called them off, Marfeau's agents ended up with the ironic task of trying to restrain the French and xenophobic monster they themselves had helped set loose.

For balance, perhaps, and to appease Father Bisson, who was angry at the notion of anyone throwing anything at the man who cooked his dinner each evening, Marfeau decided to indulge the spiritual as well. But being Marfeau, a person who dealt only in shrieking polar opposites and completely lacked a commonsense middle ground, the transition from bear-hunting the national prejudices to deifying Marilyn Aldrich and her fellow pilgrims (Kyle-Boyer excepted) was necessarily an immense distance to travel. The scoundrel preacher arranged for the entire First Communion class of Châteauroux, the next big town they came to, to line up and kiss the hand of Blessed Marilyn Aldrich, a televised display that was to set a precedent for repeat performances through the rest of France and across the frontier into Italy.

Also there were the lame and maimed: paraplegics and assorted cripples, amputees, and persons with incredible skin diseases that may have been tertiary syphilis or even leprosy. They began appearing in prearranged places—clusters of wheelchairs, crutches, braces, and bandaging—all waiting for the sight of a cured white-clad English girl astride a white mule. Only they were real and believers and not agents of Marfeau made up to look like the crippled and sick, and that knowledge disgusted Murphy and nearly drove Kyle-Boyer to the brink of apoplexy. For the preacher had simply raided the expectant terraces of the basilica at Lourdes, thrown in a few more who were carried by their families to the evangelist's tent at Clermont-Ferrand for a chance at a curing, and trucked the lot of them to places along the pilgrims' route with appropriate backdrops for filming: church steps or the memorial stone World War I crosses that littered the French villages.

There was really nothing to be done about it. Marfeau had them. Only two of their number—Murphy and Kyle-Boyer—were afflicted with the proper disgust, and no amount of protest on their part was going to stop this exploitation. Besides, Marfeau countered unctuously through Gervais, rather than being an exploiter he was a dispenser of hope-fulness. The reaction of the other pilgrims was no help at all. Jonathan Whitmore was either indif-ferent or just plain amused at the sight of the clusters of waiting grotesques they came upon. Marilyn Al-drich—still with saddle boils and still drugged against the hurt—seemed not to see them at all, even when she smiled in their general direction in her eternal myopic way, but she at least imparted some balance to Marfeau's temerity by voluntarily touch-ing her hands to their wounds, scars, and termina-tions with no apparent care for her own health. Father Bisson, who along with Kyle-Boyer and Mur-phy might have tipped the balance and forced Mar-feau to cancel this particular outrage, believed, alas, in Marfeau's divinity as much as he believed in Marilyn Aldrich's, and there was no way to convince the old priest that Marfeau was orchestrating yet an-other sham. Gervais worked for Marfeau and was afraid of him; Ricard and Lebel, still smarting with the pain of healing broken noses, seemed comforted by the sight of other bandaged casualties.

But the assaults on Kyle-Boyer the atheist and the abuse of the maimed and diseased were almost min-iscule compared to what Marfeau did to the pious youths and gypsies.

Children began suddenly showing up after the pil-grims left Châteauroux, a contingency not even con-sidered in all the meticulous planning the crusade had entailed. The first of them was a dewy-eyed young man of about eighteen who obviously had the faith. He stood waiting for them on a street corner in a tiny village, clad in something like a Boy Scout uniform stripped of its badges and carrying a knap-sack on his back. Two women hovered about him: the one—obviously his mother—weeping and kissing him good-bye; the other—probably his grandmother—deftly sewing a Cross of Lorraine to his shirtfront. In an-other moment he bade them adieu and fell into line beside Murphy, who was carrying his crucifix and dying for the chance to talk with someone new so he might get through this particular day's march without resorting again to the necessity of counting his footsteps and agonizing over his blisters.

"Are you joining us?" Murphy asked when the youth finally left off from waving good-bye to his mother and grandmother.

"*Oui, monsieur.* I'm going to walk to Jerusalem with you. Do you wish for me to carry your cross? My name is Raoul."

"Did Marfeau send you?" A rueful smile had already come over Murphy's face. It seemed a logical question. Who the hell could be expected to join them without being in the preacher's employ?

"No, I have never met Père Marfeau, but I want to receive his blessing at Clermont-Ferrand. You are the American, *n'est-ce pas?*"

"I used to be an American. I'm a French citizen now."

"I discovered *le bon Jésus* in America."

"Where?"

"In Utah, near Salt Lake City. I was walking in the desert when it happened."

"It may have been sunstroke," Murphy said automatically, amazed at the cynic he had become. Then he looked askance at the kid for a long moment. This Raoul, in certain ways, reminded him of his own son, Jean-Philippe. But the eyes, finished tearing, still had the mystic's traditional moistness in them; Jean-Philippe was hard as a rock where this kid seemed full of mush and sentiment. Murphy turned about and, except for Marilyn Aldrich, caught an inquisitive look on every face. Gervais motioned him to come to the creeping station wagon for a conference. Murphy asked the young man to carry his cross for a moment—a task joyfully accepted—and went to talk with Gervais, who had Lebel halt the Peugeot.

"Who is he?" the producer asked.

"One of those kids . . . a Jesus freak, I think. I've read about them in *Paris-Match.*"

"Ah, yes. Another American cultural export."

"He's French," Murphy said flatly. "You ought to be proud, considering he's the only one we've met so far that hasn't been one of the bad guys."

"We'll make it up to you, Murphy. Just wait and see. What does he want?"

"He wants to go to Jerusalem with us. He's really heard the call, apparently. Footprints for Jesus and all that stuff."

"All the way to Jerusalem? He's crazy," Gervais judged, hissing out his disdain Provençal-style. But the instant after he spoke, he saw the humor of it and began laughing. Lebel beside him shook with silent merriment, since his mending nose would not permit him to laugh openly. Murphy, despite his stored-up annoyance over Marfeau and his publicity tactics to date, grinned and told Gervais, "We ought to take a chance on him. Marfeau hasn't sent him, so his presence isn't likely to backfire on our little pilgrimage. And using his innocence isn't half as cruel as using those lepers and paraplegics Marfeau keeps sending."

"Perhaps you're right. Besides, we need new material. Marfeau informed me this morning there won't be any more lepers and paraplegics." Gervais sighed deeply, his disgust apparent also. "His unholiness has had to call them off because they've gotten out of hand like the egg throwers. By ten o'clock this morning he had over fifty thousand requests for a cure because of all the publicity from other paraplegics and lepers he didn't know existed. *Merde! Quel salaud!* Obviously he had to get rid of them. If it ever was known that Marfeau couldn't rid a dog of his fleas, he'd be out of business completely. Yes, I think you are correct, Murphy. The young man is an innocent, unknown to Marfeau. Filming him isn't likely to produce any kind of backfire, as you call it, equal to what has happened already on this march."

That judgment turned out to be incorrect also, though at the beginning no one might have guessed it. On camera, Raoul the pious was marvelous. Pure youth, pure French, pure Jesus freak (though well groomed), he came off in his first interviews with a trembling-voiced sincerity that no actor his age might have duplicated. Marfeau was delighted. From Clermont-Ferrand he sent champagne for the pilgrims and their keepers (but not for Murphy or Raoul) to congratulate them on their excellent good find and urged Gervais to put the *gosse* on the payroll until Gervais flatly told him the kid could not be bought. Astounded but undaunted, Marfeau galloped off in another direction. He sent his minions of agents fanning out across the country to make certain the newspapers printed the publicity release on "Raoul, Youth of France" that he had had composed. Raoul was a celebrity overnight.

Within a few days the crusade was visited by a plague that had the unholy one of Clermont-Ferrand shrieking at Gervais over the wires in a vocabulary that the senior-most truck driver from Marseille might have had difficulty matching. For other Raouls began showing up, an event that, though unforeseen, might have been highly desirable, since within four days the number of pilgrims swelled to more than thirty, and, seen on television from a distance, the entire entourage looked large and purposeful as it marched toward the Holy Land. But up close, where after the fourth day Gervais's camera dared not tread, the problem was made manifest. All the other Raouls were not like Raoul himself.

A few, perhaps four or five, were somewhat like him, of course: village kids pumped full of the slush of religious sentimentality and bent on following the cross. But the majority, despairing of hitchhiking their way out of a nation glutted for the summer with young travelers, and many short on food and money as well, apparently decided the easiest recourse for leaving France was to hook up with the pilgrims. They were of many nationalities, both male and female, smoked pot, and were, for the most part, unkempt; from talking with them Murphy learned a good number were pointedly on their way to another place that differed from what Murphy's generation had called the Holy Land: Katmandu was become the new Jerusalem, apparently. Even the disparate ones who on first arrival were headed toward Italy or Yugoslavia or Greece decided they would join up with the larger group and leave the crusade once it reached Istanbul, heading off toward Nepal through Iran and Afghanistan. Together, moving slowly through villages that now seemed plainly stunned at the sight, the combination of original pilgrims, pious youths, Katmandu pilgrims, mules, and vehicles was a ragtag affair. All in all, though, Murphy judged, it was a proper justice for Marfeau and a reminder to him that, although the original Crusades had their supposedly idealistic nucleus, they also had their hordes of mercenaries, opportunists, and hangers-on.

Gervais, for once to his credit, tried to save them from the reaction he knew would be coming from Marfeau, whatever form it took. He urged them to clean up, and for the young men to cut their hair, and resorted to filming them only in darkness when they sat smoking around a campfire and nodding their heads in lilting response to the soporific platitudes that Father Bisson had taken to dispensing before bedtime, since he had at last an audience that would listen to him—even if less than half of them understood French. But the producer's admonitions to change themselves achieved no results, and he had no success in culling any of their numbers from the ranks, and on the sixth night before reaching Clermont-Ferrand, lying in his sleeping bag beside Murphy and Kyle-Boyer, he finally gave up with an interminable long sigh on his attempts at persuasion. "I think we will be hearing from our friend Marfeau very shortly." He spoke in a low voice to no one in particular. "I've done the best I could with these *gosses*. But they think they've found a very good thing in our little crusade, and they're unwilling to change or leave. Expect the worst, and pray that it won't be quite that bad."

It came the very next night. While they camped in the city park at Montluçon, a platoon of police descended suddenly upon them and conducted a drug raid, having already cordoned off the area so none could escape. While the raid might have been an innocent-enough happening of itself, considering all the publicity the Children's Crusade was getting, the certainty that it was some move of Marfeau's was proven by the fact that all the young people, pious and worldly both, were nabbed with identical quantities of hashish in their knapsacks—this despite the vociferous protestation of many of the pious that they did not even know what the stuff was and the equally vociferous protestation of the worldly that no one who knew what it was would be stupid enough to carry hash in so obvious a place as a knapsack.

But it was all to no avail. Marfeau was cleaning house, and the police were obviously working for him. When Murphy and Kyle-Boyer bade a sad goodbye to the once-golden Raoul, Youth of France, who wept bitterly at not being able to accompany them to Jerusalem and more bitterly still at the prospect of the reaction of his mother and grandmother to the news that he was a *druggiste,* the gendarme who held him by one arm gave the two pilgrims a broad wink over the young man's head to indicate that the forthcoming justice would certainly be tempered with mercy, at least in the case of Raoul. It was. Later film footage showed all twenty-two of the Children's Crusaders being arraigned in a court at Montluçon. Raoul and his fellow pious were put on probation and remanded to the custody of their parents; the others, all of whom were foreigners, were simply declared persona non grata and deported. And Marfeau reaped reams of publicity from the incident, appearing the next evening on the nation's screens, mournful yet more righteous than Murphy thought possible, deploring the widespread depravity of youth and the violation of the sacred purpose of the pilgrimage. Ever magnanimous, he ended by welcoming young people to his great tent at Clermont-Ferrand, though clearly on his own terms. The newscaster's follow-up told that the police were beginning to despair of ever finding Suleiman's Pebble, now gone almost three weeks from the Angoulême cathedral. After bristling at the phony righteousness of the minister Marfeau, Murphy found himself cheering that emphatic blow to the treasury of organized religion.

But the word was out—flawlessly so. As if an elaborate and sensitive grapevine existed the world over among traveling youth, no more backpacking wayfarers showed up to join the crusade and spoil the image Marfeau had intended for it in all the distance that remained to walk to Jerusalem.

In the same way the gypsies, who had an actual underground communications network, learned to stay away also. Their turn came a few nights later when the pilgrims were setting up camp in a farmer's field only fifty kilometers from Clermont-Ferrand. There were about twenty of them in four motorized caravans, elaborate and gilded vehicles that testified to the gypsies' easy acceptance of the twentieth century and brought home to Murphy, as nothing had before, the notion of exactly how unusual the pilgrims and their mules must look hiking across the landscape. Apparently Gervais thought so too, and, not warned sufficiently by the fiasco of the Children's Crusade, he filmed the striking contrast between the two groups of travelers. Then he conducted a live interview with their leader, a man called Karajek, replete and perfect in a Camargue cowboy's outfit, who spoke a heavily accented Breton French into the microphone and presumably Romany in a series of asides to his followers that had them frequently convulsed with mirth. For Gervais's purpose, Karajek was the best anyone could have hoped for. The leader called the crusaders kindred spirits, since the gypsies themselves were working their way back to Brittany by slow stages after having made their yearly pilgrimage to Les Saintes-Maries near Marseille for the reveration of their patron saint. Further, he told the camera that the crusaders were noble and courageous for having undertaken so monumental a task as a walk to Jerusalem and that more than any other man alive a gypsy, a ceaseless wanderer, could appreciate the arduousness of the task that lay ahead. Then he absolutely outdid himself by having all the members of his band line up and, kneeling, kiss the hand of Blessed Marilyn Aldrich. The last and most fervent of the homage payers was Karajek. He wept as he laid his lips on her fingers.

Later, while Gervais congratulated himself on his good find and the fortunate chance to appease Marfeau just as they were entering Clermont-Ferrand, Murphy noticed the crucifix was missing. His nightly task was to make certain it was secreted away behind the sliding panel in the utility van, but lately he had grown casual about it and usually waited until just before bedtime to put it away. Now that it was gone, there was obviously only one place that it could have disappeared to.

Gervais tried a diplomatic approach to Karajek to get the cross back, emphasizing that it was made of relatively valueless bronze and calling upon the finer aspects of the gypsies' religiosity, since they themselves were returning even then from their own variety of pilgrimage. But it was like pleading with the mask of comedy: Karajek, winking everywhere, pretended outrage at the accusation, and most of the women were openly amused. Also, in addition to Karajek, there were eight men in the group, of varying shapes and sizes, all completely unsmiling, in contrast to their womenfolk, and all with the special nameless look of being loaded to the teeth with brass knuckles and stilettos. Against them, Ricard and Lebel, the two broken-nosed goons, were useless since they were merely possessed strength. Only Jonathan Whitmore, who knew what gypsies knew, might have handled one of them in a square-off, but defeating one of the gypsy men in combat left a surplus of seven to be reckoned with, and Whitmore himself laughed along with the Romanies when Gervais threatened to call in the police.

"You ain't got a gun, Gervais," Whitmore said, "and the police could tear these here caravans apart 'n' never find the damn cross if them gypsies didn't want 'em to. I say forget it. Let 'em keep the thing if they've taken such a fancy to it, 'n' we can buy a new one tomorrow in one of them religion shops."

"No, that's impossible," Gervais said. He narrowed his eyes and his glance swept across the gypsies, who had arranged themselves in a kind of defending semicircle, as if he expected to see the crucifix protruding from behind someone's back. But there was nothing to be seen, and with a resolute look of fear on his face, Gervais pronounced to no one in particular, "We must have that cross returned. It was blessed by his holiness the Pope."

"OK, if you say so, Gervais." Whitmore mocked the producer's lie. "But you know who you're goin' to have to ring up to make sure you get the thing back. And I ain't speakin' of the Pope, neither."

The next day the pilgrims departed the farmer's field to begin their final leg into Clermont-Ferrand, only they got a later start than usual because of the difficulty Gervais had in reaching Marfeau by telephone that morning. And Murphy, the crusade's resident alcoholic, noted with some astonishment that Gervais, foregoing coffee, belted down some four or five cognacs for breakfast instead. Incredibly, on his last swill, Karajek, the enemy leader, joined him for a drink. Although the two men exchanged the kiss of peace, and the gypsy women pressed gifts of wine and food on the pilgrims (all gratefully accepted; no one but Gervais agonized over the loss of the crucifix, and Murphy absolutely hoped it would never be replaced), the cross was not returned.

The crusaders trudged onto the highway, as the gypsies, strung out along a rise of the pasture, waved good-bye, singing a sad song of farewell that sounded to Murphy not unlike the eerie fados, the fate songs of the Portuguese. The women, with the breeze billowing their long skirts, reminded him of Aegean sirens, and with his bandages already chafing beneath the tough leather of his sandals, he thought how pleasant it would be to return to them and have them wash his feet with their doubtless soothing ancestral ointments. But in another minute they were gone, and Murphy found himself in curious sympathy with the words of Father Bisson that came up the line of march toward him: "They have taken the cross, but it is not wrong. They will venerate it far more than we do."

They plodded onward. About noon, two large open trucks with men packed into them like sardines came toward them from the opposite direction and stopped across the highway. Gervais left the station wagon and crossed the road to speak with the occupants of the cabs. Both trucks were lettered with identical huge signs: HERE COME THE CHRISTIAN ACTIVIST WORKERS OF FRANCE. But to Murphy they all looked like a variety of lumberjack or strikebreaker headed for a dockside confrontation. Apparently Kyle-Boyer thought the same.

"I pity those poor gypsies," the abortionist commented.

"*Moi aussi*," Murphy agreed. "I was rather hoping I wouldn't have to carry the thing any longer."

But it was not to be. In moments more Gervais returned to stand beside the others as the trucks rumbled off again.

"I suppose we'll have our cross back again in short order," Gervais said. He was slurring his words; he had evidently been hitting the cognac bottle again while riding in the Peugeot. "In a way it's a pity. That Karajek was a very winning fellow. He admitted this morning that they had stolen it. But they did it because an old woman of their camp, a soothsayer, told them they must have it if their tribe was to continue and prosper. Considering their superstitions, one really can't blame them all that much."

"That old woman—the soothsayer, as you call her —is about to be out of a job," Kyle-Boyer said ruefully.

In time, as they crested a hill, Murphy was able to look back and see the first spirals of smoke arising from the area of the gypsy encampment. In the beginning it was white, like a damp wood fire; then it turned a dirty black as the flames reached the rubber of the caravan's tires; then came a series of explosions, almost simultaneous, as the gas tanks went off. Blessedly, it was too far distant to hear the screams of pain or blood lust.

Within a half hour the two trucks returned, a man sitting atop the hood of the first brandishing Murphy's cross like the staff of a victorious centurion. The bodies of the two vehicles, filled with avenging Christians already roaring drunk on the wine they had taken from the gypsies, were also filled with the Romanies' possessions; in each truck a dozen or more men had dressed themselves in clothes taken from the women. Murphy caught the crucifix that was hurled through the air to him.

Later it occurred to him, as the trucks headed off again to Clermont-Ferrand, that if he remembered his history correctly, the original crusaders had at least waited until they got outside France before they began pillaging in earnest. But still it appeased something in him that none of the gypsies had been killed.

Neither Radio-Télévision Française nor a single newspaper in France, with the exception of a blurb in the local daily of Montluçon, reported on the gypsies' demise.

9

Marfeau

ON THE TWENTY-FIRST DAY after Murphy joined the crusade, they arrived in the early evening, exhausted from that day's forced march of thirty kilometers, at the northern suburbs of Clermont-Ferrand. While they rested on a convenient swath of grass at the edge of a gas station and the station attendants generously gave water to the three mules in a metal tub beside the pumps, a young priest drove up in a microbus and, declining to dismount, beckoned Gervais toward him for a conference. The producer, stiff from sitting all day in the station wagon, hobbled to the driver's window and was almost immediately into an argument with the priest, though too far distant for Murphy to overhear what it was: Gervais gestured emphatically toward the pilgrims, stamped his foot on the ground, and slammed the tinny side of the bus with the flat of his hand repeatedly until the priest cracked him across the jowls. Incredibly, Gervais struck back, a pent-up torrent of annoyance, clobbering the cleric and then walking quickly away, just neatly avoiding being run over by the microbus as it buzzed over onto the highway. When Gervais returned to the crusaders, Father Bisson, smoothing

102

the ruffles in his cassock, was just leaving the service station's men's room. The producer smiled politely at the old priest and then stood before the others to say wrathfully in English, "That son of a bitch!"

"Who was he?" Murphy asked.

"Not that one. I mean the boss, Marfeau. You've fallen onto a bit of luck, mademoiselle and messieurs," Gervais said caustically. *"Le père* Marfeau is having a great tent meeting tonight, and we're right on schedule. You're all to be the featured guests in front of four thousand spiritually hungry souls and more television coverage than one of Pompidou's news conferences, even though I've told that young whelp who was just here that you've marched over thirty kilometers today, haven't had your evening meal, and will probably have to be carried on stage."

"I say, Gervais," Kyle-Boyer said. "I know we owe our friend Marfeau one night of theatrics, but couldn't we possibly put it off until tomorrow? Today's march has been literally brutal, and I've not got the energy to lift a soufflé pan this evening. No one else is in very good condition either. We might be of more use to your French Rasputin if we had a day's rest."

"It's not possible," Gervais answered. "Marfeau's clients are getting restless. We were supposed to have been here days ago, and he may not be able to hold them any longer if he doesn't come up with a new distraction. We must go onstage tonight; otherwise the crowds are going to thin out drastically. . . ."

But even as he said this, Gervais's voice trailed off in dismay. Jonathan Whitmore was already asleep on his patch of lawn; Marilyn Aldrich lay with her head propped up on the neck of her white mule, which had returned from drinking water and promptly slumped to the earth; Father Bisson, looking glassy-eyed as if he were about to drop off from heat prostration, fanned himself vainly with the blocklike thickness of his breviary; Murphy had settled back against the staff of his cross, propped up against a fence, depending on the pain of its intrusion on his backbone to keep him awake. Kyle-Boyer was the worst by far; his khaki walking shorts and shirt were drenched with sweat, and his face had the beet-red look of an impending explosion.

Gervais surveyed the exhausted pilgrims a moment longer and then began to beg. "Please . . . please do this one thing for me."

"You really are quite frightened of Marfeau, aren't you, Gervais?" Kyle-Boyer speculated. "Not that I blame you, of course, considering what his henchmen did to those gypsies back there."

"And you're not frightened of him, after what you've seen? He may control the Mafia and the Union Corse for all I know." There was a kind of wonderment in Gervais's eyes as he surveyed Kyle-Boyer, and he actually advanced to lay his hand on the fat Englishman's forehead as if testing for the fever and delirium that obliterate fear.

"Why should I be afraid of him? Or the rest of us who walk, for that matter? There are limits to what he can do to us. Otherwise he's got no pilgrims and therefore no crusade. You, the warden, and your two turnkeys, Ricard and Lebel, over there, are the ones who have to worry if things run amok."

It seemed to Murphy that Gervais might have wept for the truth of what Kyle-Boyer spoke. The producer turned, seeking some sort of help from Ricard and Lebel, who sat side by side on the bumper of the utility van. But, like twins, their noses still bandaged, they shrugged to indicate their helplessness. When Gervais returned to facing the pilgrims he was smiling desperately, offering candy to babies.

"I will personally guarantee an additional one thousand American dollars to each one of you if you agree to make an appearance in Père Marfeau's tent tonight."

"Make it two thousand yank dollars 'n' take us to a restaurant for a good feed, 'n' me 'n' Marilyn goes along with you," Whitmore said. Hearing talk of money, he had miraculously awakened. He stifled Marilyn Aldrich's protest by simply clamping his hand over her mouth.

"Done!" Gervais exulted, a pitchman making a little dance. "That makes two who go along, then. And our good priest, of course." Certain in his knowledge that the priest would follow anywhere the majority went, Gervais smiled broadly at Father Bisson, who smiled in return. "What about you, Murphy?"

Murphy was sitting up by now. He had wriggled off his sandals and was picking road tar from between his toes with a bit of twig. "The bribe seems pointless to me, Gervais. It'll be so long before I get a chance to spend it."

"But will you come along?" the producer begged.

"I suppose so. If it'll save your ass from Marfeau. You're a halfway decent person. You did try to protect that Children's Crusade and those gypsies from the boss, after all."

"Thank you, Murphy. And you, Kyle-Boyer?"

"I'm too tired to be bought today, Gervais. I suppose I'll go along also. As Murphy says, you're something of an honorable chap. Just a bit flighty."

"You saw those two lorries filled with persuaders yesterday who came from Marfeau to deal with those *gitanes*. Surely you can understand why I am so? And as you yourself imply, we the keepers are disposable. You the pilgrims are not. You hold certain special options."

"I want a signed and witnessed paper on them four thousand yank dollars, Gervais." Jonathan Whitmore broke into the discussion, indifferent to any testimony to Gervais's honor or the pilgrims' options.

"You shall have it, of course, Jonathan. Marfeau himself will witness it. And I need one more favor. Perhaps two of you will volunteer to ride the mules across the city? His unholiness has no transportation for them, and they would be too skittish anyhow if they were unloaded from a lorry just before they were to go on stage tonight. A meal will be waiting for you when you arrive at the tent area."

"I volunteer," Murphy said, after trading a glance with Kyle-Boyer. Kyle-Boyer volunteered also. The empathy was immediate. With little effort the mules could be induced to make a wrong turn, and they would have a valid excuse for showing up an hour or two late. That way Gervais would be merely compromised, instead of outrightly defied, and Marfeau could go to hell; they had followed instructions, only gotten lost. Besides, Murphy remembered his promise to Monique to avoid excesses of publicity, and the televised image of her husband in a crusader's robe, on a tent revival stage, dangling idiotically on the strings of a puppet-master evangelist, could be calculated to send her through the roof of the château. No use jeopardizing their relationship any further. His drinking had been the result of boredom. After twenty-one days afoot, he craved very little of it any more. Perhaps some sort of decent rapprochement was possible, after all this was over. . . .

Murphy handed over his cross to Gervais and by himself got astride Blessed Marilyn Aldrich's white mule. Kyle-Boyer was helped by Ricard and Lebel aboard Father's Bisson's animal, and tied the lead rope of his own pack ass to the saddle pommel. In another minute, after Gervais had marked their route on a tourist map of Clermont-Ferrand, they set off from the gas station toward the city at a canter, Murphy's robe billowing out behind him in the breeze and Kyle-Boyer, with an obvious lack of expertise in riding any animal, holding on for his life.

"I take it you're as interested as I in getting out of this little evangelical extravaganza tonight, eh, Murphy?" Kyle-Boyer asked, panting even as he rode.

"Absolutely. That's why I volunteered so quickly. Why don't we go to a bar somewhere, have a few beers and a sandwich, and tell Gervais we made a wrong turn."

"Agreed. Of course, if things were in my control, I'd far rather go to see Marfeau and then get a chance to proclaim a little of my own ideology to his multitudes. But he's supposed to be so theatrically ingenious that doubtless a mechanical lightning bolt would come crashing out of the wings and smite me dead on the stage in rejection of my tenets of reason. So it's better this way—the bar, I mean. I won't be used as a pawn by any French Billy Sunday."

They cantered along until they were well away from the service station, then slowed and made their first purposeful deviation from Gervais's route, heading toward the belching stacks of the huge Michelin tire complex on the southwest side of the city. It was quickly darkening, the street lighting had just come on, and as they passed by the factory's main gate, the mules walking a slow plod, Murphy, ever attuned to the comic surreal, felt a witless giggling begin inside him at the dumbfounded reaction of the workers changing shifts to the sight of the three animals and two men—one robed and one readied for the tropics—moving past in the twilight. Eerie specters, they, the imagination's reward after eight hours of ceaseless automation. The same silence prevailed at the first large intersertion they came to, when, unsolicited, two gendarmes who had been standing on a corner stepped into the street and stopped traffic so they might safely cross but at the same time seemed too speechless even to respond to Kyle-Boyer's profuse gratitude for their kindliness. It was dead quiet, too, unnervingly so, when they entered the bar where they intended to sit out Marfeau's sermon.

The place was in a fountain square in an old quarter of the city, and, after the number of turns they had taken to reach it, Murphy had no idea how far they were from Marfeau, but he felt safe and hidden from the sorcerer. They tied up the three mules to a tree on one side of the square, stepped inside to the near end of the zinc bar, and found themselves being steadfastly observed by the barman and a group of silent patrons clustered about the beer taps at the opposite end . . . only their silence was the certain quiet of hostility rather than astonishment. Murphy sensed it in a moment; he had seen the same reproachful faces throughout France in the not-so-distant past when Algerians had walked into bars and demanded to be served.

Murphy took a hard-boiled egg from a basket before them, cracked it on the zinc, then called out to the barman, *"Une bière, s'il vous plaît."*

In response the barman, still frowning, scanned them for a long moment, shifted position several times to trade glances with his regular customers, then finally replied. *"Oui, mon père?"*

"Ah. . . . I understand," Kyle-Boyer said in a low voice. "They think you're a priest." Then Murphy understood also. It was the ultimate irreligion: a priest in a sacred bastion where priests, especially in the provincial towns, never dared enter.

"I'm not a priest, my friend," Murphy called out to the barman.

"Alors, quoi?" He came closer, no longer unfriendly, merely curious. His patrons in rhythm slid along the outside of the bar toward them.

"We're in the company of Blessed Marilyn Aldrich."

"Qui?"

"The young English girl who is making a pilgrimage to Jerusalem. She appears daily on television."

"Ah, bien compris."

The recognition was universal by now, and Murphy felt smiled on and approved. It was not often, he supposed, that genuine TV celebrities dropped into neighborhood bistros in offbeat towns like Clermont-Ferrand. Before them the barman produced two foaming beers and waved Kyle-Boyer's five-franc note back into his pocket.

"You're the naturalized Frenchman who carries the cross," one man apprised Murphy, shaking his hand and smiling.

"Oui, c'est moi."

"And you, you must be the English doctor. . . ."

Something in the indeterminate way the man left off caused Murphy to stiffen involuntarily. They might be in trouble again. Kyle-Boyer, albeit a Francophile, had for weeks now been script-reading a harangue against *la civilisation française* and the purported religious superstition of the French people. In a Paris bar he might have found droves of fellow drinkers to agree with him. In Clermont-Ferrand, where that very civilization had been bastardized hardly at all and religious superstition, if it thrived anywhere, thrived there, he would not get off so easily. Before them the barman retracted Kyle-Boyer's drink and contemptuously dumped it on the floor.

"Sale anglais," three or four men chanted at the same moment. An old one, who wore a beret, reached up and neatly knocked Kyle-Boyer's pith helmet off his head. When the Englishman bent over to pick it up, the old one kicked him squarely in the ass and sent him sprawling into his own beer. Kyle-Boyer, standing up, was the bright red color of a furnace door.

"Give me a beer!" he shrieked at the barman in French. But the words were barely spoken when Murphy felt a powerful hand grip his arm and turn him firmly about. It was Ricard the cameraman, only now he was dressed in a white intern's jacket that bore the badge of a well-known mental hospital at Lisieux, and across his face, covering his bandaged nose, he wore a surgical mask. Lebel, the other cameraman, was similarly dressed and began moving a protesting Kyle-Boyer toward the door. Ricard put down a five-franc note on the bar for their drinks, explaining to the barman and his customers, while casting solicitous glances toward Murphy, that the two had escaped from the hospital and joined some religious pilgrimage that was being staged by a young English girl. It was mere chance that one of the institute doctors had seen them on the television screen.

"Religion has frequently attracted the insane," the old one who had kicked Kyle-Boyer judged sagely. The others seemed to agree. Murphy, for his part, was caught somewhere along the incredible distance between irony and disbelief and kept trying to shake himself loose from Ricard's iron grip.

"Ricard, c'est moi!"

"Oui, mon petit, je sais."

Murphy was propelled toward the door while the barman called thanks to Ricard for the generous tip. On the outside, beneath the innocent-seeming darkness that covered the tranquil square, he was suddenly convulsed with terror: Kyle-Boyer was being bundled into a straitjacket while another unknown attendant held open the door of a white Citroën ambulance. The English doctor, his eyes tearing, allowed himself to be manipulated onto a stretcher and hoisted into the rear of the vehicle. In the periphery of his vision, Murphy saw another man leading the mules away in the direction they had come.

"Ricard, listen to me! This is madness! We're getting paid to participate in a spiritual sham. You are too. What the hell's so wrong with stopping for a drink in a bar?"

"Monsieur Murphy, please, calm yourself."

"What are you talking about? What the fuck is wrong with you?" Murphy was shouting now in English. "Leave me alone! I'm going back to Haute-Savoie!" He wriggled loose from Ricard's grip and began swinging at the big man, who for the most part easily dodged out of the way. When Murphy actually landed a few ineffectual blows on his chest, they sounded like dull thuds on the trunk of a tree.

Before him, like an automation, Ricard only repeated in the same maddeningly solicitous voice, "Monsieur, please calm yourself. . . ."

A crowd had been forming all the while, and when Murphy suddenly saw two gendarmes making their way inward from the periphery, he pushed toward them, directing them to arrest Ricard and Lebel for assault. But, he realized horrifically, they were not looking at him but rather behind him, trading high signs with Ricard. Grabbing the arm of one of the police, Murphy dragged him forward, urging him to force Ricard to remove his surgical mask and show the assembled world that he was not an institute doctor at all but a goon with a broken nose. That accusation imparted a kind of hesitancy to the proceedings, and the policeman, uncertain and fingering the butt of his revolver, told Ricard to remove his mask and disprove the claim. But Ricard countered with the neatest one-line possible, and Murphy knew he was doomed.

"I cannot, monsieur l'agent," Gervais's lackey told the cop apologetically. "The patient has TB. Tuberculosis."

"Ah-h. . . ." The recognition was universal, and Murphy watched in final despair as onlookers and police shrank back from the pariah to form a wider circle. In another instant, when the lights went out from Ricard's judo chop, it seemed the most completely expected event in the world.

Vaguely, while he was straightjacketed and loaded into the ambulance on another stretcher, Murphy saw Ricard shaking hands with the gendarmes and thanking them for their cooperation. As they drove off, a fecal smell became overpowering in the rear compartment. Beside him, on his own stretcher, Kyle-Boyer wept quietly, then said, "I suppose you realize I've defecated in my trousers?"

"Yes, I guess you have," Murphy answered, trying to control the waves of nausea that were sweeping over him.

"I say, Murphy, I wonder what sort of business we're really in for? I mean, I signed on more or less as a bit of a lark. Figured I'd gain a change of scenery, make a bit of money, lose some weight, then hop on a plane in Istanbul or some place like that when we all got tired and dispirited and head home to Birmingham. Actually, I thought we'd never even get to the Italian frontier, let alone to Jerusalem."

"We'll get to Jerusalem, Kyle-Boyer," Murphy told him emphatically. "I know for certain. They'll get us there if they have to resort to carrying us."

"This Marfeau, he must be a fiend. Worse than anyone expected. This ambulance, these extras, they've been waiting for us to do something like this. We weren't in that damn pub five minutes when they were on us. It was a test. We were set up for it when Gervais insisted they had no transport for the animals. They did it to find out who could be bought and who needed to be brutalized. We must warn the others."

"Warn them about what?" Murphy asked. He stared out the window of the ambulance past the red cross etched on the pane and watched the overhead lights slip past in quick succession. He breathed through his mouth against Kyle-Boyer's odor, then spoke again. "We don't know the extent of any danger to warn them about, and besides, we were the only malcontents in the group. Whitmore has a price for everything, and Marilyn hasn't got an opinion. Bisson would not believe anything of Marfeau except that he's a candidate for sainthood. They've got us right where they want us."

In time the ambulance slowed and began picking its way through a large field full of the Deux Chevaux and tiny Fiats of the French workers. Then they drove inside an enormous tent, whose flaps were held back by two young priests, and parked in a staging area behind a heavy backdrop curtain. Looking up, Murphy had to smile faintly despite himself. Towers of scaffolding held up a galaxy of stage lights and amplifiers; the curtain itself was an impossibly brilliant white. From its opposite side came the din of the faithful warming up in anticipation. At the edge of his vision Murphy caught sight of the inevitable long-robed youth chorus making its way into the amphitheater: the kingdom of Oral Roberts,

come for a week of brimstone and faith healing in Cedar Rapids, Peoria, or Dubuque. Except that this tent
rose from the earth in Clermont-Ferrand, France,
and Oral Roberts, unlike Marfeau, was reputed to
be a godly man. . . .

"What happened?" The voice belonged to Gervais. The rear door of the ambulance swung upward and the producer stared down at them with a
curiosity that was somehow remote. Murphy knew for
certain they had been duped by Gervais into thinking
he was the moral ally of the pilgrims, a beleaguered
man who despised Marfeau and his tactics. But
Gervais worked for Marfeau.

"The English one shit his pants."

"Get him cleaned up," Gervais ordered. "Marfeau
wants the grand march onstage in about twenty
minutes. How is Murphy?"

"Demoralized," Ricard answered. "I think he hasn't
had too much truck with reality lately. It intruded itself rather violently on him tonight."

"It was time. He has some softness of character
that needs strengthening. He signs contracts without
reading the print. It's important that he learn this
is no game. Oh, well. . . ."

The stretchers were lifted out of the ambulance and
Murphy and Kyle-Boyer carried quickly to a small
house trailer nearby that was used as a dressing
room. Inside, Gervais poured himself a glass of wine
and sat down at a table, observing the captured
twosome with a dim, pitying smile. In another moment Marilyn Aldrich and Jonathan Whitmore were
led through the door.

"What the hell are you two doin' on them
stretchers?" Whitmore demanded. "Damn! Whose
plumbin' is burst?"

"Mine," Kyle-Boyer answered, crying again. "I've
defecated in my trousers."

"What did you do that for? Why are you all
trussed up like that, you two?"

"Lebel hit me," Kyle-Boyer moaned self-pityingly. "And Ricard hit Murphy and knocked him out."

"But why?"

"Because they went over the hill, so to speak," Gervais told him pointedly. "They sinned, left camp without authorization, call it what you want. It's against the rules."

"What bloody rules?" Whitmore asked defiantly. In a way Murphy had to admire him. The Birmingham pimp was a lot of bluff he had learned in the streets, but deep down he was no coward either.

"The rules you agreed to in your contract. Remember? They stipulated, among other things, no side trips, no drinking—"

"You'd better listen to him, Jonathan." Murphy spoke quietly. "They were waiting for us to pull something. We had about five minutes of freedom. They had an ambulance, phony identification, the whole works."

"Let me add that a contingency plan has been developed for every possible emergency," Gervais said.

"Do you mean to tell me that we're bloody prisoners of these 'ere Catholics?" Whitmore demanded.

"We got one loophole, Johnny. Don't fret yourself too much." The voice, unheard before, startled everyone in the trailer. It was Marilyn Aldrich. The saddle boils gone, she was off the Darvon and had not yet applied the belladonna for that night's theatrics. For the first time since Murphy had met her, her eyes were her own, narrow slits in the made-up mask of her face. They were hard eyes, too. Responding to them, Jonathan Whitmore grew cagey, more certain of himself. They were a working team again.

"What loophole was you thinkin' of, Marilyn?"

"Padre Bisson."

She jerked her head toward the outside where the old priest, about a hundred feet away, stood at the edge of one of the high rises of scaffolding, look-

ing toward the stage on the opposite side of the
backdrop curtain. Moments before a crescendo of ap-
plause had broken loose, and now the voice of Marfeau—a distant messianic rumbling replete with the
heavy rolled *r*'s of the French workers and country
people—could be heard preaching. Bisson gazed in
rapture, occasionally nodding his head as if in agreement with the text.

"As you can see from here, Marilyn and Jonathan, that is not much of a loophole." Gervais spoke
dryly. "Do you think he'd believe anyone if they told
him Marfeau was responsible for this?" he asked,
gesturing toward Murphy and Kyle-Boyer.

"Not even if Blessed Marilyn Aldrich was to tell
him?" Whitmore quizzed. "That poor crippled English girl who was wheeled into his church for Mass
every mornin' for three months, then suddenly stood
up one day 'n' walked to the altar rail? The old
padre was so stunned he dropped his Holy Communion
all over the floor. He came down from the altar 'n'
even kissed her hands."

"Ha-ha!" The laughter, hard and calloused, came
from Marilyn Aldrich. She smiled at Gervais in triumph. Jonathan Whitmore picked up the baton, preparing to run the end of the race with it. "You got
one of your contingency plans for that?"

"Of course." The voice was bored with trifling. The
producer stretched out his arm to Lebel the goon,
who picked up an elaborately carved wooden jewel
box from atop a dressing table and handed it
over. Gervais sprang the top, and Murphy, from his
stretcher, gasped along with others at the sight. Inside, atop a cushion of purple velvet, was a
nickel-plated American Colt .45 revolver, loaded. Murphy, taught by his father to use one as a kid on
the rattlers that hunted rodents near the corn cribs,
had not seen such a gun in the seventeen years
since he had come to France. He remembered once,
when he was perhaps fifteen, holding such a weapon

two-handed against the kick and blowing the head
right off a hog snake with one shot. . . ."

"You'd actually use that on her?" Murphy asked.

"Not I, Murphy. I know nothing of guns. She
would be assassinated by a religious fanatic."

"Then what would happen to your bloody crusade,
Gervais?" Whitmore demanded. "No Marilyn, no
crusade."

"Wrong, Jonathan." Gervais eyed him levelly. "Another contingency plan. You all continue on. In me-
moriam. To her martyrdom."

"Jesus Christ!" Murphy exclaimed, turning to look
at Kyle-Boyer, whose eyes were wide with fear. Then
he watched Marilyn Aldrich and Jonathan Whitmore,
who were scanning each other thoughtfully, still not
convinced, as Murphy was, of the extent of their
danger. They had seen guns before, been threatened
perhaps in Birmingham by men who had a more nefarious reputation than Marfeau or Gervais, and basi-
cally, Murphy decided, they possessed the lower-class
Briton's universal contempt for the French, a dangerous presumption. It would take more work to bring
them around.

"You understand, Gervais," Whitmore told him
finally, "that all these complications needs a bit more
money to iron out."

"Of course, Jonathan," Gervais said, getting up to
clasp the other's shoulder fondly. "Now that we
begin to understand each other, I will tell you that
there is limitless money to be applied to the deposit
boxes in Zurich of those who cooperate. This pilgrimage isn't a game. It's work. And good workers
should be paid."

"It's almost time," Lebel warned his boss.

"Yes. Now, Père Marfeau, as you can hear, has
almost got them to the threshold of ecstasy out there.
Ecstasy is when you go onstage. You will all line
up, mules included, at the ramp entrance where Bisson is standing. When I give you a signal, begin
walking up the ramp to the stage. But slowly, keep-

ing step to the march the orchestra is going to play. Murphy, you go first, carrying the cross, and when you approach Marfeau center stage, lower the cross so he may kiss it. Jonathan, you lead Marilyn's mule with one hand and Father Bisson's with the other, and when you get to Marfeau, help Marilyn dismount. Marfeau will then come up to Marilyn, kneel, and kiss her hands. He will most probably cry. Marilyn, don't forget your belladonna, so you'll look wide-eyed, and when Père Marfeau kneels before you, implore him to stand and say loudly toward the microphone in French, *'Non, mon père! Non! Levez-vous!'*"

"What does that mean?" Marilyn Aldrich demanded.

"It means stand up."

"What about me?" Jonathan Whitmore asked. "How should I look?"

"Full of love and fine Christian sentiment," Gervais answered evenly. There was no irony in his tone; he was merely rendering stage directions. Only to Murphy, the irony the night's events contained suddenly became hopeless, and lying on his stretcher, bound up in his straitjacket, he was convulsed with mirth at the sight of Jonathan Whitmore standing before the dressing table mirror contorting the elastic of his face so that it might appear full of love and fine Christian sentiment.

Gervais, smiling somewhat, interrupted his quaking laughter. "You are to look exactly the same way, Murphy. Though I admit that in your case the condition may be somewhat more natural."

"How should I look?" Kyle-Boyer asked. His voice, submissive now, was phlegm-coated from crying.

"You are to look absolutely contemptuous of the whole proceedings, my dear doctor. Use that swagger stick of yours to the utmost advantage."

"How can I be expected to be contemptuous of

anything when you've all seen and smelled me lying here in my own feces?" Kyle-Boyer complained.

"It's easy," Gervais said. "Just think of your newly learned unrelenting disdain for the French nation and people. Your contempt for their language, religion, spheres of influence, art, music, philosophy, cheeses, and sauces. Your hatred of their bourgeois ethic, knowing smiles, Gallic noses, and their invention of the bidet, which you are shortly to use. Your disgust over the fact that, unless you fly, you English have to cross the hostile vastness of France to get down to your economy vacations in Spain and Portugal—"

"Enough," Kyle-Boyer said. "I feel restored already. Much better, thank you."

Lebel unshackled the abortionist and helped him off to find a bathroom. Ricard went outside to the utility van and returned in another moment with a change of clothes.

"How is Father Bisson supposed to act?" Murphy asked, stretching his arms to restore circulation after Lebel had released him.

"As Father Bisson will act. He'll play himself. Only one thing," Gervais proposed, the sudden tiredness in his voice real this time, not feigned. "If he gets near the microphone and starts talking about that poor drowned virgin of his, Catherine Lefrac, back in Normandy, please find a way to shut him up. Marfeau may think it amusing, but I could not listen to that story of her appearing above the waves one more time."

"Umm. . . . Yes. . . ." There was a kind of garbled agreement by everyone at the same moment, the only thing, Murphy supposed, they would probably ever be in agreement about for the rest of their journey.

The mules—Marilyn Aldrich's and Father Bisson's —were waiting for them, not surprisingly, when it was time to line up at the base of the ramp that led to the stage. Murphy helped Marilyn (her eyes now convincingly wide with the belladonna she had applied) mount up first, then old Bisson, and after a long minute of fitting the priest's feet, which seemed to have no particular power of their own, into the saddle stirrups, he retrieved his cross from Gervais and stood about listening to the gospel by Marfeau.

From where he waited, Murphy could see neither the preacher nor the audience, though he suspected it was a vast assemblage from the size of the tent. What he could see—imprecisely, because there was a single spotlight on Marfeau—was the near end of the wide arc of the cherubic chorus that ranged across the stage behind the evangelist. Their faces were uniformly rapturous, a certain tipoff that the moment of ecstasy Gervais had predicted was near at hand. Before them, Marfeau did battle with Satan, alcoholism, adultery, and the new morality that was creeping across France, a land of tradition and religiosity, emanating like a cancer from that citadel of irreligion and licentiousness that was, of course, Paris. Later, when he had sufficient strength, Marfeau promised to do battle with Paris, carry his crusade to the very center of the capital, force the Parisians to bend their knees to the power of Christ. But in Paris, Murphy surmised from the clapping and cheering of the audience, Marfeau would not fight single-handedly. An army of feet, stomping on the tent's earthen floor, seemed ready to follow him on the instant, either for the cause of evangelism or perhaps to indulge that nameless rancor toward the Parisians that Murphy had long since learned lived in nearly every provincial French breast. . . .

Marfeau, knowing apparently that the time was right, fell silent. In another minute the stomping of feet drifted off to a distant patter, and the lights playing on the faces of the youth chorus began slowly to brighten. Marfeau commenced speaking again, no longer the voice of a petulant pope seeking to set the crusade in motion. Now he spoke quietly and convincingly of faith: *la foi*.

"Get ready," Gervais ordered. He had been following the preacher's text page by page in what looked to Murphy to be a leather-bound play script. "You have fifty seconds."

Despite himself, Murphy felt a cringing anticipation, like goose bumps, come over him.

"Thirty seconds. Now, when Marfeau says the words, 'We have been given a living example of hope! She is here with us now!'—*Tu comprends, Murphy, en français?*—the orchestra will begin the march and you all start moving up toward the stage. What are you supposed to say to Marfeau, Marilyn?"

"*Non, mon père! Non! Levez-vous!*" Marilyn Aldrich pronounced, automatically speaking the words she had been constantly repeating since Gervais first gave them to her.

"Good, Marilyn. Ten seconds. . . ." Gervais began an actual countdown. When he got to zero, the producer proved only slightly imprecise. In another instant Marfeau spoke the cue line, and the orchestra broke into the strains of the march. Incredibly, like everything else he had stolen from the American gospel circuit, Marfeau had lifted the march also; it was "Onward, Christian Soldiers." Turning to exchange one bottomlessly sardonic look with Kyle-Boyer, Murphy, his cross held high before him, started toward the stage.

At the top of the ramp, he halted an instant, momentarily blinded by the stage lights. When his eyes adjusted they swept over the assemblage that he automatically numbered in the thousands, and over the youth chorus that he counted in the hundreds, and finally focused on Marfeau, standing alone in center stage behind a microphone.

Murphy was frankly startled at the sight of the preacher. Marfeau, for all his notoriety, was not overexposed, at least not photographically. Pompidou, like de Gaulle before him, had never invited the

evangelist to the Elysée Palace. His image traveled
the land in the blurred print of the newspapers,
and if, occasionally, he chanced to appear on the television screen, as he had after the drug raid on the
Children's Crusade, he was always a small, ascetic
man of God, wrapped in the folds of his Dominican
habit, his head nearly obscured by the overhang of
the cowl. For the rest of what was seen of him, his
ministry might as well have been in the catacombs.

Now he appeared absolutely demonic. He wore a
tight-fitting simple white cassock that only emphasized his thinness, and his hair—a fact unrealized
before—was darkly black and long to the level of
his shoulders. The two eyes, even from the distance
Murphy stood away from him, told the tale of the master's charisma. Beneath them, instead of mere circles,
were whole fields of atrabilious grayness that merged
into the planes of a pale, wizened face. Marfeau gestured to him, and Murphy marched slowly forward,
only vaguely aware that Jonathan Whitmore behind
him was audibly cursing and fighting to control
the two mules, which stomped about in apparent
fright after suddenly confronting the blinding light at
the top of the ramp. . . .

In mid-stage, so fascinated was he by Marfeau's
eyes, Murphy just barely remembered to lower his
crucifix so the other might kiss it. He watched as
the preacher put his lips passionately to the figure
of Christ, then felt Marfeau's grip—surprisingly
ironlike for so wasted-looking a man—on his elbow
to urge him quickly past. The reason for that haste
was easy to discern: Marilyn Aldrich's white mule
resembled a pitching ship at sea, alternately rearing
up on its hind legs and then kicking backward as its
forequarters touched down again, all in a rhythm
curiously atuned to the still-blaring music, while the
cured one, no amount of cosmetic she wore able
to disguise her fear, clung desperately to the pommel.
Father Bisson's black mule, a calmer animal, had
not resorted to bucking and merely shied a safe

distance away at the length of his lead rope to avoid being kicked. Beyond the two mules, Kyle-Boyer, composed again, had no trouble looking contemptuous of the entire proceedings as per Gervais's instructions. In fact he was absolutely convulsed with mirth. Dumbfounded, Murphy watched as Jonathan Whitmore released the lead to Bisson's mount; he almost howled himself as that animal trotted neatly across the stage past him and down an exit ramp on the opposite side, with the old priest still seated in the saddle. Then Whitmore flung himself on the neck of Marilyn's mule, and Marfeau, after making an elaborate and (it appeared to Murphy) hypnotic sign of the cross over the beast, took a firm hold of the bridle. Between them, they seemed by the time of the last few bars of "Onward, Christian Soldiers" to have calmed the animal, which stood quivering as Marfeau stroked its neck on the side toward the audience, calling soothing words toward the microphone. An appreciative gasp of awe found its way from the crowd over the endless powers of Marfeau. . . .

But the youth choir undid the work of the master. On cue, after the last faded drumbeat of the march, they rose up in a single instant from their seats—hundreds of snowy apparitions in long robes—and burst into a tumultuous "Hallelujah!" to mark their joy over the presence of Blessed Marilyn Aldrich. Her white mule simply went berserk. Marfeau had a premonition, hardly divine, of what was going to happen. Seconds before the choir leader signaled the horde to their feet, the preacher's eyes went wide with horror and he stretched out his arm, as if in warning, toward the chorus, his mouth fell open, but only a witless gurgling came out. Then resigned, he released his hold on the bridle and stepped back just in time.

"*Merde!*" the preacher shrieked—too close to the microphone, so that the curse resounded throughout the great tent—as the frightened animal rose into the air in one bound, its four legs spread awry, throwing Jonathan Whitmore off its neck and onto the stage. It touched down once, the same moment that Marfeau's fingers automatically flicked off the sound switch on the mike, then reared up on its hind legs, throwing a terrified Marilyn Aldrich to the floor.

The rest belonged to the surreal. Time slowed to the miniscule, though it could actually only have been instants, and Murphy saw with segmented clarity a panorama that no evangelist's revival meeting in history could ever have sponsored before: The choir continued on thundering out the "Hallelujah Chorus," oblivious of the carnage on the stage before them; Marfeau stood mesmerized, four fingers of one hand thrust childlike into his mouth; Jonathan Whitmore, as if he lacked the power to stand, was crawling away across the stage toward an exit; and Kyle-Boyer, convulsed with his vengeful atheist's laughter, had fallen over into a forest of potted palm plants. From the wings a cadre of Marfeau's Christian Activist Workers started toward the lunging animal, looking as if they intended to wrestle it to the stage, one of them carrying a mallet. But they were too late. Marilyn's mule reared up for one last time on its hind legs, slipped apparently in iron shoes on the highly burnished floor, and toppled over on the sainted one, still lying where she had fallen. Murphy heard a dull crack, like the limb of a tree breaking off on a subzero day. Sensing the full possibilities of the ironic, he suspected the mule had broken one of Marilyn's miraculously cured legs.

"Oh, my goddam leg is broke!" she shrieked out in affirmation.

"*Mon Dieu!*" Marfeau hissed to no one in particular. "What terrible luck!"

The white mule, scrambling to its feet, was set upon by the preacher's gang of workers, and someone offstage had the good sense to ring closed the curtain before the audience got a chance to see the giant of a man who carried the mallet smash the animal right between the eyes and knock it out cold. Murphy and the others behind the curtain, including the chorus that had finally left off singing, watched dumbfounded as they dragged it off stage, trickles of blood already coming out its nostrils.

Kyle-Boyer was the first to come out of shock. He climbed out of his palm plants and rushed to Marilyn Aldrich's side. Jonathan Whitmore was next to reach her. By the time Murphy and Marfeau arrived on the scene, Kyle-Boyer had turned into a medical professional again. He looked up at Marfeau and barked out a sharp order. "Have your men bring a stretcher, Marfeau. Her leg is broken for certain, and she'll have to be moved very carefully. I'll need an X ray before I set the leg. Is there a clinic nearby?"

"She stays right where she is for the moment, Dr. Kyle-Boyer," Marfeau said flatly. "The power of Marfeau has been assaulted by caprice, and I intend, as I always do, to make the best of an unfortunate situation. Marilyn will continue to lie there, and her broken leg will be the subject of my preaching, which will not last longer than fifteen minutes, I promise you."

"Are you mad, Marfeau?" Kyle-Boyer demanded. "Are you quite mad? She'll be of no use to you. She'll pass out from the pain."

"Then give her a sedative or a drink or something to help her. I'm going to have that curtain opened in exactly one minute. *Mes clients,*" he said, jerking his head toward the throngs in the audience, "are getting quite restless and perplexed, as you can hear. Sit down, come to order!" he called out to the youth chorus, most of whose members were standing in their places, the better to see Marilyn's collapse.

"Marfeau, I won't stand for this!" Kyle-Boyer exclaimed.

"You have no choice, doctor. Now shut up or I'll

have that swagger stick of yours wrapped about your neck. One would think you had learned enough of a lesson during your visit to the bar tonight."

"Don't worry about me, Kyle-Boyer. I won't pass out from the pain," Marilyn told him. "I wouldn't miss the chance to lie here grinnin' 'n' leerin' at that crowd out there while Father Holy Britches here tries to preach to them. I've learned a few tricks in my time, too."

But so had Marfeau, apparently. He shunted Murphy, Kyle-Boyer and Jonathan Whitmore off to the wings and then spoke briefly with a technician, pointing upward to the banks of lights several times. When the curtain drew back, there was only Marfeau at his microphone, bathed in a single spotlight, and Marilyn Aldrich lying on the floor of the stage in her own pool of light, grinning and leering as she had promised and throwing a few obscene gestures for good measure.

Only her efforts were all for naught. It was easy to see how Marfeau had gotten to be Marfeau. He spoke almost in a whisper to the hushed audience, a plaintive but nearly frightened voice that said *la pauvre anglaise* had sinned by presumption, been invested by Satan, and punished by Almighty God in that order: one, two, three. Murphy, from where he stood, could not see the assemblage but easily imagined the shaking of heads and clucking of tongues. The only universal response from the crowd, a vast sigh of relief that might have lifted the tent from its pegs, came forth when Marfeau promised to exorcise Satan that very night. For his own part, Murphy wondered ruefully what blunt instrument the preacher intended to use. . . .

But Marilyn Aldrich, lying in her pain and unfortunately not understanding three words of French, could not know she was winning nothing. She was a victim instead. When Marfeau was done, humble before his followers with the suggestion of gathering strength for the monumental task of casting out devils that lay before him, she was still awake and fighting. While she was carefully loaded on a stretcher to be carried off the stage after the curtain swung closed, she cursed out Marfeau in a bristling Birmingham cockney that restored Murphy, Kyle-Boyer, and Jonathan Whitmore to smiling with the notion that their side was getting in its licks also. Murphy was proud to be her companion.

Once off the stage, at the bottom of the ramp, her imprecations died abruptly, overwhelmed by the hoarse, wheezing sounds of an animal's death rattle. They had slashed the throat of the white mule. It hobbled piteously across the ground, its legs splaying outward, its eyes agonized in dying, blood streaking down its front and evidently pouring into its lungs, choking it.

"Oh, my God! Oh, my good God!" Marilyn Aldrich said after a moment. Then, tough as she was, she fainted dead away. The beautiful white mule, whose name had been Mirabelle but whom Marilyn called Jennifer, toppled over and died not a minute later.

Murphy vomited reflexively, as did Jonathan Whitmore. Kyle-Boyer merely shook his head in awe. Father Bisson, sitting on a barrel a short distance away, wept the pitiful tears of an old man who did not even know what he was fighting against.

10

Adieu, la France

THE REST OF THAT EVENING'S EVENTS produced no real shock. Murphy was numb. He knew the feeling; he had had it once before, in Iowa, when the tornado killed his parents and sister. It had lasted for several months after their deaths, until he flipped over the family pickup one drunken, icy night and came out of the accident scathed but alive. Then, finally, he had exploded into the proper paroxysm of rage and grief and gone on about the business of living.

But now Murphy had no hope that the slow-motion nightmare in which they found themselves trapped would be ended by anything so agreeable as a truck accident. The slitting of the mule's throat had done them all in, made them impotent to react. And when, an hour after Marilyn Aldrich was rushed off to a local hospital to have her leg set, Marfeau confessed to being not a priest at all, it seemed the most expected admission in the world.

The remaining four pilgrims—Murphy, Kyle-Boyer, Jonathan Whitmore, and Father Bisson—sat in the charlatan's dressing trailer. Marfeau, belting straight

Scotch from a bottle, was high as a kite; he even became friendly.

"I'm not a priest at all, you see." He had already stated the fact three or four times, hoping for an amazed response that was not forthcoming, so that Murphy, tired of the repetition, thought to prompt him along.

"You're not?"

"No. No, I'm not. But I've got all the papers, I know all the ceremonials, and I'm a fantastic preacher, don't you agree? You see how I can enthrall my audience. I'll bet I could get a good number of them to march off to Jerusalem with you tomorrow if I wanted."

"Thank you, no, we can barely stand each other as is without adding hordes of others. But yes, your preaching is quite extraordinary," Kyle-Boyer judged dully. "Your English is also commendable, considering how drunk you are. You hardly slur your words at all. Tell us, if you don't mind, exactly how you got to be the Catholic Elmer Gantry."

"I didn't have a divine vision, if that's what you mean." He slapped his leg, howling with delight. "But I did need a job. Rather desperately so. You see, I was in Senegal when the Empire was dismembering itself, and if I had stayed on, I'd have ended up being a file clerk for some nigger administrator, and besides being a racist there was evidently no future for me in that. They weren't promoting whites, so to speak. But happily the chancery in Dakar burned to the ground and all the records were destroyed and there was no one back in France to prove otherwise, so I became a priest. A good one, too. I have a certain charisma, you see. So I came back and established a spiritual empire among the *pieds noirs* first—an easy job, considering their needs and hatreds —then branched out to combat communism among the peasantry. Needless to say I got a little help from higher up in Paris. A few theatrical and organizational touches were imported from the American gospel circuit, and I was the phenomenon a tired, dispirited France was looking for."

"Bravo, Marfeau. But why the crusade?" Murphy asked. Their boss was biting the Scotch bottle again. Murphy reflected dimly that even in the days of his most boundless capacity for the drink he had never been capable of that.

"Oh, well, Murphy, business was dropping off, as they say. The *pieds noirs* have been back a long time now and have quite settled in. And once the farmers and workers feel the power of a little car beneath their arses on a Sunday afternoon drive, suddenly there's less need for the solace religion has to offer. It's all the fault of the economy, you see. And Christians are so ungrateful. They seem to work in cycles only. It's a historical fact. Confiscate all the little cars and throw them in the ocean, and they'd all be so very Christian again. Would anyone like a drink? Good Scotch whisky given to me by a wealthy patron. The finest. How about you, Murphy? Your friend Emile Monard tells me that if you weren't stuck in a French château, you'd be on the Bowery in New York for love of this poison."

"I'm on the wagon," Murphy told him defiantly.

"And you, Kyle-Boyer?"

"That isn't the finest Scotch, Marfeau, not nearly as good as my own brand. And I have no intention of drinking with a person who has been responsible for making me defecate in my trousers."

"As you wish, Kyle-Boyer. But as I say, I cannot perform miracles. The weakness was in your sphincter. How about you, Monsieur Whitmore?"

"Fuck yourself, Marfeau."

"Tsk, tsk! Such disrespect for the clergy. Especially when they pay you so much money for merely walking. *Et vous, Père Bisson,*" he asked the old priest, "*quelque chose à boire?*"

"*Oui, mon père.*"

Their moral barometer's acceptance instantly deflated his fellow prisoners. He picked up a glass on

Marfeau's dressing table and indicated with his finger that he wanted it filled to the top. He had finished crying now, but his eyes were red and rheumy in the parchment-white skin of his face.

"My orphanage?" the old priest asked him. "You will really build it?"

"Construction has already begun, *mon père,*" Marfeau told him, filling Bisson's glass. The bogus preacher, now drunk enough, spilled a quantity of the Scotch onto the other's cassock and giggled at his imprecision, but it seemed not to matter. "We have photographs, in fact, of the excavations and the pouring of the foundations." Marfeau opened the dressing table drawer and extracted an envelope, pulling out several photographs that he handed Bisson. Reflexively, Murphy, Kyle-Boyer, and Whitmore crowded around, each preparing to disbelieve.

"*C'est ça!*" Bisson exclaimed, stamping his foot in delight. "*Mon église! Mon presbytère!*" The old priest smiled like a happy child. He drained a huge gulp of Scotch from the glass, the near-transparent weariness disappearing instantly from his face.

"Is it true?" Murphy demanded of Marfeau. He took one of the photos from Bisson. In a large open field between church and rectory appeared a gang of workmen erecting forms for foundation footings in a dugout. In another picture the footings were already poured.

"Of course it's true, Murphy," Marfeau told him, smiling. "Our side signed a contract, and your side signed the same contract. We shall live up to our part of the agreement. It's important to remember that you must live up to yours. That way there'll be no more violence, and no more fright and shitting of one's pants."

"But the building will be so very large," old Bisson interrupted in French. There was real awe in his voice. Marfeau sat down on the couch beside him, putting an arm around Bisson's shoulder.

"One has heard so much of your good work, *mon*

père, one decided to reward you doubly. It will be four stories high. The extra two are a surprise," Marfeau told him. He took another bite on the Scotch bottle and kissed Bisson wetly on the cheek. Bisson drained the rest of his glass and kissed Marfeau also on the cheek while the preacher poured him another.

"Four stories! But now I will need eight sisters to run the orphanage!"

"You shall have them, *mon père!* You shall have them, never fear!" Marfeau promised. He drank some more, then kissed Bisson on the forehead this time, putting down the Scotch bottle and clasping the ancient's head between his hands. "He's so good, do you know?" Marfeau addressed the others. "It's truly amazing to be in the presence of such holiness."

Bisson, weeping now for joy, kissed Marfeau in turn. Murphy merely shook his head at the hopeless irony the night's events contained. Kyle-Boyer spoke out loud. "If apparent reality allows itself to be distorted one more time, I think I shall simply go mad."

"These 'ere French, they're really bloody crazy," Jonathan Whitmore judged. "I'll bet this time Marilyn comes back from the hospital cured like she was supposed to be in the first place."

"That, Jonathan, is quite impossible." Marfeau swigged on the dregs of the bottle. "I couldn't cure dandruff. Though God knows I should like to find a cure for the hangover I'm going to have in the morning. I'll bet it will be beastly. But on the other hand I won't have to bother with any makeup to seem convulsed by sorrow at your departure. I'm quite sure I'll look ghastly enough by my own merits."

They were interrupted by a knock on the trailer door, and one of Marfeau's lackeys poked his head in to inform them that the replacement mule for Marilyn Aldrich had arrived. Marfeau reeled toward a cabinet door, yanked it open, and pulled out another bottle of Scotch. He unscrewed the top, refilled Father Bisson's glass, took a long swig himself, and invited them to accompany him outside.

About twenty feet from the trailer, beneath the ceiling of the great tent, waited a farmer holding the bridle of a snow-white mule, identical—it seemed to Murphy—to the dead Mirabelle, except that it stood at least a full hand higher, wore no blinders, and seemed to have, if such a thing were possible in a mule, the relentless stare of an automaton.

"Il es très spécial, ce mule. Comme un rocher." The farmer spoke to Marfeau, seemingly oblivious, as was the preacher's employee, of the Scotch bottle.

Marfeau said nothing, only strode up to the mule and, making a fist, smashed it in the mule's forehead, right between the eyes. The animal did not even flinch. Then he kicked it in the forelegs and, ordering the farmer to pull down its head, actually bit the mule's ear like a Navajo taming a mustang, pummeling its neck at the same time with the Scotch bottle. Bisson, giggling from the drink, worked over the animal's hindquarters, slapping at its withers until Murphy corraled the old priest and pulled him away lest the beast turn out to be less serene than the owner proposed. After Marfeau planted a fierce kick in the mule's underbelly (which did make the animal flinch slightly), he pronounced himself satisfied and ordered the owner paid.

"That bloody mule ain't got any feelin' at all," Jonathan Whitmore said.

"Then for certain he's not likely to throw our white goddess off again," Marfeau said. He and Bisson had their arms about each other's shoulders, and Bisson alternately giggled and whimpered at the construction site photographs.

Marfeau's aide opened a briefcase he was carrying and took out two check vouchers that he handed to Jonathan Whitmore.

"What's these for?" Whitmore asked.

"You agreed to appear here tonight for a certain

amount, I believe," the man said. "This is the agreed-upon remuneration for Miss Aldrich and yourself."

"Go ahead and give Murphy and Kyle-Boyer some money, too," Marfeau urged. "They deserve it after tonight's little misunderstanding."

Jonathan Whitmore looked up from scrutinizing the vouchers. "Why, these is for double the amount we was promised. That's right good of you, Padre Marfeau. I'm beginnin' to like you myself, takin' care of us 'n' old Padre Bisson so fine. If you're payin' this kind of money you can tell that chum of yours, Gervais, to put away his nickel-plated revolver for the rest of the trip because he ain't gonna need it for Johnny Whitmore or his friend Marilyn."

"Boys"—Marfeau urged them conspiratorially closer —"there's more money in this than in the Bank of France for all of us, me included, if you just do what you've agreed to. That's all that's necessary! That's really all that's necessary!" The preacher chanted until his lackey told him curtly to hold his tongue. After a long moment of staring dumbly at the man, Marfeau quietly handed the bottle to Bisson, indicating that the old one was to finish it. Then, incredibly, Marfeau kissed each of them good night, ending with Père Bisson, whom he pummeled wildly on the back. In another minute the aide led a lurching Marfeau off to his trailer, after clapping his hands to summon the pilgrim prisoners' guards. Eerily, Gervais, Lebel, and Ricard appeared from beneath the stage props where, unseen, they had evidently watched the entire proceedings. The farmer led the white mule off toward an exit. The animal's plodding was the only sound in the great tent except for the flapping of canvas in the wind above them.

"As you can see, Murphy, you are not the only one who ever had a problem with alcohol," Gervais remarked. "And you should not expect Marfeau to be friendly and kissing-sweet in the morning. He will doubtless be surly and miserable and hate himself for having been kissing-sweet tonight. Oh, well." He shrugged. "At least you enjoy the luxury of a real bed tonight. You're all to sleep in that trailer over there. Let's go. It's time to rest."

The four pilgrims marched dutifully off toward the indicated trailer, shadowed from behind by their three guards. Murphy, who held up a wobbling Father Bisson, realized suddenly how very tired he was, too tired in fact to attempt a reply to Kyle-Boyer's newest appraisal of their situation. "Well, our captivity—and it must be called that, I'm afraid—seems at least a benign one."

Murphy did not believe their captivity was benign at all, and he was convinced of it moments later when Gervais locked the four of them in the trailer as they prepared to sleep. He was especially convinced of it in the morning when they were rudely awakened to find the bogus preacher sick with a hangover, surly as Gervais had predicted, and aggressively threatening, besides—particularly toward Kyle-Boyer, whom he called "shit-in-the-pants" and repeatedly tried to kick. Growing tired of the effort, he went off to a nearby hillside, where he read an outdoor Mass before a crowd that Murphy estimated to be about four or five thousand souls. Kyle-Boyer, shaking his head in stupefaction at the sight of the host of the faithful lining the adjacent hillsides and waving crusader flags and branches of palm apparently brought up by the truckload from the Mediterranean, revised his estimation of the nature of their captivity.

"No one would believe it." The abortionist spoke miserably. "Look at all those television cameras! This is the biggest fraud in modern history. Murphy! No one among all these people, or perhaps in all of France, would guess that we're absolute prisoners."

"I know," Murphy answered quietly, as Marfeau, Ricard, Lebel, and Gervais lined them up (with Marilyn returned that morning from the hospital, her leg in a cast, sitting sidesaddle on the new desensitized mule) to march in solemn procession out of Clermont-Ferrand toward Lyon and the Italian frontier. "Just look at their faces. They're utterly rapturous. They'll believe anything Marfeau tells them."

It was true. Marfeau had France believing what he wanted it to believe. They saw it repeatedly during the nine days it took to cover the distance from Clermont-Ferrand to Lyon, with crowds and First Communion classes come out to see and touch the famous Marilyn Aldrich, now properly exorcised and back on God's own track. Murphy in particular saw it in Lyon, where he had occasion to meet with his father-in-law, a perfect loon of a man swimming always against the tide in almost any instance in the past that Murphy might recall. Only now he spoke to his son-in-law from another world, believing in and reverencing the pilgrims and their pilgrimage exactly as Marfeau had intended. And after their first few words together, Murphy saw that it would be impossible to persuade the old man otherwise, to make him understand that he, Murphy, was in danger.

He encountered *le baron* as they marched through the center of Lyon along the National 7, heading for one of the bridges across the Rhône, intending to take up the National 6 that wound upward through the foothills of the Alps and into Italy not far from Turin. Murphy, carrying his cross and preoccupied with the notion that Marfeau would have them killed when he no longer had any use for them, did not at first hear the voice that called out to him from the throngs of Saturday afternoon shoppers that lined the sidewalks.

"François! Frank!" The old man left the curb, came up to Murphy, and bussed him warmly on both cheeks. He wore a dark suit, his familiar black beret, and his Croix de Guerre from the first war. With him were Luchachefsky and de la Chalonière, two old royalists, the one White Russian, the other French, with whom *le baron* plotted in preparation for the Bourbon restoration. They acknowledged Murphy with polite bows and then fell into line beside de Rastignac, all three moving toward the Rhône in a stiff military gait. Not inexplicably, Murphy was caused to think of Flaubert and the village parades of old rural France.

"Frank, you've lost much weight," the old man judged, falling back momentarily as if to admire him. "This walking is good for you, I think. But all things done in the name of God and religion can only produce good results in the end."

"Yes, perhaps, *beau-père,* but at the same time I don't drink much any more. Are you still trying to empty the caves?"

"What else can I do? The mistake was mine. I must correct it, *n'est-ce pas?*" The old man winked, his eyes twinkling. "Besides, for me the wine is like gasoline for a car. If I stop drinking it, my motor will also stop."

"You'll have a *crise de foie.* Your liver, monsieur."

"My liver is dead. It died years ago. But enough of this talk. François, I've seen you almost every evening on the television. The marvel of our technical age is that I'll be able to watch your progress nearly every step of the way to Jerusalem. Those who say technology and religion make poor bedfellows are fools. If only there had been television when Guillaume marched off to Moscow. Our family might have warned him about the czar's Tartars. But at least, by way of consolation, I'll know you are safe."

Murphy suppressed an ironic reply; there was no point in it. "I doubt we'll be seen every night after we leave France, monsieur. Perhaps once a week. Tell me, does Monique watch me? Or Jean-Philippe?"

"Monique refuses." The old man shrugged. "And I no longer permit Jean-Philippe to watch. He thinks everything is a fraud anyhow. The other night in Clermont-Ferrand when the English girl fell from her mule, he fell from his chair with laughter. *Il n'aime pas la vie spirituelle, comme nous.* Even if she were

a fraud, it must have pained her very much. He could
have been sympathetic."

"It's not his way," Murphy heard himself say.
He turned about to check out the reaction of Gervais to the presence of the three old men in the
line of march. Predictably, the producer had his head
stuck out the window of the Peugeot, his face
screwed up into a question mark. Murphy shrugged
his shoulders to indicate his ignorance of the persons
who marched beside him. Then Gervais jerked his
thumb toward the sidewalk, implying that the crossbearer was to invite his companions to leave. Only
Murphy did nothing, some resistance still alive within
him, wanting to see how Gervais himself would get
rid of the old men. Then he thought of escape,
really for the first time since they had left Clermont-
Ferrand. Nearer the river, the sidewalks were
crammed with curious onlookers, and Murphy con-
templated dashing through them, forming a flying
wedge with *le baron,* Luchachefsky, and de la Chalonière, racing to wherever the old Citroën stood
parked, and heading south on the National 7
toward the Riviera. But in the end he did nothing.
To tell *le baron* they were actually prisoners of Marfeau and his lackeys would not result in desperate
flight; the old men would simply turn about and
begin blindly fighting and end up either being clubbed
to the pavement or hauled over to the police as a
nuisance. This realized, Murphy compensated and informed his father-in-law instead that the entire pilgrimage was a fraud as Jean-Philippe had judged.

"What does it matter, François?" The old one
shrugged. "Keep on walking. It's a noble undertaking,
I think. Marfeau, for his work to bear fruit, must
promote religious sentiment, and the individual man
desperately needs an occasion for glory. Wars have
been created for that same end. Only now that
they've made war into a nuclear hell, the soldier
seeking glory on the battlefield merely faces the
risk of being fried alive. One can honor the ashes, as

I've heard it said, but the ashes cannot know they're being honored. I myself have not had a clear-cut chance since the first war. These days it appears one must be a master politician like Clemenceau or a chanteuse like Edith Piaf. There seems to be nothing in between. But you can count your good fortune. At home in Vardelle you are a hero. The people of the village light candles for you in the churches. They bring baskets of food to the château. Your picture is taped to the windows of the *pâtisserie* and the *boulangerie*. Buvais the mechanic worked on my car some days ago and charged me nothing in your honor. I myself commissioned your portrait from a photograph, and it's to hang in the great hall with your illustrious ancestors. Perhaps I'll break the line of succession and put it next to Guillaume."

"Do you think Monique will stand for that, monsieur?"

"Why not, François? Besides, she's distraught anyhow, too upset to really care what I do."

"Why is that? Because of me?"

"No, because of the death of a friend of hers, a young man who was her classmate at the Sciences Politiques. His name was Gillet, a lawyer, a member of the bourgeoisie. He was killed in an auto accident in Normandy. Sometimes in the evenings I hear her crying and she mentions his name. Perhaps she was a little in love with him before she married you. *Tu sais?*"

"Perhaps," Murphy said for his father-in-law's benefit, knowing miserably that her infatuation for Gillet had caught fire and been stamped out in a single day whose tragic event Murphy was now almost certain had been engineered by Marfeau.

"Well, no matter, François. Things can be patched up. I have some money in my sock back at the château. I think that when you reach Jerusalem, I'll buy airplane tickets to fly us there for the occasion. We can have many photographs taken of Monique and you and Jean-Philippe and me for our collection.

It will be a great time of reconciliation, *n'est-ce pas?*"

"I look forward to it, monsieur."

"Moi aussi."

They marched forward in silence for a time, coming up to the Rhône. Some gendarmes stopped traffic along the quay, and they moved onto the bridge. Old Luchachefsky said something about breaking stride lest they shake the bridge into the river, and *le baron* and de la Chalonière gravely agreed it was the responsibility of marching armies to do so. Murphy, for his part, found himself chuckling over a familiar source of amusement: the Bourbons on the march.

"How goes the restoration of the king, *beau-père?*" he asked his father-in-law.

"Always the same problem, François: cowardice and lack of funds. Oh, if only we had thought to steal that diamond from the Angoulême Cathedral instead of those fools of Basques! Think how much money we could have gotten for it!"

"Apparently, monsieur, those Basques are not such fools after all."

"Yes, they are, Frank! They are worse than fools! They are stupid! You haven't heard what happened to the diamond?"

"We never watch the television any more, *beau-père,* or read a newspaper. What happened?"

"They found a Basque in Bayonne who killed himself. He left a note saying he grew frightened because the police were closing in, so he threw the diamond into the bay at Saint-Jean-de-Luz and then took poison. Now every adventurer in the country is diving down in the bay looking for the thing, and there are two *flics* on hand for every diver. They say it's only a matter of days before someone finds it and it's returned to Angoulême."

"Incroyable . . ." Murphy murmured softly, saddened at once that the great heist that had so electrified his imagination had ended in the ignoble death of a Basque who had capitualted to his fear. He won-

dered how such a man could have had the original genius to plan the theft.

"It is not unbelievable, François," de la Chalonière said, anger rising to his eyes. "It is sad. The saddest thing possible. I myself do not condone anarchy, but at least once in life a man must rise to the bait of the spectacular, shatter laws and defy authority, punch the middle class right in its staid, ugly face to let the world know he is truly a man. But the end this Basque chose for himself—"

"*Il est fou, ce Chalonière,*" *le baron* pronounced, jabbing Murphy in the ribs. "Very crazy indeed. He would rant for days about the nobleness of man and absolutely forget about the value of the diamond to our cause. To hell with the Basque! But I can't speak of it any more. Shut up, Chalonière. It upsets me to think of it. Tell me, Frank—the English girl; is she in very bad pain?"

"No, not now, monsieur. She's taking drugs for it, of course."

"It's too bad about her background. I preferred to think of her as Jeanne d' Arc. But still, she now seems somewhat more human to me."

He said it without snickering. As usual, *monsieur le baron* was in dead earnest. Murphy and the three old royalists turned about to look at Marilyn Aldrich, who rode sidesaddle, cowed and miserable, her cast-encrusted leg hanging almost straight off in a sling. Marfeau, desperate after the night of the accident at Clermont-Ferrand to save himself from the cynics, had denounced her as a prostitute who had fallen back on her ways and was paying for it. Though that news could hardly have assured those same cynics, it at least diverted their attention. In addition Marfeau had ordered a black cross painted on the cast without really giving a reason, though it seemed as good an indictment of Marilyn's personal moral tragedy as Hester Prynne's letter. On the route of march since Clermont-Ferrand it had been repeatedly photographed, parents with grave, accusing faces had shown it to their children, and all in all, since La Belle France could be counted upon to be infinitely more fascinated by recognized unholiness than the bland end product of a miracle who had simply gotten up and walked away, Marfeau was safe for the time being. No one, it occurred ruefully to Murphy, had thought to ask out loud how a paraplegic had ever functioned as a prostitute anyhow. Perhaps it bedeviled the national mind, suggested perversions that speech was unable to describe. . . .

"She looks very unhappy, I think," *le baron* judged.

"No one looks happy," Luchachefsky said. "But who can blame them? Look at the distance yet to go to Jerusalem. Look at the mountains to be crossed in front of them."

Murphy looked up. Almost immediately beyond a traffic rotary before them, where more police were already halting cars, began the real foothills of the Alps. The distance to the Italian frontier was almost three hundred kilometers, a continuously uphill climb to an elevation of about eight thousand feet. The combination of kilometers and altitude suddenly oppressed him, making the cross he carried seem doubly heavy. It may have oppressed *le baron* as well, for he began panting heavily and fanning himself with his beret. Then he spoke. "I can go no farther, François. I need a glass of wine for energy."

"*Moi aussi,*" chanted Luchachefsky and de la Chalonière simultaneously.

"I say good-bye now. Thank God for your youth and your deep Catholic faith," the old man said. "I give your love to Monique and Jean-Philippe. *Au revoir.*" Tears came easily to his eyes yet another time, and he bussed Murphy on both cheeks in farewell. Luchachefsky and de la Chalonière followed suit. "I will write you a letter to the *poste restante* each week, François," *le baron* said. "I anticipate good news concerning the restoration before the year's end." He traded a knowing look with his two com-

rades. Murphy wondered amusedly to himself whether
they were planning to rob a bank or hold up a mail
courier to raise funds on behalf of the Bourbons. He
hoped no one got shot.

"Beware the Italians," de la Chalonière cautioned.

"Also the Yugoslavs," *le baron* added. "They are
Communists."

"The Greeks are thieves, and the Turks prefer
men to women," Luchachefsky said.

"The Arabs—" *Le baron* started to say something
and then thought better of it and merely spat instead
on the pavement.

"The Jews are no better," de la Chalonière said.
"They are of the same race as the Arabs. Come, I
know a good little bistro near the place we left the
car. . . ."

But they were already moving away. *Le baron*
turned once to wave good-bye and did not look back
again. It was the last time Murphy saw the old man
alive, and it pleased him later to remember that for
his father-in-law it was certainly one of the happiest.
Le baron, alone among all the people Murphy knew,
had been well pleased with the noble task of his
son-in-law; it was the kind of madness he had dealt
in all his life.

After Lyon they climbed steadily for more than
two weeks, past Chambéry and Saint-Michel and back
and forth up the treacherous switchbacks of the Col
du Mont Cenis, where the air was rarer and Murphy
found it exhausting to walk. Two motorcycle gendarmes negotiated the curves before them lest anyone
come careening toward them from the Italian side,
not realizing there were crusaders on the march.

On the sixteenth day after leaving Lyon, they
crossed the border in the late afternoon into Italy
at Bardonecchia. Marfeau had joined them to walk
off the last few yards of French soil, and he solemnly blessed them, sending them on their way toward the land of infidels. There were legions of

photographers and also legions of television cameras
for the leave-taking event on both sides of the frontier,
and Marfeau read a telegram wishing success from
Pompidou. As they entered Italy, the French douaniers
and the Italian customs officials and carabinieri lifted
their hats in deference to the crucifix that Murphy
held high before him as per Marfeau's instructions.
No one asked for or seemed even remotely interested
in the passports and identification papers of the pilgrims to the Holy Land which Gervais kept with him
in the station wagon. Looking back, Murphy saw that
the Peugeot and the utility wagon crossed the border
unhindered as well. Also, he saw Marfeau doing a little jig of a dance for joy. In another instant Gervais
joined him. The bogus priest and the captives' warden
embraced and leaped about together in their happiness.

Murphy shrugged and marched forward down the
Italian National 25 toward Turin, wondering when he
would see his beloved France again.

PART III
ALINSKY

11
Père Bisson defects

IT WAS FATHER BISSON who blew Alinsky's cover. He did it unwittingly, of course, by stepping out of line on his second day in Italy.

That, Murphy decided, was how long it took the priest to realize he was no longer in France (he had never been beyond the boundaries of his native country before) but in the very same nation where his supreme temporal boss, the Pope, lived. Accordingly, he resolved to go to Rome and visit the Holy Father, and after asking Murphy and Kyle-Boyer in which direction the Eternal City lay, and heedless of their protests that Rome was over three hundred miles distant, the Pope was virtually inaccessible, and Gervais would send his two goons after the old priest to drag him back, Bisson led his mule to the end of a pasture as they set up camp that evening, walked through a grove of olive trees, and was gone. The deftness of the act astounded them. Gervais, believing implicitly in Bisson's pietistic stupidity, thought the priest was in the olive grove reading his breviary and never considered looking for him until dinnertime, more than an hour and a half after Bisson had left. Murphy and Kyle-Boyer, busy setting up for the night, con-

vincingly pretended ignorance, managing nevertheless
to convey news of the coup to Jonathan Whitmore
and Marilyn.

In a rage, Gervais and Ricard made preparations
to go after Bisson, deciding not to call in the Italian
police lest the incident make the papers. Lebel was
entrusted with the Colt .45 to guard the remaining
pilgrims, and Gervais and the other goon jumped into
the Peugeot and charged out of the pasture, heading in the wrong direction, back along the road to
France, to search for the priest.

For his part, Murphy was more excited by Bisson's escape toward Rome than anything else that
had happened since he joined Marfeau's crusade. As
were the others also; they sat cheerfully about a fire,
quaffing that night's ration of wine, fantasizing over the
old priest's chances, and carefully avoiding mention of
his intended destination. Their remaining guard, Lebel,
sat on the tailgate of the utility van parked about
thirty yards distant and eyed them narrowly as if he
suspected they were in conspiracy with Bisson. But
except for not daring to say the word "Rome," it
was safe to talk. Of their three wardens, Lebel
understood English least well. By way of compensation, perhaps, he twirled the barrel of the revolver;
its clicks came audibly toward them.

"I absolutely hope he makes it," Marilyn Aldrich
said. "I don't give a care for how much money we're
being paid. Anything that puts a wrench in Marfeau's
gears. After what that rotter did to me: lettin' me
lie there with my leg busted, 'n' splittin' that poor
dumb beast's throat. . . ."

"I wonder if they've gone 'n' told Marfeau yet,"
Jonathan Whitmore wondered out loud. "God, he must
be going cray. First Marilyn breaks her leg 'n'
fucks up his whole gospel show. Now Bisson takes off.
I'll bet he decides to disband the whole crusade 'n'
let us go home."

"I never thought I'd be wishing success to a
Catholic priest in any endeavor," Kyle-Boyer said,

"but I'm sure he's going to make it. The innocent always do. And after all, Gervais and Ricard went the other way. It's logical for them to assume he fled home to France. The only real problem is that if Bisson actually does make it, I don't think he'll be able to see his beloved Holy Father. Bisson is just a country priest, after all."

"Yes, that's the sad part of it," Murphy agreed. "The Pope is virtually inaccessible. Well, let's hope he stumbles upon a general audience and at least gets a look at his boss. But can you just imagine him riding his mule into St. Peter's Square and asking for an audience?"

They howled with laughter at that notion, and Marilyn Aldrich hammered her casted leg on the ground in rhythm to her merriment. But after two days of camping in the same pasture with no news from any quarter, and Lebel glowering at the *paparazzi* to stay away from the pilgrims, the notion of old Bisson entering the Vatican, banging on the appropriate door, obtaining an audience, and introducing the Pope to his mule assumed realistic proportions. Murphy allowed himself to be convinced of it by late evening of the second day when Gervais returned to the encampment by himself in a rented car, looking tired.

"Haven't you found old Father Bisson yet?" Kyle-Boyer demanded. He had a smirk on his face that was impossible to conceal. Murphy half expected Gervais to pistol-whip him right then and there.

"Shut up, you fat English pig!" Gervais screamed. "I want to talk to all of you now. It occurs to me at long last that you people must know where he went. What about you, Murphy? You used to talk with Bisson for hours."

"I don't know anything about where he went, Gervais."

"Let's make a deal between us, fellow crusaders," Gervais proposed. "If you tell me where he's gone, we'll pick him up and bring him back unharmed.

If you don't tell me, and we find him, which we will eventually, your saintly fellow traveler is going to sustain a very bad beating. Take your choice."

"You'd beat him up, Gervais, the way you had us beaten up?" Kyle-Boyer demanded incredulously. "He's an old man. The shock would kill him."

"Probably it would. But that's Bisson's problem. He signed a contract like the rest of you to stay with the group, and his orphanage is already being built, so the fraudulence is on his part, not Marfeau's. Now let's do some thinking. Does he have any relatives in Italy or any friends that he's ever spoken of?"

"He went to Rome to see the bloody Pope," Jonathan Whitmore said. "He rode off on his mule without as much as a road map. But that's where he's goin', and we all damn well hope he makes it."

It was Gervais's turn to be incredulous. "To Rome to see the Pope? He's crazy!"

"You shouldn't have told him that, Johnny," Marilyn Aldrich said. "You shouldn't have told him one bloody thing."

"It's best I did," Whitmore said. "Because Gervais is on trial now. And if Padre Bisson comes up with as much as a scratch on him, this here fuckin' crusade is finished. 'Cause they'll have to put me in my grave before I take another step."

"May I remind you that we still have the weapons," Gervais told Whitmore levelly.

"A lot of bloody good they'll do you if your crusaders is all dead," Marilyn told Gervais. For the first time Murphy saw a look of uncertainty cross Gervais's face and decided the English were probably the master race. To a point, like anyone else, they could be bought and sold, but their capacity for moral indignation was limitless. Murphy saw it all now: An abortionist, a pimp, and a prostitute had just disclaimed their profit motive and informed their captors the game was up if their friend the holy Frenchman was as much as scratched. Murphy saw Gervais looking at him stonily and knew the man was seeking weakness.

"And you, Monsieur Murphy, are you of the same mind?"

"Absolutely, Gervais. This is the first thing I've chosen to defend in my whole life. If Father Bisson is hurt you can kill me, too. I won't walk a step farther."

"Merde. The captors are evidently now the captives." Gervais sighed. "Well, let's talk about the reality. He left with nothing but a mule. No money, no food, no passport, nothing. How far could he possibly have gotten?"

"He might be in Rome already, Gervais," Murphy said to torment their warden. "With Bisson's luck he might have run into a bunch of drunken Italians twenty kilometers down the road from here who'd pile him and the mule onto a truck and take him right to Saint Peter's for the hell of it."

"Talk some sense, Murphy. If you were driving a truck through France and Bisson was riding a mule into Paris to see Pompidou, would you load him on for the hell of it? I wouldn't. No one would. No," Gervais considered out loud, unfolding a map of Italy across the hood of the rented car, *"nos amis les italiens* may have given him food and lodging. But even if Bisson were intelligent enough to resort to hitchhiking, no one stops to pick up a mule. And Bisson, for certain, would not abandon the animal. And after two days, of perhaps forty kilometers a day, I would guess he is not yet at Genoa. . . . I think we will have our friend Père Bisson returned to us tomorrow. When I finally realized he did not go home to France I sent Ricard south along the coastal route. It should not be difficult to find an old priest riding a mule who speaks only French. . . ."

And apparently it was not difficult to find old Bisson; the difficulty was in capturing him, as Ricard glumly assured them when he rolled into the encampment in the RTF Peugeot early the next morning. He was covered with welts and bruises and the dried blood of cuts inflicted on him by a mob of café patrons in Civitavecchia when he had made the mistake of trying to force Père Bisson from his mule and into the station wagon for the return trip to northern Italy right in front of the café.

With the aid of the patrons the priest had gotten away, a continuation of the same incredible luck he had enjoyed in the more than two days of his march toward Rome, and Ricard, for his part, had barely escaped being murdered. When the wounded goon told the story Bisson had narrated before he had gotten away yet another time, the fellow pilgrims in the cleric's cheering section were absolutely unable to control their delirium. The childlike, sentimental national character of the Italians that Murphy and other French alluded to patronizingly, to conceal their real disdain for a race of third-raters, seemed to have lain itself bare for the purposes of Bisson. Not ten miles from their pasture he had encountered a wedding party that had spilled out onto the highway on his behalf and ambushed a half-empty truck with a hydraulic tailgate. They had plied the driver with wine and cheese and the bride's kisses, and Bisson and his mule had ridden well past Genoa to Livorno. From Livorno he had made it to Grosseto in a van of race horses traveling to Spoleto with one empty stall. By this time someone had taped a sign to the mule's rump that read *"a Roma,"* and outside Grosseto a farmer and his family had taken priest and mule in their truck further south to Tarquinia. The only real distance Bisson had ridden on his animal was between Tarquinia and Civitavecchia, where Ricard had both found and lost him.

In shocked disbelief, Gervais followed the trail of escape along the ribbons of his map. When his finger touched Civitavecchia, he exploded with rage.

"Civitavecchia! Ricard, you fool! Why didn't you go after him when he left the café? Civitavecchia can't be more than seventy kilometers from Rome. He might be riding into Saint Peter's right now!"

"How could I go after him, Gervais? They were going to kill me. You can't rough up a priest in Italy. They followed me in their cars well out of the city to make certain I returned north instead of south."

"Lebel, give him the gun," Gervais commanded stonily, jerking his head toward Ricard. "Ricard, break camp and march them toward Susa. Lebel goes with me to Rome. We'll return and catch up with you as soon as we find that old *con* of a priest."

"Remember our agreement, Gervais," Murphy warned their leader. "If he comes back with one bump on him, Marfeau's crusade is finished."

Too vexed to waste time, Gervais said nothing in response, only ordering Lebel to take the wheel of the Peugeot and drive like hell to the airport at Turin, where they might catch a flight to Rome. The station wagon hurled out of the pasture, gained the road in a cloud of dust, and was gone.

Ricard spoke in an unexpectedly submissive voice when they were out of sight. "Dr. Kyle-Boyer, would you please attend to my cuts and bruises?"

"Only if you agree to hand over that gun."

"I cannot," Ricard said miserably.

"Then you'll probably catch a gangrenous infection, dear fellow," Kyle-Boyer said. "There are certain occasions when suspension of the Hippocratic oath is agreeably warranted."

"Quite right," Jonathan Whitmore chimed in.

"Yes, absolutely," Murphy said, as they set about to break camp for the day's march. He hoped Ricard would die, although he did not really consider it a possibility.

Père Bisson's defection to visit his Pope was clearly the end of Marfeau's crusade and the beginning of Alinsky's, though none of the pilgrims was to know that until late the next day at Susa, about twenty-five kilometers from Turin, where they set up the tents for the night in another pasture on the outskirts of the city. Bisson returned with Gervais and Lebel at sunset. Gervais switched off the ignition and came toward the four remaining pilgrims, who had stood on his arrival. Through the Peugeot's windshield, Murphy could see scratches and bruises on the old priest's face. He had been worked over despite Gervais's assurances.

Gervais's eyes were cautious with fear. "Listen, I want to tell you all that I consider our agreement still in effect. Père Bisson is cut and scraped, but I didn't do it. That fool Lebel found him first and beat him up when he refused to return with us. You know how insensitive Lebel is."

"The dirty rotter!" It was Kyle-Boyer who spoke. "The dirty bastard!"

"Please, it's not my fault," Gervais begged. "Can't you see how apologetic I am? If I had gotten to him first, it would not have happened. Lebel will be disciplined, I swear to you! He is sacked as of this moment. Dr. Kyle-Boyer, would you please attend to Père Bisson?"

At a nod from Gervais, Ricard retrieved the old priest from the wagon. Lebel slunk out the opposite door and warily circled the vehicle. The pilgrims, silent for a moment, gasped uniformly. Lebel the goon had conclusively worked the holy man over; cuts and scratches covered his face, one eye was nearly closed with swelling, and he had lost two teeth into the bargain. Marilyn Aldrich hobbled across the expanse of pasture toward him. Bisson looked as if he were really in shock.

"*Ils m'ont battu,*" he said to Marilyn, then began crying like a child. Lebel started across the open turf between the station wagon and the safety of his lover, Ricard, who still had the gun. Reflexively, Murphy reached behind him for the crucifix leaning against the utility van, heisted it to his shoulder like a baseball bat, and swung hard in a wide arc that caught Lebel in the side of the face and knocked him to the ground. Gervais made the mistake of rushing to kneel to assist his fallen employee, and Marilyn Aldrich, with a single deft kick, lifted her casted leg into his downward-looking face and presumably broke the producer's nose. Whole geysers of blood, it seemed to Murphy, erupted all over his face. He collapsed screaming onto Lebel, and Kyle-Boyer seized the moment to rush in and begin kicking both Gervais and Lebel everywhere along the length of their bodies. Ricard, who had the gun, was almost forgotten; he stood near Marilyn's desensitized white mule, watching incredulous and openmouthed, the weapon dangling impotently in one hand, unable to shoot for fear of hitting his boss or his lover. Jonathan Whitmore, in his turn, simply walked up to the big man, removed the gun from his hand with one easy motion, then doubled him up with a fierce punch to the stomach. Murphy, ecstatic, thought of attacking Ricard. The man was on all fours, crawling along like a bear, and while Whitmore busied himself with removing the shells from the revolver, Murphy rushed over and brought the business end of the crucifix down hard across Ricard's back. The shock of that contact separated the Savior's tree from the six-foot-long alloy staff atop which it was fixed, and Alinsky's diamond popped out onto the grass.

12

The non-gangsters

"OH, MON DIEU, NON!" It was Gervais who broke the stunned silence. He patted at his bleeding nose with a handkerchief.

The diamond sat on its wrapper of purple felt, looking—against the background of that hour of sunset—as if it were absorbing all the energy in the universe into itself. It drew a mesmerized Jonathan Whitmore toward it also. He passed through the circle of onlookers and picked up the stone reverentially, holding it up to the declining light, squinting into its planes.

"This here's a real diamond, it is."

"Yes, it's quite real," Gervais acknowledged wearily, "and I'm afraid there are no longer any guards or captives among our little group of eight. We're all in the same boat now, so to speak."

"Is that Suleiman's Pebble, Gervais?" Murphy asked after a long moment.

"Yes, it is."

"How long have we had it?"

"Right from the beginning. From Saint-Aubin in Normandy."

"Of course. It makes sense," Murphy said, smiling bemusedly to himself. "I remember laughing with my father-in-law about the robbery the same week that I signed on for the pilgrimage. Evidently it was not stolen by the Basque in Bayonne who committed suicide."

"Evidently not," Gervais answered. But his gaze, apprehensive now, was not trained on his questioner. He scanned the rows of olive trees that surrounded much of their pasture. In the declining light, knobby and grotesque as olive trees always were, their trunks might have concealed hundreds of on-lookers.

"Marfeau is simply amazing," Kyle-Boyer judged. "I find some quite interesting parallels between our little hike and the original Children's Crusade. Do you remember? A monumental dupe if there ever was one: priests scouring Europe looking for orphans and other youths purportedly to fight the infidel; then they went and sold them to the North African Berbers. Just amazing! But that's what we are, the same kind of innocents. What genius Marfeau has! What crooked, incredible ingenuity! What policeman anywhere would take a crucifix from a group of religious pilgrims and search it for a stolen diamond?"

"Gervais, it isn't Marfeau, is it?" Murphy asked. He felt himself growing giddy, if that were the proper word. He saw it in the others also. Except for Père Bisson, who as usual was blocked from knowledge by not knowing English, and Gervais, who knew every-thing, they were all somehow amused—even the vic-tims of the pilgrims' attack, who had gained their feet again and were patting at their wounds. Evidently Ricard and Lebel were just hired hands; they did not know what Gervais knew.

"No, Murphy, it is not Marfeau."

"How amusing, then," Kyle-Boyer said. "We're all in the midst of someone's marvelous joke on West-ern Christianity. Who is it, Gervais? Pompidou? Golda Meir? King Faisal? Wait, I'll bet it was Harold Wil-son!" They were all laughing now.

Gervais walked to the utility van and pulled out an armful of wine bottles that would normally have done for many nights' rations.

"Yes, I'm sure it's Wilson! It's just like something that rotter would do to swell Labour's treasury."

"I wouldn't exactly berate him, Austin," Jonathan Whitmore told him. "I think it's unpatriotic to criticize an Englishman who could steal from the French 'n' get off scot-free."

"Are we working for the Marseille Mafia?" Murphy demanded. "Or the Union Corse? If it isn't Marfeau, if Marfeau's only part of the ploy, then it's got to be something big like that." Speculation aside, Murphy wanted nothing to do with either of those vaunted organizations.

"No, you're working for Meyer Alinsky."

"Who the hell is he?" Marilyn Aldrich asked.

"I don't really know," Gervais answered, handing out the wine bottles. "Not absolutely, anyhow. But then no one seems to know much more about him than I do. He holds an Israeli passport and spends most of his time in Jerusalem. He's about fifty-five and looks like one of those actors who plays Joshua or Moses in the Italian biblical epics. Also, he's enormously wealthy—one of the wealthiest men in the world, apparently. But that may be a façade, for all I know. There are rumors of tanker fleets and East African holdings, European conglomerates and American petroleum. . . . Anyhow, he copped the diamond. Marfeau just works for Alinsky. Alinsky set him up in business years ago on the off chance that he might find a use for him some day. And apparently he found it. Marfeau in one way or another enlisted all of you—through his agents, of course."

"And you, Gervais? How did he enlist you?" Murphy asked. He noted that everyone greedily accepted a bottle of wine from the producer.

Gervais bent his head back and swilled a quarter bottle effortlessly. He still held the handkerchief to his nose. "In the cruelest way possible, Murphy," Gervais answered. "It was not Marfeau, by the way, who contacted me."

"Was it the Israeli girl, the one who's your wife?" Marilyn Aldrich questioned. She took small sips of her wine, regarding Gervais pensively; the same blood that congealed on the producer's chin also dried on her casted leg.

"Yes, exactly. He sent her to Paris from Israel to make me fall in love with her. You see, I lived alone . . . I worked very hard to gain my promotions at the network . . . I guess you might say I was the perfect chump." Gervais spoke ruefully. "On the morning he came to retrieve her, we were making love when he pressed the door buzzer. She actually got up and dressed to leave as if I had never existed."

"And she's the reason you've been persuaded to set up this entire TV extravaganza?" Murphy said. "I mean, she'll be returned to you in Jerusalem?"

"Yes, she's the reason. Plus the fact that Alinsky had already bought his way through a considerable swath of executives and directors at RTF who quite obligingly encouraged me as well."

"Why did this 'ere Alinsky steal the diamond?" Jonathan Whitmore wanted to know. In the last fire of sunset he admired it still, holding it to the light and turning it over and over again in his fingers. "It can't be for the money. There ain't a fence on earth would touch this thing."

"I have no idea why he stole the diamond," Gervais said. "As you imply, Jonathan, it can't be for the money. Perhaps it was all theoretical, a test of criminal genius. The method of the heist was inventive beyond belief, and furthermore every *flic* in France now believes it's in the bay at Saint-Jean-de-Luz."

"Padre Bisson, this 'ere's the diamond that was stole from that cathedral some time back," Jonathan Whitmore tried to tell the old priest. But there was no response. Bisson had stopped crying and drank his wine instead. Whitmore turned to Murphy. "Murphy, you tell the padre what this is in French, will you?"

"No," Gervais decided. "Leave him alone. The less he knows, the less confusing it will be for him. Alinsky has a purpose for his being here, though I can't guess what it is, and as you saw from the photographs Marfeau had, the orphanage is indeed being built. It is of no use compromising the good priest's lifework with some ethical point simply because he's been trained to lunge at the appearance of ethical points."

"Do we get a chance to meet this Alinsky?" Murphy asked.

"Most assuredly, Murphy. For all I know"—Gervais swilled more wine—"he may be watching us from a limb of one of those olive trees out there. Two of his agents are anyhow, two Israelis that have been scanning us for the last month and a half since we took to the road. Why don't we build a fire for the night? When they see us all sitting down in good wine-drinking fellowship and singing campfire songs as well, they'll know for certain that this level of control is finished. They will then impose the next level, and for that reason I'm quite sure we'll see Meyer Alinsky either tomorrow or the day after at the latest."

They set about gathering wood for the fire. Murphy noticed that though it was now swiftly darkening and the crickets that were chirping and the whippoorwills that were singing might have been Israeli agents in the near distance of the olive grove exchanging coded messages, nobody seemed particularly spooked; curiosity had overcome fear. Murphy, drinking now, thought of crying out to the darkness, informing Alinsky's men that the diamond was found out—if they did not already know that fact—and inviting them to the fireside for a drink. But he did not. It would ruin the evening. Absolved from the drudgery of endless walking, the pilgrims and their wounded former wardens were in minutes more seated about the flames in the agreeable business of speculating. . . .

"How many levels of control are there likely to be?" Kyle-Boyer asked. "Now that I know what I'm participating in, I'd like to get out. If Interpol or the French police get hold of us, they'll put us away forever. Or has this Alinsky person bought them off also?"

"It's quite possible," Gervais said. "As I see it, the levels of control equal the possibilities for intimidation. And in Alinsky's case they may be limitless. Perhaps he's the most evil person in the whole world. Look what he did to me. Can you believe such a thing? Taking my wife away with a snap of his fingers and blithely informing me she was only on loan anyhow. That kind of man has a mind the devil should fear to deal with. I don't know why he stole the diamond, or why he's brought us together in this ridiculous crusade, or why he chooses to reward us in the particular fashion that he does. When I questioned him about it, he proposed rather self-effacingly that his kind of wealth has given him the liberty to indulge in all manner of philosophical speculation, and that's really all he's doing. Meerly speculating. Just playing a game because it's the only sort of thing that amuses him any longer."

"That makes us a bunch of laboratory rats in a maze of Alinsky's creation," Kyle-Boyer remarked, "no matter how self-effacing the gentleman may be."

"And it is quite a maze," Murphy judged. "An unnecessarily complicated one. But I'd say we're giving the man too much credit in supposing he might have bought out Interpol or the Gendarmerie Nationale. We're sitting here creating a hobgoblin like a bunch of kids in America on Halloween night. This Alinsky isn't even famous. I've never heard of him."

"Alinsky could not succeed at being Alinsky if you had heard of him," Gervais said, almost crying now. Released at last from what he alone had known, he was well on his way to getting very drunk. "And don't make the mistake of thinking he could not in-filtrate Interpol or the French police if he wanted to. A minute ago I said I considered that a pos-sibility. Now that I think about it, I'm sure he's done it! He's a chess master, you see, moving us, the police, the church, the press across a board that leads to—"

"You may have remembered something, Gervais," Murphy told him stonily, anxious to impose some sane control, "but you're also drinking quite a bit."

"So what? I need it. Let me tell you what I re-called, so that when you meet this Alinsky—and find him engaging and amusing, as he can be—you will not fail to take him seriously. When Alinsky came to my apartment to take back my wife and inform me that I was to be shepherding a pilgrimage to Jerusalem, he had a black book with him, thick like an accounting ledger. It was titled the Book of the Corruptibles, and each page contained a kind of chart of the power structures of what he claimed were the major institutions of the Western world—churches, police organizations, government ministries of many varieties. The list seemed endless; it was a very thick book. Of course I thought it was a lot of foolishness, an attempt to create a stupendous illu-sion, until he showed me the specific pages for my network and for a few ministries of the French govern-ment where I know people in high places. Alinsky had gotten to every one of them. His method of infiltration is apparently simple. He just draws a theo-retical line across at a certain level of bureau-cracy, proceeds to buy it out, and effectively isolates the top of the pyramid from its base. Then nothing detrimental to Alinsky's interests anywhere filters up or down without his knowledge past the barrier he's created."

"Don't be absurd, Gervais," Kyle-Boyer said. "No one has that much power."

"Alinsky does, *monsieur le docteur*. Believe me, he does. Oh, I want to get absolutely *sou* tonight. . . .

She was so beautiful, my wife. I am handsome, I know. I've seen myself on television many times. But I could not believe a woman of that beauty wanted so desperately to be married to me of all people in the world. Now I know why. . . ." Gervais stood up and began shrieking, turning wildly about in the fire-light as if he were seeking out the two Israelis in the blackness of the olive groves. "The problem with your boss is not that he corrupts others! Do you hear me, you Jew bastards? His problem is that he's so utterly corrupt himself! He violated my heart! He made me fall so desperately in love with her, and then he took her away!"

"You'll get her back, Monsieur Gervais, when the time comes," a voice called out from an indeterminable somewhere above them, its tone almost nonchalant, but omnipotent at the same time because it came through a megaphone. "But please be decent enough to remember when you need resort to racial epithets that the woman you love so desperately is also a Jewess."

The voice, that had startled them, clicked off again as abruptly as it had begun with a lingering instant of electric static. Reflexively, Murphy and Jonathan Whitmore jumped up to pull Gervais to the ground lest a bullet come winging its way at the producer. But Gervais, shocked, obligingly fell down with them. "Now do you believe what I say is true?"

"Yes," Murphy replied urgently, "but we're getting out of this! We'll put out the fire and all the lights, and Jonathan and I can try to slip off in a while to find a carabinieri station. We can't see Alinsky's men, but without a moon they won't be able to see us either."

"We'll get rid of these fuckin' white gowns 'n' blacken our faces 'n' bodies like the Tommies used to do in Malaya," Whitmore offered.

"And what will you do, *mes amis,* if you do find a carabinieri station?" Gervais asked wearily, as if he spoke with stupid children, albeit romantics. "This is all part of life, not American television."

"We could have them arrest the lot of us and put us in protective custody," Murphy retorted. "To hell with that contract we signed. As far as I'm concerned, it's invalid now because we signed with Marfeau and not this Alinsky character."

"Murphy, dear Murphy," Gervais sniffled, leaning forward to kiss him on the forehead. "You are courageous, but think what you are saying. Some nice young *tenente* of the carabinieri will gladly arrest you, thinking a big promotion is coming for having handed the thieves who stole Suleiman's Pebble from the Angoulême cathedral. He will send word up the vine until it hits the spot where Meyer Alinsky put in the blight, and it will come right down again, throwing you out in the street where Alinsky wants you, and the nice *tenente* out of a job, if not out of life altogether. I know what I am speaking about."

"But except for those two Israelis out there he has no more control on us, and we have a gun. If we could give them the slip, we might all get in the station wagon and drive back to France. We could leave the damn diamond here for Alinsky. Listen to me, Gervais," Murphy pleaded. "I know it's tough, the business of your wife, but a broken heart doesn't last forever. The world is full of beautiful women. There'll be others."

"Cherchez les photos dans la voiture." Gervais nodded to Ricard. Obediently the other went to the Peugeot and returned in a moment to the circle carrying a packet. Gervais ruffled through it and came up with a photo.

"These two persons, Murphy, are, I believe, your wife and son. She is called Monique and he is Jean-Philippe." Murphy looked closely at the images, then sighed to indicate defeat. Monique and Jean-Philippe rode horseback through the vineyards. Baudrey, the estate manager, was behind them on Murphy's own hunter.

"Who's watching them, Gervais?"

"Any number of people. But principally someone named Baudrey, who works for you and Alinsky at the same time."

"Oh, me," said Murphy. He knew he would not try to escape now. But how he hated Baudrey! Before them Gervais dug out another photo and handed it to Murphy.

"It takes awhile to cure a broken heart, Murphy, that I will admit. But two broken hearts"—Gervais slugged again on the wine bottle—"that could kill a man."

"Who is she?" Murphy asked, looking at the old woman and already knowing the answer.

"*C'est maman.*" Gervais sniffled again.

Murphy found it in him to sniffle also, as did the others. A sweet little French lady all dressed in black stood at the counter of a *charcuterie,* pointing timidly at something in a glass case. Behind her was a man in an overcoat like a leftover war-movie Nazi regarding her with the most menacing stare Murphy could imagine. Silently he handed back the photograph.

"You know, Murphy," Gervais said, "I recall something else now, concerning Meyer Alinsky. Do you remember the Six-Day War in Israel when the Egyptian Air Force never even got off the ground to fight?"

"Alinsky?" Murphy hazarded.

"I'm fairly certain. At least that was the rumor making the rounds in Paris at the time. It is said to be universally believed in Israel. . . ."

Gervais swigged again on the bottle and, released from the burden of his private knowledge, lay back and passed out. Murphy, considering that after a month and a half on the wagon he owed it to himself, decided to get drunk along with their one-time leader.

In the morning Murphy awoke with his first hangover since the day he joined the Fourteenth Crusade. Gervais was terribly hung over also, leaning weakly against one of the Peugeot's flanks and squinting into a morning sun that was already broiling hot. The producer traded Murphy an unhappy look and then indicated a cloud of dust coming down the road through the olive grove. *"Regarde."*

A black Citroën with French tourist plates floated down the waves of heat toward them. It drew up in another moment beside the remaining two mules that grazed nearby, and two men issued from it casually. They were tall and muscular, and Murphy recognized them instantly as the two Israeli tourists, once slung over with cameras, whose very same car he had helped pull from the ditch before the château on the evening he had descended the hill to the village *presbytère* to be introduced to the madness of the Fourteenth Crusade by Emile Monard.

"Shalom aleichem, dear pilgrims," one of them said. They were both smiling, neither contemptuously nor in friendliness but more in a wry good humor. "What time did the Saracens attack?"

"They were Saracens of the bottle, monsieur," Gervais told him. "We are all hung over and demoralized and the diamond is discovered, and as you gathered from all the shrieking last night, everybody except Père Bisson knows that Meyer Alinsky is stage-directing Western civilization."

"That's too bad. None of this would have happened if that schmuck over there hadn't hit the priest. It wasn't necessary." Both men looked narrowly at Lebel, who cowered on the ground in his blanket, looking as if he feared a real beating at the hands of professionals. But they did nothing. Instead, the one who had done all the talking thus far turned to old Bisson, who had come awake, and spoke in French. *"Comment vous allez, mon père? Assez fort aujourd'hui?"*

"Oui, mon fils. J'ai pris un peu de vin et j'ai bien dormi toute la nuit."

"Très bien, mon père." Then he spoke in English.

"Alinsky left Jerusalem several hours ago. He'll be landing soon in Turin, and he'll meet with us later in the afternoon at a monastery near here. The abbot is an old friend of his, so it'll be safe and convenient. My name, by the way, is Ben Bokva. This is Teplitsky, my sidekick. He speaks less frequently than I."

"Well, Chaim! I don't believe it! Chaim, darling, hello!" It was Marilyn Aldrich speaking to Ben Bokva. On hearing voices she had unzipped the front of her tent and now crawled out into the light, Whitmore right behind her.

"Marilyn, dearest, you look dreadful," Ben Bokva told her. "What happened to you? Your leg is in a cast."

"Now, Chaim, don't be coy. You been shadowin' us for more than a month now. You know right well what happened back there in Clermont-Ferrand."

Ben Bokva smiled sheepishly. "I know, Marilyn. But believe me, it pained me just as much as it pained you. Unfortunately, as you might guess, I wasn't able to come forward to offer condolences at the time."

"But now you are," Whitmore said, "'n' your condolences is happily received. Tricks comes 'n' tricks goes, but not a man jack of them was ever such a gentleman, nor paid so well as our Chaim did." Jonathan was beaming, standing in the morning sun in his jockey shorts, extolling the tall Israeli's goodness to the pilgrims at large.

"Now parts of the puzzle are beginning to fit together," Kyle-Boyer remarked. "Hello, Mr. Ben Bokva. How nice to see you."

"Hello, Dr. Kyle-Boyer. In this general friendly air of delivering compliments, may I say that I've rarely encountered a physician of your professional abilities."

"And I, for my part, would like to say that for all your alleged promiscuity, you managed to remain exceptionally clean. Not a single positive on all those Wassermanns."

"Then the credit for my good health lies finally with Marilyn. For there was no one else."

"Oh, my God." Murphy sighed, holding his head against the pain. "I can't keep up with all this."

"Do you mean, Murphy," Kyle-Boyer asked wryly, "that you've never met our Mr. Ben Bokva?"

"I've met him. I pulled him out of a ditch once. I've even met Teplitsky here."

"I've never met Teplitsky," Marilyn said. "At least I don't remember meeting him. I think he's cute."

"Mr. Teplitsky was working the French end of the arrangement," Ben Bokva explained. "Otherwise you would surely have gotten to know him. But though the good priest is probably feeling too ill to recall, Teplitsky piously attended Père Bisson's early Mass many mornings in Saint-Aubin."

"It's quite fine, I think, that we all know each other," Gervais interrupted, "but what will be our new situation?"

"You, for your part, will go on shooting film and sending it back for Christianity's consumption. Same thing as before. Only Phase Two of the Fourteenth Crusade is in operation now. That means we watch you close up instead of by telescopic lens. You could not have given us the slip last night, Mr. Whitmore, no matter how dark you had blackened your faces. The utility van is bugged for sound, you see. I guess it's rather sad that everything has come to this pass, since anyone among you who had a grain of innocence until now has certainly lost it. Most unfortunate. But we are now, anyhow, in Phase Two as I said."

"How many phases are there?" Murphy asked. "I don't want these revelations coming too fast and furious or I might go back on the booze."

"You won't go back on the booze, Mr. Murphy. You had your fling last night," Teplitsky said. "But to answer your question, there are four phases. One

was Phase 'Marfeau,' which that *con* Lebel ruined
yesterday. Two we shall call 'Alinsky Is a Benevolent
Leader,' which he is. Three is Phase 'Alinsky Is
Somewhat Harassed but Willing to Do Anything
Short of Carrying You Himself to Get You to Jerusalem.' Four is Phase 'Alinsky Kills You'—which
phase can only occur in the most incredible circumstances, which you alone can dictate, and for which,
frankly, we haven't devised a contingency plan since
it seems ridiculous to consider. That is to say, who
among you wouldn't want to have all that money to
spend? Who'd want to do something stupid instead
and have to die?"

"Quite right. It would be stupid," Jonathan Whitmore affirmed, and the others more or less agreed.
Murphy shrugged his shoulders and by way of toast-
ing the deal handed the Chianti bottle that sat on
the station wagon's roof to Ben Bokva, indicating graciously that the other was to drink. But Ben
Bokva was a teetotaler, apparently, and Teplitsky
also; the Israeli took the bottle by the neck, eyed it
with disgust, and hurled it an incredible distance
into the olive grove, where it fell through the trees
and shattered on some rocks. As always, when he
was in the company of men who had an intense personal discipline of one sort or another, Murphy felt
a consummate shame.

13

Meyer Alinsky

MURPHY HAD GOTTEN ACCUSTOMED to a certain modicum of unreality in life; living for fifteen years in a restored eleventh-century château filled on occasion with not a few grotesque participants to the twentieth century had primed him for an easy acceptance of many things. Hence the idea of meeting Meyer Alinsky in the abbot's office of Il Monastero di Tutti i Santi did not particularly unnerve him. But he feared for the sanity of Gervais. With the producer and Kyle-Boyer he rode in the rear seat of the black Citroën. Ben Bokva drove and Teplitsky sat beside him. The rest of the band, with the exception of Lebel, who was made to walk the two remaining mules as his punishment for hitting Père Bisson, followed along in the Peugeot. All the while, right up to the gates of the priory, Gervais had ranted on about how Alinsky was the most heinous human alive, and neither of the Israelis thought enough of it to silence him. Finally, as they alighted from the car, the flash of recognition came. "Murphy, I've got it!" Gervais nearly screamed. "I know now who this Alinsky reminds me of!"

"Who?" Murphy asked. His curiosity was dull. He was glad to be out of the car's confinement and able to stand away from Gervais.

"Chillingworth! From *The Scarlet Letter,* by Hawthorne, the American. Do you remember how he tortured the poor *prêtre,* Mr. Dimmerdale, until his death?"

"Dimmesdale," Ben Bokva corrected. "With an 's.' But unless you intend to flatter Meyer, Gervais, you'd better not tell him that. With his kind of ego, anything good, bad, or otherwise that reinforces his total power concept is received as a compliment. I don't say that the boss is a megalomaniac—not exactly, anyhow. . . ." Ben Bokva looked at Teplitsky.

"Not exactly." The other shrugged, in testimony to a burden they evidently shared. "But he'll do until they find a real one. Come, let's go into the courtyard to cool off."

They filed into a shaded courtyard, where a fountain sprayed, and sat down on benches to wait. A priest gave them glasses of lemonade. Flies buzzed about for an interminable otherwise-silent time until another priest appeared and spoke softly to Ben Bokva.

"*Tov.* The boss is here. He'll see you one at a time for a little private interview. Dr. Kyle-Boyer is first."

"Oh, my," Kyle-Boyer said. "I'm feeling suddenly frightened again. Here's hoping I don't defecate in my trousers another time."

"The boss is not a goon like Lebel, Dr. Kyle-Boyer," Teplitsky said. That was all. The priest led Kyle-Boyer away along an arched portico and through a heavy wooden door that closed with a reverberating slam behind them. Murphy sat and stared a long time at the fountain, thinking he was going to tell Alinsky that he needed absolute guarantees of the safety of Monique and Jean-Philippe before he would walk another step. Also that he wanted a precise answer to the question of why there were carrying an unfenceable diamond on a crusade to Jerusalem. Despite his curiosity, the deception, contrivance, illusion—call it whatever—on every level was becoming annoying. But his thoughts were broken by the sound of merriment; gales of laughter, guffawing, and gasping poured out a window above their heads that must be the abbot's office. The hilarity belonged to

Kyle-Boyer, who had entered that office fearful, and the hilarity was genuine.

"Listen to this one, Austin, listen to this one before you die! A traveling salesman pulls into Liverpool—"

Opposite Murphy, Ben Bokva and Teplitsky were smiling up at the window. Teplitsky spoke softly. "Meyer has a longer list of bad American traveling-salesman jokes than anyone in the world. If he really gets going, Dr. Kyle-Boyer will burst his plumbing and die of internal bleeding."

"Was Meyer Alinsky ever an American?" Murphy asked.

"Like yourself, Frank my friend, he was, long ago. He is not an American any longer, though." The tone of the voice indicated that the inquiry was at an end. In time the laughter subsided, and after perhaps fifteen minutes the massive door opened again into the portico and Kyle-Boyer returned to the courtyard, following the same priest. The Birmingham abortionist's face was beet red and wreathed in smiles.

"What a charming gentleman!" he exulted. "A most charming fellow. He's gone and doubled all our fees. But that's elementary. He'll probably double them again. But do you know why we're taking the diamond to Jerusalem? It's incredible. By carrying back this magnificent spoil of those awful wars, we're redressing the balance of history. The Fourteenth Crusade is undoing the work of the previous thirteen. All that raping and killing, the wanton destruction and serpentine politics, the monster lie that took the place of an ideal—we're going to repeal all that! Do you see what a monumental task has devolved upon us five pilgrims?"

Kyle-Boyer, after his appreciation of Alinsky's traveling salesman jokes, had evidently bought the gist of the man's gospel as well, Murphy surmised. It sounded like bullshit.

"Signor Murphy, *prego*." The priest invited Murphy along with a wave of his hand. "Come, please. Signor Alinsky will explain to you."

Shrugging, Murphy followed the monk through the heavy door that repeated its resounding thud, up a flight of stairs, and along a hallway until they reached an open door.

"Come on in, Murph," an unseen voice welcomed him in the same wide vowels of the American Midwest from which Murphy had once fled. Meyer Alinsky stood up from behind a rickety desk, dressed in the habit of a Franciscan, the cowl pulled over his head. He made a pious little sign of the cross over Murphy and then began to chuckle, swinging about, holding the habit in one hand like a woman with long skirts to admire himself in a full-length mirror. Despite himself, Murphy laughed also. If this were indeed the Prince of Darkness, as Gervais had suggested, he looked incredibly inept for the job. Alinsky was tall, over six feet, but with a heavy build racing toward flab that even the billows of the Franciscan habit could not conceal and a pronounced stoop to his shoulders. He had weighty jowls, like a basset hound's, that made Murphy think his face would slide off, and large sad eyes that told on the instant where Gervais's curiously diametrical judgment—that of being self-effacing—had come from. Murphy shook hands with him.

"Gervais says you're the most corrupting man in the whole world. He compares you to Chillingworth in *The Scarlet Letter*."

"Chillingworth? Isn't he the guy that did the job on the minister?"

"The same one."

"Well, Gervais is full of shit, and you can tell him I said so. I'm not Chillingworth. I'm a simple man, a bona fide phony. If anybody"—Alinsky admired himself again in the mirror with a swirl of his skirts —"I'm Cola di Rienzo."

"Who was Cola di Rienzo?"

"A wop. Someone who at the time of the Avignon

papacy almost succeeded in restoring the Roman Empire. He traded in illusion and charade, like me. He had a magnificent success, since he had no real power base at all, strictly an imaginary one. But he made it work for the most part."

"Whatever happened to him?"

"Oh, alas, the ending was sad. He blew it. Death at the hands of the mob he created. He had a fatal flaw, you see. His ego needed a constant cheering section. He stepped out onto the balcony when they were howling for his blood. But it's endemic with Italians. Mussolini went more or less the same way."

"Watch out the same fate doesn't befall you, Meyer Alinsky."

"Impossible, Murph. My ego is carefully governed. Besides, I hate crowds. The whole premise of building my empire is divide and isolate. Isolate anyone you can from anyone else. But of course, given the moral bankruptcy of nearly everything and everybody in the world these days, it's not so hard to do. No, if I'm to be killed, it's got to be at the hands of a single assassin I create."

"Oh, well, we shouldn't talk about your death at our first meeting," Murphy decided ruefully. "It seems unfair, considering your generosity. But there are a number of things I'd damn well like to satisfy my curiosity about before some inexplicable accident happens to me. Ben Bokva says you were an American."

Alinsky took his place behind the rickety desk and planted his arms firmly on the top. "Yes, I was an American. But that was long ago and far away, and I've since traded in my passport for a new model."

"Where did you come from? Someplace in the Midwest, right? Chicago, I'll bet."

"No, wrong. It was a little town in Iowa called Aruba. But I haven't been back there in ages. And I don't think any discussion of my past is particularly pertinent to what we're involved—"

"I'm a former Iowan, too." Murphy cut him off. "I know where Aruba is."

"You were? You do?" Alinsky looked shaken. A man of comfortable and somehow humorous poise, the kind that must have unnerved anyone he was really into business with, his eyes grew momentarily wide with uncertainty, then narrowed to two mistrusting slits that appraised Murphy keenly. "Why'd you leave home, Murph? I thought you must be Knights-of-Malta Irish from Boston or Philly or someplace in the East. I mean, your education in Paris, and married to that expensive French gal—"

"That was an accident, my marriage, in the same sense that leaving home was an accident. My family was killed during a tornado and I was the insurance beneficiary and there wasn't much reason to stick around Dubuque, so I went to Paris."

"They were killed by a tornado!"

It was rhetorical, in an awed voice, and Alinsky winced visibly when he said it. He stood and went to a Styrofoam beverage cooler in the corner of the abbot's office and pulled out two cans of an American beer, Budweiser, and handed one to Murphy.

"Have a beer, Murph. A remnant of home I couldn't leave behind. I drink it practically all day long because I like to keep a little buzz on. Life is more bearable that way. But listen, seriously—they got it in a tornado?"

"Yes, it was ironic as hell, and it even seems a little silly to talk about it now, but I was trying to commit suicide in the funnel and the damn thing got capricious and missed me and blew up the house where they were hiding instead."

"Jesus Christ, I should've had you better researched!" Alinsky smashed a fist on the desk so hard it nearly collapsed. "They told me you were a naturalized French drunk with an Irish last name. Instead you turn out to be my goddam alter ego. I'll bet you even went to the University of Iowa, too, didn't you?"

"Yes, class of 'fifty-five."

"I was class of 'forty," Alinsky said. "I played football there."

Of course. The realization hit Murphy like lightning. Alinsky, the great Iowa halfback whose ferocious visage had glared out of the Fieldhouse trophy cases at Murphy, the miserable undergraduate, plodding on winter mornings to the required PT courses he so detested. The same Alinsky whose pass reception and running records remained unbroken in 1955 and were perhaps unbroken even now. Then Murphy remembered something else: the advertisements in the *Iowa Alumni Review* requesting information concerning the whereabouts of Meyer Alinsky, eye-catching because they came sometimes in verse, were funny, and covered over a half page. In the beginning, after Murphy had left the university, they appeared frequently. But now when he thought to glance through the magazine, he saw them only rarely.

"People have been looking for you, Meyer Alinsky."

"Who, Murph?"

"There were ads for years in the *Alumni Review* trying to find out where you were."

"There were?" The news seemed to please Alinsky. He sat up straighter and threw back the cowl to his shoulders.

"Yes. I think it was your class secretary one time or another, then the athletic department a couple of times, and I guess some friends of yours."

"Hmm. I didn't know about any of this."

"Some years back I also remember seeing a memorial remembrance of the twentieth anniversary of your wife's death."

"Holy fuck," Alinsky said softly. He stood up, sipping from the Budweiser can, walked to the window, and stared despondently out into the courtyard while he swished the beer back and forth in his mouth from one cheek to another. Curiously, as if to protect himself, he drew the cowl over his head again. "Do you recall who placed that remembrance?"

"It seems to me it was a bunch of cheerleaders from one of the classes in the forties."

"Yes, it would have been the class of 'forty-two. They were a good gang of girls. My wife is dead now twenty-two years," Alinsky added inexplicably.

"Where did it happen?" Murphy asked.

"In Iowa. It was an accident. She's buried there, in Aruba."

"Why did you leave Iowa like that so no one knew where you were?"

"It's a private affair, Murphy, and none of your business, so don't ask me about it again. The employee doesn't need to know everything about his employer as long as he's being well paid."

Alinsky was still looking out the window, and Murphy wondered if the ensuing silence meant he was dismissed. But in another moment Alinsky turned about, and to Murphy the other's eyes seemed on the verge of real tears.

"I want to talk again about the tornado. A tornado is the only thing I was ever afraid of in my whole life. I flew a bomber during the war over Germany and almost got my ass shot off a hundred times, and don't think I much cared whether it happened or not. But those tornadoes. . . . When they'd come near Aruba I'd hide in the cellar of our house and shake like a dog. Tell me something. When you tried to kill yourself that time in the funnel and it killed your family instead, did it seem to you like the thing was—well, did it seem to you like the thing was trying to stay away from you?"

Murphy might have laughed at the preposterousness of the idea except that he saw the intensity in Alinsky's eyes. Almost involuntarily the man had pulled the Franciscan's hood close about his head.

"No, it didn't seem like the tornado was trying to stay away from me. I just couldn't get near it. It's as simple as that. You know how unpredictable they are. They can enter a town from the west, devastate it on the south end, and never touch a blade of grass where you'd most expect them to."

"Yet you wanted to die, and your family presumably didn't. But they got it and you couldn't get it. Why?"

"Look, Alinsky, let's get on with the interview. I don't see anything supernatural about tornadoes, and frankly, as long ago as it was, it's still a bit painful to recall."

"Yes, yes, forgive me, Murph. I didn't mean to offend you. My curiosity got the best of me. Listen, have another beer."

"No. I have a terrible hangover from last night, and this one tastes bad enough. I want to ask you some more questions."

"Ask away," Alinsky invited, anxious to please. He took another Budweiser from the cooler and sat quickly down at the desk, extending his hands by way of invitation.

"Why did you steal the diamond?"

It was Alinsky's turn to be annoyed. "I explained the whole thing to Dr. Kyle-Boyer. He's an articulate man. He'll fill you in on the detail. It's all based on my admittedly naïve notion of what constitutes universal retribution, but after you get the diamond to Jerusalem I'll send it back to the bishop at Angoulême and everything will be hunky-dory again."

"Nuts, Alinsky. I've already heard the explanation. History tells us the crusaders poured into the Middle East, slaughtered Mohammedans and Jews, and hauled back everything that wasn't nailed down. A single diamond traveling in the opposite direction isn't going to atone for all that. It's deeper than you say."

"If I say that's what it is, Murph, then that's what it is. Why does it have to be deeper?"

"What else could compel you to keep my wife and son prisoner?"

"They aren't prisoners." Alinsky spoke wearily. "We

had some photos taken to scare you into line in case you got really belligerent. They were taken one day, I believe, with a telescopic lens when your wife and son were out riding with your estate keeper. I'm sorry to have scared you like that. It was unfair."

"Gervais says you bought out Baudrey, the estate keeper. That part I believe. In Americanese, he's a real prick. He always has been."

"Whatever he is is your problem. Gervais was just told to tell you that. We haven't gone near this guy Baudrey. And furthermore, Gervais has informed us as a matter of duty that you receive letters from your father-in-law at the *poste restante*. If the Château de Rastignac is bound and captured and the estate keeper is holding everybody prisoner, has the old man mentioned it yet in his letters?"

"No," Murphy grudgingly admitted, that case against Alinsky's sinisterness put to rest.

"What else?" Alinsky smiled his innocence.

"What about the Basque? The one who supposedly committed suicide and left a note saying he threw the diamond into the harbor at Saint-Jean-de-Luz?"

"That was a bona fide Catholic miracle!" Alinsky exclaimed, clapping his hands with delight. "The timing was perfect. You see, he had an apartment in a condominium block I own near Bayonne and actually did himself in for reasons of Basque political impotence. But when the building manager contacted me for directions on how to proceed, the opportunity seemed heaven-sent. Especially with every cop in Europe looking for the Angoulême diamond. So I told the manager to plant the note and call the cops. Genius, huh?" Alinsky tapped the side of his shrouded head with a single finger.,

"Genius," Murphy echoed weakly. "One last question. The lawyer, Armand Gillet; why did he have to die?"

"Qui est Gillet?" Alinsky asked in French.

"That's exactly what that goony evangelist Marfeau that you set up in France wanted to know."

"Well, if Marfeau doesn't know, how the hell am I supposed to know?"

"Why wouldn't Marfeau know who Gillet was? Gillet met me in Normandy before I joined the crusade. He had all the papers ready for me to sign."

"I can give you a logical explanation," Alinsky said, sipping on the beer. "It's the best one I can offer, and you'll have to buy it or forget it. I can only suppose Marfeau contacted the law partners he usually deals with for this job, and they sent some young kid that Marfeau wasn't acquainted with off to Paris to do the legwork. Senior partners are more Marfeau's type anyhow."

"Maybe." Murphy was not convinced. "Where did you ever get the idea of setting that freak up in business anyhow? And don't try to say he isn't yours. He gave us some story about being self-made in Senegal, but Gervais told us otherwise."

"I admit it. He's mine. I set him up in business years ago, and he's proved to be very useful many times since then. But to be truthful, the idea of creating such a monster was hatched ages before in an Iowa cornfield when I had the extreme pleasure, rarely given to a young Jew, of attending a Klan meeting and hearing a widely known and respected Iowa minister shovel shit into men's hearts by the spadeful. That's power, I often thought to myself later, and I decided that sometime before I died I was going to get my very own private spiritualist shit shoveler. Hence Marfeau. It's kind of difficult to imagine anyone doing a better job than that turd, don't you agree?"

"On that point, Meyer Alinsky, I'm in complete agreement with you," Murphy said. "But if you really control Marfeau, then it makes you all the more frightening, not the simple man you claim to be and not a self-admitted phony either. Because you know and I know exactly how powerful Marfeau is in France. He could make some of those peasant followers of his jump through hoops of fire if he wanted."

"Fire is cleansing," Alinsky judged lamely. "And if owning Marfeau makes me the archfiend you're trying to convince yourself I am, then please remember I've never taken the leash off that holy man. He hasn't been allowed to sell hatred or violence from the pulpit like the Iowa preacher. Just cooling platitudes, and lots of them. Meyer Alinsky doesn't want to topple anybody's empire."

"How about breaking hearts? Is that off limits, too?"

"Whose heart did I break? Yours?"

"No, Gervais's. That was a real stinker sending that girl out from Israel to hook him into this crusade."

"Business, Murph. Strictly business. But I lost on that one." Alinsky sighed, throwing up his hands, a prisoner of fate. "Rifka used to be my Mata Hari. A real pro, too. But this Gervais, despite all those rumors of his fabulous prowess, turned out to be so lonely, so vulnerable, such a fuckin' mama's-boy milksop that in the end she fell for him. The first night he made it with her he broke down and cried. Can you imagine that?" Alinsky snorted contemptuously, getting up to pace back and forth behind the desk. "Actually cried over a goddam woman."

"Where is she now?" Murphy asked.

Alinsky took his seat again. "In Jerusalem. At my house. She's on strike and won't go out on another job. I hope this crusade gets to Israel pretty fast so I can reunite her with her gorgeous French husband and get rid of her. She failed me. She's the last person in the world I ever thought would let her emotions get in the way of a business proposition."

"Can I tell Gervais that he gets her back?"

"He's been assured of that already. But if he wants more assurance, I'll sign an agreement in blood. It'll be worth it to make sure he takes her out of my house. I can't stand the sight of a beautiful woman going to hell on her own. She sits around and smokes cigarettes all day, and she's got bags under her eyes that are creeping toward her jaw line. . . . By the way, Murph, not to change the subject, but Kyle-Boyer did make the point, though he promptly forgot it, that the contracts you signed are no longer strictly binding. . . . I'm not going to have any trouble with you about this, am I? I've offered to double everyone's fee and can produce the vouchers to prove it. You'll keep on working for me, right?"

"Absolutely, Meyer," Murphy told the apprehensive face. "I wouldn't quit this pilgrimage for anything. I've got to hang on and find out what the secret is at the end of the line in Jerusalem."

"There's no secret at the end of the line. I've laid all my cards on the table."

"Bullshit. Nobody sponsors this much money, intrigue, and planning to give Christianity a chance to redeem itself for the travesty of the Crusades when Christianity can barely remember what the Crusades were all about."

"Then we'll have to let it go at that." Alinsky smiled wanly and rose to indicate that the interview was at an end. "Next year in Jerusalem, as the Hebrews say." He extended his hand to shake goodbye, and taking it, Murphy found the hand was clammy cold. Alinsky pressed a button on the wall behind him, and almost at once the door to the room opened and the priest reappeared, awaiting orders.

"Whitmore and the girl," Alinsky directed as the monk, making a sign that Murphy should follow, started out of the room.

They were at the end of the hallway, about to descend the steps, when the voice of Alinsky boomed out of the room after them. "Now those two, Murphy, Whitmore and his girl friend—you can bet they never let their humanness get in the way of any business deal."

Murphy thought of turning around and telling Alinsky that the Birmingham twosome had done so already on behalf of Father Bisson, but he decided against it. The priest had opened the door to the outside, and Murphy followed him, dazed momentarily by the hot sun, until he reached the patches of shade where the others sat waiting.

"Signor Whitmore y Signorina Aldrich." The monk smiled at them, helped Marilyn to her feet when Jonathan did not, and urged her to lean heavily on him and take as much weight as possible off her casted leg. The three moved toward the door, Marilyn having difficulty with the rough flagstone of the courtyard, then disappeared in moments more behind the slam.

"Well?" Gervais asked. Murphy saw himself being closely scrutinized, to see if he had bought the goods from Alinsky.

"You get your wife back when we reach Jerusalem."

"I don't believe him," Gervais said flatly, a new misery coming into his eyes.

"He says he's lost her to you. That she fell for you after all, and that all he wants is for you to get to Jerusalem and take her out of his house."

"If he wants her out of his house, why doesn't he let her join me and ride along in the station wagon? I'll bet I know what the answer to that question will be when I get my turn up there." Gervais jerked his head toward the room.

"I say, Murphy, what do you think of his motive for all this business?" Kyle-Boyer had lost his previous exuberance and seemed more wary, as if Gervais had gotten to him with some real logic while Murphy was being interviewed. Father Bisson lay stretched out asleep on a bench several yards away. He whimpered occasionally from his pain. Ben Bokva and Teplitsky sat with their backs resting against the fountain, out of hearing but watching them steadfastly at the same time.

"I think it's all bullshit," Murphy judged. "Absolute bullshit. He's one big enigma, and I think he takes some sort of perverse delight in being one. Rather coincidentally, we both come from Iowa in the States, even went to the same university. But he won't say he left, and he's vehement about not going back, even though there've been people looking for him for years. By the way, he's not Chillingworth, Gervais. He said to tell you that."

"Who is he then?"

"He says he's somebody from history called Cola di Rienzo."

"Oh, yes," Kyle-Boyer said. "Cola di Rienzo was a master at creating illusions. Except of course they caught up with him in the end. He was butchered by his own mob following."

"That's not likely to happen with Alinsky," Murphy said. "He disdains crowds altogether."

They fell silent. From upstairs in the abbot's office, almost predictably, came the raucous sounds of Jonathan and Marilyn laughing with Alinsky. A staccato thumping told that Marilyn must be banging her casted leg on the floor in rhythm to the merriment. Murphy, shrugging at the incongruity of people's response to the same enigma, and bored by the prospect of waiting through the interviews of Gervais and Father Bisson, stretched out on his bench and promptly went to sleep too. When he awoke, he saw that Bisson had been left undisturbed. Ten feet away the dutiful Italian monk poured champagne for a circle of outstretched glasses. Meyer Alinsky was engaged in animated conversation with Kyle-Boyer, Jonathan Whitmore and Marilyn, and a now-smiling Gervais who had evidently been won over. Alinsky nodded benignly, as Murphy rubbed the sleep from his eyes, and then invited him to join the circle for a drink. "A little champagne, Murph? It's the finest thing in the whole world for a hangover."

Murphy stood and took his glass and concentrated on holding it steady while the monk filled it to the brim. When he looked up again Alinsky was regarding old Bisson with a curious stare, and it occurred to Murphy, telepathically, perhaps, that Meyer Alinsky knew what Murphy always supposed: that Bisson would never make it to Jerusalem.

"Père Bisson looks very peaceful, doesn't he?" Alinsky said softly. "I hope what that bastard Lebel did to him isn't hurting too much."

"Listen, Meyer," Jonathan Whitmore spoke familiarly to their boss. "There's one more thing I forgot to mention. We all want Father Bisson to go to Rome to see the bloody Pope."

"The Pope. That's a tough one. He's a hard man to get to."

"Please try, Alinsky," Murphy urged him. "It's very important to your pilgrims."

"Well, I'll give it a shot," Alinsky said without enthusiasm. "Chaim," he called to Ben Bokva, still leaning against the fountain. "Bring the book down here, will you?"

Obediently Ben Bokva left for the abbot's office, and Gervais pronounced in a distant voice, "This is the Book of the Corruptibles I was telling you about last night. It's true, you see."

"Without a book like this it would be really difficult to run a worldwide business enterprise," Meyer Alinsky said nonchalantly. "And believe me, it's taken years to put it together." He accepted a refill from the monk as Ben Bokva returned, holding the black book Gervais had described against him like a lectern. While the others crowded around, Alinsky flipped pages until he came to a double-page layout labeled *Roman Catholic Church, Italian Section*. Murphy blinked at the complexity. Rather than the expected single organizational pyramid reaching up to balance the Pope at its summit, there were four of them instead—Curia, religious orders, regular clergy, and laity —all of them in seeming competition from the range and vehemence of Alinsky's action-reaction arrows to get at the little gummed star at the top that folded into the cleft between the pages when the book was closed, and that was presumably the Supreme Pontiff. But in the last analysis there seemed only two real avenues, admittedly battlescarred, to get to the man: one through the upper crust of the laity, and another through the Curia. Alinsky shook his head in dismay.

"I'll be blunt with you, folks. The only way it looks from here to get Padre Bisson an audience would be to kidnap the Pope."

There was a kind of universal sigh from the pilgrims, and Ben Bokva seemed eager to close the book because of its weight, when Alinsky hushed them all and drew finger tracks across the pages for perhaps two minutes more, then stabbed the page in apparent recognition and called for Teplitsky.

"Yitzhak, is Cardinal Ridano's secretary still having a little thing with Arima-Ladinzi's driver?"

"I don't know, Meyer, but I think so. It can be checked on by our people in Rome."

"If it's go, take the old priest down there. Tell our friends to lean heavily on Ridano's man. Exposé. The Holy Father himself. And don't let the bastard commit suicide, whatever happens. Get Bisson cleaned up, buy him a new uniform for the audience, get him in and out, take him to the Via Veneto for a spaghetti dinner, and get him back to the group as fast as you can. No sight-seeing. They leave here tomorrow. They should be in Turin in three days."

"Right, Meyer. Shalom."

"Shalom." He waved to the departing non-gangster, who raced for the abbot's office, presumably to call Rome. Then he turned to Murphy. "By the way, Murph, you know the diamond is going back in the cross?"

"Does it have to, Alinsky? I'll be paranoid as hell crossing all those borders carrying that thing."

"You'll never be caught. Not in a million years. Who's going to search a crucifix? Are you crazy? You've got Christians or a semblance of them who're going to doff their hats like the French and Italians did back there on the frontier all the way to Turkey.

You've got Muslims in Turkey, Syria, and Jordan anxious these days to extend those elaborate old Islamic courtesies to the Fourteenth Crusade to make up for what they failed to do for the previous thirteen, even if the fourteenth is going to a Jewish Jerusalem. And undiplomatic Israelis are going to welcome the holy Christians who've walked all the way from France with a custom's check, right? Murphy, you've got the world by the ass. Even if I'd stolen the diamond for profit I still couldn't have thought of a better way to get it to Jerusalem. Now relax and enjoy your work. The fringe benefits will be marvelous. You'll see."

"OK, Alinsky," Murphy answered him, less crusty now because of the plan for Father Bisson. "I'll play along."

"Good man, Murph. Well, everybody, I've got to say good-bye. Next year in Jerusalem," Alinsky intoned, turning with the Book of the Corruptibles beneath his arm to leave and casually flipping his champagne glass into the fountain, where it splashed and sank.

"Good-bye, Meyer," Marilyn, Jonathan, and Kyle-Boyer called out in unison, obviously delighted with their boss.

"Good-bye," Alinsky enjoined, pulling the cowl over his head and shambling off, only to turn suddenly. "Hey, Murph, did you ever hear anybody back home on the prairie talk about the Kiowa and Sioux belief in a tornado god?"

"No, Meyer," Murphy answered in annoyance, sick to death of tornadoes. "And if there was a legend like that floating around, it was probably invented by some shitkicker from Missouri who needed a gimmick for his medicine show. Let's drop the tornado talk, OK?"

"Yeah, you're right. I'm sorry."

Then he hastened off, his robes flapping, back to the abbot's office.

14

Meyer's mother

ALINSKY RETURNED FROM ISRAEL four days later, as Murphy suspected he might; something was clearly unresolved in their talk of Iowa and tornadoes, the Angoulême diamond, and Alinsky's silly proposition about why he had stolen the gem.

They were past Turin, moving along the headwaters of the Po toward Chivasso on a scorcher of a day, when Alinsky abruptly pulled up beside the line of march in a chauffeured Mercedes and stuck his head out the window. "Hello, everybody. How're your feet holding up? Murph, climb in for a while. I want to talk to you, OK? Ben Bokva, I'll have him back tomorrow. How did the French priest like the Pope?"

"He's in heaven right now, Meyer. Mystical experience or something like that. He hasn't had time to eat since he got back yesterday."

"Is he on a fast or some damn thing like that?" Alinsky demanded, looking back with real concern at Père Bisson, who clung tightly to the pommel of his mule, staring ahead raptly. "He's an old man. If he doesn't eat he'll get weak and die, and then what the hell use is he to this crusade? Make him eat if you have to force it into him."

Alinsky hurried Murphy into the car, and at a command to the driver they were speeding in the opposite direction, toward Turin.

"Where are we going, Meyer?"

"To Naples. Here, have a beer."

"Why to Naples? I've never been there."

"The more reason you should go. I want you to see Naples before you die," Alinsky joked, jabbing Murphy with an elbow. "Besides, I want to talk to you about something."

"What? Not about tornadoes again?"

"Wait until we get there. But I promise it's not about tornadoes."

Contented with that promise, Murphy quaffed his beer and asked for another as the car raced toward the airport at Turin. Once there they slid through a security clearance at a gate with a simple nod from the guard and pulled up minutes later before a bright blue Boeing 707 jet that was devoid of any markings except for the code numbers in yellow.

"Is it yours?" Murphy asked, knowing already that it would be. He wondered what Meyer Alinsky's private yacht looked like.

"Yeah, it's mine. Always fueled and ready to go."

"Where do you keep your yacht?" The next question would be to ask how one displaced Iowa boy got to be so wealthy; real money, the possibilities for it, had always eluded Murphy. He decided instead to keep silent.

"I keep the Red Sea—Indian Ocean one in Eilat. The every-place-else one is in Haifa Bay. Come on inside, Frank, and meet my mother."

"Your mother?"

"Yeah. She's along for the trip. She likes to fly but doesn't like to walk, so she just sits in the plane and looks out the window at the scenery on days like today."

Murphy was amused. The scenery on one side of the plane was a broad expanse of corrugated metal hangers; on the other, far across a runway shimmering in the heat, was a cluster of oil tanks. They mounted the steps that had descended since they had alighted from the car. Once inside the air-conditioned cabin, Murphy gaped at the sight. There were but four massive reclining seat-belted chairs; the rest was plush carpeting, a bar and galley, what Murphy guessed was a parquet in-flight conference table, and fabric-paneled walls hung with obviously good paintings and broken only occasionally by a window. He walked directly to one of the paintings. "That's Matisse," Murphy judged. "It's a really good reproduction."

"It's the original," Alinsky snapped back. "The reproduction is in Paris."

Someone guffawed at Alinsky's annoyance and Murphy turned to see four people, two men and two women, breaking up a card game at a small table far forward behind the cockpit.

"Shalom, everybody," Alinsky told them. They stared at Murphy with obvious amusement. He was so used to wearing his pilgrim's robe with its crusader cross stitched to the front that he never thought of it any more, but after a moment he understood and was embarrassed—not because of the men, but because of the women. By now he had lost a lot of weight and not drunk much except for the night of the diamond's discovery, and he was dying for a woman. Both the Israeli girls were beauties. Murphy felt a wrench of pain in his groin and thought of an old American joke.

"Later, Murph," Alinsky said, thinking perhaps of the same joke. "We'll arrange a little something for you. Gentlemen"—he addressed the two pilots—"a quick trip to Naples."

The two men disappeared instantly through the cockpit door and closed it behind them. Both girls stood waiting for instructions. "Shoshanna," Alinsky said to one, "bring me the Book of the Corruptibles, will you, honey? And you, Rifkale"—he turned to the other—"bring us a couple of beers, OK? By the way, Murph, this is Rifka, whose husband is a certain French national you know named Etienne Gervais. As you can see, she's quite a lovely gal."

The flattery failed to bring out the coquette in Gervais's wife. She looked closely at Alinsky as if seeking permission, biting her lip for a moment, and then spoke to Murphy in an accent that showed she might have emigrated to Israel from somewhere in French North Africa. "You have seen Etienne? You know where he is?"

"He's about fifteen kilometers from here and missing you very much." Murphy tried consoling her anxiety.

"Meyer, can I go to him?" she begged Alinsky.

"No. You understand the arrangement, Rifka. You get him back in Jerusalem. Not until. Now, bring the beers," he ordered coldly. "Come on, Murph, I want you to meet my mother. She's in the rear watching TV."

Alinsky pointed toward a sectioned-off part of the cabin that was entered through a heavy leather-covered door.

"You were pretty rough on her, Meyer," Murphy told him on the way. "It's only a lousy fifteen K's from here."

"Like I told you before, Murph, I sent her out on a job, not an affair of the heart. If she wants the chicken she'll have to wait for the egg to hatch."

Alinsky pushed open the door. His mother sat knitting on a semicircular couch that was provided with seat belts, laughing at a film with dubbed Italian voices on the TV set before her. She had an engrossing face, the kind that Murphy would have called eternally bemused; a shawl covered her shoulders against the air conditioning and her hair was piled into a bun at the top of her head. Little old Jewish lady from Iowa, Murphy thought, inexplicably remembering his own mother's timidity. She sipped at a drink before they reached her.

"Mother, I'd like you to meet Frank Murphy from Dubuque, Iowa."

The light of polite expectancy in her eyes suddenly dimmed at the mention of the word Iowa; Murphy sensed it in an instant. Alinsky's mother extended her hand. "You're a long way from home, Francis Xavier Murphy."

Murphy smiled and understood why the sight of the robe had not perturbed her; she knew of the crusade's existence and perhaps a lot more.

"You're also far from home, Mrs. Alinsky."

"It has its compensations." She waved her hand about the 707's interior. "Meyer built us a palace in Jerusalem. It's all marble and sandstone, and it's drafty and no good for my arthritis in the winter, but it's still a palace and has lots of servants. My house in Iowa was nice, though. It was an old place that Meyer's father had gutted and insulated and rewired with central heating put in. On the coldest day in the winter it was warm as toast and had a great big kitchen. Would you like an old-fashioned?"

"I think we're being given a beer, Mrs. Alinsky."

"I like them because they're nice and sweet. How old do you think I am?"

"Sixty?" Murphy thought she must be about seventy-five if Meyer were in his fifties.

"Wrong. I'm seventy-one." Her fingers rearranged the bun of her hair, obviously pleased by the compliment. "I had Meyer when I was nineteen. He's fifty-two now. But the way he's going at it, he's catching up with me fast. People are starting to say we look like husband and wife these days."

Alinsky, his mother's husband, seemed oblivious of the conversation. The girl Shoshanna appeared, carrying the Book of Corruptibles beneath one arm and balancing the two Budweisers that Rifka was to have delivered in her hands. There was a brief moment during which Murphy thought Alinsky would explode with anger over Gervais's woman, but he did not. He handed Murphy a beer, mumbled something about the need to do some reading, and went forward, leaving the door to his mother's cubicle open, to flop himself with the Book of the Corruptibles into one of the chairs in the main cabin.

"Where did you learn to speak Italian, Mrs. Alinsky?" Murphy asked, glad the tension was gone. The television still played; on the screen Ginger Rogers and Fred Astaire spoke of love in Italian. It was absurd; they kissed with American purity long before the sworn testimony of southern European dubbing artists was even ended.

"I don't know a word of it. It's just that I've seen this film seventeen times at least. I know everything they're saying. I think I've seen every American film made during the thirties, forties, and fifties. Meyer lends me the jet to go to New York once a year to see all the new musicals and movies."

"Doesn't Meyer ever go with you?" Murphy asked.

"Meyer hasn't set foot in America since the day he left."

She said it emphatically, as Ben Bokva already had, then waved her hand to indicate the matter was at an end. Beyond the door Alinsky sipped his beer and read from the Book. His mother switched off the TV and belted herself in readiness, as did Murphy. The jet's engines began screaming in warmup, and a distant sign above the cockpit door blinked on—FASTEN SEAT BELTS—in English and French and, below those, presumably Hebrew and Arabic. At the last moment the two girls strapped themselves in and the jet taxied onto the main runway, intercepting both an Alitalia and a Lufthansa flight, and was airborne in seconds. Murphy experienced a curious lightheadedness that he guessed had much to do with being in the presence of Meyer Alinsky et al. He looked out a port window and was reassured by the sudden view of red Italian roofs, as the plane banked sharply and turned south toward Naples, that they were not going to the moon.

"Would you like to watch a movie, Frank?" Alinsky's mother asked. "I could have the girls set up the screen and projector. We have *Easy Rider* and *Gone with the Wind*. Of course we always have *Gone with the Wind*. I've seen it a hundred and forty-six times already, but I can always watch it again. That part where Scarlett O'Hara comes back to Tara after the burning of Atlanta and sees that her old life is gone always makes me cry and cry. . . ." She shook her head sadly. "We can see half on the way to Naples and half on the way back."

"Thanks, Mrs. Alinsky, but I'm not in the mood for a movie."

"How about another beer then? I want to keep you happy."

"OK, I suppose."

"Shoshanna, *motek*," she called out, "a beer for Frankie."

While the girl opened the food locker, took out a beer, and pulled the snap tab, Alinsky put down the Book of the Corruptibles, yawned, lowered the back rest of his chair to bed level, lay back, curled up in fetal position, and fell instantly to snoring. Murphy took his beer and gestured toward him. "Meyer must be having a tough day."

"Also he drinks too much," the mother said, annoyance keen in her voice. "If Budweiser's had a son, they'd call him Meyer after their best customer. He's amazing. He runs all his business from six-pack to six-pack."

Murphy laughed. They watched in silence as Gervais's wife unexpectedly produced a woolen blanket and gently covered Alinsky's form.

"They're mighty handy to have around," Murphy commented. "What are they? Cook and secretary?"

"I don't ask. A mother shouldn't. On the books it says one's a secretary and the other's a cabin stewardess. Meyer's wife died and he never remarried. Don't ask me why. He likes women but not wives.

He seems to prefer secretaries and waitresses. God knows I've met enough of them."

Murphy chuckled to himself while Alinsky's mother sighed. He looked out the window again. They were over the Mediterranean now between the Italian coast and a large island that must have been Corsica. The city in the distance had to be Bastia, from its size.

"Why are we going to Naples, Mrs. Alinsky?"

"Because Meyer's got another hair up his ass, as he always says, about some project or other, and he's getting set to buy you out, body and soul, so you'll do it for him. What is it he wants you to do?"

"I'm not sure. I'm not sure Meyer knows either."

"He knows. If he didn't know exactly what he wanted you to do four days ago when he saw you at that monastery, he knows by now. He's been up every night since then. Only be prepared. He's going to take you up to one of those old palazzi on the top of the city that he rents for effect, put his hand firmly on your shoulder, and make you a deal for half of everything you see in front of you if you just agree to do what he wants you to do. Dr. Faustus all the way. Believe me, I've seen it before, and after a cup of wine better men than you have bought the deal. Have you ever seen the Bay of Naples? No? Well, the Naples trip is the fitting climax to Meyer's art—that is, after he plies you with all the illusions of power, money and the corruptible universe that he maintains. Your head is usually spinning by sunset. Only don't buy it, because his payoffs are always funny to behold."

"Why's that?"

"Well, because he doesn't own it, obviously. Oh, he might own something down there. A tanker, maybe, or a bowlarama or a spaghetti restaurant he won in a card game or something like that. But nothing more. So beware."

"Why are you telling me all this, Mrs. Alinsky?" Murphy asked. He decided this was the kind of lady

he liked to get drunk with. If Meyer was a colossal
enigma, Meyer's mother was more enigmatic still.

"Let's have another drink, Frankie." She held up
two fingers to the girl Shoshanna, then sliced one in
half to indicate the old-fashioned should be weak.

"I'm telling you this, Frank, because I'm a two-
headed monster. One, you seem like a nice Iowa
boy to me and I'm real proud of you for walking
off your drinking problem, like your own mother
would be if she didn't get killed by the tornado. I
wish Meyer could do the same. The other thing is
I've spent fifty-two years worrying about Meyer, and
it's no use quitting now. Tell me something. Are
you pilgrims still carrying that damn diamond Meyer
stole from the French bishop?"

"Yes, we are."

"Well, I wish you'd wrap it up, put the bishop's
address on it, and drop it in a mailbox someplace.
This is bad business because it isn't business at all.
Meyer doesn't want that diamond for the money.
Nobody would. It can't be fenced and only the
lowest, dumbest crook would have it cut. This heist
has philosophical or moralistic overtones to it. When
I heard about it, I said to myself, Rachel, there'll be
more trouble than not before this caper is over."

Murphy was silent. He sipped the beer that Shoshanna had delivered to him and listened to the rattle
of Mrs. Alinsky's ice cubes. She looked steadily
through the door to the main cabin, where Rifka
stood staring out a window at the sea below.

"How's the French boy that Rifkale got herself
married to?" Meyer's mother asked at length.

"Lovesick and unhappy. What do you think of that
business, Mrs. Alinsky?"

"It's a double-edge sword, Frankie. Meyer sent
her out to get the boy and, cool cookie that she was,
she went along with instructions. Only she'd never
been in love before and she fell for the boy and
now she doesn't know what the hell's wrong with her.
She spends half her time in Jerusalem crying on my

lap. But I think I'm going to really put my foot down with Meyer to make sure he reunites them. By now she deserves him. She's paid her dues through all her misery."

"I hope it happens. Neither of them is clean enough to be Romeo or Juliet, but they're both acting like it."

"I'll take care of it, Frankie, don't worry about it. You can reassure the nice French boy." Once again she cleared the air with her hand to indicate the subject was exhausted.

"Tell me one last thing, Mrs. Alinsky, before you get tired of talking. Is it true that Meyer bought out the Egyptian Air Force during the Six-Day War?"

"Oh, that damn rumor! It's so embarrassing to live in Israel and have everyone point at me when I go shopping and hear everybody whispering, 'There's Meyer Alinsky's mother!' "

"But is it a rumor?"

"Of course it is, Frankie."

"How did it get started?"

"Meyer started it. How else would something crazy like that get started?"

She threw her hands to heaven: a millennium of Jewish exasperation. But Murphy noticed she spilled not a drop of her drink.

15

Sunset at the Bay of Naples

THE BOEING TOUCHED DOWN at the Naples airport and taxied to a distant row of private hangars, where there was a large Fiat waiting for them.

"Villa Frascati," Alinsky told the driver, and then settled back to gaze absorbedly out the window at the countryside. He had awakened perhaps ten minutes before their descent began, showered, and dressed in a white linen suit with a black tie so that now, in anyone's estimation, he might seem a self-possessed and wealthy Italian out for a drive with his confessor. Only Murphy chuckled inwardly at that assumption, noted that it was already late afternoon, and decided from the heat of the day that the sunset would be rosy and powerful for the purposes of Alinsky's extravaganza.

In half an hour, having climbed to the topmost hills behind Naples, they drew up before the gates of the palazzo Alinsky's mother had promised. Murphy whistled audibly as an attendant swept open the gates and admitted them. The style was Moorish, all in pink with arches of marble, great tiled expanses of terrace, and formal gardens and graveled parking areas surrounding the main building; pools and palm trees were there in abundance stretching out toward the balustrade. Below was the Bay of Naples. Ischia in the distance was hung over with a thin blue haze; Capri, Alinsky commented, could be seen by its lights that night.

"Do you own this place, Meyer?" Murphy asked, testing the man for honesty.

"Yeah. I don't use it all that much, but it pleases me to know it's here." He clapped his hands like a pasha, and miraculously, it seemed to Murphy, an old woman, too refined-looking to be an actual servant, appeared carrying two cans of Budweiser. Alinsky spoke to her in fluent Italian, then told Murphy, "We'll have an early dinner up on the terrace. The something I want to talk to you about we'll talk about later."

In the middle of the incredible sunset, when they had finished dining, Alinsky steered Murphy to the railing of the terrace. Lights were beginning to wink on in the city below, and the distant din of traffic that Murphy had noted on arriving seemed abated now. Beyond the port one freighter exited toward sea while another headed in. Standing there, a sudden memory saddened Murphy: the time of his parents' only extended vacation with their children, when the family had driven from Iowa west to San Francisco, the most beautiful American city, and stood in some hilltop park overlooking the bay. There Murphy, a child, had begged that they never go back, until his father, bemused and kindly, had made him understand they had no need for Iowa farmers in that particular city. . . . Alongside Murphy, perhaps Meyer Alinsky remembered a similar time, until he jerked himself alive again and toasted the beauty of Naples, gulping Soave from a brandy snifter. Murphy joined in but took only a cautious sip from his own glass; some of his more memorable drunks had begun this way, a great feeling of contentment and pleasure gone awry. He made his decision. He emptied the wine over the balustrade and put down the glass on its surface.

"Why are we here, Meyer? What's the business you had in mind?" he demanded abruptly.

"Do you like money, Murph?"

"It has its uses. A man like you should know that better than anyone. I can think of lots of things, for instance, to do with that eighty thousand bucks you're paying me for walking to Jerusalem."

"That's chicken feed. I'm talking about big money. Really big money. I'm in a position to make you a very wealthy man."

Inwardly Murphy smiled to himself. In another moment Alinsky's hand settled firmly on his shoulder, just as Alinsky's mother said it would. He reached out the brandy snifter with his other hand and Murphy heard the soft padding of the old Italian woman's feet as she came forward to fill the glass. When she withdrew Murphy spoke first. "What is it you want me to do for you?"

"I'll make you a very wealthy man, Murph, if you agree to assume the guilt of a certain murderer."

They were the least expected words in the universe. Murphy peered at him askance. Alinsky's eyes looked straight out, toward Ischia, but Murphy knew he did not see the island. They were so pained and full of anguish that for an instant he thought Meyer Alinsky, evidently a Hebrew prince, might actually break down and cry.

"Who's the murderer, Meyer?" Murphy asked in a low voice. Distantly it occurred to him, for no particular reason, that there might, beneath all the foiling layers upon layers of Meyer Alinsky, actually be a hard core, a nugget of suffering, that the layers had been created to protect.

"I don't know who the murderer is."

"Well, where did it happen? The murder, that is."

"I can't tell you that."

"Who was murdered? When did it happen?"

"I can't answer any of those questions. I'm just

asking you: Will you agree to assume the guilt in return for my money?"

"You're crazy, Meyer. I can't just decide to feel some kind of guilt because you want me to. Obviously I had nothing to do with the murder you're talking about. And if it touched you in some way, then I'm sorry for you. But if you're looking for retribution, this is an impossible way to find it."

"Why, Murph? Substitutes are legitimate." Alinsky spoke frantically. "Collective guilt has often been assumed by individuals. Look at the Nuremberg Trials, for instance. They couldn't send all the German people to jail so they sent the Albert Speers instead. Read the New Testament. What was supposed to have been the function of Jesus Christ's agony and death? All military establishments have done it at one time or another. Dreyfus got it in France, didn't he? The precedents are endless. Look at American literature. Remember us talking about *The Scarlet Letter* a couple of days ago? Didn't Hester Prynne carry the guilt for a sin that was mostly Dimmesdale's and the congregation's?"

"Yes, but Dimmesdale knew he was guilty, bore it in private, and had a far worse time of it than Hester in the end. And that's the point of all this, Meyer. Me assuming some murderer's guilt and walking it off on the way to Jerusalem would be a hollow expiation. It might satisfy you on the outside, but on the inside it would merely fill me with curiosity and do nothing more. It seems to me the whole business would be as futile as the Israeli hanging of Adolf Eichmann. Right up to the end he insisted he couldn't feel a grain of remorse."

"The hanging of Eichmann wasn't futile," Alinsky said harshly. "You weren't touched by his crimes, so you couldn't know."

There was a long silence, during which Murphy decided he wanted more wine. He picked up his glass and went to the table where the old woman had left the bottle in some ice. He filled the glass, then returned to the balustrade. Alinsky continued to look unseeing down into the city. Many lights were winking now; the sun was minutes from departing altogether. Capri could be seen for the first time.

"Why don't you let the diamond do the work, Meyer, like it's done so far?" Murphy asked him quietly.

"The diamond isn't enough any more, Murph. It needs to be a flesh-and-blood person. Before I met you I didn't think it was possible. Couldn't you just pretend? Couldn't you just get up in the morning and say, "The twenty miles I'll walk today are to satisfy my guilt for the murder that only Meyer Alinsky knows about?"

"For Christ's sake, Meyer, don't be absurd. How can I? I'd like to help, but it's impossible."

"I'll make you fabulously wealthy, Murph. Just as I promised you."

"How much would you give me, Meyer?"

"Half of everything you see before you can be yours." The hand went back on Murphy's shoulder, and with his other arm he swept magnificently over the Bay of Naples.

Murphy, for his part, sighed wearily, deciding it was time to lay on the truth. "You're full of shit, Meyer. You don't own anything down there but an Italian restaurant. You don't own this palazzo either. It's rented."

"Who told you that?"

"Your mother."

"She's lying!"

"Your own mother?" Murphy demanded in fake astonishment.

"God dammit anyhow! When did she tell you that?"

"On the plane when you were sleeping. She's not sure what you're up to, and I'm only half sure, but she thinks it's dangerous business. Anyhow, she labeled you a fraud."

"Huh! My own mother! How can she call me a fraud? I have power. She's not exactly destitute

from the lack of it. I got the French priest in to
see the Pope, didn't I? How many other men in Europe could pull that one off on so little notice? And
I'm not even a Christian either."

There was real petulance in Meyer Alinsky's voice:
a little boy angry with his mother. "Murph, do you
remember the Six-Day War? I was the man who
grounded the Egyptian Air Force."

"I heard about that one too, Meyer."

"Come on, Murphy," he snarled, smashing his
glass on the terrace in anger. "Let's get the fuck
out of here! *Ciao, signora,*" he called out to the
old woman, who waved them good-bye shyly.

"Ciao, Signor Alinsky. Ciao, Signor Murphy."

"Who was that woman?" Murphy dared to ask
as they rushed toward the car.

"She's the owner," Alinsky barked. But that was
all. They climbed into the Fiat and began the descent toward the city and the airport. It was full
darkness now, Ischia and Capri merging with the city
and shoreline lights until the whole resembled an immense necklace. Murphy, for his part, could not help
thinking that, necklaces notwithstanding, the evening was replete with symbolism: Meyer Alinsky, a
glorious full-blown sunset of illusions and possibility,
had just sunk well below the horizon in power. But
it was better this way. Despite the congenital ease of
being former Iowans and Budweiser swillers, there had
been something discomforting and sinister about Meyer.
Now it was all gone. He had been born of a
mother, a female of the race, just like anyone else.
And what a mother. . . .

At the 707 Alinsky gave the order to head back
north to Turin and then plopped angrily into a chair,
fastening his seat belt and not speaking to his
mother. Mrs. Alinsky sat reading a paperback mystery. As the jet taxied up the runway, she once
lifted her head and knitted her eyebrows quizzically in
Murphy's direction, but Murphy merely shrugged.

Becoming an ally of Meyer's mother was not his idea of good politics either.

They were airborne when Meyer called for a beer and turned to face his mother. "Why did you spill the beans, Mother?"

"To protect you from yourself, Meyer. On some days you're your own worst enemy. I still haven't figured out what this crusade business is all about, but it's a good idea to start putting the skids on it now."

"You made him think I'm a fraud, Mother. He thinks I have no power."

"You have plenty of power, Meyer. You're the man that bought out the Egyptian Air Force, after all." When she said it, Alinsky's mother began to giggle, and Murphy also tried to suppress his own mirth.

"You drink too much, Mother. Drink loosens the tongue."

"It also unleashes the imagination and makes everything seem larger than life, my teetotaler son."

"I arranged a private audience with the Pope for the French priest," he said belligerently.

"Bullshit, Meyer. This is your little old Iowa mother you're talking to. If the French priest saw the Pope, then the Pope was some little guy with a hooked nose that you had dressed up in silks and ermines for the job. The only way you could get to the Pope is through the front door of the Vatican with the rest of the tourists."

"You've really done it now, Mother. What if he goes back to the pilgrimage and tells the others what you've told him?"

"Buy him off, Meyer, so he won't tell the others. You've got a price, haven't you, Frankie? Everybody has a price. Otherwise, how could Meyer possibly operate?"

"I don't want any more money, Mrs. Alinsky," Murphy said. "Eighty thousand dollars is enough for a year or so of walking that promises to cure a host of ills. And I won't tell anyone that Meyer's a fraud. It's curiosity that's got me now."

"Stick around, Frankie," Mrs. Alinsky told him. "I have a feeling the best is yet to come."

At the airport in Turin, Murphy left Alinsky and his mother arguing inside the plane and returned with the waiting driver to join the others near Chivasso. The man did not speak to him during the trip, concentrating instead on keeping the car on the road as he hurtled through the darkness. Evidently, then, it would be Ben Bokva who would deliver up the grim warning to be silent about the day's journey and Meyer's incredible proposition, since Alinsky himself had neglected to do so on Murphy's departure.

But at the pilgrim encampment it was obvious that neither Ben Bokva nor Teplitsky had any idea where Murphy had gone or what had happened, and when the others questioned him, he originated the convenient lie that he and Alinsky had gone to Naples for spaghetti to talk about tornadoes.

"Tornadoes?" Kyle-Boyer asked. "Is he daft on the subject of those things, do you think?"

"It certainly seems that way," Murphy judged wearily, throwing up his shoulders to indicate his ignorance of Alinsky's fascination. Also he neglected, from kindness, to tell Gervais that he had met his wife so close by.

Only as he bedded down for the night, stunned by the day's events and his meeting with old Rachel Alinsky, he knew for certain it would be Meyer himself who would deliver the warning to keep his mouth shut.

It came the next morning after first dawn: an incredible scream as the blue 707, looking, with its wheels lowered, like a giant ferocious eagle, flew at them almost at ground level into the flat pasture where they had camped, sending pilgrims and mules, French former wardens and the Israeli current wardens, all scattering for cover. Murphy and Kyle-Boyer dived into the same ditch.

"My God, Murphy, what is it?" Kyle-Boyer asked, clutching his pith helmet to his head in fear.

"It's Meyer. He'd flush the toilets if he could and it's me he's aiming for, not any of you."

"But why—?" Only the words were cut off: Ben Bokva jumped into the ditch on top of Murphy.

"Murphy, Murphy, listen to me!" he begged. "Say yes the next time he asks you for anything! Make him think you agree, even if you don't! Because if he thinks he has to prove something to you, innocent people will be killed!"

Murphy nodded mutely, still dazed from looking upward. On the belly of the fuselage, impossible to see when the plane was grounded, was a large Star of David, painted in yellow. A fire danced from each of its six tips.

16

The good women of Verona

AFTER CHIVASSO, in the hot August days of the march across northern Italy toward the Yugoslav border, Murphy granted the tortured Alinsky one concession that Alinsky could not know about. When he rose each morning he automatically spoke Meyer's suggested formula: "This day's twenty miles to expiate the guilt of the unknown murderer for the crime of which only Meyer Alinsky knows." He meant to repeat it each day until they reached Jerusalem, if ever they did, his moot contribution to ameliorate the heinousness of a crime that Murphy suspected had driven Alinsky mad.

But was Alinsky mad?

"He's gone bloody fuckin' crackers," Jonathan Whitmore furiously assured them after the 707 had nearly cleaved them in half in the pasture near Chivasso.

"A dangerous psychopath," Kyle-Boyer proposed analytically, frightened again and now far less enamored of Alinsky's philosophy and purposes.

Mad, a mind contorted, Murphy was eventually to conclude, though not before he gave Alinsky a chance, conceding that in the case of the Chivasso incident allowances might be made for anger and eccentricity. But at Verona came a desperate event and all the frightening proof that was needed, and after Verona Murphy carried with him a special fear of Alinsky that would not be abated until the end of the crusade in Jerusalem.

It was Murphy, unwittingly, who prompted the event. He was dying for a woman and put in a petition to Gervais almost daily along the march from Chivasso to Milan. Gervais perfunctorily relayed the word by radio to Ben Bokva and Teplitsky, two phantoms who again hung back in their Citroën out of sight at Alinsky's command. Only nothing got back from the boss apparently—perhaps as a punishment—all the way through Milan, where Murphy, no longer abashed at wearing his monk's robe, considered diving into the rows of beautiful northern Italian women who sat in the cafés along the streets where they marched on their way through the city.

But on the outskirts of Verona, in the beginning of September, two hundred kilometers after Chivasso, Ben Bokva and Teplitsky appeared suddenly one evening in the darkness as the campfire was being lit and called Murphy, Kyle-Boyer, Jonathan Whitmore, and Gervais to the car. As ever, Ben Bokva was self-effacing; Teplitsky seemed downright embarrassed.

"It seems that Meyer's anger has finally cooled. Arrangements have been made for those of you who wish to visit a bordello tonight in Verona. Are there any takers?"

"Thank God!" Murphy twirled the staff of the crucifix he still held above his head for joy.

"One, obviously." Ben Bokva chuckled.

"And you, Gervais?"

"I cannot," Gervais said miserably. "It is because of Rifka."

"*Bien compris,*" Teplitsky said. "And you, Jonathan?"

"I gots Marilyn with me."

"Even with her leg in a cast?"

"We manages well enough, thank you."

How about you, Kyle-Boyer?"

"I have a hormonal problem, I'm afraid."

"I'm sorry for you, then. Come, let's go into Verona, Murphy. You'll have to wear civilian dress, though, since you begin to look so convincingly like a priest."

Changed back into the same clothes he wore when he first joined the pilgrimage, Murphy was driven in the black Citroën into the city. They sped in silence under the arc lights of the *autostrada* until Ben Bokva spoke, unprompted. "Except for Jerusalem, Verona is Meyer's favorite city in all the world."

"Why's that?"

"Romeo and Juliet, of course. The Capulets and Montagues."

"I didn't know Meyer was a romantic," Murphy said vexedly. "He doesn't seem the type."

"He's an incurable romantic. When he's not angry with someone, that is."

"I remember your warning, Ben Bokva. I've also seen the photos of my wife and son, and I don't believe Alinsky had them taken at long range just to frighten me, either, as he insisted. And our estate keeper, Baudrey, is perfectly capable of being bought."

"I know nothing of these things, Murphy," Ben Bokva said wearily. "I don't even know why Meyer almost murdered the lot of us with his jet back there in Chivasso. I don't want to know, either. And you shouldn't worry about it or you'll think yourself into impotence on this night of nights."

Murphy said nothing but instead gazed out on the palaces of Verona, the ancient fief of Alinsky's Capulets and Montagues, and contented himself with fantasizing about the woman who would service him that night. They turned into an ever-narrowing series of streets, heading deeper into the city's old quarter, and stopped unexpectedly before a walled villa in a residential area when Murphy had expected to be taken to the traditional street of the whores. Teplitsky alighted and rang a bell at the gates, and almost immediately the doors swung inward. Inside a number of cars were parked; as they drew up Murphy recognized, or thought he recognized, the chauffeured Mercedes that had sped him to and from the airport at Turin for his trip to Naples. Ben Bokva and Teplitsky may have recognized it also; they exchanged a speculative look so that Murphy thought to ask, "What's that car doing here?"

Ben Bokva shrugged. "I can only assume it brought one of Meyer's agents to set up the orgy. More of you were expected to come, after all."

But that was all. They were met at an open doorway by the madam, a tall and handsome woman with the bearing of a contessa who appraised Murphy knowingly and then led him through a pillared foyer, where she invited Ben Bokva and Teplitsky to wait on a couch. She opened the double doors to another room, and Murphy unconsciously gasped at the sight. In another columned hall, done all in marble and mirrors extending to the ceiling of the house itself, the women of Verona, perhaps ten of them, cavorted naked in a shallow pool with a fountain splashing at its center. Around the sides, seated in rows of plush oversized chairs, were five or six of the house's clientele in a thoughtful process of selection, oblivious to Murphy's arrival.

"Why not take a seat, Monsieur Murphy?" the madam invited. "I'll have a drink brought to you, and you can choose a friend at your leisure."

"I'll take her," Murphy returned, pointing to the nearest girl, a very white-skinned, blue-eyed blonde whose hair was long and straight to her shoulders and made Murphy think she might have been procured from Scandinavia. She emerged from the pool at a nod from the madam, draped a towel about herself, and led him out of the room by the hand as the other swimmers giggled at his anxiousness.

She skipped ahead of him down a dimly lit hallway to a room tritely labeled FELICITÉ, as others were labeled BELLISSIMA and ECSTACIE, and urged him out of his clothes in the mirrored dimness of the place. While she finished toweling down, he learned she was not Scandinavian but rather a northern Italian from Merano who spoke only pidgin English.

Murphy, already erect, lay down on the silk-sheeted bed, and she washed his body with a rose-scented oil while Murphy's one hand roamed the orbs of her breasts and the other explored the moist cleft between her legs.

"Hurry, please hurry up," he begged her as she rubbed the oiled cloth the length of his prick. He reached out, trying to pull her to the bed, but laughing she restrained him, saying emphatically, "No me. This one for you. . . ."

She pointed to a darkened corner and Murphy—who had had a premonition on first entry that there was someone else in the room, though it was soon forgotten—gasped at the naked specter that came haltingly out of the blackness, ashamedly covering the front of herself as best she could with two small hands.

"Oh, shit!" he exclaimed, watching his penis die at the shock. She was dark-haired, olive skinned, and lovely, from somewhere in the south, Calabria or Sicily perhaps, and no more than thirteen years of age at the most. Tears crept from her eyes. A virgin for sure: a decidedly unwanted gift from the bizarre Alinsky.

The blonde who had bathed him seemed perplexed at his reaction. Angrily Murphy sat up on the side of the bed and ordered her to call the madam, while trying best to figure out how to refuse Alinsky's gift.

But the refusal was unnecessary. In another moment a cacophony of shrieking began behind the mirrored panels in the room next to their own, and Murphy, hastening into his trousers, hurried out into the hallway with the blonde, who had wrapped herself again in the length of towel to see what was the matter.

There, somehow not unexpectedly, Meyer Alinsky was sparring with three of the women of Verona; from the rantings of one of them in French who repeatedly spat at their opponent, Murphy, now furious, was made to understand that Alinsky had been discovered spying on him and the blonde through a one-way mirror from the next room, something that had been that day installed for his convenience alone, and something the women of Verona objected to mightily.

Standing behind him, Murphy angled for a position to kick Alinsky squarely in the ass. But before he got his chance, the man simply went berserk, punching out at the three prostitutes and actually knocking one of them down. Murphy jumped him from the rear, trying to pin the other's arms, and as he was hurled off against the wall by the incredible force of Alinsky's rage, he saw the blur of four people rushing up the hallway toward the altercation: Ben Bokva, Teplitsky, and the contessalike madam led by Rachel Alinsky, brandishing a cane, who came up short behind her son, screamed out some invective in Yiddish that may have been a plea for forgiveness, and cracked him hard at the base of his skull. Meyer Alinsky went out like a light, falling hard onto the carpeting of the hallway. His mother, panting heavily, leaned against the wall as Ben Bokva and Teplitsky rushed to their fallen boss.

"What happened, Murphy?" she gasped out. The prostitutes had shrunk back, frightened perhaps that they might also be caned.

"Your madman of a son gave me the treat of a night out in a bawdy house and then tried to match me up with a twelve-year-old kid."

"What? Are you crazy?"

"See for yourself." He pointed to the room he had left. He was angry enough not to spare her anything. She started toward the door but made it only halfway; the virgin came slowly outward, wrapped in a sheet, tears streaming down her cheeks.

"*Mein Gott!* If she's even twelve. . . . Did you two know anything about this?" she demanded harshly of Ben Bokva and Teplitsky, who held a slumped-over Alinsky between them.

"Nothing, *Giveret* Alinsky," Teplitsky told her. "We followed orders. Meyer told us to bring Murphy here. That's all we knew."

"How did you come to be here, Mrs. Alinsky?" Murphy asked.

"I followed him in a taxi after he left the airport. I followed him because something had to happen tonight. He's only slept about an hour a day since that trip he made with you to Naples, Murphy."

She broke off for a moment and then suddenly slammed the cane hard against the wall. "What is he up to?" she screeched at the assemblage. "Does anyone know? Do you, Ben Bokva?"

"No, *Giveret* Alinsky, I don't."

"Well, if you do, you call me and tell me. Do you hear?"

"No, I won't, *Giveret* Alinsky," Ben Bokva told her flatly. "And you know better than to ask."

"Putting blind loyalty before your conscience is going to get you in trouble some day, Ben Bokva. Take him to the car, you two. Back to the plane," she ordered sharply.

They dragged Alinsky off, still out cold, and Murphy spoke. "It's lucky you didn't kill him with that clout you gave him."

"I've had to do it before. Mermelstein, our doctor in Israel, showed me just how to do it." She shook her head wearily, then revived to face the madam, her aplomb unruffled, who had watched the whole proceedings contemptuously. "Where did you find that little bambino, lady?"

"She is an orphan, madame. Your son simply

agreed to some corrupt official's price, and that's how she was procured."

"And you didn't think to say no, I take it?"

"Your son, madame, agreed to my price. It was high, given the special nature of his perversity."

Rachel Alinsky smiled ruefully, then turned in a sudden anger to the virgin. *Catholica? Israelita?*

"Catholica," came the whisper in response.

"Come on," she said, grabbing the child's hand and pulling her down the hallway, unexpectedly cracking the madam fiercely across the knees with her cane as she swept past.

"Where are you going?" Murphy called out.

"To find a convent that's still open. Back to your blessed relief, Frankie boy."

"I'm not in the mood any longer, thanks to your goddam son."

"Can't say I blame you," she remarked, as the contessalike madam whimpered nobly in her suffering.

17

The gam: Another dying

AFTER VERONA, Murphy, apprehensive over the possibility, wondered when they would see the tortured Alinsky again.

When the encounter came, Alinsky was dead. Or practicing, anyhow.

It was in Yugoslavia, in a southern province near M..kovic, when, after plodding the long corridor of relentless beauty between the Adriatic Sea and the Dinaric Alps for nearly five weeks, they met a torchlit Slovene funeral procession coming eerily toward them just after dark along a rutted dirt road that led to that night's camping place.

There were perhaps twenty people in the cortège: two priests in front swinging censers, six pallbearers who carried the coffin on their shoulders, torchbearers and assorted mourners following behind. Unexpectedly they stopped at the moment of passing, as Murphy lowered the crucifix in respect, and one of the priests asked Father Bisson in fluent French to bless the dead one.

He acquiesced, and as they lowered the coffin to the ground and removed the lid, Bisson—as if the coffin held the most expected dead person in all the world—said simply, *"Ah, pauvre Monsieur Alinsky."*

The pilgrims gasped in response. It was Alinsky in a funeral shroud, his eyes closed, his face white and drained of blood, his hands clasped over his chest.

"Au nom du Père, et du Fils, et du Saint Esprit, ainsi soit-il." Bisson spoke the blessing.

Alinsky sat up immediately, beaming through the ghostly makeup, and sang out, "Happy Easter, folks!"

"Whatever are you doing in that coffin, Mr. Alinsky?" Kyle-Boyer demanded incredulously.

"Practicing. A dress rehearsal." He admired himself in a hand mirror. "One never can tell when the day will come, and I at least want to know how I'll look."

"I kind of prefers you dead, Alinsky," Jonathan Whitmore told him flatly. "You're a lot less dangerous that way. That business of trying to flatten us with that jet airplane of yours back there was bloody crude, I think. And what you tried with Murphy here, in that whorehouse in Verona, was even worse."

"Oh, may God deliver me of my awful temper," Alinsky pleaded heavenward. He climbed out of the coffin, wiping the death paste from his face with a towel. "You can't imagine some of the trouble it's gotten me into. However, I apologize for those things and I'd like to make it up to you. We're camped about two kilometers from here with a fine larder and liquor cabinet, and since you're a full month ahead of the First Crusade, as nearly as I can calculate, I think a few days of rest and good food and drink are really deserved."

"Undeniably. But no violence, Alinsky," Kyle-Boyer emphasized.

"No violence. Scout's honor," Alinsky promised.

"Is your mother along, Alinsky?" Murphy asked.

"No, Murph, I'm afraid not."

"Then we've got no guarantees."

"Trust me, folks. And now come. Your dinner's been preparing for hours."

Though they were weary and hungry, the pilgrims' compliance was hedged with wariness. The two ships of the night set off side by side and returned to Alinsky's encampment.

At Alinsky's camp beside a small lake, where Persian carpets covered the dust on the floor of the tents, there were the expected retainers. There were also the unexpected ones: Mermelstein, the Alinskys' doctor, and Luciano the castrato.

Murphy met the former before dinner, since he was the first of the pilgrims in line for a medical checkup that Mermelstein was along to perform. The doctor was pudgy and humorous, an Amer-Israeli formerly of Chicago, with an accent that had never left him, who had apparently known Alinsky since the days of the founding of the Jewish state. In the lantern-lit tent that served as his clinic, he took a blood sample, tested Murphy's pulse and blood pressure, probed his tongue and rectum, listened to his heart and lungs with a stethoscope, pounded his kneecaps for reflex, and inquired after his liver. Then, apparently satisfied, he stared at Murphy quizzically for a few moments. "Meyer tells me you're from Iowa originally, Murph."

"Yes. Near Dubuque. Long ago."

"Hm-m-m-m. Tell me, what are you doing this for? I mean, why do you think *meshugga* Meyer has got all you guys marching off to Jerusalem?"

Murphy shrugged. "He says it's to redress the cruel balance of history from the time of the Crusades."

"I heard that one too. That's a bunch of cockamamie bullshit if I ever heard it. I'd give an arm to know what he's up to. His mother would give two. Lately, for a year now, he's been schizoid. One week the old Meyer, the generous prince. The next a *dybbuk,* a madman."

As Murphy shrugged again to indicate his ignorance, he heard on the outside the beginning of a

sweet sad song in Hebrew delivered in a high, clear
voice. It came from near the fire where Alinsky lay
sipping his beer, his head propped up against Father
Bisson's mule saddle. A love song for sure, it silenced
the buzz of conversation in the camp and the clanking of pots and pans. Only the stomping of the mules
and the chirping of crickets could be heard.

"Who is she?" Murphy asked Mermelstein.

"She's a he. Or was, anyhow. That's Luciano the
castrato. Been Meyer's sidekick since the 'forty-eight
war. Ever since Meyer gelded him. *Oy vey,* was
that a mistake!" Mermelstein slapped the side of his
head.

"You're kidding!" Murphy begged. "Alinsky did
that to him?"

"Swear to God. Luciano was an Italian yid come
to fight the same war as Meyer. Only Meyer didn't
know anything but English and a few words of Yiddish from the parents, and when he ran into Luciano
babbling Italian he thought the poor guy was an
Arab. And when Luciano didn't know about a certain
arms cache Meyer was looking for, Meyer did him
in, they say, in a room full of captive Arabs to get
the point across. Only later did someone notice
Luciano was on our side."

"Ouch!" Murphy winced, slapping his own head
also.

"You said it. The castrato's lived with Meyer and
Rachel ever since then. Solomon's own David. Calms
Meyer's rages through song. Only one I know can
shut him up besides his mother, and she uses a cane.
Oh, well, you're clean, Murph. Good luck. Send in
Kyle-Boyer, will you?"

Outside, where Alinsky's castrato still sang, Murphy
motioned Kyle-Boyer toward the tent and took his
place near the fire. Alinsky, absorbed, stared deeply
into its center while the others studied the singer of
sad songs. Fine-featured, with black curly hair, he
seemed eternally young, though Murphy suspected,
given the lapse of time since the 1948 War of In-

dependence, that he might be close to fifty years of age. Fittingly, somehow, in keeping with the biblical parallel Mermelstein had suggested, he wore a long Moroccan caftan and strummed an ancient mandolin guitar. Murphy, wondering at the growing complexity of Alinsky's empire on every possible level, could not dismiss the thought that Luciano the castrato, more than anyone else he had met so far, was a genuine Alinsky possession.

With Mermelstein done with his testing and Marilyn Aldrich's leg finally released from its cast, they took dinner around a table set up in the largest of the tents. Afterward, Murphy—as did the other pilgrims—declined to join Alinsky and Mermelstein in their tent for a nightcap. Instead he sat nearby on the outside, listening to the castrato explaining his condition in broken English to Kyle-Boyer, Marilyn, and Jonathan, who eyed him with a consummate fascination.

"Meyer think I speak Arabic, but I speak Italiano. He ask questions, but I not Arab so I not know answer. Then he do the terrible thing to me."

"Oh, my God!" Kyle-Boyer said.

But the exclamation died in the silence of shock and was replaced in moments more by the rising sounds of an argument between Alinsky and Mermelstein, who were obviously getting drunk in Alinsky's tent.

"Meyer, tell me, what are you up to with this fuckin' crusade business? I really think you're nuts. I remember you when we first came over—what you did to those Arabs. Cripes, you didn't kill them, you butchered them."

"What was I supposed to do, inoculate them? There was a war on. If they'd made me a general then, Baghdad would be a provincial capital of Israel by now."

"Some general you'd make! Meyer, I never told you this, but I saw you one night in Haifa, down in the port, dressed like a woman."

"You never saw anything like that, Mermelstein! You're lying!" Alinsky raged.

"I know I saw you. Find me another six-foot woman in Israel with cleat marks on her legs where yours are and I'll gladly retract the statement."

"Shut up, Mermelstein! Don't piss me off!"

"Meyer, it's a joke. I thought it was funny. I went home and told Ruthie about it, and we both howled. Who the hell in Israel except Meyer could afford the luxury of being a transvestite?"

Outside the tent, Murphy leaped to his feet when he heard the crack of Mermelstein being struck by Alinsky and an accompanying howl of pain. The others followed suit. When they threw back the entrance flap Alinsky was on top of Mermelstein, pummeling the doctor's face with his fists.

"Alinsky, you promised no violence, remember?" Kyle-Boyer tried to grab at Alinsky's still-flailing right arm, but it was the castrato who ended the punishment of Mermelstein; he simply grabbed Alinsky's head by a handful of hair and yanked it upward until he looked straight into Alinsky's eyes.

"Meyerle, ze Dr. Mermelstein—your friend, no?"

The words had the effect of an instant tranquilizer. Alinsky shook his head in consternation, as if trying to determine how he got to be where he was, then looked down in real disbelief at Mermelstein's bruised and already bleeding face.

"Oh, my God, what have I done? It's Saul, my own friend, that I'm hitting."

"Meyer—" Mermelstein began to speak from the carpeting of the floor, shaking his head in another kind of disbelief. "Meyer, you're going right around the bend, do you know it?"

But Alinsky did not respond. Instead he sat back, leaning against a camp chair, and began crying, great heaving sobs of remorse that sent the tears rocketing down his cheeks. The castrato comforted him, patting his back and chanting over and over again, "Poor Meyerle . . . poor, poor Meyerle. . . ."

"I wants to leave tomorrow morning," Jonathan Whitmore said flatly. "It's safer on the road than it is here with you, Alinsky."

"Absolutely," Kyle-Boyer enjoined.

"No, stay here, people," Alinsky begged through his crying. "You need the rest. I'll leave. The camp and the servants will be at your disposal. Dr. Mermelstein can stay with you. Forgive me. Forgive me, if you can."

Contrite, Alinsky got up and left the tent with the castrato at his elbow. Kyle-Boyer and Murphy helped Mermelstein to his feet. The Alinskys' doctor shook his head once again, wiping at the blood on his face with a handkerchief, and then spoke quietly. "I guess I'll have to stay on with you a few more days. That way my face will heal up some and I won't have to explain to his mother what happened to me."

He started to leave the tent but brightened at a thought.

"A few extra days off might be a fine thing. It'll give me some time to indulge in my favorite pastime. Cave searching. Spelunking. Those mountains up there have got to be loaded with caves and crevasses. Anyone like to join me?"

There were no takers; the pilgrims' communal instinct was to remain together and in camp. Alinsky, instead of waiting until the morning, left that very night.

In the morning, at first dawn, Mermelstein, accompanied by Ben Bokva and Teplitsky, who carried the necessary equipment in packs on their backs, left for a day of spelunking.

In midafternoon, Ben Bokva and Teplitsky hastened back to camp at a run to announce the terrible news that a rope had frayed and that the good doctor lay dead at the bottom of a deep crevasse.

The two non-gangsters of Alinsky set off immediately in their Citroën to notify the police about the accident.

18

Interlude in Greece

IN NORTHERN GREECE, in mid-October, there came a day when Murphy no longer had any doubt of Alinsky's menace.

On a hot windless afternoon when the sky was, as ever, inordinately blue, and Murphy, inured to the relentless Aegean beauty of bleached houses and gnarled olive trees, was thinking instead of the circumstances of Mermelstein's death, Monique and Jean-Philippe appeared. It was near Drama, about halfway between the Yugoslav and Turkish borders, while the pilgrims plodded along a tarmac road covered with an inch-thick layer of dust, that a Deux Chevaux with Greek plates approached from the opposite direction and pulled abruptly to a stop at the head of the procession. Murphy almost fainted at the sight of the occupants.

"It's my wife and son," he announced to no one in particular.

"Frank! Frank!" Monique called to him frantically. "Get in quickly! I think we're being followed!"

Murphy, too stunned to react, felt the cross being wrenched from his hands by Kyle-Boyer, who shouted to him, "Hurry, Frank, before Ben Bokva and Teplitsky get up here!"

Murphy sprinted across the road and around to the passenger door while Jean-Philippe bounded into the back seat. He had barely slammed the door shut when Monique spun the Deux Chevaux about and headed back in the direction from which they had come.

"How did you get here?" Murphy asked. Impulsively he reached over, locking her head in his arms as she drove, and planted a kiss on her cheek. She did not resist. From behind, Jean-Philippe threw his arms about Murphy's neck and hugged him tightly.

"It's a miracle!" Monique almost shrieked. She hurtled the car up the dusty road at nearly eighty kilometers per hour. Murphy was now keenly atuned to her desperation; at home, driving the Peugeot, she hardly ever topped even half that speed.

"Lefevre, the agent of these people, whoever they are, had to go to Paris on some business. Jean-Philippe and I went riding, and that *salaud* Baudrey was following behind us on your Arab. But she shied at something and threw him straight into a stone wall near the vineyards. He died instantly of a broken neck, and for the first time since you crossed over into Italy we were unguarded. We went back to the house, got our passports and money, and rode the horses all the way to the Swiss border, across the fields and through the mountains, so they couldn't find us. If we had taken the car, they would surely have caught us in hours. We got to Geneva and took a flight to Salonika because we knew you must be somewhere near from the last *post restante* address. But I'm sure someone must have observed us leaving Switzerland."

"Maybe not. Where's your father? He may have been able to sidetrack them when this Lefevre got back from Paris."

"Oh, Frank, he's dead. He's been dead for more than two months."

"But Monique, I just received a letter from him."
Murphy spoke dumbly. Somehow there was no feeling
of remorse; his skin began to crawl instead.

"Of course you got a letter. You would have received letters all the way to Jerusalem. They had
someone who was an expert forger send you one just
as before, little bits of news and the rest copied
out of Chateaubriand and Racine. Oh, Frank, who
are they? They're everywhere, and everyone seems
to be in their employ. There's no one left to trust.
This crusade you're walking in is not sponsored by
le père Marfeau as we thought. You've not been
seen on television back in France since a few days
after entering Italy. And Marfeau is dead. He slept
one night on the folds of his circus tent in the
back of a truck and was burned alive when the canvas caught fire. Arson is suspected. Who are they,
Frank?"

Monique was crying now. Bred by nuns from an
ancient past to be sage and reserved, she had reached
the bottom of her strength, Murphy saw.

His every instinct was to clasp her firmly to him
and somehow reassure her that everything would
be all right, except that she still careened up the road
at eighty kilometers per hour and he no longer had
any idea what constituted "all right." Marfeau was
dead; *le baron* was dead. And not a scrap of news
about either of them. Who knew what Alinsky intended
next?

From the back seat Jean-Philippe lay a firm young
hand on his mother's shoulder. *"Petite maman, ne
pleurez pas. Vous êtes toujours si brave."* Then, to
his father: "Who are these dirty bastards?"

Even now the language startled Murphy, as did the
tone of contempt in the voice, until he remembered
there was hardly a drop of Murphy in Jean-Philippe.
His son was a de Rastignac to his marrow. Like his
grandfather he knew no fear. How could it possibly
penetrate through the massive shield of hauteur that
kept the outer universe at bay?

" 'They' are in the employ of one Meyer Alinsky, an Israeli who was once an American and who is responsible for the theft of the diamond from the Angoulême cathedral last summer. The diamond is in the crucifix I was carrying, and we're taking it to Jerusalem."

"A jewel thief? All this is the responsibility of a common jewel thief?" Monique demanded incredulously. Still, something in her relaxed perceptibly at the disclosure. Perhaps "they" no longer had the spirit quality she had feared. The speedometer plummeted to fifty kph.

"He isn't common," Murphy warned her.

"But, Frank, answer this: Why would this Alinsky go through so much trouble just for a diamond that has to be brought to Israel? It could be mailed there. I could think of ten easier ways to get it there."

"Anyone could. But this diamond is only a symbol. The rest is incomprehensible. We pilgrims, for Alinsky's purposes, are expiating the crime of some murderer. I haven't figured out yet who the murderer is, who the victim was, when it happened, where it happened, or how. But don't ask me any more for now. It gets worse as you delve deeper."

"*Mon Dieu, très catholique,*" Monique pronounced, shaking her head in wonderment.

"*Sale juif!*" Jean-Philippe said vehemently.

"*Tais-toi!*" Murphy told his son sharply. Then: "What happened to our great friend Emile Monard who got me into this mess? Couldn't he offer any help? Didn't he know you were being kept at the château against your will?"

Monique turned her head sideways to look at him with a narrow-eyed scrutiny. Her cheeks were still wet from crying, though, and the total effect was a rarely seen incongruity. Murphy caught sight of Jean-Philippe in the rearview mirror; his son's face was a study in puzzlement.

"Frank"—Monique spoke numbly—"Emile is dead also. He died more than four months ago. I wrote you a letter immediately to let you know. I received a letter from you telling me how sorry you were and asking me to give condolences to his mother. Are you telling me that you never received my letter or returned one?"

Murphy felt a simple bolt of terror rush through him. He turned to look through the rear window in expectation, but the black Citroën of Ben Bokva and Teplitsky was not yet there.

"Monique, I never got the letter, and if you received one, another forger sent it to you. Tell me something. How did Emile die?"

"He crashed his sports car into a tree on the way south to Cannes on the National Seven."

"Then it was an accident?"

"Yes."

"Thank God!" Murphy exclaimed. He wet his mouth with saliva, feeling relief, though he was instantly guilty that the manner of Emile's death would bring relief.

"But monsieur"—Jean-Philippe spoke up—"his death was perhaps not an accident. The police were called in to look at the car. Buvais, the *mécanique* in the village, brought the wreck home to salvage the motor. He said there were tiny slits filed in the tubing that carries the fluid to the brake cylinders. Buvais thinks some of the slits weakened and the fluid was forced out, and Père Monard had no brakes when the accident happened."

"*Mon Dieu,* it's not possible! Is there anyone left?" Murphy ran backward in his memory, trying to recall any additional persons Alinsky might deem dangerous to his purposes.

"How did this madness all begin? Where will it end? Please, Frank—you drive." Monique pulled abruptly off to the side of the road and sat shaking behind the wheel while Murphy hurried around to the driver's side. With Jean-Philippe's help he somehow got her past the gearshift and into the passenger seat. Murphy hiked his robe over his knees and shot the Deux Chevaux down the road again. In a moment it occurred to him that he had not the faintest idea where they were going except that the road led to Salonika.

"We ought to go to Athens and ask protection from the French embassy." Jean-Philippe spoke as if he could read Murphy's thoughts.

"No, that's exactly what they'd expect us to do. I know Alinsky, and he's everywhere. He's probably on his way to Greece right now, since he certainly knows you've taken off. He'll have his people watching the embassy and all the airports and train terminals."

"We could go to the American embassy," Monique said. "You were an American once. If we could get them to send us to America, we'd be safe there."

"I'm sure they'd be most obliging," Murphy told her, finding it in him to be rueful even in the midst of his fear. "Especially since I turned in my American passport some years back. And Alinsky would think of that, too. No, we need a place to hide around here for a while because Alinsky will expect us to make a dash for it out of Greece. A small country hotel off the main road somewhere is what we need."

Murphy checked behind them, but the shadowing black Citroën was still nowhere in sight. Evidently Gervais was taking his time notifying Ben Bokva that the crusade's crossbearer had fled. In minutes more they came to a right-angle road that headed uphill through a heavily wooded terrain and seemed, from the map Monique carried, to wend its way through a number of villages that were speckled across a promontory behind the port city of Kavalla. Murphy eased the car off the main highway to avoid a telltale cloud of dust and halted it farther on after the first turning. With Jean Philippe he ran back to obliterate their tracks, Indian fashion, with fallen branches of pine, noting with some satisfaction that enough cars passed back and forth on the highway to keep the area eternally fogged in, so that even if Ben Bokva were on their trail he could not have accounted for them by means of a single plume of dust.

In the car again, Murphy followed the uphill route through a number of switchback curves for perhaps a mile and then stopped behind a massive boulder for cover when he realized they could again see the main road below. He told Monique and Jean-Philippe to remain in the car while he crept forward to keep watch at the edge of the boulder. Within five minutes the view was more than rewarding. About a half mile off the black Citroën skidded to a halt at the behest of the driver of a large white American car with side curtains traveling in the opposite direction. Ben Bokva bounded out of the Citroën and ran to the other car with arms open and pleading. Imperious, Alinsky stepped out and smashed him across the face with the back of his hand so that even at a distance Murphy winced; Meyer was angry again.

He watched while a furious conference ensued, during which Alinsky clobbered Ben Bokva another time, and decided after a minute that the first place Alinsky would look would be up the side road they had taken. It stood to reason. They could have gone in but one direction since Alinsky had not intercepted them. But surprisingly, a moment later when their talk was ended, both cars swung off toward Salonika and disappeared in the dust.

"They're gone," Murphy told his wife and son in the Deux Chevaux, and in relief Monique began crying all over again.

They continued along the road for at least forty miles, through identical villages where children waved from play and old men waved from the front stoops of tavernas. They passed farms where lone women worked in the fields, and ranges of hills covered over with pines, and once a monastery hanging on the side of a cliff, until the countryside finally exuded a sense-numbing quality of sameness and some hope began to rise in Murphy that for once Alinsky had been thwarted. There were so many side roads and even footpaths negotiable by the Deux Chevaux that they might find the ultimate undiscoverable place and roost there for a year, if necessary. Murphy still had money in France; if they could lay hands on it they might lease a small home and wait. The crusade would reach Jerusalem in March or April. Alinsky could not look for him that long. . . .

Before them the road topped a last rise and followed along a stone wall. They drove past two decaying windmill towers, and then the line of trees on the edge of a field gave way to an incredible view of the Aegean. In the distance, to the right, was the city outline of what must be Kavalla.

"Let's try to find a small hotel around here, Frank," Monique petitioned. "Someplace with a bottle of wine. My nerves are badly shot."

"All right. But what are we going to do about my clothes?"

"It's not a problem," Monique said. "You look like a monk, so pretend for tonight that you are a monk. You can be my brother. Take a separate room, or one with Jean-Philippe, then slip in later to sleep with me. You've lost a lot of weight."

"About forty pounds." Murphy realized how pridefully he said it. Monique leaned over to kiss his forehead, and Jean-Philippe clasped his shoulder tightly by way of approval.

"I don't drink any more, Monique, or at least not very much." Then, as if to further the advantage of his temporary moral righteousness: "How was it that my father-in-law died?"

"Crise de foie." Monique sighed heavily. "His liver. He died as he lived. He drank that swill in the caves right to the end. When the priest came to give him the viaticum he was too dry to swallow it, so he washed it down with a glass of wine."

Despite the fact of Alinsky hunting for them on the lower roads, Murphy found it in him to laugh mirthfully: the universal Irishman's notion of a good joke at a wake, the finest testimony to the deceased.

After receiving his Croix de Geurre from Pétain, old man de Rastignac had taken to the drink with such avidity that Murphy did not even know if it could be called alcoholism. It had more to do with self-congratulation. He chuckled at the memory until he realized he was the only laughing mourner. By their silence he knew that Monique and Jean-Philippe disapproved strongly. He went back to thinking of the danger from Meyer Alinsky.

In minutes more they passed through another village that was sheer white, picturesque, and poor as dirt and came to a sign in Greek, German, and French on its farther outskirts that indicated there was a hotel a short distance up a side road. Murphy turned the car and climbed the hill. The hotel was a large, rambling house affair that could not be seen from the main road. Its opposite side faced the Aegean.

When they pulled up in a tiled expanse before the main door, the hotelkeeper, a smiling and nondescript fat man of middle age, came out to welcome them in Greek, then switched to French at their behest. Inside at the sign-in desk, where Murphy and Jean-Philippe were to be given a double room and Monique a single, Murphy winced at the stupidity of a singular forgetfulness.

"Vos passeports, s'il vous plaît," the hotelkeeper asked.

Murphy smacked the side of his head in dismay while Monique casually extracted her own and Jean-Philippe's passports, then looked at Murphy as if she expected him to be carrying his in the elastic of his cincture.

"Votre passeport, monsieur le curé?"

"I lost it this morning," Murphy lied hastily. But it seemed not to faze the man. He was regretful and merely asked that Murphy fill out an identity form, reminding him at the same time to inquire at the French Consulate in Salonika for a reissue, since it was inconvenient to travel without a passport. Murphy filled out the form, listing himself as Monique's brother. Then, while they followed the hotelkeeper upstairs to their rooms, Jean-Philippe asked in English where Murphy's passport really was.

"Alinsky's got it, of course," Murphy told him simply.

"That goddam son of a bitch!" Jean-Philippe hissed. But that was all. They were the only guests in the hotel, and after they bathed Murphy and his wife sat for a long time outside on the veranda, finishing a whole bottle of retsina and speculating on their chances of eluding Meyer Alinsky. By the time the hotelkeeper's wife served them their meal they had decided to try the Salonika consulate in a week's time for a reissue of Murphy's passport and then try to flee to America for safety.

"I don't know what went wrong for Alinsky back in the States years ago," Murphy commented, "but I have a feeling the state of Iowa would be the safest place in the world for us to be right now."

By dinner's end, with more wine, Murphy became convinced of the possibilities of safety that lay in getting to America. Monique also, apparently. Later he slipped into her room, tiptoeing eagerly like a teenager off on his first sexual excursion, and made love to his wife an impossible four times before morning. . . .

It was because of the passport that Alinsky found them, of course, with the unwitting cooperation of the Greek police. The next day, at nine in the morning, the hotelkeeper knocked on the door of the room to which Murphy had just returned and informed *monsieur le curé* that some gentlemen had found his passport and were waiting down in the bar to return it. Murphy, for his part, was surprised only that Alinsky had found them so quickly. For, on waking but a half hour before, any hopes of getaway had suddenly crumbled when it came to him that all Alinsky had to do to find them was go to the police, who would have lists of all the hotel registrations in Greece for the night before. The rest would be simple. Murphy tried to imagine how many foreigners had checked in without passports; the number had to be miniscule.

With Jean-Philippe he went to Monique's room. "Alinsky is downstairs waiting for us," he told her, shrugging his shoulders. She smiled ironically in response, perhaps at the notion of how short-lived their freedom had been. But she was calm.

"What do you think he'll do to us, Frank?" she asked.

"I don't know. Maybe Alinsky doesn't know either. We'd better go downstairs and find out, though. Let's hope he agrees to return both of you to France."

They embraced a long moment, breaking only when Jean-Philippe kissed each of them while making an appropriate joke about the condemned before their execution. Then they left the room and started down the stairs, Jean-Philippe walking resolutely in front while Murphy and Monique followed arm in arm behind. Halfway down the stairs they could see into the bar where Alinsky sat at a table, dressed in a white linen suit and drinking his inevitable beer. Ben Bokva and Teplitsky, both in shirt sleeves, leaned casually against a wall. When they were almost on ground level, Murphy, who had been trying to decipher the look on Alinsky's face, felt Monique tug at him sharply.

"*Oh, mon Dieu!* Frank."

"What? What's the matter?"

"It's Gottlieb. The American journalist. He came to the château over a month ago to do an article on the restoration. Oh, Frank. . . ."

She folded against him, whatever resiliency that was restored the night before completely gone. Great shuddering sobs came out of her. Holding her, Murphy felt impotent, imprisoned by the taut weavings of the web Alinsky had spun around them.

"Frank, it was the first time we were alone with an outsider without Baudrey hanging around. I slipped him a note and begged him to take it to the Prefect of Police at Lyon, and he promised to do it. We waited for weeks for the police to come. Now I can see why they never arrived."

"You're a rotten prick, Alinsky!" Murphy screamed at him.

"Yeah, Murphy, and you're as honest as Abraham right? You signed a contract, remember? There was no escape clause in it that said you could hop in a car with your wife and just take off for a vacation in Greece. Anyhow, here's your passport. Someone found it along the road."

Alinsky stood from the table and walked toward Murphy, extending the passport, but made the mistake of passing too near Jean-Philippe, who had been eyeing him narrowly all along. Jean-Philippe lashed out, karate fashion, with the instep of his foot and caught Alinsky fiercely on the shinbone. Then, just as Alinsky was making his reflexive bend to massage the pain away, Murphy's son kicked him squarely in the crotch.

"*Sale juif!*" Jean-Philippe raged as Alinsky went down, bent double and clutching at his crotch and already vomiting on the tiled floor. Whole geysers of a yellow liquid that could only be beer coursed through his nose. Jean-Philippe got off one more kick against Alinsky's ribs before Ben Bokva recovered from his surprise and made it across the room in a lightning run to put Murphy's son to sleep with a deft chop on the back of his neck. In response, Murphy jumped on Ben Bokva's back and rode him to the floor, pummeling the Israeli's head with his fists. Vaguely, on the periphery of his vision, he saw that Monique had thrown a heavy ashtray from one of the tables at Teplitsky, who was hovering about Alinsky on the floor. Then the lights went out when Teplitsky left his boss on order and smashed Murphy over the head with a wine bottle.

When Murphy awoke the first thing he saw was Jean-Philippe tied to a chair and scowling at Alinsky, who sat backwards on another chair, looking white-faced and haggard and wiping at his sweated forehead with a handkerchief. Monique sat smoking a cigarette on a bench against the wall. Alinsky, speaking French, seemed to be trying to reason with Jean-Philippe. He turned toward Murphy when the latter sat up. "This kid of yours play football, Murph?"

"Not that I know of," Murphy said indifferently. He touched the top of his head where it was most painful and felt the strip of gauze that had already been taped on.

"Well, he ought to play football, that's for sure. He almost kicked my nuts right through the top of my head."

"Too damn bad he didn't," Murphy said. "It might have knocked some sense into your brain. What are you going to do with us? Kill us?"

"Murph, I swear to God I didn't kill the others," Alinsky pleaded. "Which did I supply in Baudrey's case, the stone wall or the skittish horse?"

"What about the priest, Emile Monard? The mechanic in the village said there were holes drilled in his brake lines. He didn't have a prayer when he wrapped his car around that tree."

"Didn't we go through a list of the dead back there in Italy? Are you trying to tell me that swinger didn't have an enemy in the world? I didn't even know the guy, Murph; he was one of Marfeau's flunkies. Maybe Marfeau did him in. Or maybe it was some rich religious lady's husband. He wasn't exactly Christianity's notion of a pious priest, I hear tell."

"Then what about Marfeau?"

"You weary me, Murph. Marfeau was a wino. Everybody knew that. He fell asleep on a truckload of canvas one night and burned to death."

"The police think it was arson."

"Burning preachers is not my style, Murph. Even if some people think they definitely need burning. A guy like Marfeau had to have lots of enemies, too. Maybe some of those Communists he was always baiting got to him. I had nothing to do with it. In fact, I regard it as a loss. Marfeau was a well-trained long-time employee."

"I don't believe you, Meyer. You're in the process of wiping out all your tracks behind you. Obviously you're not going to let my wife and son return to France."

"I'm afraid not, Murph. Not now, at least. We'll take them back to Jerusalem as houseguests. Our man Lefevre can look after the château back in France. I have a very nice house," Alinsky explained to Monique and Jean-Phillippe as he stood up. "Some people have even called it a palace. It's got a big swimming pool and stables and tennis courts—and even a soccer field for super kicker, here, to stay in shape."

"You're a rotten prick, Alinsky!" Murphy repeated. "What harm could they possibly do to you?"

"I'm sorry, Frank, but it has to be this way. It's just a little security to make sure you stay with the crusade. Anyhow, think of them as houseguests. Everything will be on the up-and-up. My mother runs the place. You couldn't have a better chaperone than a little old Jewish lady from Iowa."

"I don't even believe she's your mother, Alinsky," Murphy said quietly, the defeat spreading in him already. "I think she's a character actress or someone like that you've employed to make this whole mess more complicated. Somebody to help give you an illusion of humanness when you're not human at all. . . ."

"How would you like me to knock your goddam teeth down your throat? Or break your kid's leg over there?" Alinsky demanded, bouncing about on his toes like a boxer warming up and seizing an empty wine carafe from the bar and brandishing it over

Murphy's head. "She's my mother! There are days I wish she'd do a lot less talking and snooping, but she's still my mother! Do you understand, stupid *goy* Murphy?"

Alinsky's eyes seemed to bulge out of his head, and thick veins stood out in his hand where he gripped the decanter's neck. Murphy, fearing an instant coup de grâce, knew that Meyer Alinsky was still a very physically powerful man and might easily administer it. Behind him Ben Bokva and Teplitsky exchanged harried glances; then Ben Bokva clasped his hands together as if praying, and the expression on his face begged Murphy to agree with the boss.

"Yes, I understand."

"Good," Alinsky judged, lowering the carafe. "Come on, let's get out of here."

Ben Bokva untied Jean-Philippe and they walked outside to the veranda of the hotel, where the proprietor, looking puzzled but clearly obsequious at the same time, accepted an envelope from Alinsky. In the parking area were the white side-curtained American car and Ben Bokva's black Citroën; the Deux Chevaux was evidently on its way back to Salonika. Murphy stood a long moment looking through a rift in a line of pine trees out toward the Aegean before he felt Monique standing beside him. She was composed now, smoking another cigarette, smiling wanly, perhaps because there was no point in being frightened any longer; none of them had the remotest idea of what to expect next.

"Sois courageuse," he told her. Be brave. He kissed her gently on the forehead, then clasped hands with Jean-Philippe. The three looked toward the white car to see Alinsky hanging over a door and regarding them with a curious lack of expression, as if he were not really seeing them at all. It occurred to Murphy that there was still possibly one method of throwing a wrench into Alinsky's plans.

"Meyer," he said as he strode up to the other,

"don't even think for one minute about killing them. They're innocents."

"I have no intention of killing them, Murph."

"Bullshit, Meyer, you're lying. I'm absolutely cer- tain you intend to wipe out the whole pilgrim bunch after we achieve your purpose for you. I never really understood till now the coincidence of the others all being so isolated in life. Not one of them has any known relatives anywhere who would miss them if they disappeared from the face of the earth. Even Bisson's bishop considers him a useless and embarras- ing old man. He'd probably be happy if Bisson never showed up again."

"Bisson probably won't survive the trip," Alinsky said thoughtfully. "It's still a long way to Jerusalem. And it's true about the others; they have no one. I made sure of that. You're the only hitch, Murph. That schmuck Monard said you were a rummy that everybody would be happy to have out of the way. But the son of a bitch lied, because it turns out your father-in-law, wife, and son all loved you de- spite yourself. It's going to take a lot of thinking to get around this one."

"Alinsky, listen," Murphy pleaded. "Why are you doing this crazy thing? What's the goddam secret? Will you please tell me?"

"The secret, Murphy," Alinsky said, "is in Jerusa- lem, as any asshole should understand."

"That's not good enough. You're taking my wife and son as hostages, and I'm certain you intend to kill them. But I'm not entirely powerless. I'm going to tell the others what you're up to. There's no way you can stop me from doing that."

"Tell them anything you like, Murph. But they'll walk to Jerusalem if Ben Bokva and Teplitsky and some of the other boys on the payroll have to put one leg in front of the other for them all the way. I've planned this for too long a time to have it fucked up. Only think about one thing, and I'll be blunt: I haven't figured out yet whether they have to die or not. But if you truly want to be humane, why not spare them an agony of fear from wondering about it?"

"God, Alinsky. You're an absolute fiend!"

"Some others, my friend, think I'm an absolute saint. There's just no way of knowing, is there? Until Jerusalem, then."

Murphy felt Ben Bokva grasp his arm; then he was led toward the Citroën while Monique and Jean-Philippe were taken to Alinsky's car by two men not previously seen.

The American car departed first with the Citroën following behind in its dust along the forty miles or so of back road they had negotiated the day before, their hope for a refuge from Meyer Alinsky growing with every mile passed. When they reached the main highway Alinsky's car turned left, presumably heading for some airfield, and the Citroën raced off in the opposite direction after the pilgrims. Murphy's last glimpse of his wife and son was the sight of Jean-Philippe's fist—meant to be a clenched symbol of courage—showing through the white car's rear window. Then they were gone.

In the front seat Ben Bokva and Teplitsky sighed in unison and shook their heads.

"*Mazel tov*, Frank," Teplitsky said. "Good luck. You will have need of it."

19

The Istanbul Hilton

MURPHY, RETURNED TO HIS FELLOW PILGRIMS, mourned aloud the responsibilities of land proprietorship that caused his wife and son to return all too soon to France. To his friend Kyle-Boyer alone he told the truth, apprising him of the captivity of Monique and Jean-Philippe and of the real danger to the crusaders from Meyer Alinsky that lay ahead. Kyle-Boyer needed little convincing, and after warning that Ben Bokva and Teplitsky, though perhaps sympathetic, still belonged to Alinsky, he proposed that they try contacting Interpol at Istanbul—this, rather than escaping to a police station in a Greek or Turkish village, only to have their attempt fail because they might not make themselves understood.

Weeks later, in mid-November, when, televised, they moved past the city walls of Istanbul through hordes of curious and hawking Turks and then crossed the Bosporus by ferryboat into Asiatic Turkey, conditions seemed perfect for a breakout. During the First Crusade the army of Raymond of Toulouse, Alinsky's Christian trailblazer of yore, wintered beside the same Bosporus while Raymond bargained with the Byzantines. Eight centuries later the Four-

teenth Crusade checked into the Istanbul Hilton for
ten days of rest cure. Alinsky had thoughtfully provided for an unlimited tab at the bar. Murphy and
Kyle-Boyer shared an elegant suite; the room phone,
surprisingly, was still routed through the hotel switchboard.

On the second day, in the early afternoon, after
a waiter had delivered a bottle of Scotch for courage
to their rooms, they attempted to contact Interpol.
The job was an easy one, as Kyle-Boyer had suggested it would be; he predicted that Meyer Alinsky,
like Goliath, was about to stumble and fall because
of the prowess of a miniscule enemy he had not
reckoned upon. Kyle-Boyer merely picked up the
room phone and got in touch with a helpful young
person at the British consulate who gave him the
particulars on whom to contact at Interpol. The
switchboard operator agreeably dialed the number. The
trail of easy compliances died right there.

Murphy was to do the talking, and before introducing himself to the Interpol official, he checked
down his written list of logical procedure that he
meant to use in explaining the pilgrims' plight. The
official's name was Captain Erim, who spoke a fluent
English and inquired after the purpose of Murphy's
call. But moments after he began telling his story,
with Kyle-Boyer swigging on the Scotch bottle and
coaching him from the sidelines, Murphy understood
with a growing sense of resignation that after the
fashion of all Alinsky's doings they were in many
ways still bound and captured. He even conceded that
Alinsky had foreseen the possibility of just such an
attempt at escaping and therefore purposefully molded
the crusaders into what they were: a preposterous
anachronism trudging out of Europe and into Asia
along the ancient routes that jets flashed over in
minutes, an almost grotesque collection of human
anomalies who must seem picaresque at best and pa-
tently foolish at worst, an isolated religious farce

whose any attempt at rushing into the external world
for help would be met with gales of laughter.

At the same time he was telling Erim that he
had information about the theft of Suleiman's Pebble; that he and others were being force-marched on
a pilgrimage to Israel to expiate somebody's guilt
for a crime whose victim, time, and place of perpe-
tration no one knew; that Murphy's wife and son
were being held captive in a palace in Jerusalem;
that the mastermind of the theft and the pilgrimage
was an Israeli named Meyer Alinsky, formerly an
American, who was systematically wiping out his
tracks behind him with any number of deaths back
in France; and that Murphy was certain all the
crusaders were doomed after they reached Jerusalem.
Furthermore, he cautioned Erim that Alinsky was one
of the most powerful men in the world with his Book
of the Corruptibles that showed he had somehow in-
filtrated every power structure in the West and presumably Interpol also, and that he had a group of
agents working for him called non-gangsters. And as
evidence of this power, Murphy explained that Alinsky had bought off the whole Egyptian Air Force
during the Six-Day War and that was why it never
got off the ground to fight the Israelis. However,
there was one consolation, a flaw in the magnificent
raiment of Alinsky's influence. This was his mother,
a little old Jewish lady from Iowa, U.S.A., who was
bent on holding her son to a kind of reality, because
she feared he had drifted too far into the vortex
of illusion. This, Murphy considered, was the first
point of contact for Interpol's purposes. She at least
was logical.

There was a long silence, full of sighing, between the static crackles from the other end of the
line. Then the voice, pensive-sounding, came back to
Murphy. "Are you, perhaps, a Christian?"

"Well, yes," Murphy conceded. "I mean I was
baptized a Roman Catholic."

"And how old are you, Mr. Murphy?"

"I'm thirty-seven."

"Well, then, you're obviously not a Jesus freak. Your age would make you an old-guard Christian, probably a bit fanatical. I mean, a lot of your kind find their way here from time to time. Istanbul, when it was under the Byzantines, was called the Other Rome. It still has a traditional connection in the Christian mind, I gather."

"Look, I'm not a religious fanatic," Murphy told him, pleading now. "I'm being forced to continue on a march to Jerusalem against my will. There are four other people with me."

"And how were you initially persuaded to set off on this 'crusade,' as you refer to it?"

"I signed a contract," Murphy said weakly. Even as he said it, he felt lost. Through the window he scanned the endless expanse of rooftops, domes, and minarets that covered the hills on both sides of the teeming Bosporus, wondering where Erim the cop, their only lifeline to safety, was concealed.

"Mr. Murphy, are you perhaps of the group that I saw on television a few days ago, marching through the city gates from the Greek frontier? There was an old French priest on a mule and a young English girl on another mule."

"Yes, yes, Captain Erim, that's us. That's us exactly. I was the one carrying the cross."

"Ah, the Christ himself. Hmm. The girl on the mule, by the way, smokes hashish or something like that," the voice said reflectively, almost without interest.

"Yes," Murphy agreed. "She smokes almost constantly. How could you tell?"

"Her eyes resembled saucers, as they say in the West. A close view by the television camera heightens the effect. All of Turkey understands this."

"Well, couldn't you arrest us for smuggling hashish into Turkey? I'm sure we could sort the whole thing out once we were safe in prison."

"Impossible, Mr. Murphy. No one smuggles hashish into Turkey. It all goes out. There's enough here to keep the whole world stoned—again, a phrase borrowed from the West—for a couple of eons."

"Inspector Erim, you've got to help us! We're prisoners, nothing less, of this Alinsky person. We're being watched constantly. Will you at least agree to meet with us?"

"If you are prisoners, how are you able to telephone me? Where are you being held now?"

"We're staying at the Hilton," Murphy acknowledged, his voice a bare whisper.

Beside him Kyle-Boyer merely shook his head in dismay at the hopelessness of it all.

"Well, I think it's quite nice that you're staying at the Hilton," Erim judged. "What an elegant gay-ol. This Alinsky has certainly dealt fairly with the problem of prison reform. Is it really as fanciful a hotel as they say? I've never had occasion to go there. I'll bet this Alinsky has you all tied and bound up with the gold braid from the ballroom curtains. Where are the people who are supposed to be guarding you, by the way?"

"Where are Ben Bokva and Teplitsky?" Murphy asked Kyle-Boyer.

"I last saw them getting on a tour bus in front of the hotel with their cameras."

"They've gone on a bus tour of the city," Murphy told Erim. But he said it flaccidly, knowing it was the silliest thing he had related so far. From the other end of the line there was a long pause, filled by the exasperated whistling of wind through the cop's teeth.

"Well, Mr. Murphy." The voice came back at last. "If you think you're being held captive, but your captors are out touring Istanbul somewhere, why don't you just leave your room, take the elevator down to the lobby, hand in your room key, and check out? Then you'll be free, do you understand? But on the other hand, if I were you, I'd stay right where I was. In the Hilton, I mean. Because, even if this Alinsky you speak of is a criminal, you really can't deny his good taste. How many others do you imagine have been held captive in the Istanbul Hilton? It's a little like being taken to dinner by your kidnappers to keep up your spirits at that famous restaurant in Paris. What do they call it?"

"La Tour d'Argent?"

"Yes, that's it. I've read about it in several gourmet publications. It's really quite a fanciful place. My wife has even dined there. She is Western educated, in the French manner—"

"Inspector Erim," Murphy begged, "if we were to slip out of the hotel and bring you the diamond I spoke of that's stashed in the crucifix I'm carrying, would you believe us then?"

"Of course. But so that we don't waste each other's time, why don't you check the crucifix and make certain the diamond really is there?"

"Yes, you're quite right." Murphy put down the receiver and motioned for Kyle-Boyer to retrieve the crucifix that was propped up against a wall. While the abortionist held the staff, Murphy grabbed the cross bar and twisted until the tight-fitting piece began to work loose. When they came apart there was no Suleiman's Pebble to be found in the secret compartment. Resignedly, Murphy went back to the phone. "There's no diamond in the crucifix."

"I did not suppose there would be, Mr. Murphy." The sighing of Erim was now pregnant with annoyance. "Is there really any reason for us to continue this dialogue?"

"Inspector Erim, I must convince you of our danger."

"That's impossible, Murphy. Right now it seems you ought to be staying down on the funny farm —again, as it is called in the West—rather than the Hilton."

"Will you at least meet with us?"

There was an unexpected pause. "Will you have me to dinner at the hotel tonight? They have a cuisine française there, am I right?"

"Yes, it's famous the world over."

"No, it isn't, Murphy. But it will do for this one time. Only this is strictly off the record, not at all in the line of duty. It's curiosity that's got me now. One so rarely has a chance to meet with a Christian madman. There are so few of them roaming about Turkey these days. The reward of the Armenian massacres, I suppose. How will I know you, by the way?"

"My companion, Dr. Kyle-Boyer, and I will wait for you in the hotel bar. I'll be wearing a white robe with a red cross stitched to the front of it. Dr. Kyle-Boyer will be dressed in walking shorts and knee socks, and he'll be carrying a pith helmet and walking stick. About nine o'clock?"

"By Allah's mercy I'm sure I shall not miss the two of you." The cop snorted. "Also by His mercy I hope there is no one in that same bar who knows me and sees me. *Salaam alaikum,* Murphy."

"*Alaikum salaam,* Inspector Erim. At nine tonight."

The cop rang off in a fit of laughter.

Kemal Erim showed up in the Hilton bar at precisely nine o'clock. When he entered the room, eyes twinkling mischievously like a kid's in giddy expectation, and walked forward to introduce himself to Murphy and Kyle-Boyer, seated at a table, Murphy conceded out loud that the lithe, well-muscled young man in dinner jacket was the last person he had expected. For after speaking with Erim that afternoon, he and Kyle-Boyer had set about conjuring up the inspector's image so they would be certain not to miss him that evening and predictably came up with a bad cliché: that Erim of Interpol should be fat and pasha-like, merciless and beady-eyed, sport rumpled Western-style clothes, have ring-encrusted fingers, and be crowned by a fez (this, though they had seen perhaps less than ten of them in the city so far).

"You two are exactly as I expected," Erim told them. "Faces full of anxiety, eyes betelling the nature of your guilt."

"I'm not guilty of anything," Kyle-Boyer remarked, "except perhaps abysmal stupidity. Won't you have a drink, Inspector Erim?"

"No, I have come to eat. Cuisine française. You promised, do you remember? Let us go quickly to the dining room. But tell me, if you are not weighed down by the burden of guilt that needs lightening, why are you walking to Jerusalem?"

Murphy had scribbled his name on the check presented by the bar waiter at a hand clap from Erim, and they were moving almost at a trot out of the bar and toward the chandeliered dining room, the cop between Murphy and Kyle-Boyer, urging them forward with a firm grip on an arm of each of them. Approaching the dining room entry, Erim called out to the maître d'hôtel in Turkish, and the man, heedless of Murphy's assurance that they had a reservation, swept them to a table. Waiters appeared as if by magic, seating them. Erim unfolded his napkin, pronounced himself pleased with the table, barked "Whisky soda; make it three" at the waiters, and then homed in on Murphy and Kyle-Boyer.

"Now, gentlemen, about this guilt for which you are walking to Jerusalem."

"I tried to explain it to you this afternoon, Inspector Erim, as confusing as it sounds. We're walking to Jerusalem, carrying a stolen diamond—although admittedly I don't know where it is right now—to resolve the guilt of some murderer for a crime that nobody but this Israeli named Meyer Alinsky knows about."

"I don't believe you, Murphy." Erim smiled, laying a gentle tap of his fingers on the back of Murphy's hand. A turbaned bar waiter brought their drinks, and the cop swallowed half of his in one gulp, squiggling an ice cube about in his mouth so that it alternately puffed one cheek, then another.

"I don't believe you for several reasons. One is that the French police are quite convinced that Suleiman's Pebble is in the mud at the bottom of the bay of a little village called Saint-Jean-de-Luz—"

"And the other," Kyle-Boyer interrupted, "is that you have no information at all on our Meyer Alinsky."

"Au contraire." Erim clapped for another round of drinks. "We've got a good deal of information on Alinsky."

"You have?" Murphy and Kyle-Boyer spoke in chorus.

Heads turned to look at them, and Kyle-Boyer, trying to be surreptitious, donned his pith helmet and leaned over the table toward Erim. "You have, Inspector?"

"Yes. As I suspected, Alinsky is a trafficker. But his trafficking is most unusual. He controls the ancient penitent routes—useful only to Christians, of course—from Europe through the Muslim lands to the Mother Citadel of the three great religions, the holy city of Jerusalem. He is well known and has contacts on every level, among religious personages and government personages, to expedite the passage of the guilty."

"That is what you have on him?" Murphy demanded incredulously.

"We have much more. But none of it indicates that this omniscient expeditor named Alinsky is a criminal. His is an opportunist, perhaps, a clever Jew who understands more clearly than yourselves the nature of the extra burdens you Christians carry and has determined to turn it to a profit—"

"What extra burdens are you speaking of, Inspector Erim?" Kyle-Boyer demanded testily. "And what profit? Alinsky is paying us to walk to Jerusalem!"

"I don't believe that either, Dr. Kyle-Boyer. But the extra burden of which I speak is Christianity's Manichaean legacy of all-pervasive sin and evil and its accompanying notion of guilt. I do not speak of this from my personal experience, of course, since guilt is not an Islamic cornerstone, but it occurs to me that certainly Christianity could not endure without a briar patch like guilt, nor the briar patch of guilt without a curious religion like Christianity to tend it. After all, what other religion than Christianity has come up with a premise like original sin—to dirty mankind before it had a chance to dirty itself? This, then, is the burden of which I speak. Now, Mr. Murphy, what is it that you are guilty of?"

"Inspector Erim," Murphy pleaded. "I'm not guilty of anything. I mean nothing criminal, certainly. Of course, I do have some things to feel guilty about, like anyone else—personal things, as far as my marriage is concerned and my relationship with my son and what I've done with my life and so on. After all, I'm thirty-seven years old, and when I look back life does begin to seem like a lot of false starts and more than a bit of chaos. . . ."

"But think, Murphy," Erim pursued, narrowing his eyes like the evil pasha he was not supposed to be. "Is there not one thing that you have perhaps not told your priest in the secret darkness of the little box? One little omission graver than a faux pas?"

"Captain Erim, really!" Kyle-Boyer snorted. "If I were not so desperate to convince you of our danger, I should call you an absolute rotter."

"I will get to you in a moment, Dr. Kyle-Boyer. To speak of your guilt also. Ah, here are the drinks."

"Here also are Ben Bokva and Teplitsky," Murphy observed as the waiter put down their glasses. He gestured across the dining room to where the two Israelis, almost unfamiliar in required jackets, were sitting down to dinner with Marilyn Aldrich and Father Bisson. Erim wolfed down his drink and eyed the party at the same time until Teplitsky, seeing them first, nudged Ben Bokva, informing him perhaps that there was a stranger in their midst.

"I recognize the French priest and the girl who

smokes hashish," the cop said, "but who are the two athletic-looking young men?"

"They're the non-gangsters I told you about on the phone this afternoon. They work for Meyer Alinsky."

"I see. They are the henchmen of the expeditor, the tour guides of the penitents. Will I meet them?"

But even as Erim asked the question, Ben Bokva started across the dining room, smiling effusively as he came near their table. "Hello, Frank. Hello, Dr. Kyle-Boyer. How did you spend your day? Teplitsky and I passed the afternoon visiting mosques. This city has thousands of them. They're the most beautiful I've ever seen—"

"Ben Bokva," Murphy blurted aggressively, "this is Captain Kemal Erim. He's with Interpol here in Istanbul."

Ben Bokva seemed unfazed. "*Salaam,* Captain Erim. I am Chaim Ben Bokva of Israel."

"Shalom, Ben Bokva," Erim said, rising to shake the other's hand. "I'm happy to make your acquaintance. Where is the diamond?"

"What diamond?" Ben Bokva asked easily, smiling incomprehension written on his face.

"You know what diamond I'm talking about, don't you, Ben Bokva? I know all the details."

"Oh, all right, Captain. I do not see why you found it necessary to tell him about my diamond, Murphy." Petulantly, like a wronged child, Ben Bokva whipped over one lapel of his jacket to reveal a stickpin with a small gem, presumably a diamond, set into its head. Together, Murphy and Kyle-Boyer gasped at the neatness of the trick. Erim the cop actually snickered.

"I wear it so," Ben Bokva explained, "because I fear it will be stolen. Many Turks are masters of sleight of hand. They are thieves also. This is well known."

"Oh, ho, ho!" The cop clapped his hands in delight. "A very good joke. A very good joke indeed. The Israelis, by the way, are warmongers. This also is well known. But certainly you do not keep your marvelous diamond hidden always on the hindside of your jacket's lapel?"

Ben Bokva smiled sheepishly, actually even blushed. "When we are on the road I conceal it in the crucifix that Murphy carries. Who would think of looking for it there?"

"In a Christian artifact?" Erim bellowed with mirth. "Who indeed? Oh, how I revere such cleverness!" The cop, laughing still, got off a little love tap of a punch to the chest of Ben Bokva, who made a decorous feint, his face wreathed in smiles of apparent pleasure. Murphy and Kyle-Boyer, watching their dance, merely shook their heads in unbelieving dismay.

"But one last thing, Chaim," Erim asked. "Where is the young Englishman, the one who leads the mule of the girl who smokes hashish?"

"You mean Jonathan Whitmore? He's out taking a survey not too far from here in the Street of the Whores. You see, back in Birmingham, England, he was a procurer—"

"For her?" Erim demanded avidly. "For the blond girl who rides the mule?"

"Exactly, Captain Erim."

"Ah-h-h. I begin to see it now. One understands the special nature of this penitential excursion group. And its very humanness, too, what with this Whitmore overcome by the tug of the flesh even as we're standing here. But doubtless it's good for him—this relapse, I mean—since he will be all the more assiduous about his expiation when you return to the road. But the French priest, what of him? A holy man, *n'est-ce pas?*"

"He confesses that he did not love his God enough." Ben Bokva shrugged, a timeless judgment, perhaps, of the Levant on all the madmen of the West.

Erim sniggered; then, convulsed with laughter, he began trading shoulder punches with Ben Bokva; the Israeli and the Turk, much taken with each other, dipped and bobbed beside the table while turbaned waiters from everywhere appeared to enjoy the spectacle of their clowning. But the cop stopped it first, clutching at his stomach. "Enough, Ben Bokva, enough. I must eat. I grow weak from laughter." They hugged each other, each pummeling the other's back, and Erim admonished mischievously, "Work them hard, Chaim. Purge them of their guilt."

"Inshallah, Kemal Erim. If God wills it." Then he threw his eyes toward heaven once more, though he saw only the ceiling of the Hilton, before returning to dine with Teplitsky, Marilyn Aldrich, and Père Bisson. Erim slumped to his seat, wiping tears from his eyes. The ring of waiters clapped their appreciation before disbanding.

"That Ben Bokva is a good fellow," Erim judged. "Some of those Israelis are first-rate chaps. Good fighters, too. Happily the Jew and the Turk are not enemies, as is the case with the Arabs."

"You don't believe us at all, do you, Inspector Erim?" Murphy asked somberly.

"Of course not, Murphy. You're all a bunch of neurotic Christians. Is it so unnatural for a woman to be a prostitute? Or a man to be a procurer? Think of the pleasure they dispense. And in the case of the old priest I say that if a man cannot love his God enough, then it is the fault of God for not providing sufficient enticement. But let us eat. You are paying for my meal, are you not? It was agreed to this afternoon."

"Yes, yes, we're paying," Kyle-Boyer assured him lamely.

"Good. I needed to be certain of that before I start to work." He clapped his hands again, for a menu this time, and set about ordering. Murphy, dispirited by the notion that their rush toward freedom seemed all for naught and might even gain them more of Meyer Alinsky's ire to boot, settled for a sandwich whose innards he merely picked at. Kyle-Boyer toyed with a *salade niçoise* and a glass of wine.

Kemal Erim devastated the victuals of a six-course meal—sausage, terrine of wild duck and Périgord foie gras, sea bass in a mousseline of lobster, rack of lamb with Dauphinois potatoes and stuffed artichoke hearts, a raft of cheeses, fresh strawberries, and sherbet—punctuating the wasted minutes of waiting between courses with the clapping of hands to urge the chefs and waiters to their task. For white wine he chose a Pouilly-Fuissé. For red, two bottles of a Brouilly that he drained to the dregs. After dessert he took cognac, a cigar, and Turkish coffee, pronouncing himself satisfied and emitting a loud burp, while Murphy and Kyle-Boyer sighed with positive relief at the end of the spectacle.

"The cuisine française is the best in all the world, do you not think so, Dr. Kyle-Boyer?"

"Yes, I'm quite partial to it, Inspector Erim. But only when one's spirit is elevated enough to enjoy it."

"And your spirits are rather low, I can see. But it is because of the guilt, of course. What are you guilty of, Kyle-Boyer?"

"I am guilty of nothing!" Kyle-Boyer shrieked in the midst of occasional laughter and the tinkling of silver and glasses. Heads turned yet another time, and Kyle-Boyer, growing embarrassed, hid again beneath his pith helmet. Erim continued to fix him with a demonic stare.

"If you were not guilty, Dr. Kyle-Boyer, you would not be acting this way. But come, I know of a good place to talk of such things."

"Where?"

"A steam room. *Banle*. A Turkish bath. We will go there together and sweat it all out: your guilt and the poisons that such a delight as cuisine française perversely puts into my body."

"I'm not so sure that I—" Kyle-Boyer began and then fell silent after trading a glance with Murphy. No matter where the curiously idiosyncratic cop might lead them, it was best to stick with him, Murphy reasoned; somehow they might convince him of Meyer Alinsky's guilt rather than their own. They left the dining room, with Erim waving effusive good-byes to his new friend, Ben Bokva. Looking back, Murphy just caught sight of the frown of consternation that the two Israelis exchanged as Ben Bokva began folding his napkin.

They melded easily into the madness of Istanbul traffic with Erim at the wheel of his Volkswagen, crossed the Golden Horn at the city's center, and sped inland along the Bosporus to Bebek, a suburb. There, entering a building of vast echoing spaces and clanking doors that the cop referred to as his private club, they descended into an almost sightless netherworld of hissing steam and naked bodies where Murphy guessed the temperature might be in excess of two hundred degrees. They disrobed, surrendered their varied clothes to an attendant, and were admitted by that same person to a small steam-filled room, fecal smelling, that was dimly lit by a single overhead bulb that flickered on and off as if the condensation were shorting it out. Murphy, holding his towel to his nose against the odor, perceived they were not alone; bare kneecaps and hairy calves belonging to perhaps eight other men lined the rows of sitting platforms that ascended one wall; in one corner a bald-headed Turkish classic of a muscle man soaped a naked form stretched out on a slab stone table. Erim greeted the room at large and was acknowledged by a chorus of grunts and wheezings.

"I say, Inspector Erim, how long are we to stay in this inferno?" Kyle-Boyer demanded. Exposed to the liquid heat, he had begun immediately to sweat and now the water rushed out of him, traveled the blubbery folds of his skin, and fell to the stone floor with audible splashes.

"As long as we can bear, Dr. Kyle-Boyer," Erim answered, taking a seat on the lowest row of platforms and inviting Murphy and Kyle-Boyer to join him. "The steam, long endured, is cathartic and purgative. You will feel cleansed and lightened, eager to divest yourself of your secret guilt as well."

"I have no secret guilt, Erim," Kyle-Boyer said stonily. "Only an abiding passion to convince you that Meyer Alinsky is a fiend and we are in danger of being killed by him."

"I do not believe this, Kyle-Boyer. Alinsky is helping you. You are paying him to help you. This I understand." Erim's voice grew louder with anger, his finger jabbing the steam before Kyle-Boyer's nose. "I am here to help you too, because I know that you want to be helped. That is why I have brought you here. You Christians have confessionals, but you ought to have steam baths instead, a collective place that simulates the Christian Hell where a man can sit naked and sweating before his God and properly expiate. Does this place not seem like Hell to you?"

"Quite. But I have nothing to expiate, Inspector."

"You are guilty of something!" the cop screamed, whipping his towel about Kyle-Boyer's neck from his sitting position and pulling the abortionist's head toward him.

Kyle-Boyer began gasping for breath and, putting both hands against Erim, tried to pull away, pleading in a strangled voice, "No! No! Not guilty. . . . Erim!"

"Erim, stop this madness!" Murphy raged. He stood up, preparing in his anger to try grabbing the towel away from the cop, when he was suddenly apprehended by two naked men who dropped nimbly from the platform above him. Within seconds the others descended and clustered around, and Murphy, despite his fury at the witless Erim, found it in himself to be rueful in recognizing the name of the game. Erim had evidently planned this all along; all the naked sweating Turks served the Interpol cop.

"Fat Christian pig!" Erim shrieked, pulling Kyle-Boyer to his feet with a sharp tug on the neck collar of his towel and dragging him across the room to the

slab stone table that was readily vacated by its soap-
sudsed occupant. With the aid of the muscled swab-
ber, Kyle-Boyer was bound prone on the flat surface, looking like a walrus beached atop a rock. The
cop knelt on the floor beside the abortionist's head,
knotting and unknotting the collar, so that his muscles bulged and his face seemed apoplecic from the
effort, and screeching his demand that Kyle-Boyer
confess.

"To what, you damned Turk rotter?" Kyle-Boyer
rasped when Erim relinquished pressure so he might
speak. "Confess to what? I've done nothing! And
don't dare call me a pig! You're a pig, do you hear!
I had but a single salad tonight, a thimbleful of
food compared to the avalanche you shoveled inside
yourself. It was a disgusting spectacle. If I had not
thought that we needed your help so badly, I should
have left immediately!"

The rebuke outraged Erim. Twisting the knot tighter
still, he barked out a command to the muscle man
in Turkish, and Murphy, straining anew against the
grips of his two captors (who became three as another man threw his arm about Murphy's neck),
watched incredulously as the attendant doused a towel
in a bucket of water, twirled the ends to form a whip,
and began flailing the pink-tinted expanse of Kyle-
Boyer's great body with quick, stinging slaps. Kyle-
Boyer roared with the pain each time Erim undid
the neck collar, and gasped and rattled when it was
tightened again. In the dimness Murphy perceived
that the naked circle of Erim's men were in dead
earnest about Kyle-Boyer's guilt. Not one of them
smiled; it was not a pleasure palace for sadists apparently. Also he saw that two other figures, drawn perhaps by Kyle-Boyer's screams, had eased open the
door and entered the clouds of steam in the room.

"Erim, in the name of God, stop it!" Murphy ranted
at the cop. "With that beating and this heat and
choking him like that, he'll die of a heart attack!"

"He will not die until he tells me of his guilt."

Erim grunted. "That I can promise you. I am skilled in such matters. But perhaps you can help him, Murphy, since it pains you to see him suffer so much, by telling me of your guilt."

"I am guilty of nothing, Erim." Murphy spoke hopelessly as Erim unleashed the collar to permit a brief issue of Kyle-Boyer's screaming.

In the same moment the voice of one of the two figures who had just entered the room and come close to Murphy hissed out at him, "The wine scandal, you *tuckus!* Tell him about the wine scandal!" Murphy looked down, checking. It was Ben Bokva.

"All right, Erim, I'll tell you."

"What? What is it, Murphy?" the cop demanded, releasing Kyle-Boyer, though the muscle man continued to beat him, and bounding across the steamy darkness to stand before Murphy.

"I violated the *appelation controlée* laws back in France."

"How did you do this?"

"I artificially elevated the alcohol content in one particular year's entire vintage of Château de Rastignac."

"Ah, I see. And people became drunk because of this and fell down in the streets, and there were ensuing fist fights and automobile accidents. Am I right?"

"Yes," Murphy answered, because it seemed easiest.

"Were you discovered, Murphy?"

"Yes. The government put us out of business."

"Good!" Erim enthused, a positive relief flowing out of him. "Good! It is very wrong to disturb the normal lawful and orderly tendencies of the populace." Then he apparently told the assemblage of Murphy's crime, a long several minutes of difficult explanation, punctuated often by questioning, until everyone seemed satisfied that Murphy had indeed paid his debt to society. The three who held him released him, and Murphy felt a surprising round of approving hand pats on his shoulders; perhaps they were all police. Then Erim discerned Ben Bokva in the semidarkness. "Chaim, how did you come here? Did you hear? Murphy has confessed!"

"I heard, Kemal Erim, but he was being stubborn of course. As is Dr. Kyle-Boyer. The English are that way. . . . Kyle-Boyer," Ben Bokva called out. "Tell Captain Erim of your profession as abortionist."

"Abortionist?" Kyle-Boyer demanded, gasping out between his screams even as his tormentors continued to flail away. "Is that what you want me to confess? That's poppycock. Utterly elementary stuff. That's not what I'm guilty of at all."

"What are you guilty of?" Erim screeched. "You will tell me or I will beat you myself!"

"Yes, beat me, Erim! That's the stuff. Beat me to make me tell!"

The cop needed no urging. He ran to Kyle-Boyer, wet another towel, and began whipping the top half of the Englishman's body while Kyle-Boyer screamed doubly loud and for more. Murphy looked on in head-shaking disbelief. "Good God, he likes it!"

"Chaim"—Teplitsky spoke in English—"he'll never tell this way. And he might die. If he dies, Meyer will absolutely murder us."

"Kemal Erim! Kemal Erim!" Ben Bokva begged, starting toward the scene of torture. "Don't do this! He's an overweight man in poor physical condition. What will you do if he dies?"

"Report it as a heart attack. They are not un-known in Turkey." Erim panted from the effort of his punishing. "Now stand back!" he ordered in English, then spoke again in Turkish. Almost instantly the arms came out again to contain Murphy and Teplitsky, who stood beside him. Four men jumped through the fog at Ben Bokva, who knew better than to resist.

They watched for minutes longer through the seemingly interminable beating until Kyle-Boyer's screaming fell off into a long moaning "Oh-h-h" and he finally nodded his head in compliance with Erim's thousandth request that he confess to his crime.

"Mum . . . Mum . . ." came the barely audible words from Kyle-Boyer's lips.

"Mum? What does this mean, Murphy? Come here."

Murphy was released and went near to Kyle-Boyer's head, wincing at the tortured wheezing of air that rushed in and out of him.

"Mum. . . . I went to a flicker the night Mum died. . . . She fell from her . . . wheelchair . . . died of concussion. . . . My fault. . . ."

"That is his crime?" Erim demanded in astonishment. "For that he walks to Jerusalem? That is madness. It was an accident. That is not against the law of any country. Does he not understand this?"

But Kyle-Boyer had passed out, and after telling the obviously disappointed naked group of Kyle-Boyer's transgression, Erim bade them good-bye and everyone departed in disgust.

They roused the abortionist with cold water and, still dripping sweat, got him dressed and carried him out into the now-chilly night, placing him in the back of the Citroën. On the way back to the city, while Ben Bokva talked of calling a physician to check him out, Kyle-Boyer seemed to revive.

"Murphy," he croaked from the back seat, "do you think all of this crusading is somehow toughening us up? Making us more manly somehow?"

"Perhaps," was Murphy's only judgment.

"Well, I do. This time I did not defecate in my trousers or anywhere. I'm quite sure of that."

"That's correct," Murphy said. "You didn't."

"I think, Frank, we shall yet end up throwing a good fuck into this madman, Meyer Alinsky."

Ben Bokva and Teplitsky exchanged a quick glance; then Ben Bokva spoke. "Such a thing is not possible, Dr. Kyle-Boyer. You must not think of such things any longer."

20

A short chapter of curious reflections in Asia Minor

THEY LEFT ISTANBUL, marching in their usual orderly line away from the entrance of the Hilton, one hundred forty-two days after Murphy had joined the Fourteenth Crusade in Normandy, and began plodding eastward through the dust of still-warm days toward the mountainous interior vastness of Turkey. They were well into Muslim lands now where idle, squatting men peered at them from the stoops of village mosques and the recorded voices of muezzins sonorously chanted at them three times daily from loudspeakers affixed to the tops of minarets. Women worked in the fields tending the poppy crop, and after Bursa—the last big town they would see for nearly a month and where they turned south toward the coast to avoid the real ranges and peaks of the country's center—the roads were unpaved, more often than not, and nearly empty of vehicles.

For the first time Murphy began to feel the real, irresistible tug of the physical place Jerusalem, now nine hundred miles off, and once again, despite the captivity of Monique and Jean-Philippe that was his worried, almost total preoccupation, he was overcome by a gnawing speculation to know what secret Alinsky kept hidden there.

It was Alinsky himself who reprimed that curiosity. For after Istanbul the fiend turned benign again (relief, perhaps, that he had at last gotten his crusaders safely out of Europe and into the Levant where Jerusalem was almost visible), and Murphy began gingerly to concede to himself that perhaps the man's purposes were not entirely fraught with malice. Alinsky began sending weekly personal letters to each member of the pilgrimage—even to Gervais, Ricard, and Lebel, who still followed along in the station wagon and utility van—relaxed, even humorous missives that urged them in general to keep up their morale and reminded them that the final distance was but a sprint, that the riches of Alinsky were waiting to rain down upon them, that their purpose was noble beyond comprehension.

More particularly there was something for everyone: pious anecdotes and weekly photographs attesting the progress of the orphanage abuilding for Père Bisson; relays of back-home Birmingham gossip and untold variations of the universal traveling-salesman jokes for Marilyn Aldrich and Jonathan Whitmore; cheering news and occasional photographs of the sad-eyed Rifka for her husband, Gervais; weekly installments of a learned thesis of hormone deficiency in the human male for Austin Kyle-Boyer and proposals for a plan of treatment to which Kyle-Boyer, despite what he knew of Alinsky that the others did not, responded eagerly, praising Alinsky's beneficence; a continually implemented gay guide to Turkey, Syria, and Jordan for Ricard and Lebel, plus the inclusion of a weekly homophile newsletter from Paris.

The letters to Murphy dealt only with the subject of Monique and Jean-Philippe, and as time passed they grew more and more incredible, leaving Murphy to surmise that on their own home ground in Jerusalem the Alinskys—mother and son—were extremely charming people, as they must needs be to win over his somber offspring. For Jean-Philippe and Meyer Alinsky were getting on famously now since Alinsky had taught Murphy's son how to shoot a gun, and twice they had gone together up to Galilee to hunt wolves. The accompanying photographs, when they arrived, were simply astounding. If the letters were not postmarked in Israel, Murphy might easily believe that Meyer Alinsky and Jean-Philippe were in the South Dakota hills where he had been taken to hunt as a boy. For Jean-Philippe, tall for his age, was dressed in American jeans and a T-shirt and wore a cowboy hat on his head; he smiled effusively and brandished a Winchester rifle at the camera. Meyer Alinsky looked like an Iowa dirt farmer on a hunting trip; he wore baggy khakis and a wide-brimmed straw hat and stood beside Jean-Philippe with a curiously inane grin on his face that Murphy could only interpret as pure pleasure. He looked balanced, also, if such a thing were possible with a rifle in one hand and a Budweiser six-pack in the other. Behind the two, shimmering in the Israel sun, was the clincher: an old American Chrysler Imperial with Iowa plates, rotted rocker panels, no hubcaps, presumably broken mufflers, and a gun rack across the rear window. In Turkey, Murphy grew dizzy at the incongruity of it all.

Then he grew angry at Alinsky's rebuff in another letter that what Jean-Philippe needed most in the world to make him a decent, compassionate human being was a father who would take him in hand and shape him, instead of sitting on the sidelines, as Murphy had done, speculating on how the young man had gotten to be the way he was. He, Meyer Alinsky, had he remarried after the death of his wife, would have been proud to have had just such a son. He intended to take over as surrogate father until Murphy got to Jerusalem, and Murphy, in that sense, might consider the pilgrimage doubly beneficial to him.

Murphy's return letter to Meyer Alinsky was one

of self-justification for his inability to function as a proper father figure. He explained his basic nihilism and how it had led him into the valley of the drunks, between peaks of great energy and achievement, and proposed that what Jean-Philippe had suffered from mainly was the lack of any real consistency in his relationship with his father. So what could be expected? Also he admonished Alinsky to leave his son alone and to stop manipulating him into becoming a young Iowan so that Alinsky might relive vicariously some part of his murky past life. One Murphy being used for Alinsky's purposes at a time was quite enough.

Alinsky's reply was a curt telegram: THE LION DOES NOT TELL THE LION TAMER WHAT TO DO.

Then, as if the word *lion* had triggered a switch in Alinsky's mind, the next series of photograph-bearing letters came from East Africa, where Alinsky had taken Jean-Philippe big-game hunting in Kenya and Tanzania. Murphy merely shook his appalled head at the photos. In one, taken near Nairobi, Jean-Philippe and his new father stood in smiling camaraderie with their arms wrapped about each other's shoulders before the carcass of a rhino that they agreed they had brought down simultaneously. Later, from Tanzania, came proof of the kills of a leopard and an ibix, two nondescript antelopes, and another rhino. The scorecard by the time of the second rhino was Jean-Philippe de Rastignac Murphy three, Meyer Elkanah Alinsky two, with a split decision on the first rhino. Murphy was made further incredulous by the fact that everywhere, in every photo—dressed in ceremonial native robes, swimming in the Indian Ocean near Mombasa, riding in a Land-Rover, or astride a camel in one of the game preserves—Jean-Philippe, who had never smiled in Murphy's memory except at someone else's demise, was aglow with well-tanned happiness. The change was uncanny. Always Alinsky and Murphy's son were together. Back in Israel they played tennis, rode horses on the beach

at Caesarea, played golf, went to movies, waved
from the deck of one of Meyer's tankers leaving
Haifa Bay. . . .

In time Murphy's initial anger at Alinsky's manipu-
lation of his son turned to pure vile jealousy over
the marvelous time the two of them were obviously
having together. Meyer Alinsky, besides purportedly
corrupting everything in the West, had even managed
to undermine the single fixed quantum of the universe
that Murphy felt he might always depend upon:
Jean-Philippe's seething and relentless animosity toward the world at large.

But with Monique, who had become the special ward
of old Rachel Alinsky, it was possibly worse. Murphy
could not say exactly when her wall of reserve and
fear had collapsed in the face of those charming
Alinsky people, but it had certainly fallen by the
time of Jean-Philippe's safari to East Africa. Since
that time, in numerous Kodak snapshots, she smiled
incessantly at frequent cocktail parties on the main
veranda of Alinsky's palace that looked down on the
sandstone tints of the Jerusalem hills. And from the
occasional inclusion of a brief note from Monique in
Alinsky's letters, it seemed after a while that she
had come to consider that she and Jean-Philippe
were indeed houseguests, as Alinsky had originally
suggested, and not prisoners at all. An unbelievable
testimony to that notion came at the end of November when the crusaders began encountering the first
real frosts on the plains of Anatolia. Then Meyer
lent his mother and Monique the Boeing jet for a
shopping trip to New York, where the two women
stayed ten days in a suite at the Plaza Hotel. In
addition to their buying binge (more and finer clothes
than Monique had ever owned or thought of, charged
in a single week to Meyer Alinsky) the two had time
for sightseeing, theater, and the opera. There were
whole packets of photos, sent in a box, that were
taken in Times Square, at the UN, in Chinatown,
on the Bowery, on Wall Street, at the Statue of

Liberty, on the Staten Island ferry. The most galling of all was taken in front of the entrance of a place called Lincoln Center, of whose previous existence Murphy had not known. There, for an evening at the opera, Monique and Meyer's mother in long dresses posed with two men appropriately aged for each woman before a large wall mural that Monique wrote was painted by Chagall, who had done the Paris Opéra ceiling. (The letter included a barbed reminder that Murphy had taken his wife only once to the opera in Paris in all the time they lived in Vardelle-sur-Lac.) But for Murphy, who decided he had fallen in love again with Monique during one memorable night in an obscure Greek hotel, his jealousy at the sight of the tall and handsome man who stood beside her was bottomless. To himself, marching miserably in a monk's robe across an Asia Minor that turned steadily more chilly, they seemed larger than life, a couple seized by the camera's eye in an incredible instant of perfection like a *Paris-Match* advertisement, and he thought for a while, by way of appeasing his frustration, to smash the crucifix he carried on anything handy, except that Ben Bokva and Teplitsky might come forward from where they lingered behind in their Citroën and smash him in real earnest for his trouble. Instead, he compensated during one afternoon's march when he could no longer control his anger by kicking in sandaled feet at a rock ledge outcropping beside the road and promptly broke the big toe of his right foot. Then, while Kyle-Boyer set the toe, he penned a furious letter to Rachel Alinsky in Jerusalem, demanding to know about the handsome man, and was abashed some days later to receive one of her Hallmark "Thinking of You" cards with the simple retort: *Relax, Frankie, those guys were two queens we hired from an escort service for the evening. Keep up the good work and watch out for rocks on the road. Rachel Alinsky.*

Between the New York trip and until the time they reached the port city of Antalya—hastily crossing the snow-laden passes of the western Taurus range to get there in time for Christmas Day and a banquet with Meyer Alinsky, who was to fly in from Israel—Murphy was nearly inundated at every *poste restante* with a constant, mind-numbing photographic chronicle of the Meyer—Jean-Philippe, Rachel—Monique mutual ecstasy that Alinsky sought to convince him was real and above suspicion. The chronicle was by degrees admittedly wearing him down to the point that the rabidity of his protest against Alinsky no longer sounded convincing to him, and he found himself conjuring up plausible excuses—the very same ones that Alinsky himself had proposed earlier—to explain away the litter of corpses in the wake of the crusade's passing. And Kyle-Boyer, his stalwart and outraged friend, proved no real help to Murphy in bolstering his anger, especially after the day in mid-December when Murphy found the ex-abortionist reading a letter from Alinsky and blubbering like a baby beside the evening campfire.

"What's wrong, Austin?" Murphy asked him.

"It's Mum, Frank." Kyle-Boyer sobbed as he handed a photograph to Murphy. "They've all gone and visited Mum's grave in Birmingham."

Murphy scanned the photo in the firelight and shook his head in disbelief. Standing somberly about a headstone in a crowded cemetery beneath an ugly English winter sky were Monique and Jean-Philippe, Meyer Alinsky and his mother, and a man in clergyman's garb who must have been the parish rector. The grave was heaped with fresh flowers. The letter reported that Meyer and Jean-Philippe had flown to England to intercept Monique and Rachel Alinsky on their return from New York, and all together they had gone to pay tribute to Kyle-Boyer's mother in Birmingham. Kyle-Boyer had collapsed. Marilyn Aldrich cried also, and Jonathan Whitmore found it in himself to sniffle. As did Father Bisson, who, sick now and chilled excessively by nighttime temperatures that hovered around freezing, raised himself on one elbow from his sleeping bag and blessed the name of Meyer Alinsky through the chattering of his teeth. Murphy, who listened to the eerie whistle of the wind through the pine forests about them, neither sniffled nor sobbed nor blessed the name of Alinsky. Instead, he worked gingerly at removing one of the pair of boots he had taken to wearing because of the slush and cold from around his splinted toe and decided he was either going mad or being driven there by Meyer Alinsky.

"I'm so happy they brought glads to the grave," Kyle-Boyer said. "Mum did so love glads. Frank, I simply don't think we're in any danger from Meyer. I think we let some paranoid fears get the best of us back there apiece, don't you?"

"We'll know when we get to Jerusalem," Murphy said, curling into his sleeping bag. "But I suppose the man has a certain undeniable charm."

21

Christmas in Antalya

PÈRE BISSON DIED in accordance with Meyer Alinsky's expectation, two days after Christmas in the city hospital at Antalya.

The old priest succumbed to that bane of ancient crusaders, dysentery, and even with modern remedies the curse sapped his already feeble strength so that in the beginning of his illness he could only hold onto the pommel of the mule saddle and sway back and forth in odorific misery. When he fell off the first time Ben Bokva ordered him transferred to the rear of Gervais's station wagon, and for the next few days Marilyn Aldrich went to sit on the tailgate every few hours and spoon-feed him canned soup until he could swallow no more.

Then the pilgrims revolted for the second time on Bisson's behalf, for it was obvious that Ben Bokva and Teplitsky did not care particularly if he survived or not; they refused to march another step until Bisson was taken forward to the Antalya hospital so he might be given sulfides and fed intravenously. The wrathful Israelis consulted Alinsky in Jerusalem, and he gave his assent and also agreed that Kyle-Boyer as doctor might accompany the priest,

267

on condition that the remaining pilgrims keep walking.

The remaining ones—Marilyn, Jonathan, and Murphy—arrived in Antalya on Christmas Eve. Snow was falling on the walled Turkish town beside the sea but was unable to stick because the ground was too warm. The place was glum and sad, Murphy thought, its palm trees foreign and incongruous against the snow, and he was suddenly very homesick for the beautiful Christmases of France. The fires that burned in every house against what was a monstrous cold for that eastern Mediterranean city belched smoke that hung just above the roofs, and carriage horses tied in long lines along one broad avenue snorted and stomped and blew clouds of breath smoke into the air and were all covered over with identical funeral-looking gray blankets.

At the hospital, where they stopped first, Bisson was clearly dying. With a surprising technology that Murphy had not expected, the old priest was being fed by tubing and correspondingly drained. Kyle-Boyer pronounced the doctor in attendance first rate, and also the team of nurses, one of whom entered the private room to perfume the place with an atomizer from time to time and wipe at the sweat on Père Bisson's face. They stayed at the bedside for perhaps two hours while the priest smiled dimly at his fellow pilgrims and held hands with Marilyn Aldrich, who whispered to him in the pidgin French she had picked up on the march and made it known with frequent eye signs that Bisson's hands were cold as ice. Jonathan Whitmore tried singing Christmas carols, then gave up and instead drank arrack from a flask with Kyle-Boyer, who grew intolerably despondent and at the same time medically analytical about the fact that Bisson had certainly ridden his last mile. After a time, when the hospital staff requested they leave, they were taken along with Gervais, Ricard, and Lebel to spend the night in a heated house on the outskirts of town that Alinsky had rented for the festivities of Christmas Day.

On Christmas morning the snow ended. Christmas dinner arrived at the local jetport, flown in from La Tour d'Argent in Paris and accompanied by a chef and his helper. Meyer Alinsky showed up some two hours later, in time to distribute presents to everyone, help trim the tree, and carve the Christmas goose at the head of the table. There were ten of them to dinner, including the two Israelis and Gervais and his crew, and despite the general gloom over Father Bisson, Alinsky held forth and entertained them with hilarious stories of the ghosts of Christmases past in Israel, France, Italy, and elsewhere (but never America) until, with the help of lots of wine, their mood became buoyant and silly, and even Murphy, who harbored Alinsky a massive grudge over Monique and Jean-Philippe, felt himself capitulating. Simply put, it was almost impossible to find a focal point on which to turn the hatred he knew he ought to feel. Alinsky kept so many anomalies spinning in complicated orbit at any one time that his victims, if they could actually be called that, were always left muted and dazed. Witness Monique and Jean-Philippe, who were forcibly taken to Jerusalem to be seduced into having the happiest times of their respective lives.

After dinner they sipped cognac and sang Christmas carols in French and English for a time, until a collective recall of the fact of Father Bisson's dying only two miles off in the hospital silenced them all. They sat, unspeaking for long minutes, staring through a French-windowed wall of the house into a garden courtyard where the day was sad with foggy drizzle. Then Alinsky, sighing deeply, produced a group of blown-up photos that testified to the progress of Bisson's orphanage in Saint-Aubin, back in Normandy. The work had gone quickly and it seemed an agreeable place, Murphy thought, traditional-looking on the outside so it blended easily with the centuries-old buildings on either side of it, yet thoroughly modern within, and he had no trouble imagining it filled with regimented little boys in short pants and knee socks and administered by a group of nuns that Alinsky revealed he had been able to wheedle out of Bisson's bishop—something Bisson had not been able to do in thirty years of trying.

"My mother and Mme. Murphy spent almost a week in Saint-Aubin working out the interior decoration," Meyer Alinsky said to no one in particular. "I think they've done a pretty fine job. But their biggest problem was trying to decide on the uniforms for the boys. Mother wanted some kind of fancy jump suits, but Monique wanted the traditional shorts and smocks, and it seemed to me at the end of the last bout, Murphy, that your wife won out."

"Oh, I think the short pants are so nice," Marilyn Aldrich said. "They're so French. One of the things I always loved about crossin' over to France was seein' the little kids in their uniforms marchin' along polite as you please. But, Meyer, how did your mother and Frank's wife get together?"

"I'm the matchmaker, Marilyn." Alinsky smiled sheepishly. "You see, after Monique caught up with Frank back there in Greece during October, I invited her to come to Jerusalem for a few weeks and bring Jean-Philippe along. I knew she was burned up at Frank for signing on with the crusade, and I thought if I got a chance to speak with her for a while I might be able to straighten things out. What absolutely amazed me was the fact that she accepted!" Alinsky threw his arms toward heaven at the marvel of it. "And what's more, when she got to Israel we all got on so well I convinced her to stay until Murph shows up. Then we'll put the icing on the cake, I'll bet."

"Maybe," Murphy snapped.

He was angry with Alinsky's fabrication, but angrier still with Kyle-Boyer, his co-conspirator, who gave credence to the lie by seeming oblivious to it. Instead he gazed on, weepy-eyed, at the gilt-framed photograph he had received for a Christmas present of two Alinskys and two de Rastignac Murphys paying homage at Mum's grave.

"Where are Monique and Jean-Philippe now?" Murphy demanded.

"They've gone to Bethlehem with Mother for Christmas, Murph."

"Oh, say, isn't that a treat!" Kyle-Boyer enthused. "You know, I've never made much fuss about being a Christian and all that business, but the one thing I've always thought I'd like to do was go to Bethlehem and watch the festivities. It must feel decidedly more like Christmas there than it does here in Turkey."

"Meyer, do you suppose we'll be able to go there after we reach Jerusalem?" Marilyn Aldrich asked. "It belongs to the Jews now, doesn't it?"

"Since nineteen sixty-seven, it does." Alinsky spoke. "But sure, we'll arrange a side trip for you."

Madness, Murphy thought, extending his glass toward Jonathan Whitmore, who harbored the cognac bottle, for more of the fiery liquid: Monique and Jean-Philippe, bona fide hostages in Israel, being envied for their good fortune in making it to Bethlehem for Christmas. Madness. He raised his eyes and saw Alinsky looking toward him from across the room. Only Meyer's face was not triumphant, as Murphy might have expected, scoring its victory over other people's minds. Instead he looked contrite, pleading even, as if he were begging Murphy to join in the vast Alinsky game because really it meant no harm to anyone. Murphy decided that if he had a gun he would have plugged Meyer Alinsky right between the eyes, lest the man live to confound him yet another time. . . .

They napped for perhaps an hour, sodden with food and alcohol, dozing off in the room's overstuffed Victorian sofas and chairs, until the chef woke them for a snack of coffee and quiche Lorraine in the late afternoon. Then Alinsky and his pilgrims walked two miles to the hospital through the city. Christmas meant nothing to the Turks and it was business as usual, only despondently so, for it was snowing again, and slushy as before, and merchants and shoppers alike looked too cold to haggle.

In his private room Père Bisson was slipping steadily, and though he did not seem to recognize Alinsky at first, he did in fact realize that the photographs Meyer carried were of the nearly completed project of a good portion of his life's work. Kyle-Boyer was at great pains for the old priest to understand that his benefactor was at the bedside, and when at last he was able to comprehend, tears rolled down the crevices in his cheeks and he took Alinsky's hands in his own pitifully weak grip and pressed them to his lips in gratitude.

Everyone was crying now. Marilyn Aldrich and Jonathan wiped their faces on the sleeves of their robes, and Kyle-Boyer blubbered away fitfully into a huge handkerchief. Alinsky cried too, more perhaps from some habit of easy sentimentality then actual loss, for Bisson, after all, had not been his boon companion in the daily march of the crusaders but only a paid functionary, a purchased penitent. Murphy found it in him to weep also, tears of sorrowing certainty but also of the hopeless impotence he felt, until he looked up once at Meyer Alinsky and his sense of irony regained quick control of him. Meyer was gazing not at the dying Father Bisson on the bed beside him but at his own reflection in a small mirror above the sink in a corner of the room, turning his head in contemplation of the well-tanned face, drenched with tears, that looked as pious and God-struck as a Greco saint hanging on the walls of the Prado. Except for Murphy, the others seemed oblivious of the bizarre narcissism, until Alinsky, tired perhaps of gauging his own capacity for sorrowing, tore his eyes from the mirror, kissed the old priest reverently on the forehead, and issued the abrupt command: "Let's leave now, people."

On the way out, Alinsky, forever tipping, dispensed the usual envelopes of his gratitude to the Turkish doctor and two nurses who were on constant standby, urging them to look after old Bisson energetically. Impulsively, before the outer doors of the building were reached, Marilyn Aldrich threw her arms about Alinsky's neck and hugged him tightly. "Oh, Meyer, you're the most wonderful man in the whole world!"

At the bottom of the hospital steps the emotional winds shifted abruptly and Meyer Alinsky was into it again with the pilgrims over their refusal to continue on to Jerusalem the very next morning.

"But, Meyer, we're stayin' on with Padre Bisson until he kicks off," Jonathan Whitmore told him, frankly astonished at the notion that Alinsky did not expect as much.

"Listen, folks," Alinsky urged. "Let's not ruin a nice Christmas day. I'm not going through that bit one more time about what it says in your contracts, but it certainly never said anything about taking time off for a deathwatch. Now, Father Bisson is obviously going to die, and that's very sad, but there's nothing we can do about it. I can promise you that when he dies every detail will be taken care of and he'll receive a proper burial here in Turkey. He would have wanted it that way anyhow. There's historic precedent, after all. In the time of the actual Crusades many pilgrims who died were buried along the way. At least they were that much closer to the Holy Land."

"That's all well and good," Murphy said, "but Bisson specifically asked to be returned to Normandy in the event of his death and also that a funeral Mass be read over his coffin."

"Look, Murph," Alinsky fumed, "what the fuck do you think I am, the master mortician of the Western world? Where the hell am I going to find a Catholic priest to say Mass in the middle of

Turkey? No, you people are going to break camp tomorrow morning. There's no waiting around. That old fart could hang on for months."

"You go and bugger yourself, Alinsky!" Kyle-Boyer suggested. "We've been walking across a good deal of Europe and another good bit of Asia Minor for whatever reason with that 'old fart,' as you now so contemptuously call him, for the past half year while you've been sitting on your hinder drinking beer in Jerusalem. I, for one, will be in attendance during Father Bisson's last moments and shall also feel privileged to attend a funeral Mass in honor of that saintly gentleman."

"Oh, yeah?" Alinsky retorted. "And where are you going to find a priest to say that Mass?"

"You're goin' to find him, Meyer," Jonathan Whitmore assured him. "You've turned the whole world ass end up for the benefit of us here pilgrims in the past. You even brought the bloody Pope out of hidin'. Findin' a padre ought to be a cinch for you."

"I'm a medical doctor," Kyle-Boyer said, "and I don't give Bisson more than two days at the outside. That's all the time we need remain here, and plenty of time for you to turn up a priest from the filing cabinet of functionaries you keep on tap all about the world."

"Yeah? What do you know about anything, you abortionist schmuck, you?" Alinsky hurled furiously, throwing his arms in the air so a button popped from his sheepskin jacket. "I've said it before and I'll say it again: The lions don't tell the lion tamer what to do. All right, you get your two days, but if he isn't dead by that time, you break camp. Right?"

"Wrong," Murphy told him. "We stay until he dies, and we attend his Mass before we leave. And lastly, we see off his coffin on a commercial airline bound for France from the local airport."

"Drop dead, Murph!"

"Then I'm not walking another yard, Alinsky."

"Nor I," said Jonathan Whitmore, Marilyn Aldrich, and Kyle-Boyer in unison.

They had Alinsky again; Murphy saw it in an instant. Like the time they threw the first revolt over Bisson, presumably against the crooked preacher Marfeau, and dragged the real mastermind into the open. With Whitmore and Kyle-Boyer, Murphy had begun a barely perceptible advance toward Alinsky. And Alinsky, although a big man, had begun a barely perceptible retreat. Opposite the hospital across the narrow slushy roadway was a low wall that ringed the cliffs above the wintry Mediterranean. It came to Murphy that the three of them—each in better physical condition from all their walking than they probably had ever been in their lives before—might simply throw the beerdrinking Israeli over the edge. There were no Ben Bokvas or Teplitskys to strong-arm them now; Meyer Alinsky, relaxed in the Christmas company of his crusaders, had unwittingly walked into a trap he had not foreseen.

"All right, friends," Alinsky conceded, smiling whimsically. "I agree. Until he dies. And I supply the priest and plane trip home."

"Very good, Alinsky," Kyle-Boyer said. "Only don't attempt something expedient like pulling out the catheter tubes or the intravenous feeding to hasten his departure. In fact an additional clause of our agreement should read that one of us, not one of your fellows, should be on duty with the nurse in the room at all times until the end."

"Agreed," Alinsky said quietly, shrugging his shoulders and turning to stare out at two forlorn fishing boats that crept into the harbor below.

Whitmore walked away to join Marilyn, still on the hospital steps, so that when Alinsky turned back, sighing heavily at the variety of endless caprice that seemed to beset his crusade, he was left standing with his two main adversaries.

"You know, Murphy, you could have thrown me over that wall if you'd really wanted to. I mean, you have all the reasons, since I have Monique and Jean-Philippe in custody in Israel. Why didn't you?"

"I thought about it, Meyer. I really did. But after coming all this way it doesn't make any sense if you're willing to compromise a bit. I've got to make it to Jerusalem and you've got to be there so I can find out why the trip was so important."

"I also feel the same way, Alinsky." Kyle-Boyer spoke up. "That business of Mum's grave threw me off balance for a time, but it's easy to see now from your attitude toward Père Bisson's dying that it was merely a theatrical gesture and therefore, truly, I should really enjoy the spectacle of your body bouncing off the rocks on the way down to the water. But if that happened my curiosity would never be appeased. You're an improbably strange fellow, Meyer Alinsky."

They walked in silence back to the house and picked over the remains of Christmas dinner, and Meyer Alinsky departed after a time, deciding that Jerusalem was the best place to get his hands on a priest for Father Bisson's funeral Mass.

Père Bisson, like Alinsky, had a secret of his own that they discovered two days later, when he died his natural death in bed as Kyle-Boyer had predicted he would.

He spoke and obviously understood English as well as any of them.

The fact came to light in the last minutes of his life when his four fellow pilgrims, summoned from the house perhaps an hour before by the doctor, clustered about his bed to wait out the obvious. There, while Bisson lay gasping for breath and Marilyn Aldrich wiped steadily at the sweat that broke out on his face in evidence of his agony, Kyle-Boyer mused out loud to Murphy, "It's at times like this, Frank, that I find it easy to make a case for euthanasia."

"No, Austin, my son, never that. . . . Death is the province of God alone." The words, only slightly

accented and rising up from the thin blue lips of
the near cadaver of Bisson, shocked Murphy away
from the bed and almost onto the floor.

"You speak English!"

"Yes, Frank. Since I am a little boy." Bisson gasped
out the words. "Oh, how awake I feel now! It is
surely the end for me."

"But if you speaks English, Father"—Marilyn
Aldrich burst into tears—"that means you know I
was a hooker back in Birmingham, 'n' that I could
always walk, 'n' that me 'n' Johnny ain't married."

Bisson smiled, almost bemusedly. "Many find a
priest an embarrassment to have about, no? It
seemed more Christian to remain silent. . . ."

He smiled again; then he drifted off for perhaps
a minute, his chest heaving lightly beneath the bed-
covers, while Marilyn cried bottomlessly at the sudden cruelty of her exposé and Murphy, Kyle-Boyer,
and Jonathan merely smiled ruefully to each other
at the glorious and unrelenting ironies of their life
together. When the priest came to, it was with a start,
and he stared at Murphy, his eyes wide with terror
as if there were something momentous and undone
just remembered in the last moments. "Frank! Did
the Jew really build the orphanage in Saint-Aubin?"

"Yes, Father. We've seen many photographs of it."

"Ah-h-h-h-h." The judgment came forth as Bisson's
life ebbed away like air being slowly expelled from a
bellows. "How strange . . . the instruments God
chooses for our works. . . ."

Then his head fell to one side of the pillow with
his mouth hung crookedly open, and everyone knew
he was dead. . . .

Alinsky returned from Jerusalem with his mother
and a huge priest in tow for the funeral, and Mass
was said the next morning in the dining room of
the rented house on the town's outskirts, where, after the necessary police clearance, Père Bisson's body
lay in a coffin that was placed atop the table from
which they had eaten Christmas dinner. Besides the

remaining four pilgrims, there were also Alinsky and his mother, Ben Bokva and Teplitsky, Gervais and Lebel and Ricard, the chef and helper from La Tour d'Argent in Paris (who had stayed on at Alinsky's behest to prepare a funeral meal), Bisson's doctor and a nurse from the hospital, the chief of police from the town (whose curiosity had gotten the best of him), and the caretaker of the house and his two young sons. Outside, through the French windows in the courtyard, a band of three string instruments—a joint donation of the doctor and the police chief—played some plaintive and wailing minor-chord music of the Levant that seemed decidedly appropriate, in addition to the continuing drizzle and gloom, for a Christian funeral.

Inside, surprisingly, Alinsky's priest—an American Franciscan named Riley—eulogized Father Bisson, though he had not known him: a singsong of generalities that assumed Bisson had merely fallen in with the others along the ancient and well-traveled crusade route to Jerusalem in response to the Pope's call. As the Muslim achieves his life's greatest triumph in the pilgrimage to Mecca, so also does the Christian achieve his on the road to Jerusalem. And how pleasing would the dead priest's soul be in the sight of God since the holy man had died in the midst of his incredible trek through the heathen lands (which caused the police chief and the doctor to exchange a frown) toward the city of God. Et cetera. Murphy, for his part, merely snorted disgustedly: the Long Journey, the Rocky Road, the After Life, Seeing God. For sure the speaker of these platitudes was on Meyer's payroll.

Later, Père Bisson's body was duly bid good-bye by each of them in turn and ferried to the airport. The band, its numbers swelled to seven, moved indoors to a pile of cushions in one corner of the living room and played equally wailing but now happy village reels to which the caretaker and his sons danced on the centuries-old carpeting once the furniture had been moved away, while Alinsky, Riley, the police chief, and the doctor clapped them on. In the dining room, over cocktails before they sat down to eat, Murphy managed to corner Rachel Alinsky for a conversation.

"How are Monique and Jean-Philippe, Mrs. Alinsky?" he asked. She sipped her usual old-fashioned. Murphy had seen it made close up this time, and there was very little alcohol in it.

"They're both doing fine, Frankie. Meyer thought we might bring them along with us to Antalya, but I talked him out of it. Funerals are so depressing. No place for a nice kid like Jean-Philippe. Kids always have two left feet at funerals anyhow. And no place either for Monique, after all the time I've put in on cheering her up. Wait until you see her. Lots of new clothes and a new hairdo. She's dying to tell you about the time we had in New York. I think we almost bankrupted Meyer with all the money we spent."

"Mrs. Alinsky, who's kidding who?"

"What are you talking about, Frank?"

"How can you stand there talking about my wife and son when you know damn well they're both prisoners of Meyer in Jerusalem?" He spoke in a low voice so Alinsky in the next room would not overhear.

"I don't think about it, Frank," she answered, looking away—contritely, Murphy thought. "And I don't call them prisoners. I call them houseguests, and I do my damnedest to make sure our houseguests are happy."

"Why won't you reason with him, Rachel?" Murphy pleaded, addressing her familiarly for the first time. "You're his mother. You know how to manipulate him. Get him to let Monique and Jean-Philippe return to France."

"The big Iowa halfback's mother does not tell the big Iowa halfback what to do. And to you my name is Mrs. Alinsky, not Rachel. How do you think

Meyer would react if one of the friends he brought home from college started calling his mother by her first name?"

"I'm not one of Meyer's friends from college," Murphy told her stonily.

"You weren't lucky enough, Frankie. Because if you had been, you'd know what a good person he is, and you'd trust him to work everything out all right. Stop worrying about Monique and Jean-Philippe. They'll make it through all this."

"They will? Will you? You and Monique were in America. Is it fair to ask how close to Iowa you were able to get?"

She took a reflective sip from her drink and then looked at him with a level gaze. "With a plane crew, a driver, and two bodyguards to make sure we didn't get mugged by some dark-skinned New Yorkers, how close do you think I got, Francis Xavier? Not to the far side of the Hudson River, let me assure you. Now, is there anything else you'd like to know?"

He shook his head; she had told him everything. He watched as she turned about and headed for the burly Franciscan, who swigged beer with one arm and draped his other familiarly about Meyer's mother, calling her "Rachel baby" and not being rebuked for it. Across the room, it seemed from the fragments Murphy could catch that the priest was telling a football locker-room joke; at its conclusion Alinsky was howling with laughter, and his mother dug her fist into the priest's ribs in mock indignation, probably over some term like *jockstrap*. Murphy, for his part, traded a shrug with Kyle-Boyer. They were in Turkey, in the middle of winter, but this for sure was somebody's idea of an Irish wake.

They ate the funeral supper mostly in silence, except for Alinsky and the Franciscan, who was a fool and filled the room with ecumenical quips from an American Rotary Club meeting that Meyer and the police chief seemed to enjoy if no one else did. Then they drove out to the airport, where Père Bisson's coffin was loaded onto an Iranian jet on its way from Teheran to Paris, and stood about for more than an hour in the thirty-degree cold to watch its departure, delayed because of some technical difficulty. When it finally lifted off, only Murphy and Riley and Marilyn Aldrich stood outside. As it gained the air, the priest made the sign of the cross over the disappearing plane.

"Doesn't any of this strike you as strange, Father?" Murphy asked. "I mean, flying up to Turkey to read a funeral Mass for a dead pilgrim who was being paid by Meyer to walk to Israel?"

"No, Murphy, not particularly." Riley shrugged. "Meyer's a strange person in a way, but he's a good guy too. And Rachel's a livin' doll. They've made life in Israel a pleasure for me. I mean, I know we're supposed to go where God sends us, but to tell the truth I wasn't too thrilled about the idea of working in an all-Jewish country when I was reassigned. But they've fixed all that."

"They're Jews," Murphy said quietly.

"Well, yeah, Murph, that's their religion, but I don't think they get all that excited about it. I mean, to me they're Americans. The way I see it, they're just like me. I'm like them. We think alike. We like the same things. Meyer's all beer and football, a combination I love, and Rachel's always good for a club sandwich any time of the day or night. They're like you too, Murph." The priest tapped him on the chest. "If you understand what I'm saying."

"I'm a French national. Meyer Alinsky and his mother are Israeli citizens," Murphy told him. "How does that make us like you?"

"We're all Americans, Murph," Riley said flatly. "You don't stop being an American just by wishing it, or by brandishing a piece of paper that says you're a frog and Meyer and Rachel are bona fide Hebes. It just doesn't work that way. It's indelible, and I wouldn't be too hasty about trying to erase it. I used to read about those people—hotshots and slickers during the Jazz Age—that left for Paris and swore they'd never be back. Well, they all came back and they were damn glad to get back when the time came."

"I ought to knock you on your ass, priest, for calling me a frog."

"Try it." The mirth was back in the voice now; beneath his habit the Franciscan did a little jig in happy anticipation of some violence. The wind had suddenly risen, and blizzards of dry snow that had managed to collect in the tufts of grass on the edge of the runway blew over them in gusts. Standing beside Murphy, Marilyn Aldrich, who had truly loved Bisson, seemed oblivious to the tension, watching instead as the Iranian jet, now a mere speck, disappeared northward through the black clouds that ringed the Taurus range.

"I'm a citizen of the French Republic," Murphy retorted angrily. He was not afraid of the Franciscan even though the man was nearly as tall as Alinsky. But he was afraid of Ben Bokva and Teplitsky, should he take a swing at the priest.

"Have it as you will, Murph."

"I have no intention of ever returning to America."

"Don't bet on it, buddy-boy. Don't ever bet on a thing like that. You never know what the big dealer up there in the sky has got stacked in the deck."

They turned away from the runway as if by mutual admission of exhaustion, and Marilyn Aldrich followed in their wake.

"What the hell's Alinsky's particular hold on you, Riley?" Murphy demanded wrathfully.

"Besides the fact that when it comes to Franciscan charities he's got a heart as big as the World Bank?"

"Yeah."

"His hold on me is the pro games. God, I love that man!"

"What do you mean?"

"Every *Shabbas*—that's the Jewish Sunday except

that it comes on Saturday—Meyer has a regular group of friends in for beer and bullshit to watch films of some of the top pro games in the States the weekend before. What's your favorite club, Murphy? The Jets?"

"Who are they?"

"You don't know who the New York Jets are?"

"I haven't been to the States for fifteen years. I probably haven't been to a football game in seventeen or eighteen."

"Christ Almighty, you might at least have read about them in a paper somewhere! They took an NFL crown, after all."

"I don't particularly care about football. Can you understand that?"

"Well, what the hell do you care about? You've got to care about something! Meyer said you were a goddam rummy until he got you started on this pilgrimage a while back to save you from yourself. You're damn lucky you ran into him. You're all damn lucky, I think. That frog priest we just shipped out got his orphanage built, didn't he? And Bernadette of Lourdes back there"—he jerked his head rearward at Marilyn, who still followed behind them —"and her boy friend were yanked off the streets while there's still a chance to make decent human beings out of them, not to mention that fat English pig of an abortionist who's had to trade in his coat hangers for the last eight months or so. . . ."

Murphy turned to face the priest, incredulous at the hatred in the voice; Riley's face was suddenly red as a furnace door, and he seemed almost apoplectic. Seeing Murphy's stare, he checked himself and began breathing regularly, as if he were consciously exercising restraint.

"You ought to be happy, Murphy, that Meyer's got Jean-Philippe in Jerusalem." The Franciscan spoke quietly now. "Your son's learning to play football. Meyer spends a couple of hours a week showing him the ropes of the game. That kid of yours can put a pass through a brick wall. He can already outrun Meyer's time back in his heydey, and he's getting a pair of legs on him like a brewer's horse. You should've been the one to teach him."

"Look, he's a fourteen-year-old French boy. He plays soccer like Pelé and skis like Killy. He wasn't expected to learn how to play American football."

"Bull! That's the silliest thing I've ever heard of. You ought to be grateful to Meyer instead of bearing him so many grudges. The kid won't be the worse for it. Sports build character."

"Oh, shit." Murphy was weary of the priest. "All right, Father, I'm grateful. I'm very grateful. Only one last question. Do you happen to know why we're on this pilgrimage to Jerusalem?"

"No, I don't. Meyer didn't say. Why are you walking to Jerusalem?"

"I don't know for sure. That's why I'm asking you. He might have told you something."

Riley gave a long, low whistle, beseeched heaven with his eyes, then smiled dimly at Murphy and at Marilyn, who had caught up with them. "Look, Murph, I really don't know why you're on this pilgrimage. But I know for sure that if I was walking all the way from France to Israel, I'd at least know why I was doing it."

"The choice really isn't ours any more. We're sort of captives," Marilyn Aldrich said simply, then began walking off toward the small terminal by herself.

"Some captivity, let me tell you," Riley judged. "When Monique and Rachel went to New York, they came back with the Boeing so crammed with stuff they bought they could barely fit themselves in. Meyer spends as much time as possible with Jean-Philippe, and whenever he's around the sky literally belches money on that young man."

"You know my wife and son are hostages, priest." Murphy cut him off.

"Do I, Murph?" the Franciscan asked, his face suddenly aglow at the sight of Meyer and his mother

emerging from the terminal building. "Well, if I do,
I don't do too much worrying about it. I haven't
seen either of them chained to the wall is what I've
been trying to tell you. And I don't intend to rock
the boat either. Meyer might have a secret way down
there someplace, but I'm not going to ferret it out.
End discussion. That's it."

Riley walked away with quick steps, waving now to
his patrons, the Alinskys. Murphy followed dejectedly
behind, coming abreast of Marilyn Aldrich, who stood
staring again at the sky, buttoning the quilted coat
she wore over her robe more tightly about her.

"God, isn't it an awful day?" she asked. "Poor
Father Bisson, I think he was like a saint, don't
you, Frank? Ain't it sad he never got to see Jerusalem? Oh, well, at least he got to see the bloody
Pope."

"Yes, we can be happy for that," Murphy told
her ruefully, declining to tell her otherwise. Alinsky
and his mother and their Franciscan waved to them
as they went toward the 707. Ben Bokva called them
to the Citroën and, when they were seated inside,
told them they would begin their march again at
dawn the next day. In time the 707 screamed up
the runway and into the quickly darkening sky. As
he turned the Citroën to leave, Ben Bokva remarked
that it would take the 707 less than an hour to
reach Lod, the airport of Tel Aviv.

22

Hélas, Monique

EXHAUSTED FROM SLOGGING through the mud of winter rains and minus Père Bisson's mule, which was buried alive in a slide near Adana, they came out of the Taurus Mountains into Iskenderun near the Syrian border at the end of January to await the arrival of Alinsky from Israel and his instructions on crossing the Arab lands to Jerusalem. He showed up two days later at sunset aboard the *Katrina*, home port Haifa, flying the Israeli flag, the largest (perhaps longer than 250 feet) and most beautiful diesel yacht Murphy had ever seen. Its sudden presence among the offshore freighters and a rusting tanker drew gangs of Turks and tourists out of town to the water's edge and launched a bevy of small hawking boats away from the quays toward the splendid jewel at the same time as the customs boats departed. Instructing the pilgrims to wait for their return, Ben Bokva and Teplitsky left aboard the lighter that came in from the yacht to pick them up.

Two hours later they were back with the word—generally anticipated—that the days of their wardenship were fast drawing to a close. Alinsky deemed it too dangerous for his non-gangsters to cross into Syria, even with false passports and disguises. Also, regretfully, the pilgrims were not invited aboard the *Katrina* since Alinsky was entertaining a band of European business executives; explanations would be too tedious, and the yacht was leaving to return to Haifa before sunup anyhow. Then casually, almost as an afterthought, Ben Bokva mentioned that Monique was on board for the trip. Murphy could not go to her, but Alinsky, ever charitable, would permit him a view through infrared binoculars of his appropriated wife standing in the ship's stern.

The mere sight of Monique, after not seeing her since Alinsky spirited her away in Greece months before, was not sufficient compensation. After midnight, unable to hire a boat anywhere since the fishing fleet to a man was at its night's work out beyond the harbor. Murphy—accompanied by Gervais who suspected his Rifka might also be aboard—stripped to his shorts, coated his body with olive oil, and, warmed by wine and passion, swam the half-mile distance to Monique, only to find as he drew near the circle of light that radiated over the water from the *Katrina* that the real´ end of his marriage had begun.

Whining, minor-keyed Turkish or Arabic music resounded from on board, and when he was close enough to distinguish forms through the windows of the main salon, Murphy saw with absolute astonishment that the darkly tanned woman in a simple European-style blouse and miniskirt who gyrated sensually to the music in a circle of seated, hand-clapping men was his own wife of fabled grace and reserve, Monique de Rastignac Murphy.

"Good Jesus Christ!" Murphy screamed out in the darkness as he treaded water. "That's my wife dancing in there for all those men! What the hell has that fiend Alinsky done to her?"

Through the salon windows, where the wailing music had increased its intensity and Murphy's wife hung far back in the middle of the impromptu dancing area, her hair let down and nearly touching the floor, her stomach pulsating with the expertise of a belly dancer, Alinsky, obviously drunk, had lurched to his feet and, with his hands clapping together over his head, begun some interpretive grind of his own. In another moment Monique and Meyer moved close together, like flamenco dancers, for the music—sensuous, insinuating to Murphy's ear as sin—demanded body contact. Alinsky bent low and placed an open-mouthed kiss on Monique's neck; her eyes closed and she smiled from the pleasure of his touch.

In the sea, quickly chilling, Murphy thought of allowing himself to drown. But he continued to tread water, making small powerless circles with his arms, and watched Monique plant her tongue in Meyer's ear. Alinsky's face brightened with happiness.

"Alinsky has committed some sort of travesty in the case of each one of us," Gervais said softly, "but what he's doing to you, Frank, is possibly the worst. He did not plan this, I think. He could not have. She has chosen him."

"I'll kill him for that," Murphy raged. But his rage, short-lived, turned to another kind of astonishment as a tiny shawl-clad figure that could only be Rachel Alinsky rushed out of an unseen corner of the room, brusquely separated her son from Monique, and smashed him across the face—evidently for his lechery. The music fell instantly to silence. Many of the salon's onlookers rose to their feet and began backing off toward the walls. In the center of the room, Meyer's mother delivered a harangue alternately to her son and Monique. Murphy's wife looked chastened; Meyer looked as if he were ready to collapse.

"*Qui?*" Gervais demanded.

"*La mère. Une tempête.*"

"*Formidable.* But she offers us an excellent cover. Now is certainly the best time to sneak aboard."

"Yes, you're right," Murphy agreed. They swam around the stern to the port side of the yacht, searching for a boarding ladder or even a piece of rope hanging over the railing. But there was nothing, and, looking upward, Murphy saw that even the ship's lighter had been hoisted aboard. Then they heard the unmistakable sound of someone retching violently from sickness and saw the accompanying bilge drop into the water. Toward the stern, not far from where they paddled about, Monique supported a very ill Meyer Alinsky over the railing. Her voice, that punctuated the intensity of his vomiting, was soft and comforting. Behind them, in the main salon, the castrato now sang the saddest of sad songs in Hebrew.

"Monique! Monique!" Murphy hissed, swimming into an arc of light as close beneath them as he dared. *"C'est moi!"*

"Frank, how did you get out here?" Her voice was astonished; at the same time she heaved mightily to keep Alinsky from sliding to the deck.

"We swam."

"Well, you had better swim back. Meyer doesn't want you. You were meant only to look at me, not to touch. *Compris?"*

"Monique, don't be ridiculous!" Murphy pleaded. "He's drunk. He'll never know. Put down a ladder and let us come on board."

"No."

"What do you mean, no? Whose side are you on? You seem to forget that that prick took you and Jean-Philippe captive back in Greece—"

"We are not captives, Frank, we are houseguests. And we are enjoying it very much. I'm having some real fun for the first time in my life, Jean-Philippe has learned to smile once again, and I love being treated like a woman for a change. You never gave me any money for clothes, you never took me dancing, and in fifteen years you took me only once to the Opéra in Paris. Already we have been to the opera in Paris, Milan, New York, and Rome eight or nine times—"

"Monique!" Murphy raged up at her. "Are you having an affair with him?"

"Of course not. Rachel would never permit it. She watches me like a *duenna*. She made some sort of promise to you, I guess."

"Madame Murphy." Gervais broke an incredulous silence. *"Où est ma femme? Où est Rifka?"*

"She's all right. You are Gervais, *n'est-ce pas? Bonsoir, monsieur*. She awaits you in Jerusalem. *Oh, mon petit chou."* She suddenly comforted Alinsky, who had begun his bottomless retching again. "Look how dirty he has become! I must find a towel and get him cleaned up before his mother sees him again."

"Here, Monique, try this," Murphy urged, whipping off his jockey shorts underwater and hurling them with one deft cast at Meyer Alinsky's face. Monique, seeming oblivious to the insult, snatched them from the air and applied them to wiping the dribble from Meyer's chin and shirtfront. Gervais, finding some unknown humor in himself, pulled off his shorts also and threw them upward, laughing at the notion. But Monique apparently had no need of them and they fell back, snagging on some projection of the boat's railing.

"I'm sorry if my undershorts are clean, Monique," Murphy called to her.

"It would be a wonder if they were, from what I remember of you, Frank. Now you should return to shore before you are too chilled. You also, Monsieur Gervais."

"You've betrayed me, Monique. You've betrayed our son also. I'm going to beat the hell out of you when we get to Jerusalem."

"No, you won't, Frank. Or if you do, Meyer will have you spitted and fried and eaten clandestinely at a Bedouin feast. Now move on, we will talk calmly in Jerusalem."

"Yes, move on." The voice came from the shadows of a barely seen doorway behind Monique and Meyer. A guard who had evidently been there all along stepped forward and pointed one of the fabled Israeli *uzzis* down at the water. "Go quickly away from here before you're dragged under by the screws. *Giveret* Alinsky has given orders for us to return to Haifa. It will be only minutes more before the engines turn on."

Even as the guard spoke they heard the whir of electric motors winching up the anchor from the bottom. Murphy—despite his anger with Monique—frightened of the dark environs of ships' hulls at night, was absolutely terrified at the notion of great grinding propellers turning unseen in the waters beneath him. With Gervais close behind he sprang away from the *Katrina,* intending to make a wide arc behind the stern. Again, despite his anger, he was grateful for the kindness of the guard, who threw two life rings from the yacht, dropping them accurately between the swimmers. They were far enough away, buoyed up by the rings, when the engines came to life and the *Katrina* moved off, turning a great slow circle toward the south. Monique still propped up her benefactor against the railing.

Sorrowing, knowing he had no recourse, Murphy began swimming toward shore. "Monique," he called to her over the distance, "are you in love with him?"

She shrugged, smiling a whimsical smile that he could just discern beneath the arc of ship's lights.

"She is," Murphy said miserably to Gervais.

But Gervais, silent, evidently had misery of his own.

They kicked their way homeward toward the lights of Iskenderun, turning occasionally to watch the *Katrina* disappearing toward the Syrian coast.

Compounding the defeat, the Turkish police arrested them for indecent exposure when, stark naked, they hauled themselves aboard a fully lit quay back on shore.

23

The Arabs: A geography lesson

ONE HUNDRED AND NINETY-SEVEN DAYS after leaving Saint-Aubin on the Normandy coast of France, Alinsky's diamond, returned to its hiding place in the crucifix after Istanbul, crossed the frontier into Syria.

At the border station on the Turkish side, there was a flurry of respectful saluting by the assorted customs and military personnel. Murphy marched across the line, his crucifix held high, hearing behind him the almost baleful horn blasts of their warden Ben Bokva as he said good-bye and then swung the Citroën about and returned toward Iskenderun. At an identical border station on the Syrian side, the Arabs were waiting for the Fourteenth Crusade. Like the Israelis they possessed optimistic Middle Eastern maps of their own, and for the benefit of the pilgrims a colonel had been sent down from Damascus to interpret them. He ushered them into a sort of map room in the customshouse; coffee was served; fans whirred overhead. The colonel, a polite-seeming, poetic-sounding man, was perhaps in his late fifties; he sported a waxed moustache and had the bearing of a Sandhurst officer, Murphy thought, though Syria, if he remembered correctly, had been in the French, not British, sector after the collapse of the Ottomans.

"It has been made known to me that you are marching these many days, good Christian fellows, toward Jerusalem the holy of holies in a pilgrimage of thanksgiving for the miraculous cure afforded this beauteous young lady through the good offices of the one who is called the Christ, the Christian prophet."

He stood before them as they sat, ranged like schoolchildren, on two rows of folding chairs. In one hand was a riding crop that he used as a pointer; his back was to an as-yet-unopened wall map. He smiled benignly. Marilyn Aldrich seemed first to realize that a response was forthcoming. "Yes, yes, colonel, that's exactly why we're here. Less than a year ago I couldn't walk, 'n' now I can. Why, it was just a bloody incredible miracle is all I can tell you, sir."

"Such things are not unknown. But tell me, where is this Jerusalem toward which you are proceeding? In what place is it to be found?"

"Jerusalem is to be found in Israel," Jonathan Whitmore answered, in the cadence of a schoolboy learning by rote. He was not being facetious; before him the officer's crop swung back and forth like a metronome.

"That is incorrect," the teacher informed him.

"I say, colonel." Kyle-Boyer spoke up. "Has there been some altercation in the area that we've not heard of since leaving Istanbul, perhaps? Have the Jordanians retaken the old city?"

"No, there has been no altercation, Dr. Kyle-Boyer—not in the recent past, at least. But there will certainly be in the future."

"Well, if there's been no war, then the Jews still own Jerusalem, 'n' therefore Jerusalem is to be found in Israel," Whitmore singsonged once more.

"That is incorrect!" The colonel shrieked this time, lashing the air with his riding crop as if he were slicing someone in half. "Jerusalem is to be found in Palestine! I will give you scientific proof of this. Look!"

He threw back the cover of the wall map and jabbed his pointer at Jerusalem, a naked black dot located in the beige tints of Palestine. The map, dated 1900 and designated in English and Arabic, showed the last throes of the Ottoman Empire.

"And look again, Christians!" He flipped a page and the holy city showed itself again in the pink blob of the British Mandate, dated 1946. He thrust with his pointer and unintentionally obliterated Jerusalem from the brittle paper.

"Why he's gone bloody daft, he has!" Jonathan exclaimed out loud. "Them maps is from the time the Tommies was stationed out here. Here, colonel, let me borrow that stick of yours 'n' I'll show you somethin'." Abruptly Jonathan stood up in his robe and snatched the riding crop from the hands of the startled Syrian colonel. Stepping past the man, he began tracing an outline of modern Israel on the Mandate map, explaining to his audience as he worked. "Actually, I knows the area quite well. I made myself a few good quid back during the 'sixty-seven war takin' bets on how much A-rab territory the Jews could gobble up before the cease-fire was called. Now, you see this part of the country used to be only about fifteen miles wide at one time—"

"Incorrect! Totally incorrect!" the colonel screamed, wresting back his pointer with a single forceful motion that had Murphy anticipating the real possibility that he might smash Jonathan with the instrument. "You are absolutely wrong! Israel is an abstraction! A temporary imposition! A gratuitous intellectual creation of Western imperialism!"

"Look here, colonel, take a grip on yourself," Jonathan urged, oblivious of the riding crop as he advanced to pat the Syrian's shoulder consolingly. "I don't suppose you gets much chance to travel outside your own country, what with army pay 'n' all that, but there is an Israel. If there weren't no Israel, how come we keeps meetin' Israelis everywhere along the way? Answer that one, will you?"

"The answer is quite easy, Mr. Whitmore. Israelis, like Israel, are an abstraction also. They are
personae rather than flesh-and-blood persons, crea-
tions of hack novelists and Western arms manufac-
turing interests, not to mention their own abiding
narcissistic impulse for self-aggrandizing publicity."

"I still thinks you're daft, colonel," Whitmore assured him, astonishing everyone else with his brazenness. "You'd have to be to think the world of nineteen seventy was the same as the world of nineteen
forty-six. It's just unreal. Why, back there in Iskenderun we seen a map of Israel in the future that
made a lot more sense than this 'ere bag of goods
you're tryin' to sell us now—"

"And who had this purported map?" the colonel
demanded, smashing the riding crop on a desk top
so that papers flew in all directions. From their faces
Murphy was aware that, like himself, everyone else
was trying to flash Jonathan Whitmore the high sign
to keep silent and take his place again.

"The map belonged to a Jewish fellow named Alinsky."

"Alinsky? Meyer Alinsky?"

"Yes, colonel, he's the gentleman I was speakin'
of."

The colonel suddenly smiled condescendingly at
them, as if they were very small children; encouraging Jonathan Whitmore to sit down, he was clearly
certain of victory. "Is this the same Meyer Alinsky
who bought out the Egyptian Air Force during
the Six-Day War?"

"Yes, colonel, he's the very one."

The Syrian laughed, rich, delighted laughter that
acknowledged the marvel of the joke. He sat back on
the desk top, slapping his knees and shaking with
hilarity until tears began coursing down his cheeks.
Reflexively, perhaps, the pilgrims and the RTF crew
began laughing also, and the room filled with gales
of mirth.

"Is this not an absolutely fantastic myth?" the colo-

nel gasped out. "A genuine home-grown Middle Eastern exaggeration. It proves that Israel is an abstraction, a state of mind rather than a place! For what
other than an abstract nation would need to invent
so desperate a folk hero as Meyer Alinsky? Among
the Arabs he is a joke. Can you imagine it? To have
bought out the Air Force of a powerful nation
like Egypt? It is even said of him that he possesses
a compendium of the moral irresoluteness of the
world called the Book of the Corruptibles. Oh, let us
give credit to the imaginative genius of the fable-
making Jews! Our agents have long ago determined
that no such person as Alinsky exists!"

The colonel howled on, wiping at his eyes with a
handkerchief; the pilgrims howled along with him,
but for another reason, Jonathan Whitmore nearly
convulsed out of his chair with the singularness of his
pleasure at his victory over the illusion-loving Syrian,
a victory that Murphy desperately hoped, despite his
mirth, Jonathan would not try to score home by re-
opening the dialogue about Alinsky. But the cockney
needed no warning. In time the laughter ceased and
it was easy to see that Jonathan was tired of the
game. The colonel composed himself and stood before the Mandate map again with his pointer at the
ready.

"And now, dear children, what is the city toward
which you are marching in pilgrimage?"

"We are marching toward Jerusalem," they sang out
in unison, laughing at their perfect spontaneity.

"And where is this Jerusalem to be found?"

"Jerusalem is to be found in Palestine," they sang
out again.

"Perfect! Perfect! Oh, what masterful students you
are!" the colonel enthused through their laughter.

"Let's hear it for Palestine," Jonathan proposed
wickedly. "Three cheers!"

"Palestine! Palestine! Yea, Palestine!" they chorused, laughing and standing up to clap hands all
at the same time. The colonel ushered them out of

the room and through an instantly present, smiling phalanx of customs officials who clasped their hands warmly and otherwise pounded their backs in newly made camaraderie. With the colonel they advanced out of the customshouse toward the vehicles and the waiting mules. A soldier graciously returned his crucifix to Murphy. Before setting off, they gathered around their teacher to say good-bye.

"Whew!" the colonel exclaimed, wiping his brow. "Am I glad that's over with!"

"It was kind of instructive, colonel," Jonathan said facetiously.

"Not only that, Mr. Whitmore," the Syrian returned, winking, "but the room was bugged for sound. Do, by all means, say hello to Meyer for me when you reach Jerusalem."

"You mean—" But the sentence was never completed; they were all laughing too hard again.

Murphy, when he regained control, asked the question first. "Who shall we say is sending along greetings?"

"Colonel Z of the Syrian General Staff."

"Just Colonel Z? Does it have to sound so much like diamond smuggling and other intrigue?"

"You know that Meyer loves his little games. Colonel Z is enough. He knows who I am. I'm listed in the nonexistent Book of the Corruptibles."

"Then it's true," Murphy stammered, "about the Egyptian Air Force?"

"Of that I'm certain. It's the business of whether or not Gamal Abdul Nasser was on Meyer's payroll that's driving me crazy. Meyer insists that he was. . . . Well, shalom."

"Shalom," the pilgrims sang out. The colonel bowed deeply, kissed Marilyn Aldrich's hand, then returned to join the half circle of customs officers near the border gate. Still laughing, the Fourteenth Crusade set off down the road to Aleppo.

24

Al Hazzar, the friend of Alinsky

AFTER THE BORDER CROSSING, Murphy decided only God knew how long Meyer Alinsky had been planning the Fourteenth Crusade—though it had to be years, given the number of contingency plans that existed for any possible infraction of Meyer's stated rules. That became apparent once more on their third day into Syria when they flushed their new chaperones —Al Hazzar the Bedouin and his five tribesmen followers—down from the hills ringing the way to Aleppo.

Three days was the time it took Kyle-Boyer to figure out that in an Arab country they were free of Meyer Alinsky and his minions and that, except for the fact that the habit of endless plodding had become so ingrained in them, there was really no reason why they should not climb aboard the station wagon and utility van and ride to Jerusalem through Syria, Lebanon, and Jordan. If they traveled in easy stages, they would not arrive in Israel before mid-March; someone might be hired to walk the mules along behind them.

The realization occasioned an immediate party beside the road, and Gervais broke out a few leftover bottles of Alinsky's Beaujolais. Then they boarded the wagon and the truck and, tying the two mules to the wagon's tailgate, started off again at the speed of a trot toward Aleppo. Al Hazzar intercepted them less than a mile farther on.

Actually, Murphy had seen the Bedouins before, or thought he had seen them, perhaps: the flapping of a bright-colored kaffiyeh headdress in the morning breeze that may have been but a tuft of cloth waving in a tree; the glint of gun barrel in the sun (or broken glass instead); the shadow of a man swaying astride a camel moving against the sandstone tints of the hills that may have been only a rock formation; once even (for certain) a line of pack camels disappearing over a high and distant ridge as the sun dipped toward the Mediterranean on the other side —in any event, the unnamed feeling that they were being trailed and watched.

Murphy, his arms high above his head, was first to leave the Peugeot when the six camel riders ranged across the road, all armed with rifles or submachine guns, faces covered to the eyes, motioned them to get out.

"They're bandits," Kyle-Boyer judged in absolute fright. Together, faces covered, the Bedouins looked ferocious. The road was too obscure, the chances of army or police coming along it seemed impossibly remote.

"*Salaam alaikum.*" Murphy spoke timidly toward the Arabs.

"*Wa-alaikum salaam.* Shalom also, Murphy *effendi.*" The shortest of them, who was seated conversely astride the tallest camel, spoke. He wore what looked to Murphy to be a good quality English tweed jacket over the folds of his burnoose. "I am called Musad Al Hazzar." He removed the wrap of his kaffiyeh from his face, and unwittingly something like a collective sigh of relief burst from the crusaders; he had a demonic imp's face, watery eyes full of mirth, and a dark jutting goatee on his chin. He checked the safety on his rifle, an American Winchester, and replaced it in a sling attached to the camel saddle. The others did not.

"Can you imagine why I am here, good friends?" Al Hazzar asked, smiling broadly, his eyes twinkling.

"You work for Meyer Alinsky," Murphy speculated.

"Let us just say I look after his interests in the western Arab areas. Along with others, of course. Many others, I would hasten to assure you. But it would not be up to me, a lowly follower of the prophet Mohammed, to remind you of the loftiness of Christianity's ethic—which ethic, I might add, the West has been trying to ram down Araby's poor raspy throat for a longer time than anyone can remember. However, let bygones be bygones. This is the Arab way. Now, you signed a contract with Meyer and agreed to walk to Jerusalem. And walk you will, I am afraid, good friends. If not in shamed recognition of your violation of Christianity's august ethic, then by force of Islamic arms. These are real guns, alas. Alas, also, they are loaded. These brothers of mine you see arrayed all about you are killers from the desert. Ben Bokva and Teplitsky who accompanied you formerly are but children by comparison."

"We'll walk," Jonathan Whitmore said abruptly.

"I was sure of it, Whitmore *effendi*. Now I am sure that you are sure also."

Then—incredibly—there occurred a perfect convincing culmination to the scenario of Musad Al Hazzar's polite cajolery that Meyer Alinsky could not possibly have engineered. A vintage farm truck loaded with women field workers, except for the three men who sat up front in the cab, rumbled along the road from the opposite direction and ground to a halt at sight of the Bedouins, who had swung about in their saddles from curiosity. In the narrow confines of the road there was no place to turn the truck around, so it was simply abandoned by the three men and perhaps twenty-five women, some carrying babies under their arms, who ran screaming with fright a short distance along the road, climbed a low hill, and disappeared entirely from sight over the other side. The whole terrified exodus had taken perhaps all of forty seconds. In its aftermath there was but the staggered idling of the truck's badly timed engine, which had not been turned off.

"Syrians," Al Hazzar judged, shaking his head and spitting on the ground. "Does it not seem strange that the greatest Arab caliphate once existed among these people? Allah himself could not define how they have gotten to be so. Oh, well, we must leave you now to your task and set about our own. Walk sagaciously, dear Christians. It is not long to Jerusalem, and when you arrive we shall have some marvelous parties to celebrate your triumph. All of you and I and Meyer and Mother Rachel and Monique and Jean-Philippe and Rifka and Father Riley and Ben Bokva and Teplitsky. A veritable week of feasting and drinking is planned. We shall break all the world's records for the consumption of spirits. Good-bye."

"Will we see you again?" Marilyn Aldrich asked, for no apparent reason.

"*Inshallah*. If God wills it. But I promise to wave to you from time to time so you will know you are not abandoned. Now good-bye again."

At a click sound from Al Hazzar the Bedouins turned about, rode an identical distance down the road to where the Syrians had fled, and then mounted the low hill on the opposite side and quickly disappeared into a grove of pines without once looking back.

"I wonder how he got to be on Meyer's payroll?" Jonathan Whitmore asked as he untied the mules from the Peugeot's tailgate.

"Who knows?" Murphy answered. "But after all we've seen so far, we must suspect that everyone from here to Jerusalem is on Meyer's payroll."

They set off, marching again, past the still-idling

truck, not bothering to speak to the three men who peered warily over a hillock at them, trying to ascertain if the coast were clear.

Al Hazzar waved twice along the road south of Aleppo that led toward the frontier of Lebanon into which they were to cross to avoid the mountainous Syrian interior: once near Jisr esh Shughur and another time near Homs, before the border was reached. Each time the pilgrim bunch dutifully returned his greeting en masse, even feigning enthusiasm lest the Bedouin realize how badly demoralized they were over the necessity of achieving the last leg of their grand trek under a fully armed guard that was hardly ever seen. Their method of communication was absurd. Each time they came to a town of moderate size it was Murphy's responsibility to go to the telephone exchange and wait for a call from Al Hazzar that often originated from a tap on the line somewhere up in the distant hills. And the conversations were annoying, often threatening, for Al Hazzar, for all his endless Muslim fatalism, was a real worrywart when it came to pursuing Alinsky's business. The pilgrims' most innocent conversation with any Syrian anywhere—a thing impossible to avoid in the curiosity-ridden Levant with its deep-seated traditions of hospitality—sent Musad Al Hazzar into the worst paranoid imaginings that Alinsky's crusaders were asking everywhere for some sort of protective asylum.

Once in Lebanon, near El Hermel, Al Hazzar's fears put him over the edge. In this country of many Christians, priests emerged with their entire congregations in tow, as they had back in the rural sections of France and Italy, to bless the pilgrims, ply them with food and gifts, wish them well, and hold up their sick and maimed to the eternally myopic gaze of Blessed Marilyn Aldrich. On their third day in the country, near Baalbek, after slogging their way through what seemed, disgustingly, to be endless

corridors of litter patients, Musad Al Hazzar appeared
to them unexpectedly after nightfall. They were
camped, blessedly, in the inner courtyard of a Maronite church whose use a priest had generously offered
in order to protect them from the reported approach
of busloads of suppliants coming upcountry from
Beirut. Murphy grilled chicken pieces and shashlik
over a brazier. Kyle-Boyer prepared *hummus* and a
salad. Al Hazzar rode his camel up to the courtyard's outer wall and peered steadfastly down at
them. "What the fuck are you doing in this place?
Come out at once! Meyer will have Lebanon obliterated if he thinks these people are giving you asylum!"

"Al Hazzar," Kyle-Boyer called up, "be so kind
as to go and bugger yourself, will you? We are not
seeking asylum. We are resting for the night. And I
assure you more than anything else I want to get
to Jerusalem."

"You're lying, Kyle-Boyer!" the Bedouin shouted.
Then he stepped from the camel's back, placing one
well-booted foot atop the murderous shards of jagged
glass that rimmed the wall and preparing to jump
into the courtyard. He leaped, the folds of his
burnoose hooked on the jagged edges, and Musad
Al Hazzar, the trusted agent of Meyer Alinsky, fell
ingloriously head first to the packed earth of the
courtyard. Murphy, the pent-up rage over too many
intimidating phone messages from Al Hazzar erupting
from him, raced across the yard and punched the
unarmed Arab squarely in the nose as he tried dazedly
to rise to his feet. From the brittle crack everyone
knew the nose had to be broken; Musad Al Hazzar
went out like a light.

When he awoke to a ring of solicitous pilgrims
(solicitous because they were terrified by his yet unseen desert brothers), the fight was knocked out of
him. Kyle-Boyer ministered to the nose with a cold
pack made from a linen tablecloth given by the
Maronite priest, who had then fled and hidden inside

the church when he learned the courtyard intruder was a Bedouin. Al Hazzar, lying on the earth, had turned once to check for the presence of his camel, who stared unblinkingly over the wall at the goings-on in the court, and then sat up, indicating to Kyle-Boyer that he had had enough of the cold pack. The bleeding had ended.

"The nose is, I take it, Dr. Kyle-Boyer, broken?" the Bedouin asked.

"I'm afraid so, Sheik Al Hazzar," Kyle-Boyer returned obsequiously.

"Ah, a cyclic life indeed. This is the second time now that it has happened, and both times in connection with my friend Meyer Elkanah Alinsky." Rheumy-eyed, the Bedouin stared off at the moonlit belfry of the church and sighed a great sigh from deep within him; he had relaxed again, become the noble Muslim fatalist once more.

"Indeed, Sheik Al Hazzar? Alinsky was involved before?"

"Yes, in Cairo, during the war. It was Meyer himself who broke my nose that time, plus three or four ribs if I remember correctly."

"What was Meyer doing in Cairo during the war?" Murphy asked. "He should have been in school in Iowa."

"Not Cairo in Egypt. Southern Illinois. Kay-roh. But he was in school, a halfback for the University of Iowa. The very incident of which I speak took place one Saturday night after the Iowa-Southern Illinois game when Meyer scored the winning touchdown. Alas, I aligned myself with a group of vengeful Illinois partisans in many cars laden with lengths of chain and sections of pipe and pieces of rubber hose, and we followed after the Iowa team down to Cairo, where they meant to add insult to injury by celebrating their victory in the bars of that town before they recrossed the Mississippi to their fief of hogs and corn, profaning as it were the sacred soil of Illinois. . . ."

"Indeed?" Kyle-Boyer prompted. Murphy kept himself from bursting out with laughter. The three English, gathered around Al Hazzar, were absolutely fascinated by the tale of two nation-states in the American midlands.

"Indeed, Dr. Kyle-Boyer!" Al Hazzar emphasized, struggling to his feet, the rage of thirty years still alive within him. He beseeched the heavens with open arms, calling down the gift of tongues from the legions of Arab poets who had preceded him. "Indeed, I tell you! And mind you they had no grounds for proper celebration. There were many questionable calls, clipping penalties which were ignored. And the referees were on the take. This was known by everyone. The Iowans had bribed them in advance of the game.

"But as I have told you our partisan group set out for Cairo, and when we arrived we found the Iowa team in a particular saloon, all boisterous and unrepentant, having frightened most of the Illinois patrons. except for a very brave few, right out the door. But we were not afraid! Oh, let my memory's recall be total and exact! May Allah himself govern the truth of my tongue so that not a degree of unlawful exaggeration come from it, but yet may he not let me understate any of the horror of that evening, so ingrained is it in my soul!"

Before the pilgrims, seated on the packed earth, Musad Al Hazzar the *rawi,* the storyteller, stripped himself for action, pulling off the tweed coat first, then dropping the leather crisscross of bandolier from his chest, and lastly plucking off two arm garters so that the sleeves of his burnoose hung loose and long and ready for dramatic emphasis. His nose had begun bleeding slowly again, and just as he accepted a handkerchief from Marilyn Aldrich the doors to the courtyard burst open and his five Bedouin followers, on foot and with their guns at the ready, charged inside. Al Hazzar stopped them with a wave of his hand and bade them sit in another semicircular row behind the pilgrims. They did so eagerly, like children, knowing that their leader was telling a tale. Up close—so close that the butt of one of their rifles rested casually against Murphy's rump—they smelled like goats.

"'The bar itself in this particular saloon of which I speak was typical of American bars of that period," Al Hazzar explained quickly, his eyes meeting those of each face before him in turn. "It occupied nearly the entirety of one wall, was long and straight, though curved at both ends, and carved of oak or some other fine wood. Such beautiful things are rarely seen in these modern times. However, I digress. . . .

"We entered the saloon as I said, some twenty of us, and immediately spied the Iowans all clustered about their hero, Meyer Alinsky, at the far end of the bar. . . ."

"*Yâ Allah! Yâ Allah!*" the Bedouin brethren chorused, a grave note, like dread, in their voices.

"The Iowans seemed not to see us. But even as we moved forward, determined to punish them for their unsportsmanlike conduct of that very afternoon, the bartender whipped out two six-guns and ordered us to deposit our chains and pipes and lengths of hose on a nearby table."

"Ooo-ah. . . ." Incredibly, Murphy realized, the sound was communal; he himself had participated in its utterance.

"What happened, Sheik Al Hazzar?" Marilyn demanded.

Al Hazzar grew conspiratorial, coming closer, closing himself in flowing sleeves. "I said then to my Illinois brothers, 'Let us do as he commands.' It must be understood that this bartender, probably of Teutonic extraction, clad in a bowler hat and long white apron, possessed of portly, likable jowls, was most probably a good fellow under normal circumstances. But such a person, a novice to arms, is most dangerous when flustered and might do much harm unwittingly. At the same time he had two Colt forty-fives which can blow a hole in a man even that wide." Al Hazzar emphasized the statement by blowing his breath through a doughnut-size hole formed by his fingers.

"Wa rahmat Allah!" the Bedouins choroused.

"We laid down our arms to relieve the bartender's nervousness and took our places in gentlemanly fashion at the nether end of the bar, away from the Iowans, and were promptly served by the now-peaceable bartender. Alas, this tactical diversion proved to be my downfall. You see, when I arrived in America to pursue my engineering degree, I took to all things American most avidly. Instantly enamored was I of American football, girls, and cars, American styles of dress, and—unhappily for this poor Muslim you see before you—American spirits also, particularly rye and bourbon whiskeys. Unhappily, I say, because I had come from a race among whom alcoholic beverages were not tolerated, so I had absolutely no way of calculating their effect on me. Usually they smote me down, though I understood this only the next morning. But on the night in Cairo of which I speak, my anger was changed to outrage because of the spirits, and I could contain myself no longer at the sight of the Iowan, Alinsky, guffawing out loud and flushed with victory at the other end of the bar—"

"So you took a shot at him with the bartender's gun, right?" Murphy prompted, certain he knew the ending.

"No. Instead I leaped onto the bar and raced the full length of it to where the Iowans clustered and dived at Meyer Alinsky, intending to knock him down and thrash him good. . . ."

"What happened? What happened?"

"By Allah, to this very day I have never understood. I awoke the next morning in the hospital, my nose broken and bandaged, four ribs cracked, and my left arm broken in two places. My attack was completely

routed by Alinsky. It is said that I dived directly
into his right fist and thereby lost the nose immediately. After that I remember nothing. Apparently
I was thrust rudely to the floor. My ribs were
stomped upon and then my left arm. Only Allah may
say if I might have lived, had not the Iowans
dragged Alinsky off and knocked him out cold with
a whiskey bottle."

Before his listeners Al Hazzar's eyes welled with
tears of sorrow or shame and he hung his head,
dabbing at his eyes with Marilyn's handkerchief. The
pilgrims stared at him in blank astonishment at
the incredible tale of the first meeting of Musad Al
Hazzar and Meyer Alinsky. Behind them the
Bedouins rocked back and forth; behind their veils
their eyes welled with tears.

But the *rawi* was not done. He paused a moment longer, a record machine changing a disk, then
began again, the poetic cadence of classical Arabic
transmitting easily to English as before. "But Allah
was merciful. He meant for Meyer and me to be
friends."

"Yâ Allah! Yâ Allah!"

"The very next day he came to the hospital to
visit me, tears of remorse in his eyes, bemoaning
the burden of his awesome temper which frequently
caused him grief. He begged my forgiveness and out
of respect for my bravery knelt on the floor to kiss
the one good hand left to me. Truly his remorse
was boundless. Immediately he had me removed to
a private room with my own private nurse. He chose
to pay for the entire cost of my confinement. My
room was filled with beauteous flowers, and my favorite bourbon was delivered clandestinely to me—"

"And you forgave him, obviously," Kyle-Boyer
urged.

"Not immediately." Al Hazzar shook a finger at
them in emphasis. "Meyer visited me many times,
driving down from Iowa as often as three times a
week, and each time we spoke of the need for a

retribution. Both agreed it should be so, since the notion was endemic to both Arab and Jew, and besides, I had suffered so one-sidedly in the affair. But the means to this retribution was difficult to determine, as you might expect, though finally we hit upon a solution. When I left the hospital we were to go, each of us with a friend as a witness, to a cornfield near the Southern Illinois campus where Meyer was to be chained to a telephone pole and I was to enjoy the privilege of flailing his naked back with a length of rubber hose for three full minutes."

"Jesus Christ!" Murphy exclaimed. "What happened?"

"I could not do it." Al Hazzar sighed. "The Arab is not a pig. I attacked him, after all. He was only defending himself against my fury. And think, had I not been so drunk, and thus uncoordinated, I might have killed him. Anyhow, Meyer was unchained, and there in that cornfield we exchanged the kiss of peace and have remained friends ever since that time. Such a worthy friendship, in fact, that I even conceded to cross over into Iowa numerous times after that to visit with Mother Rachel and Yakov his father in Aruba. But of course the war was in progress at that time and we were soon to be separated. Meyer joined the American Air Force, and I, because I held a British passport, went into the Canadian Army. We corresponded for a time, but, after the nature of all friends separated, our letters grew less frequent. My own father died right after the war, and I—*Allah akbar!*—became leader of my tribe. Life was less kind to Meyer. His father died also, and then, alas, his young wife of but a short duration, a Christian girl from Missouri whom he cared for very much—"

"Oh!" Marilyn Aldrich interjected, instant tears flashing to her eyes at the suggestion of the love story. "I'll bet it's because of her that Meyer seems sad so much of the time."

But before her, Al Hazzar shrugged with apparent indifference. "In my opinion his sadness was to have come from a monogamous culture. At the time I consoled him by letter as best I could, but I spoke to him plainly. Even then I had four wives; if one should die, three should remain to comfort my sorrow and therefore the loss was not total. And more might be added to the list to further temper my sorrow. Indeed, I urged him to join me in Palestine, into which many Jews were pouring after the war—"

"Do you mean that's why Meyer ended up in Israel?" Murphy demanded, stupefied. "For a polygamous marriage?"

"No, he came to fight for the Zionists in the war of nineteen forty-eight. He bought a surplus Dakota and flew it from Chicago to an airstrip near Beersheba in the first days of the fighting. Many whom you know came with him at the time. Mother Rachel was on board, and Mermelstein the doctor—who died, alas, some months ago in Europe—and Teplitsky, who was but a child in his mother's arms, she a woman who abandoned her cowardly husband in Chicago to fight for the Jewish state. Also, Chaim Ben Bokva came then with his parents, as a child of about five, though his family name then was not Ben Bokva but an American name, Kavarsky. Others came also, about ten I think, mostly young men. Some died in the fighting; most of the survivors returned to America after the war was ended. But I will tell you, Christian pilgrims, it was an unspeakable joy for me to meet my friend Alinsky at that time." And Al Hazzar flapped his arms in some witless conjuring of happiness.

"It was, I take it, after the cease-fire that you occasioned to meet Alinsky, Sheik Al Hazzar?" Kyle-Boyer asked.

"No, Dr. Kyle-Boyer, it was the very night that Meyer landed in Beersheba. Did I not tell you this?" The Arab looked perplexed but also as if he might faint dead away from the pain that must be recurring in his nose. "From the beginning I had thrown in my lot with the Jews. This was in the time before my lord Hussein was made king of Jordan and I was hating his Hashemite uncle and father before him and would not swear allegiance to them. The Jewish leaders came to me and I struck a good bargain with them for land and grazing rights round about Beersheba after the war in return for the help of myself and my warriors in the winning of it. As the fighting commenced, our first task was to make safe the nearby airfield where the supply planes from the outside would land. You can imagine my absolute astonishment when on the very first night of our commission the third plane to come winging its way out of the infernal darkness like a great hawk and pounce down on the humble desert runway between our lines of torches was piloted by none other than my greatest and truest friend, Meyer Alinsky. In fact—I remember it so well—the first person down the ladder once the engines were silenced was Mother Rachel herself."

"Did she kiss the earth?" Murphy asked distantly, his mind busy imagining the scene, doubtless fraught with emotion, of the Midwestern expatriates tumbling tearfully out of the Dakota to touch the sands of Eretz Israel.

"No. . . . No, I recall now that she did not," Al Hazzar answered, just as distantly, perhaps refocusing the ancient scenario in his own mind. "No, the first thing she kissed was me; then she said I looked very thin and I should eat more; then it seems to me she complained about the heat quite a bit, and the dust; and then she asked me about snakes and scorpions and malaria and the proper drinking water. Yes, she asked about all those things while the others were weeping and, as you have suggested, kissing the earth from reverence. Lastly, she asked me for directions to the ladies' room, and when I grew mirthful and proposed that all the desert might serve her well, as it had done others for centuries, she began weeping and screaming that she wanted to return home to Iowa. . . . In fact, as I think of it, she has never liked it in Israel. I wonder why she came in the first place?"

The question hung a long moment in the air. Al Hazzar's battered face was screwed up in the arduousness of trying to decipher the mystery. Then he shrugged and his eyes brightened appreciatively.

"But let me tell you what happened when Meyer Elkanah Alinsky descended from the Dakota. Immediately he wept, not for the sight of the land of Israel but for the sight of me. We embraced, both of us weeping now, and then my tall Jewish friend lifted me up affectionately and swung me about in the air many times. When he put me down he snatched the helmet from a Zionist soldier and bent over to center the ball. I yelled "Hike!" grabbed the old pigskin, and took off like blazes down the runway toward the end zone, dodging the Iowa defense all the way. I could feel Meyer's hot breath on my back, but the first time he laid a hand on me was just as I sailed over the goal line for an Illinois touchdown, so that it profited him nothing at all. You can just imagine the anger he felt!"

"Yâ Allah! Yâ Allah!" came the unexpected gloating of the Bedouin chorus, followed unexpectedly by a volley of rifle shots that ripped into the night sky and sent Alinsky's pilgrims diving for cover. Before them an incredible metamorphosis had taken place: Al Hazzar, an imaginary ball tucked beneath one arm, raced back and forth in the church courtyard, weaving, dodging, deflecting imaginary opponent tacklers with his other outstretched arm; on the sidelines his desert minions fired their magazines empty, then rent the air with a prolonged spasm of whooping when their leader apparently crossed some inevitable goal line and collapsed in safe exhaustion beyond, still in possession of the ball. In turn each of the Bedouins ran up to Musad Al Hazzar and joyfully

kissed his outstretched hand. When the last of them was done, the diminutive Southern Illinois quarterback, blood streaming anew from his nostrils because of the exertion of his running, collapsed flat on the ground in a dead faint.

In another moment the Maronite priest crept timidly into the courtyard with another cold pack of ice wrapped in a tablecloth. Kyle-Boyer ministered once again to the splayed nose while Al Hazzar's warriors watched with childlike fascination. Alinsky's pilgrims and the RTF crew quietly sipped beer and wondered aloud at the anomaly of everything that touched upon the fathomless mystery of Meyer Alinsky. The *rawi's* tale done, it only assured that nothing in the universe was in its intended place.

Thus, just before bedtime, it came as no particular surprise that the Bedouins who had so precisely chorused Al Hazzar's story understood not a single word of English among them.

25

A question of divinity

ONLY DAYS AFTER LEAVING BAALBEK, the pilgrims had to take to the hills with their Bedouin chaperones for safety.

Incredibly, in half-Christian Lebanon someone had actually gotten up and walked, standing up from his wheelchair after touching Marilyn's robe as she rode past on her white mule. The miraculous cure, instantly publicized, brought an emotional mob to Zahle, a medium-sized town in eastern Lebanon, and in that town's main square the crusaders were faced at three o'clock on a hot afternoon with a crowd that went wild. The crucifix that contained Alinsky's diamond was seized from Murphy's hands and passed rapidly among the suppliants, many of whom pressed the figure of the Christ violently to their lips. Marilyn Aldrich's shining white robe began disappearing from the hemline upward, shredded away by an army of frenetic ants bent on acquiring what might become a relic. Kyle-Boyer pulled himself atop his pack mule for safety, and Jonathan Whitmore began punching indiscriminately at those accosting Marilyn's robe, evidently amazed, from the look on his face, that they seemed completely disinclined to punch back.

There were no police to be seen. Murphy, still trying to retrieve his crucifix, understand vaguely

314

from the blaze of horn sounds in the distance that
a monster traffic jam had been created in the approaches to the square and decided that nothing like
the local riot squad might be counted upon to get
through to them in any event. But still he had not
anticipated the coming of Al Hazzar, and his surprise was total when the chieftain and his Bedouins,
normally illusory spirits shadowing the pilgrims from
distant forested hillsides, charged into the square at
full gallop to the rescue, mowing down suppliant
Christians and swinging deadly rawhide whips in the
air by way of emphasis. Horrified, standing frozen
in the carnage of wheelchairs and crutches that the
camels' renewed charging had created, Murphy saw Al
Hazzar snatch the purloined crucifix away from the
lips of a young man, then thrash him once cruelly
across the back with a snap of the whip that drew
blood, punishing him for daring to trifle with Alinsky's possession. Within moments, it seemed, of the
Bedouins' appearance, Murphy, Kyle-Boyer, and Whitmore were loaded bodily onto already saddled extra
camels that did not kneel, and hastened out of the
square, down narrow streets past lines of jammed
cars (where the Bedouins seized the weapons of a
jeepload of police), and out of Zahle to the nearby
hills. Murphy, his cross shoved through the cincture
of his robe for safekeeping, clung frightened to his
saddle pommel, trying to adjust to the swaying, lurching gait. Above his fear he was able to marvel at the
speed of a camel running at full clip.

They stopped to rest for the first time about ten
miles away from the city, finally clear of the trailing
carloads of zealots who regrouped after the shock of
Al Hazzar's attack had passed and came after them,
either to pursue the sacredness of Marilyn Aldrich or
to save her from the Bedouins. The camels were
made to kneel, side by side, in a small clearing in a
scented woods of cedar and pine. Al Hazzar, the first
to alight, undid the wrap of his kaffiyeh, exposing
his bandages and the deep pockets of bruise that

clung like quarter moons beneath his eyes. He
stared a long moment at fabulous Mount Hermon
to the south, covered with snow from its midpoint
to its summit, and smiled almost wistfully, perhaps
at the notion that it looked so distantly safe and
clean. Then he turned to face Marilyn Aldrich, who
had been helped from her mule. Her long white robe
had become a tattered miniskirt. For the first time
since the crusade left Normandy, Murphy saw that
she had long beautiful legs, albeit scratched.

"Those Christians are absolutely fanatically crazy
people," Al Hazzar judged, gritting his teeth in anger
and working his worry beads swiftly through his
fingers. "Islam has always understood this." His
eyes fell on Murphy's crucifix, lying against the saddle of a squatting camel, and he lifted it up scowling,
staring closely at the impaled figure. "This Christian
prophet, this Christ who is said to be both a god
and a man, what if he is but a fraud? What if he
was no more than a cunning Judean who thought he
saw a way to rid his land of the Romans, only
to have the scheme backfire and end in his crucifixion?
A great irony, would you not agree? Especially considering the wars, the massacres, the armies set
destructively in motion as in the time of the Crusades in the very name of that crucifixion. . . ."

"I would remind you, Sheik Al Hazzar," Kyle-
Boyer told him gruffly, "that the slate of Islam is
not lily white and pure either. The Arab armies also
went proselytizing with the sword. Why, if they hadn't
been stopped by Poitiers or the Turks at Vienna,
all of Europe would be a continent of wogs and
mosques today—with the obvious exception of England, of course."

"Islam is the voice of Allah himself, through
the mouth of his prophet Mohammed. I will not
hear it defiled, Kyle-Boyer." Al Hazzar pounded the
butt of the crucifix's staff sharply against a rock. "It
is an intelligent and comforting belief. It teaches
temperance and has codified a body of law in the

Koran under which a man might consider himself honored to live. It teaches also the place of women in the world. Could you imagine anything like this happening to a Muslim woman?" He gestured with the crucifix at Marilyn Aldrich, who leaned against a tree and stared vacuously off toward the peak of the same Mount Hermon at which Al Hazzar himself had smiled before her.

"I do not choose to defend the function of Christian womanhood to the likes of you, Al Hazzar."

"Defend it, Kyle-Boyer? You would do better to repudiate it. To elevate a woman to the position of a deity, to actually revere her as if she possessed the ability to walk on air or to eliminate the curse of leprosy with a touch of her hands, is foolish. For she will come to believe it, she will take airs upon herself, and after that she will never be useful to you again. The profound wisdom of Islam has always understood this. Otherwise excess will occur. Look at Christianity. What of the mother of the prophet? I have seen the great cathedrals of the West built in her name. I have witnessed festivals in her honor. Often it seems to me that the Christians have forgotten the prophet himself, choosing the woman as substitute. What of you, Whitmore? What will you do for future employ if your woman here chooses to be known as a saint?"

"She is a saint, Al Hazzar," Jonathan Whitmore said calmly, regarding Marilyn rapturously. "I seen the miracle myself. That poor bugger reached out and touched Marilyn 'n' then he stood right up out of his wheelchair and walked. She must be a saint."

"She is a prostitute." Al Hazzar sniggered contemptuously. "A prostitute who agreed for the price of forty thousand American dollars to fake her own miraculous cure and then ride a jackass to Jerusalem in an act of sham thanksgiving."

"Mary Magdalene was also a prostitute," Kyle-Boyer retorted, "but Our Lord loved her nonethe-

less. She is now venerated as a Christian saint. Evil
is not unredemptive."

"Ah, I see the problem." Al Hazzar smiled
wanly. "A problem that my brother Meyer could
not have foreseen. The ugly ducklings have become
glorious swans, according to the cliché. An alcoholic,
an abortionist, a prostitute, and her procurer are no
longer merely the bearers of Alinsky's diamond to
Jerusalem—"

"That was before, Al Hazzar," Jonathan Whitmore
interrupted. "We're different now. We've changed. After walkin' all the way from Normandy behind the
cross in the company of a holy man like Father
Bisson, 'n' then seein' Marilyn's miracle like we did,
we couldn't be the same as we was. Me 'n' Marilyn
could go back to Birmingham, but we couldn't live
like we did. Murphy ain't hardly touched a drop
since he joined up, except for the few times we all
got awash together. And Kyle-Boyer himself has said
he couldn't go back to scrapin' babies."

"Divinity everywhere." Al Hazzar snorted. He
turned and spoke in Arabic to his five Bedouins,
all of whom squatted in a uniform line, wrapped
to eye level, their rifles planted on the ground before them. Their response was gales of laughter, and
they tamped the earth before them with the butts of
their guns. One of them spoke, gesturing frequently
toward Marilyn Aldrich, accompanied again by the
mirth of his fellows.

"They do not think you have changed. They do not
believe in Marilyn Aldrich's miracle either. They think
it is the work of Meyer Alinsky, playing a game for
his own amusement."

"It was a miracle!" Jonathan Whitmore shouted.

"Do you also believe it to be so?" Al Hazzar
demanded of Kyle-Boyer. "You, a medical doctor?"

"Yes, absolutely. I was there. I saw it. Given
even the madness of Meyer Alinsky, there could
be no profit to be gained from having that person stand up out of his wheelchair. No, that man

was a paraplegic. He was not Alinsky-sent. We have witnessed a miracle."

"And you, Murphy?"

"I don't believe in miracles," Murphy heard himself say. "I can't think of the reason for it, but Alinsky must have sent that man out on a job."

"You have the wisdom of Islam in you, Murphy, to say such a thing. It is no wonder that Meyer speaks of you always in a special voice and full of awe. But it is as you say. The man had to be sent by Meyer. I shall ask him as soon as we reach Jerusalem, and I guarantee you what his answer will be. But come, we have rested long enough. I will send one of my men back to deliver instructions to Gervais and his crew. We must be well into the hills for safety from the Lebanese police by night."

"I'm not going on with you, Sheik Al Hazzar," Marilyn Aldrich said abruptly. "I'm going back to Zahle. There's lots of sick people back there who need my help. I could cure lots more than I already have."

"*La!* I will not permit it!" Al Hazzar screamed, brandishing Murphy's crucifix at her. "Meyer will not permit it either! Be reasonable, I beg you. For you to go back to Zahle might be worse for you than you think. For not only would you cure not one of those poor hopeful Christian idiots, but they in fact might turn on you and rip you to pieces once they understood you had failed them. I know these people; they are spirit worshipers of a technical age. They can be very dangerous when their belief in the mystical goes unrewarded."

"They won't harm me, Sheik Al Hazzar. They're good people. I sensed it back there. I'll go among them and cure as many as I can lay hands upon."

"Do you really think, Marilyn Aldrich, that you have the power to cure men's deformities?" Al Hazzar asked the question bemusedly, a squint-eyed, speculative look on his face. In his absorption he tapped one end of the crucifix's crossbar against a puffed-out cheek.

"Yes, I believe our Lord Jesus has given me the power to heal the sick and the lame."

"Then would you be kind enough to have a look at the foot of my loyal follower here, who is called Hassan. He has a most peculiar ailment, even since the moment of his birth, I am told."

Al Hazzar spoke in rapid Arabic to the one called Hassan, who stood up from the line of squatting Bedouins, walked forward a few yards without a perceptible limp or lurch, and then sat down again. First he dropped the wrap of his kaffiyeh to reveal a surprisingly old but almost handsome face framed in a snow-white beard. Then he began removing the boot from his right leg, struggling with it until the actual sight of the foot it had covered—gnarled and calloused like the well-worn head of a walking stick—produced a general wince of revulsion from the attentive pilgrims. A chock of rubber, carved perhaps from a truck tire, was strapped to the limb, completing the outline of the inside of the boot. Mischievously, old Hassan wiggled his toes at them in the air.

"Cure that, Marilyn Aldrich, and you may return at once to Zahle." Al Hazzar smirked at her.

Incredibly, Murphy felt his heart begin beating furiously at the possibility that she might do just that. She smiled beatifically at the Bedouin elder, moving slowly toward him so that his mask of mischief became uncertain and he looked long at his leader, Al Hazzar, and once even turned back to his fellows, who were suddenly oblivious of him, staring raptly instead at Marilyn Aldrich.

"Give it all you've got, Marilyn honey," Jonathan Whitmore exhorted her. "Tell him to take off that rubber brace so it'll be easier for the foot to fill out and become whole again."

"Put the power of the Lord Jesus into that poor man's battered limb, dear Marilyn!" Kyle-Boyer urged,

passionately kissing her hand as she moved past him.
"For you have the power of the Lord in you! Oh,
how I have sinned and defiled His name!"

Change nothing, O Lord! Murphy, who was bent
on picking up his check, retrieving his wife and son
in Jerusalem, and returning home to France begged
heaven. He watched as Marilyn knelt before old
Hassan, staring myopically at the fear in his face
as if currents of curing grace were meant to streak
out of her eyes, then laid her hands upon the foot,
undoing the fastening straps of the rubber block. Then,
unbelievably, while Musad Al Hazzar gave way to his
own variety of fear and clutched reflexively at
Murphy's arm for strength, Marilyn Aldrich bent
over and kissed the ugly limb.

Murphy's prayers were answered; the foot remained
as before. Al Hazzar breathed a sigh of profound
relief and released Murphy's arm. Marilyn Aldrich,
Jonathan Whitmore, and Kyle-Boyer stared unblinkingly at the stub, their faces mirroring their absolute
disbelief that the power of the mediatrix had failed.
Old Hassan wiggled his toes before her face again,
and the Bedouin brotherhood let out with a joyful
chorus, firing their rifles into the air yet another time
so that two camels, from fear, leaped to their feet
and bounded out of the clearing. *"Yâ Allah! Yâ Allah! Allah akbar!"*

Hassan stood up, not bothering to return the rubber brace to the foot, and performed a kind of
limping, mocking dance around Marilyn Aldrich, who
had burst into tears, still kneeling on the ground.
His fellow Bedouins clapped hands to its rhythm,
and Al Hazzar tamped the earth with the staff of
the crucifix he still held.

"I don't understand what happened. I put all my
power into his foot. I could sense it," Marilyn Aldrich lamented.

"He weren't no Christian, Marilyn," Whitmore
consoled her. "He's just a bloody Mohammedan. That's
why the foot didn't come round."

"Yes, that's it exactly, Marilyn." Kyle-Boyer reasoned for her. "We'll take you back to Zahle. There are many Christian cripples there. We can establish a shrine in the town and build a hospital to house the sick and the maimed—"

"You English have gone absolutely mad," Al Hazzar decided quietly. Then he turned to Murphy. "I have seen this before. When the British were in Palestine we would often find mad Englishmen wandering through the Negev or in Sinai looking for their Jesus. It is the fault of the climate, I think. The heat fries their brains."

"It's not March yet," Murphy answered. "It hasn't been particularly warm thus far."

"It must be the distance, then." Al Hazzar shrugged. "We are a long way from England." Turning, Alinsky's friend shouted a command again in Arabic. Two of his men sprang up and dragged Marilyn Aldrich to her feet and, almost before she thought to protest, forced a gag into her mouth. Two more grabbed Jonathan Whitmore, who for once, perhaps because of his continuing disbelief in the lack of miracle, was slow to respond to the assault, and knotted a rawhide cord around his wrists. Kyle-Boyer was thought ineffectual, perhaps; droop-jawed, he stood alone, dimly perceiving, his eyes seemingly absorbed by old Hassan attaching the rubber block to his foot and then pulling his boot over the whole. Marilyn Aldrich was carried to her mule and her hands tied to the saddle pommel. Whitmore, also gagged, was thrown over a camel's saddle, his body tightly wedged in the crook, another cord run from his wrists to his ankles beneath the animal.

"We must leave quickly and head higher up into the hills," Al Hazzar urged. "The police may have heard that volley of rifles celebrating the glories of Islam." He gazed about for a long moment, frowning at the assemblage of animals and humans he meant to lead over the mountains back into Syria, and then fixed Murphy's crucifix that he still held in one hand with a look of impossible rage. "Bah! I could kill someone for the indignity that this religion has forced upon me! To become a fugitive in the lands of these dog-mating Lebanese and those pig-raising Syrians! Now we must travel by night, fleeing from police and Christians everywhere—"

Al Hazzar could not find words to finish, apparently; he looked a moment longer at the crucifix and then flung it away from him on the ground, even though it contained Meyer Alinsky's diamond. But he had certainly not reckoned with the reaction of Austin Kyle-Boyer.

"You shall not defile the sufferings of our beloved Savior!" the ex-abortionist shouted, and then wound up before anyone could think to stop him and hurled a right hook in the direction of Al Hazzar's face. His great ham of a hand instantly flattened the Bedouin leader's mending nose, though it did not bowl him over; a Rorschach print of bright red blood spread across the bandagings.

"Oh, no, it is not possible," Al Hazzar lamented, sitting down heavily on a rock. He shook his head from side to side and touched the nose gingerly; his warriors seemed too astounded to reprimand Kyle-Boyer for the attack.

"Henceforth I shall champion our blessed Lord's cause with every last fiber of my being," Kyle-Boyer proclaimed ecstatically. "With all my powers and strengths." Before him, on the ground, Musad Al Hazzar pulled off the now completely soaked bandagings.

"I have always observed that a Christian understands nothing of the bottomless depths in the well of his Christianity until the chips are down," Al Hazzar said. "And I do not mean this as a compliment to you, Dr. Kyle-Boyer."

Then he wrote out a note of instruction for Gervais, Ricard, and Lebel, dabbed it with a bit of blood, and dispatched old Hassan the cripple to deliver it. In another moment he lay back and passed out yet another time, presumably from the pain.

26

The great Damascus ride-past

KYLE-BOYER, NEWLY CHRISTIAN, was remorseful. Al Hazzar was wrathful and would not speak to anyone except his followers for days.

The Bedouin leader's nose, by then thrice broken in some connection with Alinsky or his purposes, was repaired by a young doctor in a fedayeen camp higher up in the hills, just short of the Syrian border. Afterward they crossed into Syria illegally, between border stations, with the help of those same fedayeen and picked their way across the mountains for nearly a week toward Zebdani, the first big town on the Syrian side, traveling only at night, the camels' feet bound against the treacherous beds of shale, fearful of meeting a Syrian patrol, which would certainly try to return them to Lebanon to face charges for the violence of Zahle. They camped near Zebdani for some days while Al Hazzar awaited the return of old Hassan and news of Etienne Gervais and his RTF crew.

Hassan, his Bedouin radar faultless, entered the camp toward dawn of the third day with a letter from Gervais explaining that the three Frenchmen had crossed into Syria and were busy filming refugee

camps at the emphatic suggestion of the Propaganda
Ministry and that they would continue to do so
all the way across the country in the hope of keeping the Baathist regime appeased. They planned
to rejoin the crusaders in Jordan at Al-Mafraq.
In addition they had received a communication
from Alinsky in Jerusalem warning all concerned,
Bedouins and pilgrims, to proceed cautiously and
avoid the environs of Damascus at all cost; the
Syrian police had posted a reward for the capture
of the Bedouins (though not for the pilgrims) and
also, in Damascus, a city of many Christians, a pietistic
fervor was abuilding for the sight of the fugitive
mediatrix, Blessed Marilyn Aldrich, and Alinsky
commanded that under no circumstances should a
repetition of the events of Zahle be permitted.

"Bah! Shit!" Al Hazzar cursed, throwing Gervais's
letter into the fire. "Meyer is truly testing my love for
him. This mission was to have been an easy task,
easier than driving sheep to better pasture. Now,
since we are criminals, look at my alternatives."
He sighed, pulling a well-worn map from his saddle-
bag. "Either we go east into the desert and make a
wide loop around Damascus and cross over into the
most inhospitable part of my lord Hussein's Hashemite kingdom, or we are forced to try our luck in
a corridor but thirty miles wide between Damascus
and the Israeli lines east of Golan, one that is sure
to be filled with the Syrian military."

"Which will take longer, Sheik Al Hazzar?" Jonathan Whitmore asked.

"The desert route obviously, you fool. Longer by
perhaps two full weeks. The other is much shorter
but far more dangerous. There are no Bedouins there,
so no one to trust. We must go the longer route."

"That's too bloody far," Whitmore judged. "Are
you a gamblin' man, Al Hazzar? The cockney narrowed his eyes cagily. In the week since his woman,
Marilyn, had failed to cure old Hassan he seemed
to Murphy to have returned to being Jonathan Whit-

more again, disavowing, apparently, his faith in the possibility of the miraculous.

"I am said to be the best poker player in the Levant," Al Hazzar stated flatly, "though there is a Greek in Cairo who fancies himself thus also. But he has refused all my challenges to this day."

"Have you got a deck with you?"

"Always."

"Let's pick high card."

"And the stakes?" Despite the bandages and blotches of bruise, Al Hazzar's eyes grew keen with excitement. Automatically, not looking behind him, he removed a poker deck from a side pocket in his camel saddle, telling his tribesmen what was at hand; they clustered around, squatting on the ground, rubbing their hands together in anticipation, casting evil eyes at Whitmore.

"If you picks high card," Jonathan told him, "we goes the way I know you intends to go, the long way. If I picks high card we go straight down that little corridor you're talkin' about 'n' takes our chances with the military. Agreed?"

Al Hazzar's face, despite its covering, was obviously screwed up in the consternation of trying to decide on the odds.

He spoke again to his followers, and an earnest dialogue ensued during which old Hassan even shook his fist at Whitmore. Then Al Hazzar spoke, his eyes riveting Whitmore's face. "If you win they say the way through the corridor is not safe. But they hate you for the trouble you've caused them and wish that I take the chance so you might be beaten and suffer humiliation at the behest of Allah, plus the discomfort of the long route."

"You A-rabs is a very sportin' kind of people," Whitmore pronounced. "I've always maintained that. You shuffle, Al Hazzar."

"Yes. Then you shuffle, Whitmore, and we choose. And Allah grant high card to his servant Musad Al Hazzar."

Al Hazzar's virtuosity with a deck of cards was indescribable, Murphy thought. But Jonathan Whitmore's was even better. Done shuffling, he fanned the deck into a wide arc on a blanket spread out on the ground. Al Hazzar chose a card, then sat back, smiling broadly across at his opponent. "The king of hearts, Whitmore *effendi*. You will have to choose fortuitously indeed."

Jonathan Whitmore picked up a card, smiled broadly in his turn, and held it up to show. Impossibly, like a preshoot-out scene from a bad Western, it was the ace of spades.

"That is not possible!" Al Hazzar shrieked. "Such things occur only in cowboy films!"

"Yeah, I seen 'em, too, Al Hazzar. Then one cowboy gets mad at the other 'n' he stands up from the table 'n' shoots. Only I ain't got a gun 'n' the blooming deck belongs to you, so I didn't stack it. Now, unless you intends killin' me, I understand we goes down the corridor, right?"

Al Hazzar studied Whitmore for a long moment, then shrugged. "It must be the will of Allah who has deserted me that we go that route. It is too singular a sign to be otherwise." He acquainted his followers with the news, and to Murphy they looked disbelieving to a man, though obviously awed at the same time by Whitmore's certain magic.

Afterward, while they waited out the day until darkness, Murphy spoke to Jonathan over a noonday meal of mutton and rice.

"Your luck is incredible, Jonathan."

"Bullshit, Murph. I got my hands on that deck two days ago 'n' marked that ace so I could set 'im up for that little roll. Any fool could tell from lookin' at that map that we was gonna have to go the desert route, 'n' I had to think of some sick way to change the minds of six Bedouins armed to the bloody teeth."

"You've saved us quite a bit of traveling, in any event."

"That ain't all, Murph. I'm gettin' rid of Mr. Musad 'n' his goons for us, too. I figure the odds are two to one that the Syrian military will intercept us 'n' haul our chaperones off to jail. It's them they want, not us, 'n' even if we are in the country illegally we can always say they brought us in. Then I'll be even with that wog for sayin' Marilyn ain't holy 'n' can't perform a miracle. She can, I tell you. The reason that bugger Hassan's foot didn't get better is 'cause he's a Mohammedan, not because Marilyn ain't got the power."

"What will you and Marilyn do when you return to England and reality?" Murphy asked, trying to make a joke and dimly incredulous that the very worldly Jonathan still believed in his woman's divinity.

"Set up in business. Like a faith healer, you know, Murph? I'll be the manager 'n' Marilyn can do the cures. We'll set up a kind of temple in Birmingham. I was thinkin' about askin' old Austin to come in with us, sort of like resident physician to certify the cures. It makes it a lot more legal when you got a doctor on the premises. But that's all gonna happen later. First things first, I always say. The next project is to make sure the sheik of Araby ends up in a Syrian jail, even if I have to do a little loud whistling to alert the troops to the fact that we're sneakin' about."

Whitmore began whistling almost from the moment they broke camp that night, and consequently he rode the next seven nights that it took to reach the safety of the Jordanian border gagged and ignominiously tied to his camel saddle. His plan for the capture of Al Hazzar and his warriors failed miserably, for Al Hazzar, though duped at cards, was in his element when it came to evading military patrols. They avoided roadways, except to scurry across them, and kept to fields, forests, and the innumerable wadis that pierced the land everywhere like earthquake fissures; once they even threaded their way for miles along the bottom of an irrigation ditch, the camels knee deep in the brackish water, the two mules immersed to their bellies.

The environs of Damascus, the place of Al Hazzar's greatest apprehension, proved to be the easiest to navigate. The sky was overcast that night, with the moon only fleetingly seen, and, except for the huge general glow of Damascus to the east, the only lights were those of the villages and farms between which they threaded their way, keeping to the fields, churning a damaging wake through what seemed like an endless sea of sugar beets. They rode in two columns, Bedouin next to crusader, Murphy first in line beside Al Hazzar, his crucifix wrapped in cloth so as not to reflect any moonlight. About 3 A.M., with the city lights slipping behind them, Al Hazzar gave off a great sigh, his breath smoking in the chill air, and broke silence for the first time yet in all their furtive night traveling.

"I tire of all this sneaking about, Murphy. Do you not also? Musad Al Hazzar was not meant to hide by daylight, his nerves a-tingle with the fear that the barking of some dog will end in a jail sentence. Bah! I hope the reason Meyer stole that diamond and enlisted you people to walk to Jerusalem was at least an intelligent one. Otherwise this seems stupid, a kind of playacting—except for the fact that Syrian patrols fire real bullets."

"You don't know why he stole the diamond?" Murphy asked. He was surprised at the levelness of his own reaction. He felt baffled rather than anything else; all along he had assumed Al Hazzar was such an intimate of the inscrutable Alinsky that he would know the reason for sure, but at the same time he had considered it useless to inquire.

"No. How would I know? He tells me nothing of this, though we are brothers in this life and unto the next. Indeed, he offends me on this point. Riley does not know either. Nor Mother Rachel. The castrato knows, I think, but he would not tell me, and one cannot threaten the castrato for the information, for as the castrato always says, he has nothing more to lose." Al Hazzar sighed deeply, his frustration revealed. Overhead the moon broke through the clouds, and turning, Murphy could see the other studying him closely above the level of his kaffiyeh. Then the Bedouin spoke again. "But tell me, Murphy, Meyer has not spoken to you either of his purpose?"

"He did once, back in Italy, but it was a lie. I have no real idea what it's all about. Just a couple of guesses."

"I have guesses of my own, but I always end up abandoning them because they make no sense to me. Besides, it is impossible to know what is happening on the inside of Meyer. He has a demon living there, something restless and tormenting. He is rich and powerful, but not satisfied ever. And worse, he has an ambivalent character. I have observed this often in the Jews. One part is like the Arab; he will take your eye if you take his. The other part is like no one else on earth; if you take one of his eyes, he will invite you to have the other. Meyer is forever somewhere between the two. Look at the castrato. First he ruins him; then he becomes his patron from remorse."

"It's something of the same thing with my wife and son, I think," Murphy said pensively. "Alinsky took them as hostages in the beginning, just to make sure I stayed in line and kept marching. But it's different now. It's easy to sense, too. As if their captivity has gotten beyond his control and they've become family to him—or worse."

"You speak truthfully of this, Murphy. Unwittingly, he was seduced by them. He fancies Monique but can do nothing, because among Meyer's strange codes one dictates that he cannot tarry with a married woman. And Jean-Philippe has become a son to him, nothing less. He teaches him sports and riflery, all those things I suppose he would have taught his own son if ever he had one back in America."

"You mean he's raising the kid the way I should have, don't you, Al Hazzar?" Murphy demanded testily.

"Judge for yourself, Murphy. I cannot. Perhaps these things were no longer important after you moved to France and began your drinking."

Murphy shrugged. "I don't drink any more. That part of my old life is ended for sure. And it occurs to me that my marriage may be ended once I get to Jerusalem. Monique likes nice things, and I certainly won't be able to keep her in the style she seems to have gotten used to with Alinsky. I doubt if Jean-Philippe will want to return with me either. In fact, I don't know where I'll go. I don't want to spend the rest of my days in that drafty château back in France."

It had been his first thought in ages about the future after Jerusalem, Murphy realized dimly. But of one thing he felt certain: Ahead was an open-ended possibility. The past would never be reclaimed—should not be, in fact.

Above, the sky began showing streaks of brightening in preparation for the dawn. Soon, like the rats Al Hazzar had taken to comparing them to, they would go into hiding for another day. A curious pleasure stole into Murphy as he glanced sideways again at Al Hazzar. The bouncing gaits of their two camels synchronized perfectly; they cleared the green sea of some farmer's sugar beets like twin hulls of a catamaran.

"Murphy, I would tell you something since I have come to like you well during our travels together. You are a rational man, not given to superstitious nonsense like these three English with us."

"What is it, Musad Al Hazzar?"

"Guard yourself well when we reach Jerusalem, for I fear what will happen there."

"Why?"

"Because Meyer seeks more from this pilgrimage than he tells, and now as I think of some things

we have discussed in the past I grow more frightened. For instance, a year ago he told me he had
need of a vengeance. I pleaded with him. 'Meyer,
my brother, if you have need of a vengeance, I
would be honored to achieve it for you.' But his
course was not logical. He would not name his
enemy so that I might put a bullet right through
the man's heart and fulfill—"

"That would be too simple for Alinsky." Murphy
interrupted the other. "If you killed his enemy outright, Meyer wouldn't gain one iota of the satisfaction
he would be looking for. Better to keep the pot
boiling and heighten the complexity and draw out
Meyer's perverse enjoyment to the last tender mor-
sel. What did he do for an alternative? I can't
guess."

"Do not speak lightly of this, Murphy. I have
more to tell you. When a bullet through the heart
was not enough, he looked about for other means.
By Allah I am ashamed to tell you how he began.
He demanded that I take him, a non-Muslim, to Mecca
to ask the *khadis* about the nature of vengeance. Into
the very place of the *kaaba* itself! I protested I could
not, that it was sacrilegious to do so, but Meyer is
very persuasive. So we went. His Arabic is excellent,
and we dressed him as a pilgrim and were not de-
tected, even though I feared the curtain of the *kaaba*
might rise into the air and fling itself down upon me,
suffocating me for punishment."

"They might have killed him if they had found
out, am I right?" Murphy demanded, incredulous at
the notion of such brazenness.

"Absolutely. They would have torn him to pieces.
I was drenched to the skin with fearing all the time.
And the trip was useless besides. He was told exactly
what I told him he would be told. The glorious Koran
is quite explicit about retaliation. Payment is due in
like kind. But that was not good enough, so we
went elsewhere to ask about the nature of vengeance,

a silly thing to do since the Koran tells all there is to know."

Al Hazzar began his exasperated sighing again, throwing his hands skyward, his breath smoke rising in clouds. Murphy, aflame with speculation, thought he saw a disparate universe of pieces coming suddenly together, the same way he sensed the troubled Al Hazzar saw it too. Also he remembered the night of the sunset over the Bay of Naples when Alinsky had begged him to become surrogate for an unknown murderer. It astounded him to realize that every morning since then he had spoken Alinsky's formula for the assumption of that murderer's guilt.

"Where elsewhere, Al Hazzar?" Murphy asked, certain he already knew the answer, or at least part of it.

"To Rome to see His Highness, the Pope, and later to England to see His Lordship at Canterbury, where Meyer bought me this fine tweed jacket you see me wearing to appease me. But what they said to him pleased him very much, I think, for he came away from Rome saying he thought he had found the method for his vengeance. When he left England he was certain he had found it. But he did not speak to me of it precisely."

"He had nothing more to say after that? Simply that he had found the way?"

"Yes, Murphy, one thing. He spoke often of the Christ, the Christian prophet. He had become fascinated by the Christian belief that the one, by his death, had redeemed the many. He spoke of it often with Father Riley and consulted scholars at the university in Jerusalem. Then he stole the diamond from the Angoulême cathedral. . . ."

There was a silence while they moved on for perhaps another minute; then old Hassan came abreast of them, whispering urgently to Al Hazzar and pointing upward at the increasing brightness of the sky. But Alinsky's friend ignored his man and unexpectedly seized Murphy's free hand, pressing it to his lips after he had dropped the kaffiyeh from his face.

"Beware, Murphy. Take special care when you reach Jerusalem. I think you are Meyer's Christ. Not only do you carry the cross into that city, but he believes you are divine."

"I?" Murphy laughed despite himself. "I used to be an alcoholic."

"Little matter. In Iowa the tornado refused to kill you, even when you wished it. Meyer speaks of it always. He holds you absolutely in awe."

"If I'm the Christ, who are the others?" Murphy asked, jerking the crucifix behind him.

"Company, perhaps, so you do not grow lonely. But Meyer cannot intend them as victims, the way he intends you, I think. They are not worth it. Privately I hope they die for the sake of their country, for they will doubtless do more harm than good if ever they return to England with these notions of that prostitute's holiness in their heads."

"Do you suppose, Al Hazzar, that Meyer will actually have me crucified when we reach Jerusalem?"

"I see you are amused, Murphy, and I will admit that all this conjecture seems crazy. But even though I love Meyer, I fear him also. He laughs, he plays, he is self-effacing and pretends innocence, but at the same time he has much madness in him. This crime he seeks a vengeance for has driven him there. He is not yet done with you. For your own sake I will watch you closely in Israel."

The dawn was almost total now, and old Hassan, growing more agitated by the minute, began actually whining with fear at his first sight of an army convoy climbing the face of a distant hillside. They fled the sea of sugar beets and descended into a nearby wadi, racing along its course for perhaps a mile until they came to an abandoned, half-destroyed village that the Israelis had swept through before halting their advance in the Six-Day War. They picked their way through the eerie silence between mounds of rubble and entered the courtyard of the mosque whose dome had collapsed inward. They prepared breakfast, ate, then bedded down to sleep into the late afternoon, except for taking their turns on watch. But Murphy, thinking of Meyer Alinsky and the proximity of Jerusalem, could not sleep. Al Hazzar, thinking perhaps of the same things, did not sleep either. Instead he sat staring through the battered doors of the mosque to the darkness inside, working his worry beads through his fingers. . . .

After three more nights of clandestine travel they came at dawn to the border of Jordan, their timing perfect as Al Hazzar had intended. On the other side, in the kingdom of Hussein, were more than a hundred of the Bedouin leader's followers on camel and horseback and in pickup trucks waiting for their appearance. Ten or so had already crossed into Syria and overrun a small outpost, whose four guards, looking terrified, were tied to a nearby tree. Crusaders and Bedouins together rode the last two hundred yards or so at a gallop into Jordan and into the midst of the waiting greeters, who rent the morning stillness with delirious shouts and the burst of rifles fired into the air. Al Hazzar and his five men of Alinsky's mission each emphatically spit on the soil of Syria before they crossed the line, then conversely kissed a framed photograph of the mustachioed young Hussein before alighting from the camels. Vaguely, Murphy decided before sitting down to breakfast of cakes and tea that if Israel possessed a real secret weapon, it had to be the Arabs themselves. . . .

In time two jeeploads of Legionnaires came to investigate the noise and shooting, but apparently recognizing cousins and brothers among the horde of Bedouins, they also sat down for a snack of cakes and tea and did not seem remotely concerned about the four Syrians still tied to their tree across the line.

27

Yerushalayim, capital of the Jewish nation

THEY BEGAN WALKING AGAIN toward the city from the Syrian border according to Alinksy's instructions, accompanied now by perhaps thirty remaining Bedouins of Al Hazzar's tribe, who rode in two files on either side of the main road to Amman. All the Arabs came from the environs of Beersheba, in Israel, and meant to return there by the same illegal means that brought them to Jordan in the first place. But they were clearly at home in either country. The crusaders were compelled to halt often and drink many cups of spicy cardamom coffee, as Al Hazzar and his entourage visited with a vast assortment of relatives and friends in villages and small tent compounds.

At Al-Mafraq, as per plan, they rejoined Gervais, Ricard, and Lebel and the two RTF vehicles and learned that Gervais, who had shot miles of film footage in the Syrian refugee camps, had mated his sense of outrage to his hatred of Meyer Alinsky and was on a violent anti-Israel diatribe, intending to return the film to France once Jerusalem was reached for the purpose of producing a damning documentary. Al Hazzar, apprised of the plan, seized the film and burned it in a roadside ditch.

"How can you do that?" Gervais screamed, his face apoplectic, wanting desperately to punish Al Hazzar but fearing his thirty followers. "You're an Arab, too."

"Without a doubt," Al Hazzar told him calmly, "but not a Palestinian. There is a difference. I swear allegiance to my lord Hussein, though I live in Israel and these people have nearly wrecked his kingdom. Soon a reckoning with them will be in order."

"Your attitude is outrageous, Al Hazzar," Gervais persisted. "Is it right that the price of ending the Jewish diaspora should be the beginning of a Palestinian diaspora? Have you no compassion at all for these poor people?"

"Do not speak to me of compassion, Christian Frenchman. It was the crimes of you, a Westerner, and others like you who drove the Jews back to this land in their desperation for survival. If you choose to lay the blame somewhere, begin at the beginning. But I will listen to no more. I am a Bedouin, leader of my tribe. The Bedouins have lived in this Levant since the first moment and will continue until the last, and my responsibility alone is to preserve my tribe, no matter what becomes of the Palestinians or the Israelis. For now, the Israelis suffice. They pay good wages to those who will work, and there is social security. The men of my tribe are eager to grow old and begin receiving their benefits. Hassan, *leke*," he called to his old favorite, speaking to him in Arabic.

The cripple came forward and in answer to Al Hazzar's command produced a savings bank deposit book that he carefully unwrapped from a plastic covering. Giddy with pleasure, he shoved the open book before Etienne Gervais's nose and pointed to the last recorded amount. Gervais, an emotional person forever beset with abstract principles that Murphy supposed the young man had acquired from too much reading and too little living, merely shook his head at the hopeless irony of events. But he was further overwhelmed. From the other Bedouins bankbooks appeared like swarms of locusts and were passed about in some Levantine variety of a potlatch ceremony. One man, whose assets totaled 5,245 Israel pounds, explained to Murphy, with Al Hazzar the wise leader translating, the miracle of bank interest and how it produced increments for which a man need not even work, then kissed the hand of the chieftain who had first led them into high finance. In the end, after perhaps thirty minutes, they set off again down the road to Amman. Al Hazzar, riding his camel beside Murphy, who walked, shrugged his shoulders and winked down at the crossbearer. "Gervais is a young hothead. When he gets to Jerusalem his Jewish wife will change many of his attitudes."

"Some of what he says about those refugees is true, Al Hazzar, and I think you know it."

"Perhaps, Murphy, but when one has but 5,245 Israel lire in the bank, one cannot afford to be a humanitarian as Gervais would like. Enough said. Let us march on."

After Amman they turned west, toward Israel, the magnetic tug of the holy city irresistible now, Murphy excitedly imagining his first sight of the place, its special tawny color, as Al Hazzar lovingly described it, spread out over the many hills.

On the east bank of the Jordan River the Bedouin leader returned the pilgrims' passports, properly stamped for a legal entry into Hussein's kingdom, and bade them good-bye, casting a contemptuous evil eye on everyone except Murphy, whom he reminded in private to be especially cautious, assuring the crossbearer that he, Al Hazzar, would be waiting in Jerusalem and meant to keep a close eye out for Murphy's safety. Their passports were stamped on the Jordanian side, the now-familiar salute given by the military, and Alinsky's diamond crossed the river to the west bank, the Israeli side, where they were welcomed to the Jewish state by an Army colonel—a government representative—who praised their fortitude in walking so far for so noble a reason and assured them the climax of Jerusalem was close at hand. On the opposite bank, where the Bedouins had already begun moving southward to the place below the Dead Sea where they intended to cross into Israel, only Al Hazzar remained. Murphy turned once after passing through the border station to wave a fond good-bye to the man, but Al Hazzar, for whatever reason, did not respond. . . .

The climax of Jerusalem was somehow anticlimactic in fact. It rained that day in early March, two hundred forty-three days after Murphy joined the Fourteenth Crusade, two hundred forty-eight days after Alinsky heisted the diamond from the Angoulême cathedral.

The city, first seen from the Mount of Olives near Et Tur, was not tawny colored at all. The rain, perhaps the last of the winter, had fallen steadily since dawn, soaking the pilgrims to the skin and wetting the city's buildings so that on a sunless day, to Murphy, they seemed gray and sad like the winter face of a northern city, and not the fabled face of Jerusalem the Beautiful.

As Saint Stephen's Gate, the entrance to the Old City, Ben Bokva and Teplitsky waited for the crusaders in their Citroën to pass along Alinsky's final instructions for disposing of the diamond. Accordingly, after about five minutes of interviewing with an Israeli TV crew, they marched through the gate to the Via Dolorosa and followed the Way of the Cross, forcing their path through swarms of hawkers, tourists, and a few bona fide pilgrims, none of whom seemed either to be particularly daunted by the steady drizzle or to have the remotest knowledge about the Fourteenth Crusade and where it had come from.

The letdown was absolutely devastating; the sense of their perfect uniqueness among all the creatures on the earth an illusion. . . .

"Jerusalem seems not particularly ready for us,"

Murphy said to Kyle-Boyer, his bemused sense of
the real irony total when he devilishly stopped in
mid-procession to autograph the Bible of an American woman from Oklahoma City and then posed for
photographs for a group of British tourists. He leered
at them, delighting them, leaning heavily on the staff
of his cross, Kyle-Boyer waving a small Union Jack
in the air, until they were confronted by an angry
Ben Bokva, who had come forward to find out the
reason for the delay.

"You don't frolic on the Via Dolorosa. Is it necessary for me, a Jew, to instruct the lot of you in
the significance of this place and the Crucifixion of
Jesus Christ, especially when you've walked all this
distance to reenact that very event?"

"Is that what we're doing?" Murphy interrupted
the other. "Reenacting the Crucifixion?"

"Exactly. Hold your cross up, Murphy. Think
of what you're supposed to be doing and comport
yourself with dignity. This is the way to Calvary,
after all."

"All right," Murphy agreed, amused now at
Teplitsky's attempt to shake off an Arab relics ped-
dler who was purveying fragments of the True Cross.
"If that's what Meyer wants, that's what he gets. It's
his money, after all."

In twenty minutes more of beating off tourists
and hawkers they came to the Church of the Holy
Sepulcher at the end of the Via Dolorosa, the place
of Calvary and the entombment and resurrection of
Christ. They entered after tying up the mules outside, and Ben Bokva directed them through the dimness and chanting to the Roman rite altar where
Murphy—as per instruction—handed the cross con-
taining Alinsky's diamond over to Riley the Franciscan, who blessed it, apparently prayed deeply over it
for a long silent minute, and then, looking at the
pilgrims but not really seeing them, said with a
sudden intensity, "Now may God Almighty deliver
our brother Meyer from the torment that infests him!"

In seconds more he was gone, as if fleeing, his cowl pulled over his head, taking the crucifix with him. The pilgrims emerged from the church, grateful for cleaner air after the all-pervasive incense in the interior, in time to see Riley hurry up to a black American limousine, hand Meyer Alinsky the crucifix through an open window in the rear where he sat with his shawl-covered mother, and then climb quickly into the front seat beside the driver as the car began moving off. Alinsky, his face incredibly wan and pale—demonic-looking, Murphy judged—did not acknowledge his pilgrims as he rode past, even though Marilyn and Jonathan waved to him. Nor did Riley, his cowl pulled closely about his head, choose to look at them. Only Rachel Alinsky stared at them, the pain and fear in her face obvious to anyone. Then the car was gone, heading toward the Jaffa Gate and into the new city.

"Very sinister," Kyle-Boyer, a distant voice, surmised. "Very sinister indeed. Can that be all there is to this?"

Ben Bokva and Teplitsky peered in the direction the car had taken, their faces devoid of any expression. In time Ben Bokva said simply, "Wait here awhile. Someone will come to pick you up."

Then the two Israelis walked away down the Via Dolorosa, presumably toward their car, without ever once looking back.

The rain was abating now, and for lack of something to do they crossed the wet cobbles of the square to a small kiosk where the four ordered glasses of steaming tea. Murphy, leaning on one side of the kiosk, traced the Hebrew script of a candy bar wrapper through a display case window. Then, for no reason at all, it seemed, he began to cry a little.

They were all crying and sipping their tea when the station wagon that Alinsky had sent to retrieve them pulled up in front of the kiosk.

PART IV
ALINSKY'S DIAMOND

28

Such good haverim

THE STATION WAGON TOOK THEM from the place of
Golgotha through the Jaffa Gate, then westward
through the new city to the far outskirts of Ein
Kerem where Alinsky's palace—justifying expectation
and then some—was fixed to the edge of the final
promontory that gave way to the long descent that
reached down toward the Plain of Sharon, Tel Aviv,
and the sea. Bronzed gates opened at their approach;
inside the walls, despite the graying of the accompanying sandstone beneath the rain, was a dazzling
landscape of biblical mosaics—Solomon, David, and
hordes more of the Old Testament crew—that awed
the crusaders to silence as they pulled up beside
the American limousine that had carried off Alinsky,
his mother, and Riley the Franciscan not long before. The two RTF vehicles were already there, and
a line of other vehicles, including the old Iowa Imperial with a Winchester positioned on its rear-
window gun rack.

They stepped out of the wagon, testing the silence
for ambush, noticing one by one the armed guards
stationed about the walls and in the beautifully
manicured formal gardens. The first sign of move-

ment was Jean-Philippe bounding by twos down the long wide flight of stairs that led to the main house, dressed in whites and sweated as if he had just come from playing tennis.

"Papa! Father! *C'est moi!*"

Then Murphy's son was upon him, already taller than his father, embracing him powerfully about the shoulders and lifting him off the ground in little jumps as he leaped about in a delirium Murphy would never have thought possible.

"How have you been, Jean-Philippe?" Murphy asked huskily, his pride boundless at the notion that his fellow travelers so obviously approved of the young god.

"I am well, Father! *Très bien!* But my mother has not been so very good, and it is necessary that you beat her up a bit."

"What? Why?"

"I'll tell you, Father, and I hope it doesn't hurt you too much, but she's enjoyed herself far too well in this place. At first we had a conspiracy that we should only pretend so Alinsky would grow less suspicious of anything we did, but after a time she did not pretend any longer and *vieille* Rachèle has had to watch her like a mother superior."

"Ah, that. Yes, I saw your mother in action back in Turkey." The anger Murphy had walked off between Iskenderun and Jerusalem suddenly rekindled itself and roared on to bonfire proportions. He was on the verge of shrieking out some invective against Alinsky when Jean-Philippe silenced him with a sharp grip on his arm.

"*Regarde, papa,*" he said disdainfully. "The whole court is coming to meet us now. Solomon, the Queen of Sheba, the court jester, Rachel Alinsky, and all the servants."

They looked up to see Meyer, Monique, the castrato, and old Rachel Alinsky descending the steps toward them through the drizzle that had begun again, followed by a gaggle of household servants in timeless

Middle Eastern livery, carrying water basins and towels, glasses, ice buckets, and bottles of liquor, two of them actually swigging on a whiskey bottle behind Alinsky's back on the way down. Alinsky, between the two women, wearing a striped, belted caftan and sandals, was beaming, holding his arms open in welcome, his earlier sinisterness completely dissolved. Monique, unsmiling but incredibly beautiful, her hair pulled Nefertiti-like into a beehive atop her head, wore a long robe, black and flowing and threaded with gold, the perfect raiment, Murphy surmised dimly, for someone who by now undoubtedly saw herself as consort to a Hebrew prince with a mini-palace in the Jerusalem hills. Old Rachel Alinsky, forever the bellwether of good sense, wore a neat, modern pants suit. A plastic rain hat covered her head.

Murphy wondered where and why in the enormous house the crucifix and diamond he had carried so far lay hidden. . . .

"What a wonderful thing you've done!" Alinsky enthused. "You must be so proud of yourselves!" He waded into their midst, taking Marilyn Aldrich into his arms first, hugging her to him, kissing her warmly on the cheeks. Then in quick succession, pummeling their backs at the same time, he pumped the hands of Kyle-Boyer, Jonathan Whitmore, and Murphy, exclaiming each time, "If only Father Bisson were here with us now to share this moment! If only he were here. . . ."

But Murphy accepted his congratulations only perfunctorily. He stared wrathfully at Monique, who stood at the bottom of the steps, her eyes humbly downcast, not yet having met her husband's gaze. Then, when Alinsky released his grip, Murphy stepped forward and slapped Monique hard across the face. She yelped with the pain, the beehive of her hair collapsed into a sudden fluff, and small tears began sliding down her face, dragging the Nefertiti eye shadow with them.

"Murph. . . ." Alinsky's response was a kind of plaintive reprimand, half recognizing that it was Murphy's right to do what he had done. Monique's eyes were still downcast; a servant had given her a handkerchief.

"Murph, please, not today of all days," Alinsky went on, making the peace. "Don't run the wonderful thing you've done because your imagination has run away with you—"

"Crack her again, Frankie!" Rachel Alinsky urged fiercely. "And don't worry about your imagination running away with itself. It couldn't catch up to some of what's been going on around here. I've always heard French women were fast, but Madame de Pompadour here is going to make the Guinness Book of World Records for sure this year. And to think poor Jean-Philippe has had to watch this spectacle all along. His own mother! A tart!"

"Mother, you're exaggerating," Alinsky protested angrily. "You ought to keep quiet before somebody gets the wrong idea."

"Don't tell me I'm exaggerating and don't tell me to keep quiet. If your poor father—*aleve shalom* —were alive today, he'd take you out to the shed and shred your *tuckus* good for carrying on with another man's wife."

"Mother," Alinsky beseeched, "hasn't this been painful enough for everyone by now? And let my poor father rest in peace. Think of the deep meaning of this day."

Alinsky tried patting his mother's rain hat, a patronizing, placating gesture, but she brushed his hand angrily away and took a few aggressive steps toward him. "What is the meaning of today, *meshuggana, dybbuk*? Can you tell me now at last? I'd give my right arm to know the meaning of all this horseshit with the robes and the crucifix and the diamond and all that walking—"

But then they were interrupted by the whine of a low-geared vehicle from outside the walls. In an-

other moment the gates swung open to reveal Al
Hazzar at the wheel of a Land-Rover, its wipers
swinging in a sluggish arc in the drizzle before his
face. He drove inside, parked near the other vehicles, and swung down to the ground as Alinsky's
mother called out to him, "Musad, hurry over.
Meyer is about to tell us the meaning of the Fourteenth Crusade."

"By Allah, I too should like to know, having
traveled with it a good distance. What is it, Meyer?"

"To prove to these people, all of whom I found
in various unfortunate circumstances, that even in
this overwhelmingly technical day and age a triumph
of the human spirit is still possible."

The answer begot a long moment of silence and
digestion. Alinsky's mother was first to respond, after
a disbelieving snort. "Meyer, it's not possible for that
story to change one more time. There are not that
many possibilities available. I think I've got notes
already on forty variations or so. The point is, now
that you've got them here, what are you going to
do with them?"

"Kill them, what else?" He grimaced at her as
the assemblage exploded in laughter. "Really, Mother,
first I'm going to offer them a drink. After walking
twenty-five hundred miles they certainly deserve one,
don't you agree? Then I'm going to invite them inside, since it's wet out here, before they think we're
rotten hosts by treating them to a bitter family feud
before offering any hospitality."

"You're right, Meyer, offer everybody a drink.
That should solve everything we don't understand
about the Fourteenth Crusade. It always has in the
past, hasn't it? And if you'll take my advice, everybody, stay out here instead of coming in because
it's not half as damp out here as it is in there."

Then she turned on her heel and, with a surprising litheness for an old woman, surged up the
steps toward the main house as Alinsky, seemingly
oblivious to her departure, ordered the servants to

their task of dispensing drinks. Murphy and Kyle-Boyer both took Scotch. Murphy watched detachedly as Monique accepted a glass of champagne and then walked to stand beside Alinsky, who still beamed on the grouping. She stared at Murphy a moment, smiled wanly, then turned away. In that instant Murphy knew for certain she was gone (even though he had surmised as much the night of the swim in the Bay of Iskenderun) and that no matter what occurred there would be no return to the château in France to take up the duties of dried-out father and husband with Monique at his side. Jean-Philippe seemed to sense it also. Shrugging his shoulders, he exchanged a glance with his father, the bemused smile of a wise young man who had learned much since Alinsky spirited him off to Jerusalem lighting his face instead of the clouds of anger Murphy had grown accustomed to over the years. One promise lined the horizon, though, Murphy suddenly decided. Without Monique, he and Jean-Philippe would still be together, and they got on well with each other now. The future need not be necessarily unhappy.

The bizarre, drizzled-upon cocktail party became the setting for a series of Shakespearean asides. Kyle-Boyer was first. Standing to the left of Murphy, who was sipping his drink, he spoke quietly. "I'm sorry about the wife, Frank. I know deep down you cared for her quite a bit. But Meyer isn't really to blame, you know."

The castrato was next, swinging toward Murphy, conspiracy in his face. "A very great quandary, Murphy. Monique want Meyer, Meyer no want Monique. Maybe it is necessary you take her back." Then he was gone, to be replaced by Al Hazzar, who seemed already to be feeling the effects of his first drink.

"You have lost her, Murphy," Al Hazzar pronounced, enunciating so loudly that Murphy surmised Alinsky must surely have heard the Bedouin. "Also, my brother Meyer is lying about the reason for the

Fourteenth Crusade. But doubtless we shall find out later."

"Doubtless," Murphy agreed. But that was all. The rain halted, though the sun did not immediately appear, and magnificently, pastorally, Alinsky swept them up the long expanse of steps to the house, waxing excited over the numbers of banquets and parties that had been planned in their honor. At the top, behind the balustrade, they looked east to a suddenly startling view of Jerusalem where the mists were clearing from the ranges of domes and minarets and towers. Alinsky, his arms fanning out to embrace the holy city, asked them suddenly and unexpectedly, "Are you really content with the wonderful thing you have done?"

"Oh, yes," the pilgrims chorused, Murphy speaking the words so emphatically that he was astounded to hear his own intensity.

"You should be," Alinsky advised them benignly. "Few people are ever given the chance to redeem their sordid pasts as completely as you have." Then, before anyone could follow up with even a polite defense, he looked down the stairs behind them where the liveried servants slowly climbed upward, most of them nipping from the bottles they carried, and his brows knitted in fury. "You bastards! Stop drinking my liquor! You should be ashamed of yourselves in front of our guests!"

"Look who's talking," one woman, the oldest of the group, said to the others. "The old *shikker* himself." It was audible enough so that everyone standing above on the terrace heard her. In response, Alinsky, seemingly impotent, stamped his sandaled foot angrily into a puddle, creating a small splash, and stalked off into the house, muttering about the servant problem in a socialist country, leaving his guests behind. Monique followed dutifully after him.

"So much for the grand entry into the palace of Meyer Alinsky," Al Hazzar noted, winking facetiously.

"Nothing ever works quite the way Meyer intends it. Perfection constantly eludes him. Wouldn't you know that Nature would even conspire to cheat him out of an earthquake on his Good Friday?"

The Bedouin shrugged, his face no longer evincing the humor he had apparently felt. Then Riley the Franciscan came out to welcome them, smiling effusively, shaking hands everywhere, no longer the mournful recipient of Murphy's cross. In another minute they were joined by Gervais and his Rifka, both looking tousled and sheepish yet decidedly pleased, as if they had just left off making love. Everyone congratulated them on their reunion before entering the broad, marble-lined foyer of Alinsky's palace, where Richard and Lebel, another set of lovers, were stupefied at the treasures contained within. All the *haverim*—the very good friends—were together again.

That night was the first of the week-long series of planned testimonials to the pilgrims. Murphy prepared for it pleasurably with a long hot soaking in a cavernous sunken tub, a session with a barber and manicurist sent to his rooms, and then nearly an hour with a Moroccan masseur who kneaded 2,500 miles of the relentless march out of his limbs until Murphy simply fell asleep under the man's hands. When he awoke, some force of habit deep within him still not believing in the journey's end, he headed for his crusader robe, hanging on a wall hook. But the Moroccan deflected him toward a wardrobe where his evening clothes were already laid out. When he was dressed, the clothes perfectly cut, the white dinner jacket at least three sizes smaller than the last jacket he had worn back in France, Murphy, embarrassed but unable to control himself, took some sort of narcissistic fit in front of a full-length mirror. Dear God, the fringe benefits of Alinsky's madness! He had lost at least fifty pounds, his body was slim and hard, and he radiated health

and a new youthfulness—ten years younger than the
bleary-eyed, puffy drunk he had known in France—
and something else. It was in the eyes: an indom-
itable self-confidence. He saw it all now. Albeit in
company, he had bested the rigors of a 2,500-mile
march. How many other men, moving relentlessly
toward the prescribed containment of their forties,
could claim that feat? Not many, he decided. Murphy
smiled proudly at his image; the Moroccan nodded
approvingly. Then they went forth to the victory banquet. . . .

Outside his rooms, Alinsky's house was pervaded
by a kind of frenzy. The testimonial was to be held
in a large high-ceilinged hall that the Moroccan, evidently become Murphy's valet, winkingly referred to
as "the throne room." It was a virtual madhouse
when Murphy arrived at the doors, with Arab,
Jewish, and Christian leaders squabbling over the right
to preferred seating nearest Alinsky and his crusaders at the head table on a raised dais. As
Murphy was being seated, Alinsky and Kyle-Boyer
actually punched each other over Kyle-Boyer's insistence that an empty place be left at the head table
in honor of Father Bisson, who of course could not
be with them. Marilyn Aldrich and Jonathan Whitmore, seated side by side, appeared radiant and
serene at the same moment, observing the pande-
monium before them with unseeing eyes, a fact certi-
fied by Murphy's Moroccan, who acknowledged that
Jonathan's Moroccan had procured for them on request that afternoon a notable grade of hashish.
Correspondingly, the servants appeared drunk, reeling
about and trying to serve a first course to yet-
unseated guests; the band played, discordantly, barely
unrecognizable music from the American thirties and
forties. To Murphy the only sanity seemed to be at
a small corner island of a table where Rachel Alinsky, Riley, Al Hazzar, Jean-Philippe, and the castrato
sat together, all talking in a hushed, serious way, and
he longed to leave the head table and join them.

Riley gave the invocation, and later, though many were not done eating, Alinsky began the main address, essentially a recapitulation of his statement of earlier in the day that during the Fourteenth Crusade he had been all the while funding a potential triumph of the human spirit. Except that now he included biographies and waxed with a negative eloquence in turn on the nature of the nefarious backgrounds he had helped redeem.

The other pilgrims were mute, fascinated, Murphy could see, with the total rush of their old lives back at them across a banquet table. But Murphy, when his turn came, after the first few repetitions of being referred to as "one of the most notorious drunks in France," thought he could not stand much longer the sight of all those assembled faces staring up at him. He remembered the vision of the new man in the mirror—the same man those tables of onlookers were viewing now—and in the next moment went blind with rage at being called "the lord of twelve thousand unmarketable bottles of wine," a phrase that could only have found its way into Alinsky's text from the traitor Monique.

Murphy stood up abruptly from his place at the head table, preparing to leave the room and knocking over his chair in the process. "That's enough of that horseshit, Meyer! There was nothing in that all-encompassing contract of yours that said we had to writhe to death with embarrassment over the misfortune of our past lives once we got to Jerusalem!"

"Murph, please," Alinsky pleaded, anguished rather than angry over the interruption, cupping one hand over the microphone before him. "There are many important people here. A lot of them are religious leaders—"

"Fuck 'em!" Murphy hurled back. "They've got dark places in their hearts too!"

"Murphy, I've been working on this speech for months! You don't want to spoil the whole affair, do you?"

"You're damn right I do!" Murphy yelled, moving past the lectern on his way out.

Alinsky tried to grab his arms and restrain him, but it was Monique, sitting to the right of Alinsky, who leaped up and planted herself firmly in Murphy's path. "Frank, please sit down! Meyer has been working so hard on his speech. He's been practicing for weeks."

"Ah, poor Meyer," Murphy intoned sarcastically, thinking to clobber his wife once again before the larger audience. "Haven't you got an ounce of loyalty left in you for me, Monique? Do you really want to sit here and listen to that awful righteous rendition of our old life?"

She was a menacing she-lynx now. "Yes, Frank. The better to remind me how awful it was! You ought to listen, too; then you'll thank *le bon Jésus* that Meyer Alinsky came along and saved you from the death march on which you were so relentlessly swilling—"

"Shut up, Monique! I'm Francis Xavier Murphy, not Barrabas!" he screamed to the banquet guests. "I'm leaving! And if you're not absolute asses you should leave too!"

"Murph, please," Alinsky begged, tears welling in his eyes. "Just let me finish my speech. I'll pay you plenty for it. . . ."

But it was no good. While Murphy shoved Monique back into her seat, Kyle-Boyer snapped out of his trance and joined the revolution, standing to leave also.

"Frank, Austin"—Alinsky was whining now—"please. . . ."

"Don't let him talk you out of it, Frank!" came an admonition from the rear of the hall in a shrill voice. It was Rachel Alinsky, standing on her chair and brandishing a tiny fist toward the head table, with Al Hazzar trying vainly to restrain her, and the castrato balancing her and giggling with amusement. "Meyer Alinsky, have you lost your mind for good?"

she demanded. "Since when in five thousand years of Jewish history can we afford the luxury of a righteous ass? You'd actually think you'd never done one questionable thing in your whole life."

"Mother, my speech—" Real tears now, flowing down his cheeks.

"Give it, Meyer, if you want. Then I march up to that podium and follow it up with one of my own. Beginning with a certain indiscretion you once committed in the cathedral town of Angoulême, France, that some of these religious leaders might be interested in hearing about."

"Mother, please, let me do it my own way. . . ."

"No! Play some nice music!" she shouted at the band. "Jerusalem has had enough revival-tent inspiration for one night."

Not improbably, the Arab band began playing, at the fall of a baton, an ill-chosen sweet-sad song from the American thirties—"Three O'Clock in the Morning"—but not loud enough to drown out Alinsky's rantings.

"Mother, you've ruined my banquet! You know how long I've planned this!"

But the rantings fell on deaf ears. Alinsky's mother had dragged the castrato to the floor, and together they fox-trotted on the periphery of Meyer's banquet. The guests squirmed about in consternation; then one man and his wife got up and began to dance also, and soon there were ten or twelve couples on the floor. Murphy, too fascinated to leave, watched Alinsky, who surveyed the ballroom that his mother's treachery had created in a soundless panic. Just as he opened his mouth as if to begin screaming again, a waiter tipped an entire tray laden with bowls of fruit into the middle of a still-seated tableful of guests. The chaos that broke loose then was capped by Alinsky, who, suddenly enraged and finding a target, picked up the lectern at which he had been speaking and hurled it at the waiter.

"Out! Out! Everybody get the hell out of here! The party is over!"

The guests—some fearful, others decidedly angry themselves by now—marched out of the great hall until there was no one left but the pilgrims, Meyer's mother, Riley, the castrato, Jean-Philippe, Al Hazzar, Alinsky, Monique, the band—still playing—and the couple who had first followed Rachel and the castrato to the floor—still dancing. Alinsky, his head down on the table, sobbed into his arms. Monique comforted him. A few waiters hung about, glowering at Alinsky for throwing the lectern at one of their number. In time the music ended, the dancing couple departed, and Meyer Alinsky, clearly devastated and with a handkerchief masking his face, left the table with Monique supporting him and went off to his rooms. Murphy, shrugging at the eternal irony of events that surrounded Alinsky and everything he touched, went off too, abruptly tired and irritated at the cheat that the testimonial banquet had turned out to be. He locked the door to his bedroom and, on the advice of his Moroccan, carefully checked his bed for scorpions and snakes.

Before he slept it came to him that he could not possibly stand much more of Meyer Elkanah Alinsky.

He was awakened in the morning, just after dawn, by that worthy, looking very drawn and haggard indeed. Alinsky sat cross-legged on the floor beside Murphy's bed, apparently thinking it unnecessary to explain how he had entered the locked room, and apologized for the travesty of the night before.

"Murph, I'm so sorry. Honest to God. I've been thinking of you people as statistics for so long that I couldn't see you as human beings with a lot of undiscovered pride. How can I make it up to you?"

"Not by dumping more money into the till," Murphy said, annoyed. "The most obvious way is to suspend that week of commemorative chaos you've got planned for us."

"Agreed. I decided that last night anyhow. Come on, Murph, let's you and me take the bus down to the sea and spend the day on the beach. I've been wanting to talk to you for a long time now—since Naples, in fact. Besides, it'll be a madhouse around here today with all the diplomatic corps and the rest of the guests who've been invited to the other parties calling to cancel when word gets out about what happened last night."

Complying, Murphy took breakfast with Alinsky. Then they left in the limousine for the Jerusalem main bus station to catch the shuttle for Tel Aviv. Once in the terminal it was easily apparent that Meyer Alinsky was an Israeli version of a folk hero. Commuters pointed at them, stood about them in little whispering knots, occasionally smiling toward Alinsky, who acknowledged them with a practical, frugal smile. Aboard their bus, the driver came back to shake hands obsequiously with the man who had bought out the Egyptian Air Force, and up front a group of perhaps twenty children on an outing began singing as the bus left the terminal and clattered out of the city and down the main road to Tel Aviv, the name of Meyer Alinsky emerging again and again from the indecipherable Hebrew verses of the song. Alinsky laughed with pleasure despite the gray of his hangover.

At Tel Aviv, where he signed autographs amid the confusion of the bus station, they changed buses for the beach at Bat Yam, where another all-too-expected anomaly came to light.

The man who may well have been the richest in the Middle East refused to pay admission to the beach. Instead, while Murphy discovered his sense of humor fast returning, they sneaked along the periphery of a barbed-wire fence to an obscure point out of sight of the villas on the ledge above and wriggled like fedayeen beneath the bottommost strand of wire, which one held up for the other.

"This is insane, Meyer," Murphy protested, laughing at the same time at the sight of the paunchy Alinsky nearly burrowing into the strip of gravel that ran beneath the fence until the sand of the beach was reached. "It only costs a few *agorot* to get onto the beach anyhow."

"It's the principle of the thing, Murph; I'm a great defender of principle. The beaches should be free." Alinsky grunted. "The idea of the municipality charging for their use is totally unjust."

"Principle, shit, Meyer. You create the ones that suit you, and that's the truth. In accordance with what principle did you take my wife and son to Jerusalem as hostages?"

"That was Alinsky's Creative Destruction Principle. The one that proved to you that three de Rastignac Murphys had come to the end of their rope and needed separate outlets to a new life. I provided them for you, didn't I? Besides"—he was panting as he got to his feet and began to walk toward the sea—"they weren't hostages. They were houseguests. I've told you that before. And they're free to go any time they like now that you're in Israel."

Murphy had also scrambled to his feet. "Are you sure Monique wants to leave? She seems madly in love with you."

"That's her problem, Murph. It's not reciprocal. And by the way, I don't like to criticize you, especially after what you've done for me, but you could've given that woman a few extra francs to spend. Or taken her out to dinner a few times. It would have made all the difference in the world, believe me. When she first got here she fought me tooth and nail, but with a few little gestures on my part, what I'd consider just normal generosity toward anyone, she fell apart so completely I had to lock her out of my bedroom.

"And one thing on that score, Murph," Alinsky went on, laying out a blanket. "I swear to God Almighty I've never slept with her. Even if I'd wanted to, I couldn't. You can ask my mother about that. After we got back from Turkey on the yacht that time, Mother slept outside my room in a chair for about a week to make sure nothing happened. And she threatened to cane Monique a few times and even tried it once."

"Good," Murphy heard himself say, positioning his towel near Alinsky on the uncrowded end of the beach toward the misted outline of Jaffa, Tel Aviv's sister city, and thinking at the same time how distant Monique really had become, a specimen object for their analysis. "Only one thing, Meyer. I'm sure Monique won't return to France with me, and as a matter of fact I don't want her to. Jean-Philippe will, but I think your courtesan houseguest will have to stay here and depend on your generosity for a time longer until she decides which of the marvelous avenues you've opened to her she's going to choose."

"That's not possible, Murph. She has to leave. I don't want it to seem as if I'm kicking her out now that I have no more use for her, and I'm sorry, too, for the trouble I've caused you, but I did it quite unwittingly. No, there are one-way tickets to Paris on two different flights ready for everyone on Monday next. One is for Monique. She leaves then."

"You couldn't keep her here even for a month, Meyer? Until I'm able to dispose of the château and figure out where Jean-Philippe and I are off to?"

"Sorry, Murph, but I don't expect to be around Israel too much longer myself."

"Where are you going, Meyer?"

"Away. . . ."

The answer told him nothing, and Murphy was suddenly seized with the notion that Alinsky intended somehow to return to the hated, unmentionable, yet (Murphy's instinct certain) equally loved America. He propped himself up on one elbow, watching his adversary. Alinsky stared unseeing over the Mediterranean, in his eyes the same tortured look that Murphy remembered from when he stared out over the Bay

of Naples the night that Alinsky played Satan to
Murphy's Christ.

"Meyer. . . ?"

"Yes, Murph?"

"I did what you asked me to do that crazy night
in Naples. I offered up each day's march to expiate
the guilt of the murderer you spoke of."

"Did you, Murph? Did you actually do that?"
Alinsky turned toward him, his face suddenly trans-
ported, a disbelieving wreath of a smile—beatific
even, making Alinsky seem childlike—etched across
it.

"Yes, Meyer. I mean, it was little enough to do
since the thing was torturing you so much."

"It was a wonderful thing to do, Murph!" Alinsky
exulted. "It was a blessed thing to do! God love
you, Murph, for understanding that!" Then—the least
expected event of all—Alinsky threw his arms about
Murphy's neck, crying into the hair of Murphy's
head, saying over and over again, "Thank you,
Murph! God bless you, Murph!"

Murphy was too astounded to be embarrassed at
the emotion of the other's display. Released and
gasping for breath, he was only vaguely aware
that a beachful of Israelis were staring at them
with unabashed curiosity.

"I prayed you'd be good enough to consider doing
that for me, Murph."

"Meyer, tell me something. . . . Your vengeance,
the one you went to Mecca and Rome and Canterbury to find out about—has it been achieved now?"

The reaction was a surprise. The wariness of the
old Alinsky seemed gone; instead there was a kind
of sadness over the discovery. "Who told you about
those trips, Murph?"

"Al Hazzar. He's very worried about you."

"My desert brother talks too much. But yes, the
vengeance is achieved. Mecca was no help. It was
after Rome and Canterbury that I understood the
way."

"Hence the crusade? The journey of expiation?"

"Precisely."

"And the diamond?"

"A symbol."

"And the crime?"

"To be revealed in the future."

"And the murderer?"

"Still unknown."

"And the victim or victims?"

"Long dead and gone."

"Ah." It was the end of the litany then, most of which Murphy thought he understood now except for one thing. "Meyer, your mother—why is she giving you such a hard time?"

"She doesn't believe in diamond thefts, Christian pilgrimages, or vengeance as a Jewish prerogative," Alinsky said bemusedly.

"She certainly gave evidence of that at last night's banquet."

"Yes, that's why we're not having any more celebrations. Instead we leave tomorrow on a bus tour of the country. We'll visit every place in the land, have ourselves a ball, and get back in time for everyone to leave for Paris on Monday."

"That's it?" Murphy inquired speculatively. "That's all there is to it?"

"What more do you want, Murph? Enough is enough, wouldn't you say? Even I tire of playing Alinsky's games."

They stayed hours more on the beach, not speaking any longer except to shoo away people who came to introduce themselves to Meyer Alinsky. Toward sunset, Murphy, used to the habit of walking, grew restless and marched along the feathering edge of the surf toward the pink-tinted outline of Jaffa, pursuing the litany the two had spontaneously sung and wondering in his endless frustation about the crime. He thought of it, too, on the bus trip back to Jerusalem, undisturbed despite the joyous clapping and singing of a crowd of Hassidim as the groaning bus crept up the last hills into the city.

The secret—the riddle at the center of all the other riddles he thought he had deciphered—hid for sure in Jerusalem, Murphy guessed. He hungered to know it. Ever a romantic, and conscious of the enormity of all those centuries of history that overlay these hills, he looked at the spotlighted silhouettes of the Old City walls and decided there was never a more perfect place in all creation to contain the reason for Alinsky's madness.

The crusaders, Alinsky, Al Hazzar, and the castrato left the next morning aboard a special air-conditioned bus with a bar and galley for their alternative tour of the land of Israel. They went south first, to the Dead Sea via Bethlehem and Jericho of the appropriated west bank, then into the moonland reaches of the Negev, a washboard of hills and wadis where hobbled Bedouin camels lurched across the roads, seemingly untended, their owners never seen.

They stopped a half day at Masada, place of a Roman siege and a Jewish mass suicide, and Alinsky eulogized the Jewish dead. They stayed a night in Eilat, swam in the morning in the waters of the Red Sea, then left for Sharm El Sheik, the new Israeli possession, surprisingly developed, that guarded the entrance to the Aqaba Gulf.

The bus cut across Sinai and the carnage of the Six-Day War, passing close to the Israeli rear lines of the Suez Canal. Then they came out onto the Mediterranean beaches of the Gaza Strip and played there for two days, avoiding the occasional refugee camps, before continuing north again into Israel proper. They stopped for two days in Tel Aviv-Jaffa, then went farther north along the coast road to Haifa and past to the spectacular cliffs on the Lebanese frontier.

They turned inland to the hills of Galilee, where Alinsky delightedly showed the troupe places where he and Jean-Philippe hunted wolves in the old Imperial. They visited the Galilee towns of Safad, Nazareth, and Capernaum and, on the Sunday of the return to Jerusalem for Monday's departure to Paris, took a long reflective lunch on the grounds of the monastery atop Mount Tabor, overlooking the hazy ranges of hills and the Sea of Galilee, shimmering and blue, far below.

Kyle-Boyer, easily mellowed these days, raised a wineglass on high over the land of Israel and proclaimed, with tears in his eyes, "God's blessing on this holy land. It must never again be overrun and fall victim to violence!"

"It shall not be overrun," Alinsky enjoined sonorously.

"It must ever remain the Jewish state," Kyle-Boyer went on. "A unique act of justice among all the injustices of this dreadful century!"

"It shall remain," Alinsky echoed him.

"Returning home to Europe, we shall take renewed energy from the sacredness of this land!"

Alinsky did not respond this time, but Murphy, reading his mind or thinking that his lips had moved, thought he heard the words: "You shall not return. . . ." Al Hazzar and the castrato, sitting side by side and each apparently deep in his own thoughts, exchanged a quizzical glance for the briefest moment, then looked away again.

They returned to Jerusalem that night, the bus, high-powered and comfortable, roaring into the city. Everyone was drunk, and the castrato led a sing-along in fast hand-clapping Hebrew. No one knew the words, but everyone sang.

29

A humane revenge?

By sundown Monday, Alinsky's vengeance, for whatever its worth, was achieved.

But there was absolutely no hint of this at five in the afternoon, when Alinsky gave a champagne sendoff for his crusaders on the upper-level veranda that faced the rosening domes and towers of Jerusalem. Below, in the parking area before the gates of the walled enclosure, was the RTF station wagon, already loaded with luggage and waiting to bear the pilgrims (with the exception of Murphy, was was to leave on a later flight with Monique and Jean-Philippe) and the RTF crew and Rifka Gervais to the airport at Lod for their departure to Paris.

The gathering was full of toasts and well-wishings, most spurious and lighthearted, until Alinsky distributed their paychecks and they arrived at the moment that Murphy surmised would be inevitable, for the pendulum of the crusaders' emotions had shifted dramatically and the final verses of their pilgrim epic had become nothing less than a love song for Meyer Alinsky.

"One cannot say it too often, but this is truly the finest thing I have ever done. Nothing more in my life will equal it, I know. Thank you, Meyer Alinsky, for teaching me the nature of Christian humility." It was Kyle-Boyer again, absolutely sodden and blubbering great tears, holding up his champagne glass in tribute to Alinsky, who sat, looking embarrassed, on the railing of the terrace. His mother, her eyes still disbelieving but nearer to being convinced, had changed tack and now stood beside her son, warily glowing with pride, if such a thing were possible. But Kyle-Boyer was not yet done: "And I salute you further, Meyer. For if the way of my life can never be the same again, neither will my weight and girth. And for that perhaps I owe you even greater thanks."

The howling of laughter done, Etienne Gervais was next.

"Your ways are your own and very strange, Meyer. But if it were not for you I would never have known my beautiful Rifka. I kiss you for that."

Unabashedly, Gervais, ancient enemy of Alinsky, who had so often called him a Jew derogatorily, stepped forward and planted a kiss on the matchmaker's forehead while the pilgrims and the rest of Alinsky's entourage—Ben Bokva and Teplitsky, Al Hazzar, the castrato, Rachel Alinsky, Riley the Franciscan, and the servants, who were naturally nipping at the champagne they were serving—stood clapping at the act.

Marilyn Aldrich followed suit, simply taking Meyer's head in her arms and holding him to her for a long minute. Her eyes were misted and she was crying a little, but she was in complete control. Murphy, so used for 2,500 miles to looking backward at her clinging in a drugged daze to the pommel of her saddle, was astounded at the transformation wrought in her by the journey's fulfillment, and also by the attack of Alinsky's army of beauticians, hairdressers, and wardrobe mistresses. Her beauty, once a speculation, a promise, was now confirmed. Flaxen-haired, sloe-eyed, healthily tanned, clad in a simple light-blue belted dress and low-heeled, comfortable-looking shoes, she forced perhaps the ultimate testimony from her benefactor Alinsky by causing him to stand and walk admiringly about her. "Beautiful. How very beautiful you've become, Marilyn."

It was self-respect he had given her, not actual beauty, Murphy suddenly thought, forgiving the crazy Iowa Jew the travesty of Monique that he had clearly not intended. The others saw it also, even Monique, Murphy suspected, in the moments of wind-filled silence that followed. Alinsky's Fourteenth Crusade had involved a miracle, after all, but it had occurred at the end; it had nothing to do with the sham of the beginning.

"We can't never go back to the fleshpots of Birmingham, Meyer." Jonathan Whitmore gave out the news in cockney speech, though in blazer and club tie he no longer looked like a cockney. He sighed at the apparent loss, nonetheless.

"And the temple-of-healing idea?" Alinsky kidded him. "With Marilyn working the cures?"

"Scratch that one too, Meyer. No, it's a quiet country inn for us. Far off the M-One. Quiet and respectable. Out near Nottingham or Lincoln perhaps."

"With nothing illicit on the premises?"

"Well, we might water the whisky a bit for remembrance' sake, but that'd be the long of it, I think. One thing, though, Meyer, if you was agreeable, we might have a kind of anniversary party there every year. On us, of course. There's three of us in England already, 'n' Frank could come over from bloody France, 'n' you always seem to be able to come 'n' go as you please anywhere—"

"That sounds like a fine idea, Jonathan," Alinsky said kindly, "and thank you for thinking of it."

"Yes." There was a kind of garbled agreement and then an embarrassed silence. The real innocence of the worldly Jonathan Whitmore—who understood stilettos, stacked decks, and the mystery of odds on horses—was a spiritual innocence, Murphy supposed: the kind that failed to know that certain purifying rituals, unlike championship football seasons, were irretrievable once done. There would be no yearly gathering in Lincolnshire or Nottinghamshire: just as well.

Murphy was last. Before approaching his prince he looked a long moment at Monique and Jean-Philippe, who stood near each other but decidedly not together, and considered he owed Alinsky no thanks whatever on that score. Perhaps later, when certain ambiguities cleared. Monique patted at real tears with her handkerchief—but they were sorrowing tears, because she was being forced against her will to leave the man she preferred to remain with in Israel. Jean-Philippe, cheated by both his drunken father and the intriguing Alinsky out of the special joy of his teen-age years, watched the exchange with his usual caution.

Murphy extended his hand to shake with Alinsky. "Thanks for giving me the chance to dry out, Meyer." He meant that part of it. Then, symbolically, he dumped the champagne over the veranda railing.

"You're welcome for that, Murph. I only wish it could have been me in your stead."

There was nothing more to say. They stood about awkwardly, the travel fever growing apace like that of hotel guests departing a tropical paradise and suddesly struck with the reality of return to a distant northern place of chill and indebtedness. Besides, so much had already been said. In time, after another nervous refill of their glasses, a servant came onto the terrace and announced it was the moment to leave.

In near darkness they filed down the stairs to the lighted courtyard, still bidding good-bye, Murphy the recipient of most of the hugging and kissing now, an absurd exchange of addresses suddenly taking place. At the station wagon, Gervais and his Rifka claimed the rear seat, Kyle-Boyer, Ricard, and Lebel took the middle, and Marilyn and Jonathan the front, Jonathan driving and receiving detailed instructions on where to leave the vehicle at the airport so it might be retrieved and returned along with the utility van to France.

Unexpectedly, though, Riley the Franciscan wedged himself into the front seat beside Marilyn, asking Jonathan to drop him off at the priory on their way through the city. "Rachel, darlin', keep the kettle on," he called out happily to Alinsky's mother. "I'll be back for a sandwich and some coffee tonight about ten."

"OK, Aloysius. But don't forget to come over. We've got a lot to talk about, you and I."

"I'll be over, Rachel, but I don't think we have all that much to talk about," he returned, winking at her. "I still don't know what your son Machiavelli here was up to"—and he jabbed Meyer lightly in the stomach—"but he's managed to make a few very happy Christians out of these rogues in the process."

The warning of their impending deaths shone then in Meyer Alinsky's face, Murphy would ever afterward recall. It was Riley who had tripped the switch. Alinsky's color became ashen even beneath the glow of tan, and he trembled as he set his champagne glass down atop the piles of luggage on the Peugeot's roof rack and took a viselike grip on Riley's arm as it hung out the wagon's window. "Aloysius, stay for now, will you? I'll have one of the drivers run you into town. I want you to bless the crucifix before I turn it over to the Franciscan order."

"Aw, Meyer, I'll do it tonight. There's a bunch of instant pilgrims from Chicago going to be at the Dormition Church in about fifteen minutes, and I'd better get my tail over there to take up a collection. With all the time it took to get that crucifix to Jerusalem, it can wait a few more hours for a little holy water."

"Aloysius, please!" Alinsky begged, opening the door a crack against the other's resistance, trying to pull him out of the car. But it was no good. Riley laughingly fended him off and Jonathan Whitmore lurched the wagon forward through the gates into the distant orb of the rising moon, blaring the horns and blinking the lights like a party of mad revelers on their way to an evening wedding. Murphy, still watching Alinsky, comprehended in the instant of their departure what must needs happen and opened his mouth to shout a warning after them. But the words, from horror, were frozen in his throat.

"Good-bye! Good-bye! Shalom! Shalom!"

"Long live Meyer Alinsky!" Kyle-Boyer called back at them, hanging far out his window. "Long live the Jewish nation!"

"Good-bye, Riley. Forgive me," Murphy heard Alinsky say, and he gulped down the champagne he had retrieved from the wagon's roof. The amber tail lights receded, the horns still blared, as most of the remaining party surged back up the stairs to the open terrace for a better view along the road away from the house before the vehicle turned out of sight. Alinsky followed determinedly in their wake; Murphy trudged doggedly behind him; only the castrato remained below, suddenly wracked with sobs that many mistook for another kind of sorrowing.

On the terrace again, where Alinsky steadied himself by tightly gripping the railing, they saw it happen. The Peugeot, trailing a long plume of dust behind it in the twilight about half a mile away from the house toward the Ein Kerem suburb, was suddenly lifted off the ground by the force of the incredible explosion that went off beneath it, only to be slammed back to earth an instant later by the clap of fury emanating from the other charges planted in the roof-rack luggage. It sat tortoiselike on its frame, within seconds a fiercely burning funeral pyre from the ruptured gas tank and whatever other fuels Alinsky may have chosen to apply, the reverberations of the dual explosions echoing again and again across the Jerusalem hills.

No one—please God—could possibly be left

alive in that inferno, Murphy thought distantly, yet he was hardly surprised when four Arabs, pale ghosts in the moonlight, suddenly appeared from the brush on either side of the road and methodically sprayed the remains with machine-gun fire before melting back into their cover. In their aftermath was but the roaring sound of the fire and the weepings of the castrato below. There was not a whisper from the watchers on the terrace, only a kind of mute shock that was a long time in registering.

Murphy stood between Alinsky and his mother. Her eyeglasses reflected the grisly pyre. Behind them the eyes seemed pensively calm, as if, for her at least, the final piece of the puzzle had just been fitted in place. Behind her, Al Hazzar and Jean-Philippe, both horror-struck, had gripped each other's arm from some unthinking reflex. Like Murphy himself, neither understood the reason for the destruction. Nor did Monique, who looked as if she might begin shrieking except for the handkerchief she gripped tightly between her teeth. Alinsky was first to break the silence.

"Those damn fedayeen! No one is safe anywhere in Israel!"

"You did that, Alinsky," Murphy told him flatly.

"The men who fired those machine guns were not fedayeen, Meyer," Al Hazzar said in a hoarse whisper. "They were not Arabs either. They were your boys."

In response Alinsky shrugged, the guilt acknowledged but certainly unfelt. He turned and walked to the table, where the champagne still sat cooling in buckets, and calmly poured himself another glass. The others (with the exception of Jean-Philippe), for the lack of knowing what else to do, did exactly the same thing. The mood was an impressive calm now, woven from fibers plucked out of the surreal. The scenario of death out there was the aberration, a bad Israeli film about the irresponsible viciousness of the national enemy. In the distance the wail of police sirens grew louder as several jeeps approached from the city; at the same time the American limousine rushed through the compound gates to intercept them and doubtless deflect them from the house as per plan. Murphy sipped at his champagne and then turned to Alinsky, after a long reflective look at the cremation of his companions in pilgrimage. Curiously he felt no malice. Alinsky smiled at the leaping of the flames; he was quite, quite mad.

"You screwed it all up, Meyer. I was your Jesus Christ, after all. I should have been the one to go."

"Leave it to Meyer to pervert the Christian myth to his own ends," his mother said quietly. "Only God could say what changes the world would have known if Meyer Elkanah Alinsky of Aruba, Iowa, had been around in Jerusalem two thousand years ago."

"Mother, today of all days I don't want to have to listen to you any more."

"Well, you're going to have to listen a little longer, Meyerle. Not only did you just kill eight innocent people to gain that goddam revenge you've been looking for for the last twenty years or so, but one of them happened to be your old mother's beau, a Franciscan priest named Aloysius Riley."

"I never liked him anyhow, Mother. He wasn't right for you. He had a price for everything."

"Who doesn't? And women are supposed to come with dowries anyhow. The point is that after he came to Jerusalem I wasn't a lonely old woman any more. It was nice to go out to dinner or to a movie somewhere with him. You could have saved him—and the others." She frowned at her son in consternation for a brief time, then asked simply, "Frank was right, wasn't he, Meyer? He was the one meant to die. I remember how carefully you looked for him. He absolutely delighted you: a *shikker* Christ. Why did you spare him and kill all the others?"

Alinsky regarded his mother as if he were totally mystified that she failed to comprehend. "The tornado, Mother. He turned out to be an unbelievably bad choice. That he came from Iowa was a brilliant coincidence. But if the tornado god refused to kill him, how could I do it?"

"You're gone, Meyer," Murphy told him. "You're not eccentric. You're absolutely around the bend. You've become fiendishly inhumane!"

"On the contrary, Murph. I'm humane and compassionate in the extreme. I killed them at the noblest of their miserable lives. If they had lived it would only be downhill again. After a time the money would have run out, and Austin, by degrees, would be back to scraping babies. Marilyn would soon be upstairs turning tricks again to keep up the payments on their country inn, since the gentry would avoid it like the plague once they found out two cockneys were running it. When the bloom came off the rose for Etienne and Rifka, there would be religious warfare all over the apartment. No, in the nature of all the vengeance the world has ever known, this was certainly the most humane. Is the vengeance of Alinsky at all comparable to the crimes of Hitler or Joe Stalin? Ask yourself that, Murph."

"A vengeance for what?" Murphy screamed at him. "For what? Will you tell me? What was worth the lives of those eight people?"

"I think, Mother," Alinsky said quietly, "that it's time to take our friends down to the treasure room of this here particular castle."

But his mother did not respond. She had collapsed into a chair, whining piteously. Alinsky bade Murphy, the castrato, and Al Hazzar to follow him into the house.

30

A case for euthanasia

THEY WENT DOWNWARD into the bowels of Alinsky's palace, through the viewing rooms for films
and the weekly football games, through a locker
room—where Alinsky extracted a Budweiser from a
refrigerator—that led into a squash court, along the
edge of an indoor swimming pool, then across the
wide expanse of an underground garage filled with
varied unaccountable vehicles, until they came to a
massive steel door set in a concrete framing that
made Murphy think for no particular reason that
they were at the entrance to the house's furnace
room.

Alinsky, with Budweiser in hand, rang a bell
beside the door. In another moment they heard
the padding of feet ascending the steps. A bolt slid
behind the door, and the portal swung inward to
reveal a Bedouin woman, her face littered with
blue tattooing, who looked questioningly at Alinsky
for a moment, surveyed his companions, then seemed
to Murphy to give a kind of gasp of pain before
she turned and led them down the stairway, her
clanking jewelry echoing along the walls. Below, from
the low whir of machines and the universal antiseptic
hospital smell, Murphy suddenly knew with an in-

stinct more certain than any before that Meyer Alinsky's wife, who was supposed to have died years before in Iowa, still lived on in this subterranean place.

The realization numbed him to a fantastic calm. The castrato's reaction was identical, Murphy supposed, because he had known from the very beginning. Only Al Hazzar evinced a head-shaking disbelief at the sight of the shrunken, white-haired husk of a woman on the bed in the middle of the room, being fed and presumably dilated and respirated and drained by a myriad of catheters and tubes that led to and from the complex of humming machinery that lined one wall. Behind her, at the head of the bed, was their leader perhaps, a stoic cyclops of a pulse recorder with a single red dot creeping across the eye of its screen. Curiously, for no decipherable reason, since Murphy guessed heretofore only five or six people could have known of her existence, her name was attached to the bed on a metal tag: Catherine Raabe Alinsky.

"Has she been like this for twenty-two years, Meyer?" Murphy asked, his voice resonant-sounding in the room. It seemed impossible that the answer might be in the affirmative.

"No. No one could be like this for twenty-two years. It's about a year and a half now that she began slipping so badly. Which explains," Alinsky concluded sadly, "why I was in such a haste to get the show on the road."

"Meyer, my brother, in Allah's name, why could you not have told me of this?" Al Hazzar begged.

"What could you have done about it, Musad? What could anyone have done about it?" The question was a cry of anguish, the love story certain now; all the sanity in Meyer Alinsky had died twenty-two years before of a broken heart. Sobbing, Alinsky sank into a chair the Arab woman had set beside the bed and laid his head against the paltry outline of his wife's right leg beneath the covers. More chairs

were brought and ranged about the form, and Murphy, Al Hazzar, and the castrato took up their places
for the feast of sorrowing, Al Hazzar unexpectedly
whimpering, blowing his still-healing nose in the folds
of his kaffiyeh, the castrato wailing a high-pitched
chant, its words, Murphy surmised, those of the
professional mourners of his Italian past.

Murphy had no tears. In the last little wave of
shock his mind could possibly absorb, it came to
him exactly why they were there. This was to be
Catherine Raabe's last day in life. All the preparations had been made. He looked across the bed,
past Alinsky, to the wall of blown-up photographs he
was just now seeing for the first time. They were
all of her, seized instants of perfection out of the
purer American past: the cheerleader leaping toward
a brilliantly clear Iowa autumn sky; the girl on the
sorority house steps; the prom queen; the homecom-
ing float rider; a floppy-hatted Dietrich astride the
running board of a Ford car with spoked wheels; a
reflective, spread-eagled moment in the Iowa grass
with a daisy growing out of her mouth. More:
ringlets of curl were everywhere. Something suggested that she threw back her head a lot, laughed
in a clear, tantalizing way, was unconscious of any
need for poses. She had been beautiful, evidently,
granddaughter or great-granddaughter of Scandinavians
or Germans, a middlewestern type. But there had
been lots of them, even in his time, Murphy suddenly
thought sacrilegiously. Many look-alikes. Heirs to the
legacy of golden hair, clear skin, and fine teeth. The
nation's middle was littered with them. Then, seeing
Alinsky's anguish once more, he chased the notion
away, focused purposefully on a profile of her caught
unawares, speculating on something unknowable, perhaps, far off in the future. . . .

Below the pictures the Arab nurse sat against the
wall, tears streaming down her cheeks, alternately
raising her arms and letting them fall to her knees
with a slap. No sound came from the tortured open-

ing of her mouth, and Murphy understood that, following the strange nature of all Alinsky's carefully chosen
retainers, she was certainly a mute.

"I even had her taken to Lourdes!" Alinsky
shrieked suddenly, the rage recurring so unexpectedly
that he squeezed the beer can and a geyser of liquid
shot into the air onto the bed linens before he
hurled it into a corner. The act seemed to stir his
wife; she opened her eyes, turned her head slightly
toward her husband, and, Murphy thought (hoped?),
showed the merest spark of recognition.

"Do you know how she got this way?" Alinsky
asked of no one in particular. "How she got to
spend twenty-two years of her life as a vegetable
and ended up with tubes feeding and draining her
and even a machine to help her heart beat, and not
ever a chance of recovery?"

"How did it happen, Meyer?" Murphy asked softly
after a moment, when he sensed the question was
not rhetorical. "Who did it?"

"Christians did it, Murph. Back in Aruba, Iowa,
one snowy December night during a time of my life
when I was so in love with her that my heart
would start pounding like crazy when I saw her coming down the street to meet me. On that night the
police came to tell me they'd found her mugged
and bloodied and lying in the snow, robbed and
beaten on her way home from doing volunteer work
at the hospital. She was two months pregnant at
the time."

"Ah. . . ." Murphy was incredulous that the
sound—actually a sob—came from himself. He saw
it all: a Fitzgerald landscape; the snowy, beautiful, windless nights of Iowa towns with the great
naked elms that lined every street bearing witness
to the promise of the reunion of the lovers; the
studied dullness of the heartland lit by an unquench-
able flame.

"I was sitting before the fire waiting for her to
return." Unprompted, Alinsky supplied the rest of

the scenario. "Then that stupid bastard of a police chief came to the door to tell me my life was ended. They'd banged her head against a hitching post and made her into this." He pointed at the form again. "More merciful to God they should have killed her then instead. . . .

"It deranged my mind, Murph," he said simply, reacting across Catherine's legs to take Murphy's two hands in his own. "It made me sick. Even then I knew what was happening to me, but there was nothing I could do about it. I'd wake up in the mornings and swear to take a grip on myself, but in an hour I was gone. That's when I started the drinking, too. Catherine was in the hospital, and I was walking or driving around Aruba looking at people's faces, at their shoes for scuffs, at their hands for scratches or bruises, at anyone and everyone hoping I'd see some sign, a snicker, a wink between two people, the look in someone's eye that would tell me that person was the one, or one of the ones. Do you know something, Murph? I was born and raised in Iowa, and for the first time in my life I understood that I was a Jew, an outsider. I understood then what the blood that flowed in my veins had forgotten since the family left Russia. That town was a whole wall of faces guarding a secret. They knew who did it. Even all the ones who dared to come to the house to present condolences, they knew too. . . ."

"Meyer, you're exaggerating. You've got to be. It was the shock taking its toll. Those Iowans weren't animals. If they'd known, they'd have gone to the police."

"No, Murph, you're wrong!" Alinsky raged, his eyes distended as if ready to pop. "They hated our love, our happiness! I understood this only later. And it was someone from the town. I'm certain of it. When that schmuck of a police chief came up with absolutely nothing day after day, I brought in private detectives from Chicago. They made the rounds of the bars; some even worked in our packinghouses to hear anything they could. They never found out who, but they told me it was someone from Aruba. . . ."

There was nothing to say. Alinsky was convinced. Even if it were not someone from the town, Murphy decided, the detectives, sensing his madness, may simply have told him it was to placate him and depart with their fees.

"And so you came here and brought her secretly on the plane the night we first met in Beersheba and played touch football on the airstrip," Al Hazzar said. He had stopped crying; his eyes were glazed and vacuous as if he could no longer support the burden of being Meyer Alinsky's friend.

"Yes, Musad, she was aboard that night. While we fucked around with a football they got her off unseen."

"Ah, me." Al Hazzar shook his head. "And poor little Aruba, Iowa? What did you do to the town, Meyer? Certainly you did something to it."

"I punished it. I destroyed it," Alinsky said distantly. "Not physically, of course, but economically it's been ruined. I closed down the stockyards and packinghouses and then bought out and shut down everything else. Every time the Chamber of Commerce tried for a revival to bring in new business or industry, my agents made sure nothing moved. There can't be ten people living there now. Only the keepers of the cemeteries. Everyone who had to make a living moved away."

"That wasn't revenge enough, Meyer?" Murphy demanded angrily, pulling free his hands. "Eight people had to be killed into the bargain? Do you think your Catherine Raabe would have approved of that?"

"Why don't you ask her what she approves of, Murph? If she could answer she might tell you. She was a sainted woman. She loved everyone. But even in her case twenty-two years of a life lost might have changed her thinking a bit."

"You did a fiendish thing, Meyer."

"No, Murphy." Alinsky smiled wistfully. "As I said before, I did a compassionate thing. It had to be compassionate, you see, because the vengeance was for her. I had to make it worthy of a great love; I had to find a special way to temper it. The blind inhumanity of men toward other men was inappropriate here. How could I simply have gone out and mercilessly killed eight poeple in the name of my beloved Catherine? It wasn't possible. No, the vengeance was necessary, but it was also necessary to deify the victims first."

"Yet there was a time you would have settled for one, wasn't there, Meyer? I was to have been the one."

"Yes, Murph, but life is enigmatic, n'est-ce pas? Even the most planned-out and willful decisions of men become caprices of destiny, and I have a profound respect for the tornado god. But you're not finished yet. There's an even greater purpose in your being alive than I could ever have seen when I went looking for you or someone like you a year ago. In my stead you'll be even further able to temper this vengeance with justice. You'll be more the Christ than ever."

"What do you mean, Meyer?"

"Why, Murph! You're the one to rebuild Aruba! Don't you see it?" Alinsky stared at Murphy with a look that suggested it was Murphy, in his incomprehension, who was the actual madman.

"But what about you? Where will you go?"

"Meyerle." The castrato spoke. "It is time. The police may come to the house because of the explosion."

"Yes, yes, it is time, Luciano. You're right."

The castrato took Alinsky's diamond—not seen since before they tried to contact Interpol in Istanbul—from a small pouch and handed it across to Alinsky, who had begun crying quietly again. He turned it over in his fingers for a brief time, holding it up to the light and inexplicably smiling through his tears at the reflection of its facets. Then with two fingers gently placed on the atrabilious pouches beneath his wife's eyes, Alinsky opened them and held the diamond before them.

"She always did love bright things. . . ."

There was an awed, hushed response to the symbolism of the act. Murphy, unconsciously touching the woman's arm with his fingers, felt Al Hazzar take a panic grip on his arm; the castrato wedged the end of his caftan into his mouth. Some flicker of a smile, an almost imperceptible momentary brightness of the eyes, told she had seen. The hand of the arm Murphy touched, shackled at the wrist lest the intravenous tubing be disturbed, moved slightly, the fingers spreading clawlike as if she meant to reach up and touch it. Almost tauntingly Alinsky moved the diamond before her eyes; they moved back and forth slowly, following the bright trajectory.

"Oh-h-h . . ." came the collective sigh, pent-up air releasing from the giant bellows of the Universe.

"She sees it," Alinsky said in a low, hoarse whisper. "She understands."

He wept violently and smiled delightedly at the same time, and then grabbed Murphy's arm. "Do you see, Murph?" he begged. "Do you see how she understands?"

Alinsky was very near the end of his own life now, Murphy thought. There was nowhere else to go. He had come to this. In the anguish of twenty-two years of love unrequited, cruelly destroyed, seeking an island, a haven of peace, he had persuaded himself the sensorium of her mind registered the glittering object. But Murphy could have wept for another reason. The diamond might as well have been a newly minted coin; the woman before them on the bed understood nothing of love, or the supposedly tempered vengeance that love had prompted. Murphy was absolutely sure she did not recognize Meyer Alinsky.

"She understood, Meyer," Murphy said quietly.

"Yes, that is evident to me also, Meyer, my brother," Al Hazzar lied.

"Yes, Meyerle," the castrato assured him. "She knows."

A final reassurance demanded, Alinsky turned to the Bedouin nurse. She nodded her head in emphatic agreement, the coin mask of her forehead clanking to the rhythm of the falsehood.

"In God's name, I loved her so much!" Alinsky shouted, his eyes gone wild again. "She knows it was a vengeance God would approve of. I could never commit outright murder in the name of our love. The whole world understands this. . . ."

"Yes, Meyerle," the castrato said again, seeming wearied. "But we have spoken so often of this. The agony is over now. The time for her relief is at hand."

"Yes." Alinsky was calm now. "Yes, the time of her relief has come. She has certainly deserved it."

He turned to the Bedouin woman again, gained her attention, then shifted his eyes to a small boxlike cabinet on the wall nearby. Murphy guessed that the box contained the circuit breaker that would silence the life-sustaining machines that hummed about them.

In response the woman shook her head no and then buried her face in her hands. Alinsky looked to the castrato. "Luciano?"

"*Lo*, Meyerle. You have paid or forced people in the past to turn the world upside down, to create reality for you when it suited you, and illusion when you could not longer stand the reality. This one thing you must do alone. Luciano has done enough for you. Even after you did the terrible thing to me, I stayed by you and sang the sad songs of lovers that you wished always to hear. I can do no more."

"Musad," Alinsky begged Al Hazzar. "Will you?"

"*La*, Meyer. You would ask a man who spends his passion and fondness among four wives to do

this? I have always accounted you more intelligent.
For me the act would be simple murder. I would never
love a woman this way."

"Murph?"

Murphy grew taut with anger, withdrawing from it
all. He must be more objective or cruel, climb swiftly
out of the charlatan Alinsky's net. "No, Alinsky.
You provided the vengeance, as you saw it. You
provide the relief, as you call it."

Alinsky stood, placing the diamond in his shirt
pocket; wracked with more sobs, he went to the wall
cabinet and opened the door. The circuit breaker
was there: the old-fashioned kind with a handle
that one simply pulled downward to break contact.

"Ours was a very great love," Alinsky assured
them, wiping his nose on his sleeve. "One of the
greatest the world has ever known."

"Yes," Murphy answered after a moment of silence, a rush of sacrilegious thoughts flying out of
him: that the love was happily nipped in the bud
before it had a chance to fade, then fester, like
his own and Monique's; that the past, growing distant and desperately lacking at the same time, tended
to aggrandize itself; that Aruba, Iowa, Meyer and his
Catherine notwithstanding, had to have produced
some of the humblest innocents of the universe, on
whom all of this would certainly be lost. . . .

But then Alinsky pulled down the circuit breaker.
Instead of the commemorative blinking of lights like
that of the power drain of the electric chair that
Murphy was expecting, the machines simply hummed
to a halt. The slowly traveling red dot of the pulse
recorder staggered abruptly, then died altogether as
the screen went blank.

Catherine Raabe Alinsky still lived, but it would
be only a small matter of time before she was
gone. Her husband came back, sat down again, and,
crying softly now, laid his head on her shrunken chest.
Once he half rose to plant a kiss on her bloodless
lips, and another time, though she could certainly

not comprehend, spoke to her passionately. "In twenty-two years, Catherine, I have never touched another woman. I swear it to you."

That pronouncement stunned Murphy and Al Hazzar, though evidently not the castrato, and they exchanged an incredulous glance. But knowing Meyer, it had to be true. In a more pragmatic moment Murphy certainly would have deemed the man more stupid than mad, only now his wife was clearly dying. The pathos charged back into Murphy, and he found himself thinking again of the incredible anomalies that fashioned the lofty totem outside the lodge of Meyer Alinsky: his wife, a blond-haired, blue-eyed *shiksa* cheerleader of Missouri dying in the antiseptic dungeon of the record-setting Iowa halfback's palace in Jerusalem. Enough: Murphy could bear no more.

As the Catholicism of his youth eased cautiously back, Murphy heard somewhere within him the melody of the sad Requiem of the old Latin Mass, but he could not remember a single word of it. Al Hazzar rocked back and forth without a sound, and in her chair the Bedouin nurse took off her headdress to expose her long gray hair and began casting off her jewelry in mourning. . . .

In half an hour or so the life was gone from Alinsky's wife. In the last minutes Alinsky had stopped crying and merely rested his head on her chest, which ceased its minute heavings, and, wide-eyed, smiled at her face, which seemed incredibly peaceful in death, remembering perhaps years before how young and fine and lovely the face had been.

In time Murphy and Al Hazzar pulled Alinsky to his feet and half carried him from the bedside toward the steps that led upward to the garage above. The castrato walked before them, saying in a kind of sing-song voice, "Poor Meyerle. Poor, poor Meyerle. What he has done to Luciano the castrato is nothing compared to the evil God has done to him. . . ."

Behind them the Bedouin woman began removing

the catheters and tubing from Catherine Raabe Alin-sky.

Occasionally she halted, throwing her arms ceiling-ward, the blue-spotted face a mask of sorrowing, her tongue lolling out of her mouth as if she would wail.

But, appropriately, no sound came forth.

31

A revisit: Cola di Rienzo

UPSTAIRS IN THE THRONE ROOM the queen mother was holding court. Rachel Alinsky sat in a suggestive throne of a chair, no longer content with the sipping delicacy of an old-fashioned but drinking straight bourbon from a water glass while a bottle stood on a table beside her at the ready. When they entered the room she was shrieking at Ben Bokva in a Middle Americanese Murphy had not thought her capable of, pointing through a window and across an expanse of terrace to the distant place of the catastrophe along the road from the house where the dome lights of four jeeploads of police whirled in the darkness and a single fire truck hosed down the smoking carnage.

"Ben Bokva, you go out and bring those police to this house right now! Meyer is going to jail today for what he did out there!"

"*Giveret* Alinsky"—Ben Bokva pleaded with her —"he's your own son!"

"Yeah, and Aloysius Riley was my own boy friend! That's why I'm drinking straight bourbon, honey," she suddenly announced in an aside to Jean-Philippe, who sat on the floor nearby, dressed for no apparent reason in Western clothes and a hat and wearing a six-gun at his hip exactly as Murphy had seen him in the photographs of the Galilee hunting trips. But Jean-Philippe merely shrugged in response and then spat on the floor. Nearby on a divan sat Monique and Teplitsky. Monique was crying fearfully, perhaps in expectation of her own death, certainly no longer in love with the madman. Teplitsky, the moralist of Alinsky's two favorite henchmen, sat dazed and numb-looking; clearly, Murphy judged, he had had no idea what Alinsky intended for the pilgrims.

Drying his eyes, Alinsky walked forward and stood before his mother while Murphy, Al Hazzar, and the castrato formed a half circle behind him. Imperiously, Rachel Alinsky held out her glass for a refill of bourbon while she eyed her son narrowly. "Well?"

"Catherine is dead, Mother." He spoke in a phlegm-coated voice.

"I'd say it's about time, Meyer, wouldn't you? Did she like the diamond?"

"Oh, yes, Mother." Alinsky smiled, clapping his hands delightedly. "She loved it. Her eyes brightened so much when she saw it. You just wouldn't believe it."

"Be sure to write the Bishop of Angoulême and tell him. I'm sure he'd be ecstatic to know his diamond met with the approval of a cheerleader from Missour—"

"And she understood, Mother." Alinsky interrupted her, oblivious to the insult. "She understood that I had avenged her—"

"She understood nothing, you damn fool!" his mother raged. "The diamond was your symbol, not hers! The same way this cockamamie crusade scheme was yours! A piece of stained glass chipped out of the bishop's window would have done the same trick down in that cellar! But enough of that. We've all had enough symbolism to last us until the end of our days. The question is what are you going to do now? Your original intention was to bump off Jesus-Christ-Murphy here and make his death look like an accident and send the others back to where they came from with no one the wiser. But then you discovered Murph was a long-time favorite of your tornado god, so plan A became plan B and eight people are dead instead of one. Now, what's plan C, I wonder? Because the way I figure it, Ben Bokva won't talk, nor Luciano, but Teplitsky's had it, and Madame de Pompadour, Jean-Philippe, Musad, Murphy, and myself are all set to sing to the cops like canaries once the shock wears off. In fact, I'm calling them right in here now."

"No, you're not, Mother," Alinsky said, smiling softly. "You should know by now that your little boy doesn't have one plan but five. Ten even, sometimes. And I've arranged for one more contingency, haven't I, Jean-Philippe?"

"Oui, Monsieur Alinsky," Jean-Philippe said, smiling softly himself. He stood up, tall and lean, movie-star handsome in the tight-fitting Levi's, and tipped his hat slightly forward: a young gunslinger in town, looking to carve his first notch. Alinsky moved onto center stage, certain there was no one behind him, his smile peaceful now in the extreme. Horrifically, Murphy understood that a macabre dance of death was being enacted. His voice, like everyone else's, froze once again in his throat. He saw the glass begin to shake in Rachel Alinsky's hand, the bourbon sloshing all over her dress.

Alinsky stopped, made a lightning feint with his right hand toward his pants pocket, then threw his arms up in the air to show he was unarmed. Jean-Philippe whipped out the six-gun and blasted Meyer Alinsky twice in the stomach, slapping the hammer both times. Alinsky, his hands on high, smiling bemusedly now, fell to the floor.

He had, Murphy thought vaguely, well . . . he had welcomed the bullets into him.

"Merci, Jean-Philippe. . . . Merci bien, mon fils,"

Alinsky gasped. Then his head fell over to one side and he died. And just like in a Western, blood began instantly coursing out of his mouth.

"You all saw that. He drew on me first." Jean-Philippe spoke to the assembly in much practiced and perfect Americanese.

"Yes," Rachel Alinsky answered, "he drew first." Then she burst into an old lady's wailing tears. "*Aleve shalom,* cowboy son of mine, and the many other things you were besides."

Murphy fainted dead out on the barroom floor not too far from Alinsky's body.

32

All Rachel's lost children

WHEN MURPHY CAME TO, Ben Bokva was into it again with Rachel Alinsky.

"*Giveret* Alinsky, we must call in the police immediately!" Ben Bokva was shrieking at her. "That kid is going to pay for gunning down Meyer! Meyer didn't even have a gun on him!"

"Do you mean to call in the police for that same Meyer who had those eight innocent people who weren't wearing asbestos suits fried to a crisp out there about an hour ago? Are you also talking about that Meyer who had this kid all set up and programmed to do exactly what he did five minutes ago?"

"He's a murderer!" Ben Bokva screamed, pointing at Jean-Philippe, who slouched against a wall, eyeing the Israeli menacingly as if he meant to use the six-gun again.

"Don't you know a mercy killing when you see one, Ben Bokva? You schmuck! You hypocrite! Thank God he's dead and out of his misery! Sit down and shut up! I never liked you since you were a kid!" She threw her glass of bourbon at him, a near faultless shot that sent most of the liquid sting-

390

ing into his eyes. Against his wall, Jean-Philippe laughed mirthfully at the sight.

Monique stood up from the divan and stared a long moment at the dead and bleeding Alinsky, a curious look of repugnance spreading across her face as if she had, in the same instant, disclaimed knowledge of him, disavowed his memory. Then she fled from the room, stopping only near the door to call back to Murphy. "Au revoir, Frank. You'll file for the divorce in France, won't you? But with a minimum of publicity. If I file it is useless. A woman has so little chance of winning, and especially after the events of this last year to my credit. No one will believe them. . . ."

"And Jean-Philippe?" Murphy called after her.

The mention of her son's name seemed to sober her. Disheveled and splotchy of face from the weeping, she forced a smile that produced an opposite effect, made her look grotesque and a phony altogether. "Jean-Philippe, you will return to France *avec ta maman?*"

"*Jamais, madame,*" Jean-Philippe said wrathfully. "I wish never to see you again for the rest of my life."

Monique merely shrugged, her duty discharged, the insult perhaps expected. Then she turned and ran away, her hurried footsteps echoing down a marbled hallway. Jean-Philippe exchanged a look with Murphy, a genuinely sardonic smile for so young a face, and then said to his father, seemingly for no reason at all, "I think, Papa, when it is time for me to marry I shall choose an Italian woman. They are said to be very faithful."

"Yes, I've heard that also," Murphy agreed, lying instantly to mask the sorrow of his terrible failure. But it had been coming for years. The de Rastignac Murphys were all fallen apart now and it was quite irrevocable.

Ben Bokva, cowed from his bath of bourbon,

a dumb ship adrift without a rudder, spoke to Rachel Alinsky. *"Giveret* Alinsky, tell me what to do."

"You and Teplitsky take Meyer's body down to the hole with Catherine and get that blood mopped up. The police are bound to come here sooner or later. Luciano," she ordered the castrato, "telephone Shimon the lawyer and tell him it's time. He'll understand. And tell him not to forget the embalmer. Ask Shimon to come as quickly as possible. When he gets here we'll all sit down for a little conference and try to work out some more details."

They watched dully as Ben Bokva and Teplitsky set to their task, Teplitsky pulling down a curtain in which they wrapped the body, simply rolling it over until it was covered, then hoisting it unceremoniously between them and carrying it quickly from the room. Al Hazzar brought two wet towels and a small bucket from behind a corner bar and knelt on the floor to mop up Alinsky's blood, periodically wringing the towels into the bucket. When it was done and he was still kneeling on the floor, he looked up dazedly at Alinsky's mother and asked simply, "Mother Rachel, what else will you have me do?"

"Please wait for now, Musad, until Shimon comes."

"As you wish."

"What about us, Rachel?" Murphy heard his own voice begging directions.

"You wait too, Frank. I'm going to need your help to at least get this show as far as the airport."

"Yes, of course."

"Jean-Philippe," she commanded, "it's time to change out of your costume now and get rid of that six-gun. The police will be here in a little while looking for some more answers."

"Yes, I will do it now, Mère Rachèle," he answered, getting up quickly and rushing off to do her bidding.

The police came finally, in five minutes more,

getting past the roadblock Alinsky had sent out from the house when some higher echelon officers began arriving from the city. But they ran headlong into old Rachel's inspired actress's tirade of abuse on the Israel police for allowing a fedayeen ambush to occur only a half mile from her home. The tide was swiftly turned, and the police, possibly fearing demotions, slunk from the house away into the night to look for Arabs.

After their departure, the lawyer named Shimon arrived, a man of gently ironic mien, tall and thin, with glazed, dark-circled eyes and a small goatee, black though his hair was nearly gray. There was an air of imperturbable calm about him, a sense of having seen it all; the proof perhaps was on his left arm, revealed by his short sleeves, a concentration camp tattoo, a number that Murphy realized—absurdly—was exactly that of the license plate of his Peugeot back in France except for the first digit. When Shimon stepped onto the veranda overlooking the lighted courtyard, all the participants in the final act—Murphy, Al Hazzar, the castrato, Ben Bokva and Teplitsky, Jean-Philippe, and Rachel Alinsky—were seated about a table waiting.

The lawyer walked up to Rachel and kissed her softly on the forehead. "Shalom, Rakhel."

"Shalom, Shimon. The day has finally arrived, yes?"

"Yes, Rakhel, according to Luciano it ended very nearly the way you said it would. Perhaps there is no wisdom like that of a mother. No sorrow like hers, either."

Alinsky's mother nodded her head toward the explosion site. The harsh glare of an acetylene torch lit the scene eerily; they were cutting the bodies free from the wreck. "Did you know anything about this, Shimon?"

"No, Rakhel. You know better than to ask that. I handled most of your own and Meyer's affairs. But Meyer was a brilliant man. I worked for him on only very disparate pieces. No one could have understood it would come to this. He made certain no one could see the connections. . . ."

It was easy to believe; no one questioned him further. He sat down at the table's remaining place and nodded his head toward the gates of the house where the servants were streaming outward on foot toward the city, sounding the house's death knell, stealing its wealth.

"The fortress is truly falling, Rakhel," Shimon judged bemusedly. "All the rats are returning to the safety of the city sewers. Your treasures will be bought up by rich tourists and spread the world over."

"Yes, the general is dead and everyone will soon know it," she agreed, also somehow bemused, delighted even with the metaphor. "Banana republics are notorious for not ever lasting too long. Jewish ones have even lesser odds. There goes the generalissimo's French whore. Historically they're always the last to leave."

They watched over the balustrade as Monique, carrying two suitcases packed so hastily that frilly things like underwear and the sleeve of a dress hung outside, hurried down a stairway toward the parking area and then ran from car to car looking for one with a set of keys in the ignition. Murphy and Jean-Philippe were in hysterics of laughter. Wife and mother had become altogether a bad joke and it was much, much better to laugh than to cry.

"Who has the keys to those cars?" Rachel asked.

"I do," the castrato answered. "You want I give her one, Rachel?"

"Yes, to Meyer's old heap of an Imperial. That will be a fitting vehicle for my lady's departure to the airport."

The castrato searched in a pouch he carried at his belt like a king's agent, found the keys, then stood up and called to Monique in his high shrill voice, *"Madame, ici,* the keys for the old Iowa car."

"Oh, mon Dieu!" Monique exclaimed, stomping one foot on the pavement. *"Madame sa mère* exacts her final revenge, *je crois!"*

Rachel Alinsky stood up and shook a little-old-lady fist in the air at her adversary. "Be lucky you're riding, *putain!* It goes when you push the button marked D."

Shrilly laughing, the castrato threw down the keys. They fell on the pavement and Monique scooped them up, ran to the Imperial, and threw her suitcases into the back seat. Then she started the car; it erupted in a roar of rusted broken mufflers and clouds of smoke from an engine badly in need of an overhaul. As she pulled out, Murphy saw that Meyer's Winchester still rested astride the gun rack across the back window. Then she was gone, the last Murphy ever expected to see of her, nearly sideswiping a gatepost on her way out. They all followed her departure a long silent minute until she had maneuvered around the distant police jeeps and disappeared. Murphy, once conditioned by her to carry a heart full of guilt, felt suddenly and conclusively unburdened. . . .

"So, Rakhel." Shimon brought the meeting to order. "Where are we now? Meyer of the thousand faces and million contingencies is dead. You yourself had only one plan for all these years, but now even that begins to look like a Balinese dancer with several heads and many arms." He reinforced the judgment by inclining his head toward Al Hazzar, Murphy, and Jean-Philippe in that order. "Sheik Al Hazzar I know well. Both you and Meyer loved him dearly, so he is beyond reproach. But what of Jesus of Nazareth and Billy the Kid here?"

"The basic plan still holds, Shimon," she told him. "Meyer and Catherine are to be buried in the Jewish cemetery in Aruba, Iowa, by sundown tomorrow, and Murphy and Jean-Philippe are welcome to come along."

The lawyer nodded his assent, not an iota of surprise anywhere in his face. But Ben Bokva, quite expectedly, rose out of his chair in disbelief. *"Giveret* Alinsky, how can you do this? How can you take them back to Iowa when you know what happened there? Every good Jew would give his arm for the chance to be buried here. You would dishonor him by taking him back to that place?"

"I've told you before, Ben Bokva, shut your mouth!" she shrieked at him. "I've paid my Jewish dues for the last twenty-two years and I'm tired! I'm going home and taking Meyer and the wife with me to bury them, and then I'll have a few years of peace, God willing, before I die."

"She's not even Jewish." Ben Bokva made one last feeble try.

"I'm sure something has rubbed off on her in all these years," Shimon responded dryly. "Now, it has been suggested you be silent," he warned, extracting a sheaf of papers from a briefcase. "To business, *haverim*. I did some checking in the car on the way over. Sundown in northern Iowa tomorrow is approximately six-ten P.M. Iowa time. That means with proposed flight time, allowances for refuelings in Rome and London, customs check in New York, picking up that rabbi cousin of yours, Rakhel, in Chicago for the burial, plus travel time overland from Cedar Rapids to Aruba, you should depart Lod airport no later than two A.M. in the morning."

"Not much time, Shimon," Alinsky's mother said doubtfully.

"Admittedly. But the embalmer is already at work. I brought him with me and saw him downstairs to the dungeon. He'll provide the coffins also, quite simple ones as you specified. A good number of other things have already been taken care of. I'll go down the list, Rakhel, and you stop me if you think of anything."

"Yes. All right."

"The plane is fueled and ready at Lod. It's in the hangar, so it won't attract any attention when it's time for loading. I've called the standby crew and they've filed the flight plan—"

"No dignitaries. No ceremonies at the airport." She cut in on the lawyer. "We're leaving by the back door."

"A small ceremony might be in order, Rakhel," Shimon tried. "He did a lot for the country, after all. Remember the Six-Day War."

"*Shumdavar,*" she said sharply. "Nothing. And I do remember the Six-Day War. Meyer spent the whole time on his ass here praying the Jordanians wouldn't bomb his beloved house."

Shimon traded a tolerant smile with Teplitsky, then said in a quiet voice, "I assure you, Rakhel, his praying was only in thanksgiving for the fruit of his larger efforts."

"Cut it out, Shimon. Not you, too," she rasped. "You're supposed to be the sensible one. Now, what about money?"

"It will be delivered by courier to the plane in New York after the customs people leave. Unfortunately, during the customs check the coffins will have to be opened for inspection."

She shrugged. "What about embassy clearance, Shimon? The burial permits?"

"Updated month after month, just as you instructed, for so many years I can barely remember now how long it's been," Shimon said wearily, shifting more papers. "So all that remains, as nearly as I can tell, is to wire your cousin the rabbi Ushpizai in Evanston, Illinois, to meet the plane at O'Hare airport in Chicago, and also your friend, Police Chief Morain, to have two graves dug and readied in the cemetery at Aruba by tomorrow sundown—"

Shimon suddenly stopped and stared unseeing a long moment off toward the lights of the city before he spoke again. "Rakhel, this LaVerne Morain, your police chief—what does he look like?"

She stared at him in consternation. "I don't know. Like a police chief, I guess. Why do you ask, Shimon?"

"Curiosity, I guess. I mean, I've been issuing checks to him once a month through a Swiss bank for the last twenty years to take care of your house in Aruba and the Jewish cemetery. I just wondered, that's all."

"Like a police chief, that's what he looks like. The same way Ushpizai looks like a rabbi. That's all I can tell you."

"Do not be too disappointed on your return, Rakhel. Prepare yourself for it," Shimon cautioned her earnestly. "Ushpizai and Morain will be old men you will hardly recognize. Aruba, we are told, is a ghost town on poisoned land. You cannot go back to the world of nineteen forty-eight in the American Midwest and live your days out as before, because Meyer's madness cheated you out of twenty years of a life you preferred instead of the one you had to live here in Israel. . . ."

"I pay you for legal advice, Shimon. My dreams are private and extralegal, and right now my mind is flaming with them. What gives you the right to dump a few tons of unsolicited Talmudic wisdom on me today of all days?"

"I survived the camps, Rakhel," he answered, brandishing the tattoo. "It hasn't exactly made a sentimental fool of me. Believe me, there's no return. The old Ford motorcars will all be in junkyards, and the windows of the ice cream parlors boarded over."

"Forgive me, Shimon," she said sadly. "I've read all my Fitzgerald even if I haven't lived it. I should know better. What else is there?"

"The money, the properties, assets, investments. . . . The one thing about Meyer that wasn't a façade was his wealth."

"You head that legal team of his, yes, Shimon? Meyer told me once he had made provisions about that in the event of an accident. Everything liquidated and into Swiss accounts, I believe."

"*Tov*. It's as was discussed. The last thing, Rakhel, it would seem to me, concerns your traveling companions for the journey home. You're too old to do all this alone."

"For sure Ben Bokva, Teplitsky, and Luciano," she answered. "They're all long since promised."

"I also would come, Mother Rachel," Al Hazzar said quietly, "to accompany my brother Meyer to the last moment."

"Thank you, Musad. God love you, too. And you, Frank, would you come? Perhaps you could stay on in Iowa with me for a while to help with the re-building of the town?" The excitement grew in her voice; she reached out her hand, clasping Shimon's left arm, unwittingly covering the concentration camp tattoo. "That's what the money in the Swiss accounts is for, Shimon, do you see? Some things Meyer did can never be justified, but Meyer's money can go a long way toward helping. Even if we're the only ones who know. . . ."

Shimon stared at her quizzically for a time, a kind of wariness in the knit of his brows. Then he placed his own hand over hers, smiling and nodding his head enthusiastically as if the notion, gradually taking shape, had become a fixed quantum. "Yes, Rakhel! Yes, I can see it now. It's perfect! I would never have thought of it. What of it, Francis Xavier Murphy? Will you stay with her? I must have the security of that knowledge, for the others will return here for certain."

"Meyer already proposed that I do that exactly," Murphy said, watching the play of lighted shrubbery in the wind below them, knowing even as he spoke the words that he meant to acquiesce. "I'll go with you, Rachel."

"And you will stay to help me rebuild?" she begged.

He made ease of it. "Yes, I suppose I will. I

don't really have too many other options, do I?"

"No, you really don't, Frank," she assured him, clapping her hands together to expel the pent-up nervousness. "I don't mean to imply that you've failed, but you have burned a few bridges behind you—with a little help from my son, of course."

"Just as well," Murphy judged. Then there was a silence, and all eyes were on Jean-Philippe.

"What about you, Billy the Kid?" Shimon asked softly.

"*Pas à l'Amérique.* I don't wish to go to America, Papa."

"You'd go back to France to that mother of yours?" Rachel Alinsky demanded incredulously.

"*Non.* To Italy, madame. I will go to live with Uncle Pietro and Aunt Eustacia in Milan, Papa. They like me very much. Remember?"

"Yes. Yes. They're wonderful people." Murphy became suddenly enthused at the solution, recalling Monique's cousin Pietro, a straightlaced and well-funded architect whose hospitality verged on the boundless, whose disapproval of Murphy's drinking had verged on the murderous.

"And his wife, this woman Eustacia, is she a good woman?" Rachel questioned critically.

"She's the mother of fourteen children," Murphy answered. "If she's not a good woman, at least she doesn't have time to play around, if that's what you mean."

"That's what I mean," she said. "All right, Jean-Philippe, you may go to Italy."

"*Merci, mère Rachèle.*" He kissed her cheek. Murphy saw that his gratitude was genuine.

"Shimon, what about the bodies out there?" Alinsky's mother remembered with a sudden start; small tears flashed instantly to her eyes again. In their preoccupation with dismembering Alinsky's empire, they had somehow forgotten his sacrificial victims.

"I'll arrange for the bodies to be sent home for proper burial after identification. Their pay vouchers will be honored also. The monies are to be donated to their favorite charities."

"But how will you know where to bury them? How will you know what their favorite charities were?" Murphy demanded, fearful suddenly that their remains might end up in desecration in some potter's field for unclaimed Christians in Israel, that someone on the Alinsky legal team might pocket the money.

"All the information was relayed to my office last week when you were off on the bus tour of the country. Meyer, I suppose, took elaborate pains to gather the facts from each person individually. If only I had understood. . . ."

Shimon threw up his hands, disavowing any responsibility with the claim of ignorance. But Murphy on the opposite side of the table suddenly lurched to his feet, his fists clenched in fury in his certainty that Shimon, for all his soothing equanimity, had been an actual conspirator of Meyer Alinsky.

"Shimon, you prick! Do you mean to tell me that a list like that shows up on your desk and you're not able to put two and two together? Not even to suspect what he was up to?"

Al Hazzar and Teplitsky restrained Murphy. But Shimon was defiant; he stood also, taller than Murphy, holding his own ground on his side of the table, pounding a fist for emphasis.

"My God, Murphy, what do you think I am? The Almighty himself? Your name was on the list, too, along with those of your wife and son. I told you before, Meyer never provided connections. Supplying that list at the same time he instructed me to purchase plane tickets for Paris was just typical of the way he did things. Planes crash from mechanical failures, you know. Terrorists bomb them. I had orders to get tickets for two different flights on the same day. Do you think in my wildest possible imaginings I suspected Meyer might blow two commercial jets out of the sky? Be reasonable, Murphy, I beg you."

Again, the perfect good sense of things, uncontestable. Murphy sat down again in defeat.

Then there was nothing else, everything said perhaps, any other words anticlimactic certainly, until the Bedouin nurse came suddenly onto the terrace, looking like a true Medusa, her black eye shadowing streaked across the blue tattooing of her face, tears roaring from her eyes. Soundless, unable to release the pain from within, she embraced Alinsky's mother, who stood for the event; the two women, weeping, rocked back and forth, Rachel Alinsky suddenly providing the sounds of limitless pain, the Bedouin woman openmouthed and mute.

33

Yad VeShem

AFTER SHIMON DEPARTED to his remaining tasks, there were—in the wake of the day's incredible events—almost inconsequential things to be taken care of. In the brilliantly lit, unstaffed house where their now-unhurried footsteps were muted along the corridors, Murphy packed a bag, trying besides his toilet articles and changes of underwear to remember what he might need in the tentative early April days of Iowa. Then there remained but his recently returned passport, inoculation card, and some traveler's checks in dollars. He smiled agreeably at the meager collection of possessions left to him in his thirty-eighth year and decided that one of the acknowledged maxims of starting over was certainly to take as little as possible from the old life. So far he was complying admirably.

About eleven thirty, with Al Hazzar, Jean-Philippe, old Rachel, and the castrato, he went to the gigantic kitchen for a late supper of cold chicken and ale, where they ate with the staff silver, the staff having stolen the good stuff. In the beginning they spoke little, except for Jean-Philippe's acknowledgment that Teplitsky had already telephoned Pietro and Eustacia

403

Malatesta in Milan and received assurance that they
were eagerly expecting him. He would travel with the
others to the airport, take a later El Al flight to
Rome, and then fly Alitalia up to Milan, where
Pietro would pick him up.

But for the moment, at least, that was the end of
it. There was no talk between father and son of
meeting again. Time would cure the thing, Murphy
supposed, erase the image of Billy the Kid from his
mind. Someday Jean-Philippe might consent to visit
the States, and Murphy might introduce him to the
America of the seventies that he himself would have
to begin learning all over again. Perhaps it would
be the other way. Murphy to Italy to visit his son.
But that would take time also. Pietro Malatesta, for
all his good family-man qualities, was a righteous bastard. It would be years before his anger over the
divorce from Monique would abate, before Murphy
—even Murphy on the wagon—would be welcome
again in his house.

Rachel Alinsky broke the ensuing silence, looking
at a distorted image of herself in the great slab side
of a stainless steel food locker. "I'd like to create
some sort of tribute to the eight, more than just a
proper burial and giving the money Meyer promised
them to some charities, but I'm too numb to know
where to start. The shock doesn't have anything to
do with Meyer and Catherine. It's the others. They
were all innocent victims. Riley, especially. I suppose
the horror will surface somewhere, maybe back in
America in the future before I die. . . ."

She stopped speaking and took a reflective sip of
her ale before she began again.

"I remember one night years ago I went to Yad
VeShem, the Place of Remembrance, with Shimon,
who lost a wife and four children in the camps. And
he told me that after the liberation by the Allies he
wandered all over Germany looking for them or
some news about them, but there was nothing, and
finally the Red Cross confirmed they'd all been killed.

But he felt nothing, he said, the thing was pushed too far down inside him, until one day in Haifa in the early fifties he saw a woman who reminded him of his wife and he just plain went berserk and was taken to a psychiatric hospital for about six months. Can you imagine keeping something like that repressed for so long? I wonder if that will happen to me? I mean because Meyer was my son and some people would say I've given birth to a monster. And he killed Riley. I should hate him for that. Riley was my only real friend in twenty-two years in Israel."

"I should not worry, Rakhel."

The voice came from the shadows of the entryway to the kitchen. Startled, Murphy knocked over his glass and it shattered on the tabletop. Shimon, unheard, had returned to the house and stood listening. Now he entered the room, wearing a black skullcap on his head.

"None of it was your fault, and there was nothing you could have done to prevent it, since you had no idea what Meyer's monomania intended. Even he had no idea the eight were to die in the beginning. Murphy was the intended victim. That seems certain. And when he first telephoned me this evening, Luciano told me that, above all else, Meyer tried to prevent Aloysius from leaving. At least that attempt bespeaks his capacity for humanity. The rest was his madness, and we both well know Meyer's madness was not inherited. His childhood was normal and healthy. It was the crime against Catherine that infected his mind. Go back to Iowa, and think only of those happy days in that place. You have no reason to go berserk as I did."

He patted her hair as if she were a child.

"But the others. . . . I wonder, Rakhel. I overheard you speak of a tribute to be left behind. It would not be improper, you know, since everything is being terminated for you in Israel. Some sort of monument to the memory of their innocence is what I was thinking."

"A sort of Yad VeShem for the Christian victims," Murphy suggested ruefully, thinking how few were eight compared to six million.

Shimon shrugged self-deprecatingly, sensing Murphy's irony. "A very small Yad VeShem, Frank. A crude sort we might construct ourselves on the spot of the catastrophe rather than leaving it to a monument maker after everyone has departed. It would have more meaning that way."

"Yes," the castrato enthused. "We could make a cross lying down on the hillside near where the car is burned. There is much rock out there."

"Yes, Shimon," Alinsky's mother agreed. "That would make a fine gesture. Something to give my conscience a little peace besides."

"We should go now then," Shimon urged. "We do not have a great deal of time."

Together they left the kitchen, trooping upstairs through the empty house and out to the cars. In the parking area they selected the limousine, the castrato driving it through the gate and then through the moonlit night to the place where the burned-out shell of the Peugeot sat alone on some suggestion of hindquarters, the front half, the engine hanging downward from it, bent upward at the frame, presumably where the force of the first explosion had hit it. The second, evidently, had smashed in the roof, collapsing its pillars. Thus with the doors forced shut it had become a grisly pyre from which no one left alive might escape. Holes had been cut by the police torches in the twisted roof and tailgate to remove the bodies. The monument builders all sat a long moment in the limousine, looking at the wreck, until Al Hazzar broke the silence with a consideration that had doubtless been on everyone's mind.

"There is no odor. That is very curious. Perhaps

the firemen used some sort of chemical that did away with it."

They were out of the limousine now. Murphy walked toward the hulk of the Peugeot, expecting a wave of heat to meet him. But there was none, and when he tentatively touched it, the metal was as cool as the night air. Also he wondered vaguely why there were no sightseers.

"Rakhel, I think that hillside over there would do nicely," Shimon said. "There is a lot of good-sized rock there, too."

Nothing more was said. Murphy and Al Hazzar went to the designated hillside, pulled the low clumps of brush out by the roots, and threw them into a ditch. Shimon traced out the outline of a cross in the earth with a stick, the main shaft perhaps twelve feet long, the cross bar about half that size. The castrato turned the car about so that its headlights illuminated the area, and they set to work carrying rock—much of it blasted from the ledges to create the roads that led to Alinsky's great house—and stacking it along the outline. Shimon admonished old Rachel in the beginning to sit in the car and wait until the job was finished, but she refused, bending over in sprightly little-old-lady fashion to pick up rocks, her only concession to Shimon's concern being that they were smaller than anyone else's.

In half an hour they were finished, the neat heapings of stone reminding Murphy of some overly large shallow grave of times past on the American frontier. When the last stone was placed (covering a plastic-wrapped list of the victims' names that Shimon had written in Latin and Hebrew script) a police car came by to check on the activity and informed them that the reason there were no sightseers was because of a roadblock being maintained farther along the way toward Ein Kerem. Further, they told Alinsky's mother they had scoured the hills and found no traces of the fedayeen who had pulled the job. Then, preposterously, as if the word had triggered a recognition, one of the cops got out of the car and began frisking Al Hazzar, demanding even that he remove his kaffiyeh, until Shimon, enraged along with the others, shoved the cop back inside the car and bade them depart because a commemorative service was about to take place.

When the police were gone, the five stood before the headlights of the limousine so that their shadows were cast over the cross on the hillside and all bowed their heads. After a moment of silence during which Murphy could not pray or even think, Al Hazzar asked, "What shall we do? What shall we say of them?"

"You're the only Christian here, Frank," Rachel Alinsky said, "and they were all Christians except for Rifka. Perhaps you could say a Christian prayer?"

For a moment the request baffled Murphy.

Then it came to him, the words of the Roman Requiem he had carried deep inside him since the day he had buried his parents and sister in Iowa so many years before, and he spoke them toward the cross that marked the place of Alinsky's own holocaust on the Jerusalem hills:

"May the souls of the dearly departed, through the mercy of God, rest in peace. Amen."

"Amen," came the general echo.

Then they returned to the car and Luciano wheeled it about and headed it back toward the still-lit house, empty except for the Arab nurse, Jean-Philippe, who slept, and presumably a mortician. In the back seat, his arm about Rachel, who sniffed softly now, Shimon broke down and cried outright for the first time, wiping at his tears with a handkerchief.

"Ah, Meyer, Meyer," he said. "May God, recognizing your madness, forgive you for what you have done."

34

Inheritor of the Book
of the Corruptibles

THEY LEFT ALINSKY'S PALACE without taint of majesty in a kind of microbus brought up from the subterranean garage. Up front, nine passengers were crammed onto the two seats (the Bedouin nurse to be dropped off in the city), and in the rear were the coffins of Catherine and Meyer and the small scatterings of their luggage for the journey. It was 12:30 A.M., about one and one half hours in advance of the proposed departure, time enough to reach Lod airport and board the 707 but scarcely enough time to attract any attention to the fact that they were fleeing the land of Israel.

Just after they passed through the gates, Rachel Alinsky seemed to remember that the house was for the most part fully lit, and she told Teplitsky to return and throw the main switch and lock the doors behind him. He left the vehicle, and in another minute the lights went out and the house was suddenly vast and ghostly in the moonlight, the soft night wind blowing the great curtains with their biblical motifs of Solomon and David outward onto the upper terraces where the doors had inadvertently been left open. Teplitsky rejoined them and the castrato

409

drove on, everyone else turning back reflexively to watch the house diminish behind them.

"*Mein Gott,* am I glad to be out of that place!" Alinsky's mother affirmed. "It has to be the draftiest house in the world. I've been in agony with my arthritis in there for the last fifteen years. . . ."

Murphy smiled inwardly, as he supposed the others did also, hearing her, thinking to himself that the agony of her arthritis must have been nothing compared to living with but never completely understanding Meyer's monomania. But his thoughts were cut off as they drove past the place of the ambush and the burned-out vehicle and the little Yad VeShem they had created earlier that night.

"Tomorrow I'll have the memorial ringed about with barbed wire and put up a notification sign of some sort," Shimon promised. "Israelis have an intense respect for memorials. So much in the Jewish past to memorialize, you know."

But there was no response. Farther along, the single police jeep roadblock saw them coming and pulled out of their path to let them pass, not bothering to halt them for questioning, the two cops merely observing them curiously as they slid by.

They negotiated the twisting, dimly lit streets of Jerusalem's new city, passing the Knesset and the Hebrew University on their way out of town. There were few cars and fewer pedestrians, and in the distance, when they could be seen, the walls of the old city were almost white in the light of the perfect moon. It was an incredible beauty that Murphy would never forget, and he suddenly wondered to himself if, in creating that evening the burnt offering to his love, Meyer Alinsky had profaned or exalted the Holy City. Thrown to the moralists, the question might take generations of squabbling to decide.

The Bedouin nurse alighted from the vehicle before the Central Bus Station; soundlessly, not looking back at them, covering her face and gathering

up her robes about her, she fled from them, her
meager satchel of possessions bumping her legs with
the motion, running into the middle distance until
she seemed to vanish in a puff behind the sudden
cloud of diesel smoke from a bus pulling out of
its stall, gone. . . .

At the city's outskirts they picked up speed, moving down the steep and curving highway that led out
of the Jerusalem hills toward the Plain of Sharon. They
rode in silence except for Rachel Alinsky, who spoke
each time they came to the signpost of a village on
the way down, pronouncing its name carefully, as if
she were transcribing phonetically. At Ramle, a big
Arab town where they turned north to head off toward Lod, Shimon finally asked her why she was
doing it.

"Because I'm never coming back, Shimon. I've
got all the sights and smells of this country in my
memory; now I'm just adding the last few sounds as
well."

For certain she meant what she said and no one
questioned her; one Alinsky at least had put reins
to the Fates. Past Ramle, where the night air grew
warmer, they opened the windows of the microbus
and the vaunted fragrance of orange groves—a lushness Murphy hoped would be his own last sensation
of Israel—rushed in at them.

They entered the airport, and the castrato halted
first in the commercial departure area to leave off
Jean-Philippe at the El Al lounge. Billy the Kid
(dressed again in Western style) descended, taking
with him a small bag he had packed and checking
its contents on the outside while Murphy clambered
out to join him. Jean-Philippe shuffled about a moment in the ghoulish purple of the overhead arc
lights, said something of a cursory good-bye to everyone in English, then compulsively jumped back inside the vehicle across the knees of Shimon and
Teplitsky to kiss Alinsky's mother on the forehead.

"Merci, vieille Rachèle. I carry your memory with me always."

Her tears that had started again when he left the bus gushed forth now. She took his head in her arms, holding him tightly to her and kissing his forehead, telling him in a raspy voice, "Be a good boy, Jean-Philippe. Play lots of football, screw all the girls you can get your hands on, and don't think too much about any one thing."

"Oui, madame," Jean-Philippe agreed. The others laughed mirthfully at her advice, despite the nearness of the coffins. Then, with Murphy, Jean-Philippe walked inside to the airline check-in counter, past the scrutiny of two soldiers who apparently decided there was no need to frisk them, and confirmed his reservation. He handed in his bag for weighing, removing from it first a single package that he tucked beneath one arm, then moaned at the counter girl's advisement that his flight, delayed one hour for certain, would not leave for three more.

There was another shuffling silence while Jean-Philippe adjusted his cowboy hat, then took it off, flailing imaginary dust out of his jeans and jacket. Peering past their reflections in the plate-glass windows, Murphy saw that all the occupants of the microbus were watching them steadily. Murphy proferred his hand, and Jean-Philippe took it, squeezing an iron grip.

"When shall we see each other again?" Murphy asked, smiling sadly.

"After some time, Papa. When the divorce is finished I would like to visit you in America. To see the states of Wyoming, Utah, Montana, and Idaho and the cowboys who live in these places."

"That would be fine. We could take a camping trip together. They have these wonderful camper vans in America that I've read about."

"Yes, I have read of them also." Jean-Philippe spoke brusquely now, impatient for the good-bye to end.

"What's in the package, Jean-Philippe? Something for your Aunt Eustacia?" Murphy said desperately, nodding at the package still wedged beneath Jean-Philippe's arm.

"No, Papa, it is the Book of the Corruptibles."

"You're kidding me. How did you get hold of that?"

"Alinsky gave it to me. Part of his motive was sentiment, I am sure"—Jean-Philippe shrugged, dismissing sentiment as evidently worthless—"but the rest was a case of genuine admiration. He told me he could think of no one who would put it to better use."

"Sorry to disappoint you, *mon fils,* but that book could prove to be nothing more than a lot of horseshit. A lot of Meyer Alinsky was façade, you remember."

Jean-Philippe smiled kindly at his father. "I remember. But I lived with Alinsky constantly, Papa, while you worked for him at a distance. The book is real. Whoever possesses it possesses real power."

"And what do you intend to do with it, may I ask?"

"I intend to become the richest man in Europe. Nothing less."

"The task is worthy of you, Jean-Philippe."

"Yes, it will give me something to do."

Then the restless shifting again. Murphy shrugged a few more times, feeling foolish indeed, seeing once again the busload of his fellow travelers peering steadfastly in at them from the outside. "Try not to take it too hard about your mother, Jean-Philippe. A lot of it was my fault, you know."

"Peut-être." He shrugged. Then he grew vehement. "But I will never forgive her. You were always an outsider, but we were alike, she and I. We were de Rastignacs. We were French. We had a pact together against Alinsky, and she broke it. She even tried to sleep with that kike bastard! I heard her begging him one time to fuck her!"

Murphy lashed out, slapping Jean-Philippe hard across the face with the flat of his hand; Murphy's son looked back at him with absolute astonishment.

"Forget that business about your mother, Jean-Philippe! Forget that business about kikes, too! If you intend to spend the rest of your life hiding behind all the prejudices of that seedy old French de Rastignac nobility of yours, you'll end up in worse shape than I was with the drink!"

A fist came back at Murphy—his own son's—and connected hard with his nose in the El Al lounge, knocking him to the floor. "No matter what happens to me, *mon cher,* de Rastignac ancestry or not, no kike will ever convince me to play the part of Jesus Christ in the last half of the twentieth century and actually have me believing it sometimes. Imagine"—he spoke in a contemptuous voice to the onlookers in general: a few stragglers of passengers, the airline counter girls. two police security guards, and about ten soldiers—"imagine this poor man walking all the way from Normandy in France to Jerusalem carrying the sins of mankind on his poor shoulders."

Murphy, on the floor, put a handkerchief to his bleeding nose and thought he was going to begin laughing at the absurdity of it all. It had to end this way. The final curtain call: Jean-Philippe de Rastignac Murphy standing in the middle of an armed camp of a Jewish nation shooting off his mouth about kikes. Murphy saw that a general anger was spreading from those who understood English to those who were being made to understand. There were about ten *uzzi* machine guns in the place. Not unaccountably, Murphy thought of the St. Valentine's Day massacre. Then he thought of getting to his feet and somehow restoring a face-saving order before he rejoined the others outside in the bus.

"What's this rot about kikes? And what are you doing on the floor, sir?"

The voice came from the Israeli sergeant major,

middle-aged and trim, holding a revolver on Jean-Philippe. He was all spit and polish, impeccably English with a handlebar moustache, a graduate, Murphy supposed, of the British Army or the Jewish police under the Mandate.

"It's all right, sergeant. The young man is just a bit outspoken. I'm his father."

"I should say he is outspoken. And if you're truly his father, you should be standing here and he lying there with a bleeding nose instead of vice versa."

"I am quite ungovernable," Jean-Philippe told the officer with a level gaze. "I have experienced a lot for my age."

"You run the risk of being quite dead for your age, running off at the mouth the way you do, young man," the officer told him with an equally level gaze. Then he turned to Murphy. "Now, sir, if you are his father, off the floor with you and discharge your paternal duty at once."

"Yes," Murphy agreed. He sprang from the tiles and while Jean-Philippe still sized up the Israeli, Murphy nailed him with a right hook that sent his son reeling to the floor. There was a round of clapping and cheering in the lounge, and the officer pumped Murphy's hand energetically.

"Good show, sir," he congratulated him. On the floor Jean-Philippe was actually laughing, his better nature, hidden in a perverse place, unlocked by the chastising blow from his own father that he had wanted all along. Outside, the castrato honked his horn impatiently.

"I've got to go now," Murphy told the officer. "He's got a flight to Rome to catch in about three hours. Keep an eye on him, will you?"

"My pleasure, sir. I'll give him a cram course in Jewish history."

"I think he's already had one these past months," Murphy answered distantly. "Perhaps that's why he's acting the way he is."

Then Murphy waved to Jean-Philippe, who waved

in return, and headed out to the microbus. He climbed inside. "The old French anti-Semitism again, I presume," Ben Bokva guessed dryly.

"Yep. Exactly."

"That will never cure," Rachel Alinsky said in a low voice. "He hasn't got an ounce of Murphy in him. He's a de Rastignac to his marrow."

"Yes," Murphy agreed. But somehow he was proud also. "Meyer left him the Book of the Corruptibles as a testimony."

"He did?" The question came from Ben Bokva. Then he began laughing, almost hysterically, rocking back and forth in his seat, his humor—also locked up evidently in a perverse place—suddenly exploded. "Oh, God! How perfect! How absolutely perfect! The remnant of Western civilization that's left to us now will never be the same again once that *putz* of a kid gets started."

"That's not funny. He's just a little boy." Alinsky's mother silenced him. "Come on, Luciano, let's go."

35

The funeral ship

THE CASTRATO DROVE to a private hangar, and they were admitted by two security guards. Inside, where it was brilliantly lit by an overhead galaxy, the blue 707, gleaming stunningly, the funeral ship of Meyer Alinsky's last voyage, sat waiting, a tractor attached to its front landing gear in preparation for towing it outside for the departure. The security guards locked the doors behind them; then everyone, with the exception of Alinsky's mother—the retainers, plane crew, and guards—helped unload the two coffins from the rear of the microbus and carry them up the long incline of a walk-up ramp to the inside of the jet, setting them side by side in the middle of the plush carpeting of the main cabin that had been nearly emptied of its usual fixtures.

The hostess for the trip, the girl Shoshanna of the earlier flight Murphy had made with Alinsky, escorted them tearfully to the rear cabin where, unexpectedly, the movie screen was exposed and ready as if this were a conventional voyage toward the fulfillment of one of Alinsky's schemes somewhere in Europe. Quietly old Rachel told her to remove it. By her manner, Murphy—and the others, he supposed—quickly understood that Shoshanna had no idea her co-hostess, Rifka, was dead.

"Say nothing," Rachel warned as the girl left the cabin and they took their places in the belted lounge chairs. Then Shimon, the only one not accompanying the funeral voyage, prepared to say good-bye.

He shook hands all around, lastly handing Rachel Alinsky a manila envelope with the necessary documents they would need to clear customs in New York. Then he kissed her warmly on both cheeks, saying simply in English, "Peace at last, Rakhel, eh? I regret that you leave Israel, but Iowa will be kind to you also. You have always loved it so."

Then he stopped a second time before Murphy.

"Take good care of her, Frank. You will not go unrewarded for this, you know."

Murphy merely nodded, anxious to be off, irked by the promise of money. Shimon, understanding, turned and quickly departed. Through the open door from the rear cabin he could be seen adjusting his skull cap and pausing a moment over the two coffins; then he touched two hands to his lips, laid one each on the tops of the coffins, and after a moment went outside and down the ramp and was gone.

"Shimon is certainly one of the finest men who has ever lived," Rachel judged. There was a kind of universal agreement.

"After the horror of the camps and all that he lost, I think the time came when he arrived at a certain inner calm that nothing else could brutalize." Al Hazzar spoke distantly. "He served Meyer faithfully, but he could not be bought and sold like the others. He had none of that arbitrariness in him. And he was good for a person like Meyer. Often they talked together for many hours, and afterward Meyer was at peace for a time. I have witnessed this myself."

"I'm sorry I blew up at him back there in Jerusalem," Murphy said. "What I accused him of was preposterous."

"It sounds as if we're eulogizing Shimon," Rachel said. "Make them sound more like accolades. A man who understood that I wanted to leave quietly, without any fanfare, deserves accolades for complying, don't you think?"

But her suggestion of accolades for Shimon was interrupted by the noise of argument from the boarding ramp, not yet removed, and in another moment it was apparent they had not been quite able to sneak out the back door of Israel. Despite the best efforts of the girl Shoshanna and a crew member who had rushed back from the cockpit, three policemen had managed to force their way on board. They halted beside the coffins for a brief time and removed their hats, inquiring in Hebrew to know which was that of Alinsky. Shoshanna indicated the correct one, and one of the policemen unfolded a very faded Mogen David, an Israeli flag that may have been flying somewhere over the airport or a police post that very night, and spread it over the top of the casket. The frayed edges hung down to the carpeting, and it had two fist-sized tears in the middle of the star through which the surface of the coffin could be seen.

"How the hell did they find out?" Rachel Alinsky asked peevishly, getting up and walking out to the police. Murphy, watching her receiving the police condolences, considered there were a myriad of possible ways they could have found out—the American embassy staff, the plane crew, the household servants back in Jerusalem, the doctor embalmer, even the security men at the gates of the hangar. When she returned after politely shooing the police from the plane, ordering the ramp removed, and making certain the door was locked, she sat down and smiled resignedly at Murphy. "Guess who?"

"Jean-Philippe?"

"Good to the very last drop." She sighed. "He knew the last thing I wanted was any publicity.

We'd better get out of this hangar before the Army shows up."

She telephoned the cockpit, spoke briefly in Hebrew, then told everyone to fasten seat belts. They heard the loud whirring of electric motors that presumably opened the doors to the hangar, then felt a gentle lurch as the tractor drew the 707 outside into the purplish light of mercury arc lamps.

The jet engines started up, warming perhaps for five minutes or so before the plane began slowly taxiing to the runway for takeoff. Murphy, watching the lighted enclosure of the Lod main terminal and control tower slip past, tried to think of some epic solemnity—the perfect one for the first moment of being airborne—to describe the final departure of Meyer Alinsky and his beloved wife from the land of Israel. He rushed, seeking analogies, through the Old Testament, Greek mythology (albeit ill-remembered), bits and driblets of the bardic tales of Europe, purposefully circumventing *Romeo and Juliet*. But nothing came out, except for some reference to the phoenix rising from the ashes that it seemed impossible to correlate, so he gave up and found himself thinking instead of Jean-Philippe waiting for his own departure in the El Al lounge and wondered if his son had yet managed to drive the outwardly unflappable sergeant major into an insane rage.

The jets began revving in earnest and Murphy braced for the takeoff as the 707 accelerated forward, desperately searching for the words or the sensation to encapsule it all, but his thoughts were interrupted by Ben Bokva's sudden cry. *"Giveret* Alinsky, look! The Army!"

Outside, in the bluish darkness, two troop carriers raced down the swath of grass beside the runway, their headlights bouncing in the turf. Atop one of the vehicles a soldier, braced in place by his fellows, madly waved the Mogen David in the air, the six-pointed star brilliantly lit by the spotlight of the second troop carrier following behind. Then they were gone, left behind in the jet's sudden ascent as the voice of a crew member in the cockpit came over the address system in Hebrew.

"They thank Meyer for his part in winning the Six-Day War," his mother translated. "If only they knew. . . ."

Airborne, the plane circled once over the Plain of Sharon and the winking lights of Tel Aviv. Looking down, Rachel Alinsky suddenly asked an impossibly lame question in English. "Does the Tel Aviv sewage still go into the sea down on the waterfront?"

Ben Bokva looked at her, astounded. "Yes, I think it still does, *Giveret* Alinsky."

"Hm-m. You'd think they would have gotten around to doing something about that after all these years."

Her kind of mind, capable of incredible feats of detachment, was a generous gift from the Creator, some people said; Murphy thought that also.

Then there was no more. The 707 headed out over the dark Mediterranean on its journey north toward Rome. The winking lights grew dimmer as it climbed, and after a few minutes, looking behind him, Murphy could no longer see the land of Israel.

Exhausted by the passionate events of the day, drained by the death-loving energies of Meyer Alinsky, Murphy fell almost instantly to sleep.

He came partly awake when the Boeing settled down with a gentle lurch at Fiumicino in Rome for refueling, but stayed longer in the cobwebs, enjoying the end of a dream of lovers, erotic and beautiful at the same time, played against an Elvira Madigan lushness of springtime colors. The dream was about Meyer and Catherine, young and somewhat divine and running happily through Iowa meadows (a strange explicitness: they had cut classes that afternoon), and intermittently stopping, kissing, searching each other's eyes, then lying, blemishlessly naked, in concealed places where the sun still shone to make love.

Murphy, excited by their lovemaking, was also possessed of an erection. Then he came fully awake, his shoulder shaken urgently by Al Hazzar, who stared pointedly for a moment at the bulge in Murphy's crotch, then nodded his head through the door to the main cabin. Disbelieving the apparition, Murphy stared. The Pope sat beside the coffin covered with the Israel flag, holding the two hands of a sniffling Rachel Alinsky in one of his own, speaking to her softly, gesturing with his other hand in a wide arc so that two accompanying clergy, who stood behind him, shifted away in the cramp of the cabin to avoid the holy touch.

The Pope looked in at Murphy momentarily, a withering glance, and Murphy's erection died instantly, his penis become a dead tendril, his mind however overcome not with guilt but with a stupendous excitement. It was all true! Everything! Alinsky had known the Pope! And old Père Bisson had kissed that worthy's hand before he died, and not the hand of some made-up character actor. There had been no act of fraudulent contempt on Alinsky's part. What he promised, the man had delivered. Bug-eyed, Murphy turned to the others; they were drinking coffee and staring at him rather appraisingly, he thought.

"So now you believe?" Teplitsky asked the question.

"Yes, I believe," Murphy said. "I believe everything."

"And the Book of the Corruptibles?"

"Yes, I believe."

"And the Egyptian Air Force?"

"I believe that, too."

"Is there anything else you need confirmed?"

"Naples? Did Meyer really own half the city?"

"No, that was a lie for sure," Ben Bokva answered. The four—Ben Bokva, Teplitsky, Al Hazzar, and the castrato—erupted into a properly subdued kind of belly laughter at the notion, tears of merriment rushing down their cheeks. Then the castrato spoke in a piercing voice that Murphy supposed the Pope in the main cabin could not fail to hear.

"Napoli! Who want to own Napoli? Very dirty city, Mafia everywhere, full of *gonifs*. Napoli easier to steal than to buy, yes? Everybody help you. . . ."

In time the Pope rose, and the two clerics accompanying him aided Rachel Alinsky to her knees in the carpeting. Murphy slid to his knees also to receive the Pontiff's blessing. Al Hazzar, the only other one who could see into the main cabin, stood from respect and indicated that the others should do so as well.

Kneeling, watching the dark hollows of the Pope's sad eyes in the other cabin's shadows, a sudden tremor passed through Murphy. He had a vision, anachronistic, of another time and place, a medieval city perhaps, where he wandered frightened and alone through misted nighttime streets, meeting only one other person, a plague warden, a gentle, deathless man (yet thanatophilic) with the selfsame sad hollow eyes as those of the Pontiff. Then, some instinct in Murphy, almost ungovernable, made him want to rise, enter the place of the coffins, and warn the Pope not to lay his hand on Rachel Alinsky again, not even to look at her. She had far to travel still, much to do before the soundless angels came for her, perhaps now not even time enough to do it all. . . .

The Holy Father raised his hand. Murphy heard the words of the benediction spoken in Latin and in relief crossed himself, as did the Pope's two clerics, then stood again as the Pontiff looked to the rear cabin to exchange a small wave with Al Hazzar, whom he had met with Alinsky, before turning to leave the plane. Rachel Alinsky braced herself against the outside door, looking after the departure for perhaps a minute, then returned slowly to the rear cabin, shaking her head sorrowfully.

"It was all true," she said, blotting at her tears.

"He did know the Pope. And all these years I called him *meshuggana* and a liar and a self-deluding fool and all the rest of it. . . . May God rip out my tongue for what I've said."

She was drained. She fell to quiet whimpering in the depths of her chair, and through the window, Murphy watched a big Fiat limousine and its police-car escort glide silently away into the 4 A.M. mists, saw the refueling crew replace their hats after the parting, then the ramp being removed and Shoshanna closing the door to the jet. In another minute she came to the rear cabin and handed Murphy the folded cloth that one of the accompanying clerics had given her. It was the Papal flag. The collection was on its way.

In minutes more they took off from Rome, heading north again to their next refueling at Heathrow in London.

True dawn came over the foothills of the Alps on the Italian side just as they passed over Cortina. Murphy, his cheek pressed against the chill of rarefied air at the window, looked down through the masses of broken clouds at the jumbled mountain approaches to his beloved France.

Curious it was to be returning this way, not even able to touch down, a mere passing over, so many months after they had walked the breadth of the country, a petulant, quarreling gaggle of Christians convinced they were on a fool's errand being paid for by a fool, a banal imitation of the medieval European jihads. How they had erred. It had turned out to be far more than a mere evoking of the past; it had become instead a death march of the present, a qualified revenge of the tragic Alinsky, who had seemed at times a terrible fiend and now, in death, a hapless and pitiable rag doll of a man. . . .

Unaccountable tears came to Murphy's eyes. In the long run, he decided, it was perhaps best they did not touch down in the land of the Franks; he did not need to be reminded of the variety of carnage he himself had left behind after seventeen years there. Monique, a closet hellion, was loose and slavering now, and who knew where she was going, especially with the impending divorce? And what would become of Jean-Philippe? Inheritor of the Book of the Corruptibles, he was the worst possible recipient on earth, in Murphy's estimation, since he would put it to real use. The world had yet to hear from Jean-Philippe. Murphy, staring miles off into the future, saw another of life's rueful anomalies: himself, a kind of Cassandra of the cornfields, living out his days in Iowa with a new American wife, trying hopelessly to convince anyone that the famous, high-living, and fantastically wealthy Jean-Philippe de Rastignac Murphee (the kid would doubtless Francophize his name, once done with his parents), of whom they read so much in *Time* and *Newsweek,* was Murphy's own son.

Bitter . . . bitter . . . Murphy thought, and suspected this was no way to wing one's way to a new life. He turned to see Rachel Alinsky regarding him steadily. She said nothing, merely pressed the call button as he wiped away his tears, and when Shoshanna appeared at the cabin door she ordered two bottles of champagne for breakfast.

Everyone drank—even Ben Bokva and Teplitsky —giggling witlessly as the ancient regions of France fell swiftly behind them. Savoie gave way to Burgundy, Burgundy to Champagne, with Paris just barely visible to the west when they called for two more bottles. Paris behind them, they descended gradually over the fields of Picardy into the real northeast of France. Over Artois they called for two more, finishing the dregs as Calais and the channel became visible.

At Heathrow, in a snow-white fog—an island-wide phenomenon that could be seen from the sunny coast of France—the plane, empathizing perhaps, set down with a hard lurch. They were all quite looped by the time the Archbishop of Canterbury came aboard. Rachel Alinsky, smiling unrelentingly from the champagne, went forward to speak with him. In the well-lit cabin the prelate, kindly-faced and white-haired and dressed in an intelligent gray, clerical-looking suit, clasped Meyer's mother's hands in his own as had the Pope, and though he spoke to her in a low, sympathy-laden voice, at the same time he seemed baffled by her levity. Murphy and Al Hazzar, sitting side by side and framed in the door-way, smiled moronically out at the clergyman, and he raised his head occasionally from his conversation with old Rachel and smiled benignly back at them.

But despite the perfect ambiance of the outside, the curling fog that enveloped the funeral ship, the eerie, cautious movement of all things through it, the visit was no good. All the mourners had drunk too much champagne, and the bright-eyed, ascetic-seeming cleric in the main cabin—doubtless lover of God, a crucible of Christian optimism—had not the power to sober them. He had no death in him, the way Meyer had had death in him, the way the Pope, the plague warden of Murphy's frightened vision, had had at least the suggestion of death in him. Rachel Alinsky stood first, indicating the con-ference was over. The Archbishop handed her the folded flag of the Church of England (which she placed dutifully beside the Papal flag atop Meyer's casket), bussed her cheek, waved good-bye to Al Hazzar in the rear as had the Pope before him, then exited quickly into the enveloping fog. He seemed to have no escort; perhaps he had even walked out to the refueling area.

Alinsky's mother, looking suddenly very tired as if she had come down from the champagne in one quick tumble, walked slowly to the rear cabin and took her seat again. She was silent for a moment, then released a long sigh. "I don't think he did Meyer much good. He seems only to think of one thing at a time. . . ."

"He was not completely satisfying to Meyer. You are right about that, Mother Rachel," Al Hazzar said. "He spoke only of love and forgiveness, of the triumph of God's justice in Eternity. Meyer, alas, was looking for justice in the here and now, not the hereafter."

"And the Pope?" Murphy demanded testily, the coiled snake of his childhood's Catholicism slashing out in attack. "Did the Pope advocate outright revenge?"

"No, of course not," Al Hazzar answered with a shrug. "But he didn't say no, either."

With the plane refueled and the flight crew changed, they set out for America. Murphy fell asleep almost instantly after they had climbed above the fog and into the brightness above the clouds and were effortlessly crossing time zones westward, dreaming of the new life to come and of the most profound sort of death dance he meant to participate in for the rest of his days: between himself and a used-car salesman, waltzing around the flanks of a gleaming used Lincoln Continental that Murphy wanted desperately to own while trying not to show it. . . .

He woke when the landing gear dropped with a *clunk* sound and looked down to the line of surf frothing the beaches on the south shore of Long Island of America that he had not seen in seventeen years. There were houses of villages and older towns and planned developments, then miles of brick row housing back to back that merged with industry and the taller buildings of small cities, all of it streaming toward the distant incredible skyline of New York. The land seemed unbelievably overpopulated. The shadow of the 707 below them passed over not a single open, untenanted place.

A surge of panic entered Murphy. The American nation, grown sophisticated enough to eat out its entrails over the affair of Vietnam and still survive,

ALINSKY'S DIAMOND

was no longer young. It was no longer the yawning portal through which the hapless of the world streamed for safety, either. It was not limitless, or infinite of power. Fearfully Murphy wondered if it would have room enough or them.

The jet touched down gently, past a line of other planes waiting for takeoff that seemed endless, the airport a fantastic congestion.

"The wandering Jews are home again," Rachel Alinsky pronounced. But the profundity fell on deaf ears. They were all too busy staring out the windows.

Murphy felt like a timid little-boy visitor in the nation of his birth.

PART V
THE LAW OF RETURN

36

Aruba, Iowa, U.S.A.

THOUGH MORE THAN TWO YEARS HAD PASSED since the return to America, Murphy could still remember the events of that first day with absolute clarity.

At Kennedy they passed quickly through customs, refueled, flew across the pre-spring bleakness of the American landscape to O'Hare in Chicago, where they picked up Rachel Alinsky's cousin, the ancient Rabbi Ushpizai, then landed for the last time, just before noon, at the Cedar Rapids, Iowa, airport. Fifteen minutes later the funeral ship turned about and began the long and tedious flight home to Israel with Ben Bokva and Teplitsky, the henchmen of the avenger, on board; Alinsky's mother, convinced that they had murdered Mermelstein in Yugoslavia, would permit them to accompany the coffins no farther.

In the aftermath of their parting it became apparent that the meticulous Shimon had omitted one detail: No arrangement had been made for transporting the coffins the four-hour distance to Aruba. In a real panic the remaining members of the cortège—old Rachel, Murphy, Al Hazzar, the castrato, and Ushpizai—ranged about the terminal trying to rent a truck or two station wagons from anyone, for Hertz and Avis had nothing but sedans available. Finally Rachel convinced a farmer with an old three-quarter-ton pickup to drive them to Aruba. He complied not for money; his service was a testimony to the remembered greatness of the Iowa halfback, Meyer Alinsky.

They set out on the final leg of their journey, the farmer shaking his head in unabated amazement at the burden his truck carried. But they were not alone. The laughing demons who had hounded most of Meyer Alinsky's passage through life had flown with them from Israel and now ranged about the sputtering truck as it made its way to northern Iowa. And in death they had one final clout in store, a singular cruelty made known at the Jewish cemetery of Aruba.

At the cemetery gates were an ancient pickup and a car, the latter a remembered Chevrolet from the early fifties with the dim lettering "Police" on its hood and front door. The farmer brought his truck to a halt beside the police car and an aged cop, as old perhaps as Ushpizai, dressed in a hanging sack of a uniform and wearing a gun at his hip that seemed ready to drag his thin, consumptive-looking frame to the ground, stepped out. A woman —his wife, Murphy guessed—opened the other front door. Two men—the grave diggers, certainly—got out of the rear.

"Rachel? Is it you after all these years?" The cop squinted at her through thick glasses as they climbed down from the truck.

"Yes, LaVerne, it's me."

"Jesus, Rachel, we've gotten old, haven't we?"

"It's been twenty-two years, LaVerne."

He came closer. His wife, similarly desiccated, limping with a cane, came round the nose of the car. "Welcome home, Rachel."

"Thank you, Betty. The house looks wonderful. We saw it on the way in."

"There's two or three folks hung on and kept up their properties. But did you see the rest of it? The town just seemed to die like it was cursed after your family left."

She gave a shudder, while Rachel Alinsky responded with a few quick nods. There was a strained silence; then LaVerne Morain said, "The graves are ready, Rachel. It's good that you dug 'em up to bring 'em home after so many years, even though there isn't much to bring 'em home to."

"Dug them up?" Rachel questioned. "LaVerne, they died just yesterday in Israel."

The cop squinted at her disbelievingly, turned once back to his wife, who had a baffled look on her face as if she had not heard correctly, then marched forward to Rachel Alinsky, putting his fingers to her cheek as if to ascertain she were not an apparition.

"Rachel," he said desperately, "that's not possible."

Murphy had no inkling of what was to come. Old Rachel Alinsky did, though, of that he was certain. If not the whole of it, then undoubtedly a good part. Her eyes widening with the onslaught of the shock, she advanced a step or two after the police chief removed his hand from her cheek and took a grip on his arm. They all pressed close upon him.

"Why is it impossible, LaVerne?" she asked hoarsely.

"Why, Rachel, that Mr. Shimon who sent the checks every month told us they died in a plane crash in nineteen forty-nine."

"When did he tell you this, LaVerne?"

"When we found out who beat up and robbed Catherine that night in the snowstorm."

"LaVerne. . . . What are you saying?"

"Swear to Jesus, Rachel. What year was it, Betty?" He turned to his wife, squinting in the arduousness of trying to remember.

"It was after the war in Korea, Rachel. It was the same year Joe McCarthy was on the television every day. Nineteen fifty-three, I think."

"That's it, Rachel!" The cop slapped his thigh.
"That was the very year. There was three of them.
The one boy got it in Korea, the second went and
hung himself, and the third came back here scared
to death that the Lord God was out to punish him
and confessed to the crime. They were passin' through
that night on their way to Chicago and needed some
money for gas and tried to stick her up. But
Catherine fought back and in the scuffle she fell
against a hitchin' post and that's how she went into
the coma. The third boy went to jail for a while,
but he'd be out long ago by now. Anyhow, that's
when Mr. Shimon told us they had died and that
he'd pass on the information to you, but that you
was livin' in Switzerland like we figured and you
intended stayin' on there—"

Impulsively, Murphy reached a hand beneath her
elbow to steady her, but she jerked away, clenching
her fists and reaching up her arms to flail them at
the heavens, shrieking out, "Shimon! *Lama? Lama?*
Chazar! Why did you do this to us?"

Al Hazzar jumped into place before her. "Mother
Rachel, I will kill him myself! I will make him eat
his own liver before he dies! I swear to Allah I
will return to Jerusalem tomorrow to do it!"

But Rachel Alinsky, her fists clenched to her breasts
now, only swayed her head back and forth, her
shock and sorrow too bottomless for sound. LaVerne
Morain, looking clearly stricken, kept asking again
and again, "Rachel, did I do somethin' wrong? I
shouldn't have said that, right?"

But it was the castrato's privilege to speak the
truth next, and he gave the summation, his eyes
staring into the graveyard at the thin shaft of a
monument crowned by the Star of David, the name
Alinsky seen on its face from where they stood.

"Meyerle's revenge was not really Meyerle's revenge at all. It was Shimon's. Shimon lost everything
in the camps, and others must to suffer from it.
Meyer was only the tool for Shimon's vendetta all

these terrible years. . . . Tsk, tsk. . . . There is no need for killing Shimon," he added, almost as an afterthought. "Shimon will be dead when we arrive at home to Israel."

"Oh-h-h. . . ." The bellows of the universe, then, someone's price paid for something anyhow.

Alinsky: victim or victimizer? The question came dimly to Murphy as Rachel Alinsky collapsed like fluff into his arms.

Ah, poor, poor Meyer. Victim. Victim, for sure.

Al Hazzar and the castrato departed Iowa for Israel the next day, and Murphy and old Rachel were left alone to mend in the great Georgian brick house of the Alinskys where the clocks had stopped in the year 1948.

During the first week they made tentative forays into the world. Murphy went to Mason City and bought his Lincoln Continental; the day after, they drove it to the farm, fifteen miles from Dubuque, where Murphy had grown up. The place had been bought out years before by some conglomerate operating from Chicago, and the land was a vast tillage, not even the foundations of the house or barns or outbuildings remaining. They walked through the newly plowed fields, ate a kind of commemorative picnic of greasy fried chicken and bad New York State wine where Murphy thought the house should have been, and ended up ironically being kicked off the place by an overseer in a jeep who first gave them a lecture on littering.

In the next week they went to Missouri, to Hannibal, to find the Raabe family and tell them that Catherine had passed away and was buried in the Jewish cemetery in Aruba, Iowa. During the trip south Rachel was nervous with anticipation. She had never met Catherine's parents. They had refused to attend the wedding.

Somehow, completely expected, they lived in a cracker shack set on a foundation of random cinder blocks. Murphy went first to speak with them while Rachel waited in the car and found they were confirmed and virulently practicing anti-Semites who believed Catherine had died back in 1948 anyhow. There was no reason to awaken the dead; Murphy left their porch steps, promising to forward a check for ten thousand dollars, their reward as beneficiaries of an old insurance policy, at the same time inventing the lie that would make certain Rachel Alinsky was not ever going to meet them.

When they returned home to Aruba in the early evening, there was a telegram awaiting them from Israel.

The air was still warm, the spring become a strong-willed certainty, and they sat on the front porch, each three drinks to the good, before they dared open it. It was from Al Hazzar. Murphy read the words aloud:

SHIMON DEAD BY OWN HAND. BURIED KYRIAT GAT SAME DAY AS MEYER AND CATHERINE. SALAAM ALAIKUM U RAKMAT ALLAH U BARAKAT.

"It's all over, then," Rachel Alinsky said softly.

"Are you sure?" Murphy asked. He supposed his smile was quite ironic despite himself.

"I'm sure."

"What does the Arabic mean?" he said after a moment.

" 'Peace and the blessing of Allah be upon you all the days of your life.' Leave it to Meyer to have an Arab friend with a hopeless gift of poetry."

He did not respond. They ate a quiet supper, watched some television; then, when he was sure she slept, Murphy left the house with a shovel, drove out to the Jewish cemetery, and, about two feet down in the fresh earth of the grave where the lovers slept side by side, buried between them the diamond that had been given him by Rachel for safekeeping.

Then, with the old life, its protagonists, and its symbolism safely underground and he hoped, reposing in peace, Murphy drove away from the Jewish cemetery to begin the new life, the rebuilding of Aruba.

The destruction was not complete, not in the sense that Murphy, who had seen Germany in the still-lingering rubble of the early fifties, had visualized before his return; it had not been bombed, at least. But two full years after the burial of Meyer and Catherine, except for Sundays, his day still began at dawn and ended with the sleep of a good conscience around midnight.

The work of his mornings, however, he gravely conceded, might be played out soon—possibly within a year. For the job of repopulating Aruba after Meyer had turned it into a ghost town was going at a fantastic rate. Almost daily now, Murphy met with representatives of various firms for long drink-less lunches to discuss the acquisition of space in the rapidly filling industrial park on the north side of town near the Interstate. Otherwise he made spot checks, driving out to the burgeoning acres of development-style ranch houses and apartment buildings that were intended for the influx of workers, to make certain the zoning regulations were being rigidly adhered to. Or to the great packinghouse of the Alinskys, where the air was rife with the droppings of hogs and steers, and which was now again in full operation and run as a cooperative by as many of the former employees as Rachel was able to lure back into town. Or to the nearly completed first-development stage of the Meyer Alinsky Community College, his mother's keenest project, where faculty interviews were being frantically conducted in anticipation of the fifteen hundred students already accepted for the first term that was to open in less than a month.

One afternoon per week he met with the newly

formed town council. But it was easy going there.
He merely informed them of Rachel's suggestions,
which became almost instant fact. Murphy decided
that none of them understood it was Meyer Alinsky
who had nearly obliterated Aruba from the earth,
but all understood full well that Rachel was footing
the bill for the restoration. Consequently the town
was compliant and full of her personal little touches.
The business district was Gay Nineties, with old brick
and gaslights; the young people could dance themselves to death to rock music, as long as they did
it behind an ice-cream-parlor façade. When the question of buying police cruisers had come up, Rachel,
leafing through a glossy magazine, had been pleased
by the sleek aspect of Thunderbird advertising and
ordered four of them for the Aruba Police Department.

But the work of his evenings might never be
concluded, Murphy considered, for it was heavy
with the longest of long projects.

After dinner he labored doggedly at the literary
epic that Rachel had commissioned him to write:
*The Fascinating History of Meyer Alinsky and His
Forebears.* It was to be a work of thirteen volumes,
modeled on Proust's *Remembrance of Things Past,*
and Murphy—after a whole year of research and
digging through family memorabilia, reading the
crabbed, handwritten letters of relatives, and squinting at stacks of faded old daguerreotypes that por-
trayed various Alinsky men and women in the garb
of Orthodox Jewry worn in their Russian past and
early American present—had completed but one vol-
ume: the tempestuous crossing after pogrom number
? on the Italian ship *Calabria* from Odessa in the
Crimea to New York to begin the new life.

But he knew he was on the right track; his
patroness was well pleased. Reading it, Rachel had
wept over nearly every sentence, confirmed in her
judgment that the Alinskys were truly a tragedy-
ridden establishment. Murphy was inclined to agree,